THE BOOK OF
GHOULS

A CTHULHU MYTHOS ANTHOLOGY

FEATURING STORIES BY

DAVID HAMBLING ~ C. T. PHIPPS ~ PHILIP HEMPLOW
MATTHEW DAVENPORT ~ ERIC MALIKYTE

Contents

The Book of Ghouls
The origin story of Lovecraft's eaters of the dead

H. P. Lovecraft was obviously fond of ghouls. They crop up in several of his stories, most notably *Pickman's Model* from 1927. In one sense, we have a very good idea of where Lovecraft's conception of ghouls come from—they can clearly be traced to Arabian folklore, as we will see shortly—but beyond that, they present an interesting puzzle.

Lovecraft's other monstrosities are very much of his own devising. The semi--vegetable Elder Things, the weird, conical Great Race of Yith, the tentacled Spawn of Cthulhu and the amoebic Shoggoth all came from his febrile imagination, along with the indescribable Dunwich Horror. These are aliens with no link to myth and legend.

The Mi-go might, in theory, correspond to the Tibetan migou, otherwise known as the yeti or Abominable Snowman. This was in the news in Lovecraft's day. But his winged crustaceo-fungoids whispering in the dark bear no resemblance to the hairy humanoids reported by mountaineers, and described in Himalayan folklore.

Lovecraft avoided traditional horrors like demons and werewolves. *The Shunned House* is a decidedly science-fictional take on the old haunted house genre, and *The Case of Charles Dexter Ward* is his 'scientific' explanation for vampire tales. *Dreams in the Witch House* recasts the traditional witch as a mistress of multidimensional space-bending geometry. Lovecraft wanted to break away from the hackneyed Victorian tropes of deserted abbeys and abandoned castles, and bring horror into the age of science—and science fiction. But apparently ghouls, though ancient, were too dear to him to ignore, and did not get the science fiction treatment.

The Thousand and One Nights, popularly known as Arabian Nights, had a powerful effect on the young Lovecraft which never quite wore off. As he wrote:

"How many dream-Arabs have the Arabian Nights bred! I ought to know, since at the age of 5 I was one of them! I had not then encountered Graeco-Roman myth, but found in Lang's Arabian Nights a gateway to glittering vistas of wonder and freedom. It was then that I invented for myself the name of Abdul Alhazred, and made my mother take me to all the Oriental curio shops and fit me up an Arabian corner in my room."

S. T. Joshi notes in his epic Lovecraft biography *I Am Providence* that Lang's edition had not been published when Lovecraft was five, but he did acquire it later. He suggests Lovecraft's first taste must have been an earlier collection of tales, such as 'The Arabian Nights' Entertainments: Six Stories,' translated by Jonathan Scott.

All the Western versions of ghouls derive from European translations by Antoine Galland published between 1704 and 1717. It was Galland who introduced the now-familiar motif of the corpse-devouring ghoul. In particular, in '*The Story of Sidi Nouman*,' he says ghouls are monsters who 'in want of prey, will sometimes go in the night into burying grounds, and feed upon dead bodies that have been buried there.' Galland also mentions a character called Amina, who, though recently married, prefers the company of the graveyard ghouls to that of her husband.

These two features, the eating of the dead and the frequenting of graveyards, were purely Galland's own inventions and do not appear in the Arabic originals. Further, while in Galland's version the ghouls are described as male, the originals seem to be exclusively female.

The traditional Arabic ghoul or 'ghul' is a monster that inhabits deserts and other desolate spots, and preys on travelers. Ghouls sometimes abducted children, and often took on the form of a beautiful woman to lure their victims, or called out in a female voice. In their natural state though, ghouls are described as being particularly ugly.

Ghouls were said to mislead travelers by lighting fires, presumably tricking them into thinking there was a camp or other habitation nearby. They were said to possess 'a thousand wiles' for catching victims.

In one such story, related by the tenth-century storyteller al-Aşbahânî, two men traveling on business meet a strange woman who accompanies them on their journey. When they stop, the woman goes over a rise to relieve herself in private. When she has not returned after an hour, one of the men goes after her. He does not return either, and after a while the second man follows. He finds—of course—a grisly scene: his companion is dead and the 'woman,' now revealed to be a monstrous ghoul, is eating his liver. The traveler escapes by invoking the name of god, a method of overcoming ghouls common in tales in the *Arabian Nights* and which works much the same way as a crucifix repels vampires.

Arabic ghouls appear to be related to the spirits called Jinn, though there is much debate on this topic. According to the thirteenth century storyteller al-Qazwīnī, when devils tried to eavesdrop on Heaven, God drove them off with meteors. Some of the burned devils fell into the sea and became crocodiles, others fell on the land and became ghouls.

The Arabic ghoul was a dangerous spirit of lonely places. The Western version was a more physically bound creature, a corpse-eating hybrid of Jinn and hyena, which eats dead bodies.

Lovecraft himself added an important twist to the ghoul tale. Lovecraft's ghouls are former human beings, people who have gradually transitioned into monstrous form. The implication is that ghouls have a similar life cycle to his Deep Ones, who appear human as children before changing in later life. This draws on one of Lovecraft's own deepest fears, that of 'tainted blood' and that a seemingly healthy individual's life would be blighted by something emerging from their heritage later on. This is understandable given that Lovecraft's own father died of syphilis when the boy was eight, and the disease may be passed down to children.

In Lovecraft's version, ghouls may also appear as changelings, swapped with human children in the cradle. This is a direct borrowing of the traditional folkloric motif of the fairy changeling, but with the difference that the ghoul-baby grows first into a human-seeming adult and then into a monstrous form.

It is not clear whether Lovecraft intended ghoul-isms to be a family trait like hereditary madness, as seen in 'The Rats in the Walls' and the affliction of the population of Innsmouth in *The Shadow over Innsmouth*, or something else entirely.

Lovecraft liked to base his work on the latest scientific findings. He had no time for the supernatural. In his stories. Magic is just multi-dimensional geometry, and his monsters are from other worlds, not the Other World.

But Lovecraft does not explain how ghouls came to be. More recently we have seen a science fiction take on ghouls in *Fallout:* they are humans exposed to radiation which gives them a corpse-like appearance, effectively eternal life, plus a tendency to cannibalism and turning feral. Maybe Lovecraft would have taken a similar direction if he had a little more interest in speculation about the effects of radioactivity, but, as things stand, his ghouls remain tantalizingly unexplained.

This, then, is the challenge we set our writers. If they are not evil spirits cast down to Earth, an option we can dismiss in Lovecraft's materialistic worldview, just what are ghouls? How did they come to have this curious, parasitic relationship with humans? Are they really human, or just apparently so? How do they become the monstrous beings we see in Pickman's paintings? What light can modern science shed on this hideous transformation?

Read on, and discover….

David Hambling
Norwood 2024

Ethical Consumption

By C. T. Phipps

Chapter One

"From ghosties and ghoulies. And long-leggedy beasties. And things that go bump in the night, Good Lord, deliver us!"

—Traditional Scottish prayer

*B*ut gradually the truth dawned on me: that Man had not remained one species but differentiated into two distinct animals: that my graceful children of the Upper-world were not the sole descendants of our generation, but that this bleached, obscene, nocturnal Thing which had flashed before me, was also heir to all the ages.

"Mr. Jameson," the voice of Professor Warner drew my attention from my e-reader, where I'd been sneaking peeks at *The Time Machine* by H.G. Wells.

"Yes, Professor?" I asked, looking up.

I was sitting across from the Professor in a passenger car compartment on a train currently heading deeper into Scotland. Fields of purple heather and bracken raced by outside. Professor Niles Warner was a somewhat stereotypical image of a white-bearded academic, with a tweed jacket, khaki pants, and an upper crust New England accent that made him seem like a throwback at modern

Miskatonic University. His assistant, Lisa Delapore, a mixed European and South Asian Goth, with a nose ring,

seemed even more incongruous. She was dressed down for this journey with her sweater and jeans but still looked significantly more punk than I guessed most of this part of the country had ever seen. I had to admit, I fancied her and been working up the nerve to ask her out for a drink, but given she was a grad student, and I was in my second year, I doubted that was going to happen.

Sitting next to me was my somewhat chubby friend Karl Butcher, and he was giving me side-eye for reasons I didn't quite get. Both of us had agreed to sign up for Professor Warner's class pretty much just to fulfill our history degree requirements. However, Warner had taken a shine to me and I'd been chosen for the Armitage Award, meaning I didn't need to entirely drown in student debt along with side jobs. The price, though, was that I had to keep taking Professor Warner's classes on theoretical anthropology and by theoretical, they should have said goddamn mad.

Karl, for reasons I didn't understand, had continued taking the classes alongside me and seemed a lot more into them than I'd ever been. He also seemed to resent me for reasons I didn't understand. Maybe he was jealous of my getting the award—but that didn't make sense since he could afford to buy Miskatonic University a new department if he wanted. His parents owned a good chunk of King Beer and its five breweries.

"I was wondering if you were paying attention," Professor Warner said, staring at my e-reader.

I put it away. "Sorry, sir, I didn't realize this was a lecture."

"Never turn down an opportunity to learn, Mr. Jameson," Professor Warner said, "Especially when it's on a free vacation."

"Yeah, Rick," Karl said, making a mocking noise with his tongue. "Ya need to pay attention *in class*."

I grimaced. "Yes, sir."

The four of us were heading to Bean, Scotland, located in Bennane Head, north of Ballantrae Bay and southwest of Girvan. It was a town primarily famous for the fact the Sawney Bean family of cannibals had allegedly settled it, and also for a popular brand of pickled herring, at least according to its Wikipedia entry. It wasn't exactly my idea of a vacation spot, especially given the fact my mother had come to America to get away from Scotland, but everything was paid for by the university. Besides, it was a chance to get closer to Lisa, and if I was ever going to make my move then it was probably going to be in a cold and wet place where there was nothing to do for ninety miles.

"I was talking about my theory of the Ultraterrestrial civilization," Professor Warner said. "Modern human civilization is something that dates back roughly six thousand years, with oral history preserving work from close to ten to thirteen thousand years. However, the archaeological evidence from the so-called Hyborian Age could well indicate an entire additional human historical era that we are only now recovering remnants of. But what if they are just the tip of the iceberg? What if, underground, an entire epoch of human civilization existed that could well upend our understanding of the fossil record?"

Yep. Goddamn mad. "Sir, a lot of the evidence of the Hyborian Age has been called into dispute," I said, reluctantly questioning my professor's conclusions once more. It was exhausting work, and every time, I kept wondering why I bothered, but my inner wannabe history professor couldn't help itself. Besides, Professor Warner had to like something about what I said, since he was the one who recommended me for the Award. "If there really was an entire pre-human race of history around the time of *homo erectus*, don't you think we'd have more evidence?"

Or any evidence?

Any at all?

I didn't say that last part, of course.

"Ah, but there is evidence," Professor Warner said. "It is just located underground."

"Yeah," Karl said, speaking in his obnoxiously loud voice. "It's underground, numb nuts."

"Like *Homo floresiensis*, better known as the hobbit," Professor Warner said. "For centuries considered a myth, until remains were found in the Liang Bang cave in Indonesia in 2003. Further cave excavations turned up several more skeletons."

"Didn't forget Liang Bang cave, did ya?" Karl said, rolling his eyes.

"Which is why we're investigating the Sawney Bean clan as a possible tie-in to the surface world," Professor Warner said. "Which I trust you did your homework on, Mr. Jameson?"

"Yessir," I said, remembering the gory, lurid stories the Professor had me going over.

"Please summarize your research findings for us," Professor Warner said, testing me. "Just to show how good a job you've done."

I took a deep breath. "The Sawney Bean clan was a cannibal clan of forty members that existed in Scotland during the sixteenth century. They allegedly killed over a thousand people during a span of twenty-five years."

"Allegedly," Professor Warner said, snorting. "Please go on."

"Their leader, Alexander Bean, was born in East Lothian and supposedly married to a witch named Black Agnes Douglas. They robbed and cannibalized several victims before settling above a coastal cave system and founding the village of Bean."

"Hell of a founding father story," Karl said, chuckling.

"Supposedly, the town was founded by Thomas C. Bean," I pointed out. "A local dry goods salesman who was possibly a smuggler and fence, using those cave systems. They used the money from their legitimate and illicit activities to fund a successful mining operation that lasted several generations. The town denied the Bean clan existed as anything other than Anti-Scot propaganda for the better part of two centuries."

"It is my belief that Thomas C. Bean is the fictitious of the two," Professor Warner said. "Alexander Bean made contact with the subterranean civilization and they provided him with gold as well as other precious metals while inducting locals as members of their sinister ghoul cult."

"Right, sinister ghoul cult," I said, trying to figure out how to indulge the professor's lunacy without affecting my grade or standing at Miskatonic. "Well, supposedly, Alexander Bean and Black Agnes had eight daughters and six sons. The family was all inducted into the same robbery and cannibalism that their parents indulged in. Plus, they were inclined toward incest and the siblings wed each other."

"To keep the bloodline pure," Lisa Delapore said. "The Dutch noble family, the Martense clan, soon found itself engaged in similar practices of cannibalism and incest when they moved to the Catskill mountains. There's long been suspicions that they, too, were part of a larger collection of ghoul worshipers."

I didn't get Lisa's fascination with the macabre, but I wasn't a Goth girl—which might have explained why college had been nothing but a dry spell since I'd arrived on campus. Part of it might have been that Miskatonic students came in two varieties: the very rich who were getting their Ivy League degrees before entering politics or lobbying, and the very weird who were attracted to the school's reputation for taking

crackpots seriously. Lisa was clearly one of the latter. Karl had been one of the former but, well, was now one of the latter. If I had a lot more money or a lot more interest in the weird, I might have had a better social life.

"Damn rednecks," Karl said, clearly trying to appeal to Lisa. "Of course it's the hillbillies who became cannibals."

Lisa glared at him, as if he'd insulted her personally. "My great-great grandfather supposedly traced the Delapore line back to one of their own estates here in the United Kingdom. He claimed he discovered an entire underground city underneath Exham Priory."

Karl grimaced.

"What happened to him?" I asked.

"He killed a friend of his, ate him, and was committed to a mental hospital," Lisa said, sounding oddly proud. "Thankfully, he was rich, and they released him twelve years later. That's where my branch of the family came from. Sadly, Exham Priory was something he willed to the government with secret instructions he didn't pass down to any of his adopted descendants."

"Sounds…neat," I said, grimacing. Maybe I should just do what other guys on European vacations did and try to hook up with a local girl. I wasn't sure, however cool and hot she was, that hooking up with a girl who admired her cannibal murderer ancestor was a great idea.

"Exham Priory was my original planned location for an investigation," Professor Warner said, frowning. "Unfortunately, during World War II, it was used as an artillery shelling range before the entire valley was flooded over to create Exham Lake."

"Mmm hmm," I said, nodding along. "That is a shame, sir."

That was always the case with Professor Warner's theories and quests for proof. Innsmouth being home to a cult of fishmen? The town had been bulldozed to the ground in the 1920s. Dunwich being home to practicing sorcerers? Died out long ago with their possessions incinerated as junk. An actual fucking underwater city containing some kind of squid Godzilla? Well, no one was willing to pay for combing every inch of the ocean to look for it.

Four possibilities emerged: the professor was the victim of an elaborate conspiracy trying to cover up the truth, the supernatural somehow didn't want to be found, the supernatural didn't exist, or Professor Warner was such a bad scientist that he couldn't have proven a link between smoking and cancer.

"Please continue," Professor Warner said, gesturing to me.

"Well, the number of dead bodies kept increasing and the town developed a bad reputation for disappearing travelers as well as heavy banditry. The Bean clan hanged several innocents in show trials and probably disposed of the evidence." If they ever existed. "Eventually, though, the Beans failed to capture one of their quarries: a trained soldier on his honeymoon."

"They ate his wife though, right?" Karl asked, grinning.

"Yes," I said, grimacing. The tale had given me nightmares despite being just a bunch of words. "The husband, his name wasn't recorded in any of my research, held them off long enough to be rescued by some nearby fairgoers and they took him to the local magistrate. James the Sixth of Scotland, better known as James the First of England, sent out an army to deal with the Bean clan. The town was no help, and Alexander Bean's mansion was empty, but they found their cavern hideout with bloodhounds. The evidence was apparently so overwhelming that they were all universally condemned as witches. The women and children were burned while the men were castrated, drawn, and quartered."

Karl crossed his legs. "Eesh."

"Alexander Bean's last words were 'It isn't over, it will never be over'."

"It's terrible the way that the Old English and Scottish theocracies persecuted alternative religions," Lisa said. "Many cultures have engaged in ritual cannibalism."

"Yeah, I think the *killing people* in order to *eat them* kind of precludes claims of religious persecution," I said, sarcastically.

Lisa narrowed her eyes. "You are so *intolerant*."

Yeah, we weren't going to happen. Probably for the best. If we did hook up, we possibly had a couple more years of working together if I could leverage the Armitage Award for a graduate degree in history. That meant keeping the professor happy with my critiques, though. "In any case, there's actually another legend that they didn't execute them at all but just detonated gunpowder at the entrance to the caves and sealed all of the clan inside."

"They could still be alive then!" Karl said.

"Uh, no," I said. "Because they'd be centuries old."

Karl snorted, way more into this legend and the occult than I was. There had

been a time when my friend had been as skeptical of the occult as I was, but now he seemed every bit as obsessed as Lisa and Professor Warner. I wanted to think he was just trying to get with Lisa, which was a pretty sexist and shameful view—I knew Karl, and that was less disturbing than my millionaire friend sincerely wanting to find lost cannibalistic underground civilizations.

"Interesting fact," Professor Warner said. "James the First was the monarch who wrote the *Daemonologie*, one of the most extensive treatises on the differences between white and black magic. He also was the monarch to sanction witch trials. Is it possible that some of what was found among the Bean clan fell into his hands? Or was the whole affair what started him down the road of occult investigation, like accusations that witches tried to kill him with a storm? Especially given Queen Elizabeth, his predecessor's, own relationship to the occult with Doctor John Dee?"

Or maybe James I was a religious nut raised by a religious nut, specifically John Knox, was what I could have said but didn't. "The nearby town of Girvan has an additional legend about the mythical clan. They claim one of the Bean clan daughters left the clan and took up residence locally. When they discovered her heritage, they hanged her from a tree she planted called *The Hairy Tree.*"

Lisa spoke up, making an interesting addition to the legend. "*Cultes des Goules,* by Francois Honore-Balfour, actually references a version of the Sawney Bean legend in the original French language edition, though it's curiously omitted from the seventeenth century English language translation—probably because of the content. You see, that version mentions the human followers of the Bean clan-cult were executed and the caves sealed over. However, the daughter of the Bean clan was actually arrested and taken to King James' court, where she was interrogated on the nature of witchcraft. The book suggests that King James was overwhelmed with lust for her and made her his mistress."

I grimaced. I hadn't bothered checking out the French edition of *Cults des Goules.* "Yeah, it makes sense the English translation would leave out accusing a British monarch of witchcraft and monster sex."

"I thought James the First liked dudes," Karl asked, confused.

"You can like both," Lisa said, annoyed. "Also, ghouls can shapeshift and frequently had lovers of both sexes."

I blinked. "Yeah. Okay."

"Monsters and unconventional sexuality are intrinsically intertwined," Lisa said, suggestively, and looking straight at me.

I wasn't sure how I felt about that, given my decision just moments before to not try to pursue her. Was she interested? Had I just not been picking up the signs?

Karl glared at me.

"In any case, Ms. Delapore had the fascinating theory that Anne Murphy, alleged mistress of James the First was, in fact, actually Anne Bean operating under her married name. Under this theory, Anne Murphy returned to her long-lost hometown with her second husband, Martin Fitzroy. A recognized bastard of James whose mother is unknown but could have been Anne Murphy herself."

"Keeping it in the family," Karl said, chuckling.

Yuck.

"They acquired the Bean lands and have been dwelling there ever since," Professor Warner said. "At least until the 2020 pandemic when the last remaining direct heirs of the family died out and Murphy Manor became property of the town itself. I believe we will find secrets to the lost civilization of the ghouls both there and within the caves below. Or, at least, an insight into the Sawney Bean legend as well as its relationship to the Ultraterrestials."

"We're just going to march up and ask to poke around their local historical landmark?" I asked, wishing I'd paid more attention to the specifics here.

"Oh no," Professor Warner said. "We've rented the house for the weekend on Airbnb. Quite expensive, too, as it's the local Meat Pie festival."

Chapter Two

I wanted to control my sarcasm. I'd gotten much better at it. My mother was Scottish, and my father was Italian, so, really, it was a miracle that every word out of my mouth wasn't pure snark. However, looking upon the sight that greeted us after we stepped out of the train station, well, I couldn't hold it in anymore.

"Yes, Professor, clearly we have come to the dark corners of the Earth," I said, sighing. "We are among a heathen people who will show us their pagan magic as well as introduce us to their chthonic masters."

A banner saying, WELCOME TO MEAT FEST 2024 hung over the front of a cinema directly across from the train station, as people dressed as various slasher movie villains walked down the street. The theatre marquee was visible with CANNIBAL HOLOCAUST, THE HILLS HAVE EYES, and DEATH LINE.

Bean was not the kind of decaying, hellish fishing town I'd been envisioning from my investigations. I'd been expecting something gray, cheerless, and probably a few decades behind the times. Which, yeah, was probably racist against my mother's people. Instead, Bean seemed like an ordinary town in every respect, the cars modern, and the atmosphere suffused with a general sense of cheer for their local festival. Every other building was a tea shop or a place selling local produce—heavy on the tartan teacloths, whisky, and enough shortbread to choke the Loch Ness monster (present in plush form). I could see, in the distance, they'd set up a fair with amusement park rides and lots of booths with a decidedly horror theme. If it wasn't the middle of July, I would have said it was a pretty good Halloween display.

To the professor's credit, he seemed to realize this trip was probably a bust. "It would seem in lieu of recent economic woes affecting the British Isles, the locals have decided to lean into their infamous reputation rather than deny it."

"You don't say," I said, lifting my suitcase in one hand as my duffle bag rested on my right shoulder. I'd always been strong as an ox and my father had said that if academia didn't work out, I could always dig ditches for a living.

Dick.

"Also points for using the word chthonic," Professor Warner said, showing he at least had a sense of humor about all this.

"The commercialization of the Sawney Bean legend does serve the purpose of raising awareness of local legends and customs," Lisa said, sounding as disappointed as the professor but doing a better job of hiding it. No one hated Goths for making the dark and spooky more family-friendly—for the normies—more than Goths.

"I'm actually with Rick here," Karl said, looking around, annoyed. "This is a horrific misrepresentation of the local heritage and religious rituals born here."

"I didn't say that," I replied, annoyed at Karl putting words in my mouth. Personally, I was of the mind that if the Sawney Bean legend were true, which was a big if, then they were a bunch of serial killers rather than anything connected to either pagan religion or primordial underground humans.

"Good evening, lads!" A woman's cheerful voice spoke up nearby. "Welcome tae Scotland."

I turned my head and almost immediately found myself dumbstruck by the woman before me. She had beautiful skin, long black hair, and piercing blue eyes. She was dressed in a plain green dress and sweater, but wore them like high fashion. I was tongue tied just looking at her. There was a kind of instant eighties movie music montage and kismet, I felt. Either that or I was really, really desperate after deciding it wouldn't work out between me and Lisa. She was carrying a bunch of folders and I noticed she was standing next to an SUV.

"Lads and lass," Lisa said, unhappily.

"Oh right," the woman said. "I am Annie Devlin, and you must be the American Miskatonic Party! I am here to guide you through our wonderful town's sordid, murderous history as well as set you up in Bean Mansion for the weekend. Tomorrow, we have a fun day planned of spelunking as well as exploring heritage sites."

It took us all a second to tune into her accent, but I got there first.

I turned to Professor Warner. "You hired a tour guide?"

"It seemed the most expedient way of getting through the bureaucratic red tape that was impeding our investigation," Professor Warner said, lightly coughing and turning his head.

I was starting to wonder if the professor was just as much of a fraud as I was. It was starting to look like he'd set himself up to do the bare minimum of actual research, let alone archaeology, while letting the University pick up the bill. If that was the case, then he'd gone up in my estimation significantly. The wonders of tenure in action.

"As you can see, we're in the middle of Meat Fest 2024! A local celebration of meat pies, steaks, sausages, lamb, venison, and stews. No pork, though. Local taboo. Don't expect to find any missing travelers in your meals, though. We save that for ourselves. Haha, just a bit of Bean humor there," Annie said, continuing to talk in her cheerful sing-song voice. It was clear she was doing her best to suppress her local accent and speak with a lighter, more comprehensible tone—at least to American English speakers.

"What if you're a vegetarian?" Lisa asked, getting a weird expression on her face as if something about the woman was putting her off; something more than just the occasional hostility a territorial person might have to a newcomer in a small group.

"Then you're just shite out of luck," Annie said, not missing a beat. "Meat Fest is a carnivorous festival and you're about as lucky to be vegetarian here as a teetotaler in wine country. However, I will assure you that the people of Bean are great believers in ethical consumption."

"Which means what?" I asked, just happy to hear her speak.

"We believe in free range handling of our domestic animals," Annie replied, speaking less like she was reading from a script and more from the heart. "None of those cramped stalls and other awful conditions that so many cattle and other poor creatures are shoved into. No being horribly pumped with drugs and steroids either. Not that we don't give them the benefits of modern medicine, mind you. Here in Bean, our livestock are treated as beloved members of the family."

"Until you kill and eat them," I replied, following that train of logic to its natural conclusion.

"Yup," Annie said, unfazed. "It's the circle of life."

I wasn't sure that was actually a circle, since the meat eaters seemed to be getting the better end of things. I was definitely interested in what she had to say though. Not just because she was incredibly attractive, but also because I was really hungry and didn't have any objections to eating animals. As long as I didn't have to see how the sausage was made, so to speak, I was happy to wolf down meat in all its forms.

"Indeed," Professor Warner said, staring. "While I appreciate this wonderful insight into the local festival, I'd like to get ourselves set up at Bean Manor first."

"Are you sure?" Annie asked, sounding genuinely disappointed. "I have lunch already reserved at the Devil's Pit barbecue. It's really an experience."

"I'm afraid so," Professor Warner said.

I had to admit I was disappointed myself.

For a variety of reasons.

Bean Manor was another location that didn't exactly meet with my "haunted house" expectations for this trip. I'd been imagining decaying walls, ominous shadows, and creaking doors with an antediluvian sense of dread seeping from every corner. Instead, once we arrived at the building a few miles out of town, it felt like the kind of spruced up mansion you'd see on television. Hell, James Bond's mansion in *Skyfall* felt more intimidating and oppressive.

Indeed, the place had a fantastic view of the ocean from its cliffside placement, and I just wanted to go out on the balcony and soak up the sea air. The facilities were another sign the trip was a bust, as any place which had wireless internet (Annie had the password), electricity, and indoor plumbing wasn't likely to be the home of eldritch abominations.

"Doesn't look like the home to a bunch of cannibals," Karl muttered, sounding almost disappointed.

"Well, this isn't the original Bean Manor," Annie said, still in tour guide mode. "The original Bean Manor, if it ever existed, was burned down by the party assembled by James the Fourth during their attempt to cleanse the region of banditry. This house was actually built by Anne Murphy and her husband, Martin Fitzroy, before being renovated in the early twentieth century after a housefire."

Professor Warner was oddly looking over every little nook and cranny of the place while Lisa seemed to be soaking up the atmosphere like it was a spiritual experience. She even had her little psychic crystal necklace out around her neck as she spread out her arms in opposite directions. Karl, by contrast, looked bored and annoyed with everything he was encountering.

"What caused the housefire?" Karl asked. "Angry villagers?"

"Faulty wiring," Annie replied. "Sadly, not much of the original Murphy Manor remains."

"You say Murphy Manor," I said, looking at her. "Wouldn't it be Fitzroy? I mean, why call it Bean Manor today?"

I was going to do at least a little research here, even if I thought this was an enormous waste of time. Besides, it was an excuse to spend some time with Annie.

"That is a long story," Annie replied. "Martin Fitzroy married Annie Murphy, his father's mistress, but actually served as stepfather to her existing child, James Murphy. It was believed that James Murphy was James the Fourth's bastard, as was Martin, and thus James Murphy was Martin's little brother, but King James never recognized him. James Murphy would eventually go out and become a famous sea captain, marrying seven times as well as keeping numerous mistresses in the town. Most of the town can trace their lineage back to him, these days. His latter descendants were less prolific, and the male line died out—"

"In 2020," I replied, repeating what I'd said to the professor. "So, it was renamed Bean Manor after the town when it became public property. Got it. It's not named after the Sawney Bean legend at all."

Annie smiled. "Correct. Yes, as you may have guessed, the village is leaning heavily into the old story."

I looked into her eyes. "What's your take on it?"

Annie smiled brightly. "I believe every town is entitled to one good scary story. Bean just happens to have a bunch."

"So, I take it you don't believe Alexander Bean was married to a witch and in contact with a bunch of underground-dwelling monsters," Karl said, clenching his fists. He was reacting intensely to all of this.

Professor Warner glared at Karl as if he'd given away the secret. The professor may have believed in utter nonsense, but he had the good sense to not advertise it to the world.

Lisa facepalmed.

"Oh, you mean the ghoul legend?" Annie asked, surprising everyone. "How there is a vast city of underground-dwelling pre-humans living underneath Bennane Head and the Bean clan was a bunch of their worshipers, learning the worship of K'Tullu and Yog-Sothoth among other fell practices."

Everyone stared at her.

"Yeah, that," I replied.

Karl looked at her if she were suddenly a glass of water and he was a man dying of thirst. "So, you have heard the stories?"

"In America, a hundred years is a long time, and in Scotland, a hundred miles is a long distance," Annie said, paraphrasing the old joke. "Bean is a relatively new community in Scotland, and it predates the age of your country twice over. I looked up you Miskatonic folk when you made the arrangements for your stay, and it was quite the read. You can find anything on the internet these days. Aye, I've heard the stories told about my hometown. However, you'll find that ghouls are just another name for very common legends. Underhill-dwelling monsters are just the same fairy stories from all over the isles: redcaps eating the flesh of the living, changelings being substituted for human bairns, and hideous monsters taking the shape of beautiful women to seduce men into siring half-human offspring. Old Francois Balfour just slapped an Arabic name on 'em and gingered it up for his scary book."

"An all-too-common perspective among my peers, Ms. Devlin," Professor Warner said, unhappily.

Despite her flippant manner, it was strange for a random tour guide to be familiar with a 17th century book of occult mysticism, even if the Bean clan was mentioned in it. "I suppose the age of the book has lent it a certain credibility."

"Pfft," Annie said, smirking. "The seventeenth century is yesterday. *Cultes de Goules* is only old to Americans. It's like believing H. G. Wells got his idea for Morlocks from Bean just because he stayed the weekend here."

"Oh, he did?" I asked, happy to discuss that factoid with her. It was a surprise to find someone who had a knowledge of my area of specialty without getting drawn into the utter quackery that it seemed to induce in just about everyone else.

"They're real," Karl muttered under his breath. "They're real."

Damn, he really had drunk the Kool-Aid. I needed to talk to my friend about this, but maybe after we were out of Scotland and had a little distance from the subject. Besides, he didn't seem like he wanted to be told that there was no Rapunzel or gingerbread house in the woods.

Instead, I looked at Annie. "Listen, this is going to seem forward, but would you like to discuss this further? Professor, would it be okay to go have lunch with her? It seems like everything is set up here and—"

Professor Warner, sadly, killed my hopes of asking her out. "I'm afraid that's not going to be possible, Mr. Jameson. We must prepare for exploring the caves under Bennane Head."

Gee thanks, Professor. "Ah."

"You won't be getting much luck out of that exploration," Annie said, a pained expression on her face. "The caves are only six hundred feet deep. It was meant to be the base of Alexander 'Sawney' Bean, but there's no city to be found there. Maybe if it was like Tolkien's *The Hobbit* and the goblins opened the Earth to swallow people but—"

"Don't encourage him," I said aloud, before realizing I had. Shit.

Professor Warner just shook his head. "Ms. Delapore?"

Lisa lowered her arms, apparently having finished whatever psychic woo or magic she was trying to do. "I definitely feel something here, Professor. I think we're at the center of it all."

"Excellent," Professor Warner said. "Ms. Devlin, you have been extremely helpful, but I think we'll be working alone from this point onward. If you could leave a number for where we can have our meals delivered from, that will be all."

Annie realized she was being dismissed and another pained expression passed across her face, but inflected with something approaching pity. Whether it was for me or the entire group was impossible to guess. Maybe a little bit of both.

"Good luck with your studies then," Annie said, looking at me. "Another time then."

Yeah, that wasn't going to happen.

In the distance, a storm started to pull in from off the coast. It wasn't exactly supernatural, this being Scotland and all, but it reflected my mood perfectly.

Chapter Three

The rest of the day was miserable, and the night wasn't much better. The storm meant we didn't get to explore the Sawney Bean caves, but it wasn't like there wasn't a huge chunk of information about them on the internet. We could have stayed in the Miskatonic Library and looked at pictures the local tour guides had taken for us. They were on the town's website for Chrissake.

Professor Warner set up a bunch of kirlian cameras, air pressure monitoring devices, brain wave recorders, and other machines of dubious practicality throughout the house. I didn't bother questioning them, even though we were supposed to be hunting a lost civilization, not ghosts. Karl refused to talk to him throughout the encounter and practically bit my head off when I suggested we sneak out for a pint. Lisa was also in full witch mode, seemingly soaking up the weirdness of Murphy Manor / Bean Manor despite the place having been re-constructed in the frigging *seventies*, according to the brochure left by Annie. Hell, I'd grown up in a house older than that.

About the only thing to recommend the trip was the fact that the Devil's Pit barbecue was a living argument for Scottish meat cooking. We'd risked the rain to get down there and had our meal against the professor's request. If Chef Gordon Ramsey hadn't already destroyed that reputation, the fantastic meat extravaganza I had there would have been the final blow.

By the time I went to sleep, I was determined to just suffer my way through the rest of the trip and start to figure out options other than the Armitage Award. I was not a good fit for all this weirdness, and not even a free trip to Scotland was worth it if I had to spend the entire time debating UFOs and mole people. I just wanted to relax and put anything spooky from my mind.

So, of course, I had nightmares that would have given Wes Craven pause.

I dreamed of the primordial inhabitants of the British Isles, naked and carrying items of stone, fleeing in terror from the bipedal wolf-faced monsters that poured out of the ground and dragged men as well as women to their doom.

I saw ancient stone monuments erected throughout pre-submersion Doggerland, marking the spots where the ghouls lurked underground. The first villages and agriculture were accompanied by tools. Futile attempts to fight back nevertheless emboldened the people, who began to worship the wolfmen's gods and call upon things from the sea to fight them.

I saw the relationship between the wolfmen and the humans change as the former set themselves up as gods. They assumed human forms and demanded blood sacrifices, willingly offered by the priests to allow the numbers of the surface dwellers to grow.

I saw ghouls begin to claim human brides and husbands, creating strange mutant hybrids that could shapeshift and walk between the worlds. The ghouls, for that was what they were, humans, and their hybrids were at last one people, or at least something approaching one people.

That was when the Others emerged from the ground. Hideous, white-skinned blind creatures that had been raised in the darkness from the ancestors of humanity, kept in pens and bred like cattle.

The Others slaughtered ghouls, hybrids, and humans alike before devouring them like their masters had them. Semi-intelligent, cannibalistic, and mutated by the hideous experiments their former owners had performed on them, they spread like a virus through the tunnels of the Earth, raping and pillaging until they formed a new species of humanity.

Us.

"Ah," I said, waking up with a ringing in my ears. I was inside one of the upstairs guest bedrooms, still in my boxers and a t-shirt, with the storm still raging outside. It was two a.m. and I had a massive headache.

I was also hungry.

Really hungry.

Shaking my head, I slid out of the bed and put on a pair of sweatpants before heading into the rest of the manor. There was a banging noise that only got louder after I left my room, and as much as I wanted to see if there was any leftover food from the Devil's Pit, that seemed something worth investigating.

Much to my surprise, I had to head into the mansion's cellar to find the source of the noise, which was much louder than I'd expected and sounded like someone chopping wood. Mind you, I'd always had good hearing.

There, among a bunch of empty wine racks, paint cans, and other leftover materials from Murphy Manor's renovation as an Airbnb, I saw Professor Warner, without his shirt on, hacking into the wooden wall paneling with an ax. Surprisingly, the professor was pretty ripped for a man his age and looked like an old professional wrestler. I needed another second to process this, as he was *hacking into the wall with an ax*.

"Professor, what the hell are you doing?" I asked, staring at the sight and wondering if I was still dreaming.

"Come here, boy, give me a hand," Professor Warner said, taking another swing and then pausing for a moment to catch his breath.

"You do realize we don't own this house, right?" I asked, staring.

"I said come here and help!" Professor Warner shouted, meeting my gaze with intense eyes that put Karl's, earlier, to shame.

"Right," I said, walking up to the wooden paneling and pulling on it. The professor had made a dent in it, but it wasn't until I put my back into it that I managed to rip several layers of wood free. I wasn't sure what I was even trying to accomplish, until the last layer gave way and exposed a staircase.

It wasn't a normal staircase either, made of wood or concrete, but something that looked to have been chiseled and carved out of the cavernous walls that surrounded it. It was, by itself, a pretty impressive find, as the crudeness of the carvings made me think it had been cut centuries ago, rather than years. I could see fairly far down the steps— I'd always had good lowlight vision—but there was something about the yawning abyss below that made me sick to contemplate.

I could feel the wind rushing up from the sea below, no matter how strange an architecture that would require. I could also hear the crashing waves. This was definitely an entrance down to the Sawney Bean caverns below. It didn't change much, but if the professor was willing to pay the price for repairs, then he'd actually made a genuine discovery: yes, it turned out that the locals once had a passage down to the cave system.

"Behold!" Professor Warner said.

"Congratulations, Professor," I said, trying and failing to contain my sarcasm. "You've discovered a hole in the ground."

"A hole leading to the caverns' true entrance!" Professor Warner said, staring with what I could only describe as madness in his eyes.

"True entrance?" I asked, wondering what the hell he was talking about.

"The one in the front would never serve as the true entrance to the Ultraterrestrial's lair," Professor Warner explained. "The Bean clan would need their own private, hidden entrance for communicating with their masters. The front might have contained bodies, an abattoir, or stored victims for King James' goons to find, but the actual center of the cult-clan's rituals would have to be behind walls of solid rock. This is just like the Delapore estate! A secret entrance covered up to hide the town's dark, forbidden history!"

I pitied Professor Warner in that moment more than I was angry for wasting months on his so-called research. "Except there's other possibilities here too. It could be a priest hole for Catholics during the time of Protestant repression. It could be a smuggler's den down there, or it could be one of the landowners just wanted to expand his house into the caverns below for storage and did a shit job of it."

Professor Warner wasn't looking at me, though. "Do you know why I selected you for the Armitage Award, son?"

He'd never called me son before, and I wasn't sure I liked it. "Because you respected my academic prowess and skepticism?"

Professor Warner scoffed as if that were a particularly ridiculous answer. "Your mother, my boy."

"My mother?" I asked, really hoping this wasn't going to be about how my mother had traded sex for my scholarship. The fact my mind even went there should tell you about the likelihood of that being the case, which was sadly non-zero. My mother had always been a wild one and it wouldn't have been the first time she'd cheated on my dad. He tolerated it with good grace, and honestly seemed a little afraid of her at times.

"Yes," Professor Warner said, his voice distant and echoing as he kept his gaze focused on the stone steps before us. "Your mother, Mary, saved my career. My sanity, even."

That remained to be seen. "What do you mean?"

"Do you remember the Arkham subway collapse of '92?" Professor Warner asked.

"I know *of* it," I said, wondering what he was getting at.

Like Boston's subway system, a lot of state money and government pork had been spent trying to expand the underground railway system that had existed since the 19th century. Questions of embezzlement and mismanagement of materials had dogged the effort for decades, though. The project had been started in my dad's era and carried on well into mine. The 1992 Collapse had almost, if you pardoned the pun, derailed the whole thing.

I didn't know much more than any other Arkham local, but the local mobsters (we still had Irish ones instead of Russian) had apparently been substituting poor-quality cement among other materials while pocketing the difference. When they'd opened the first functioning subway stations of the expansion, the entire thing had collapsed and a train full of passengers had been buried alive for a week. Thirteen people had died and twenty-three more had been hospitalized with permanent injuries, ranging from brain damage to lost limbs. Last I checked, the State of Massachusetts was still dealing with lawsuits related to it.

"I was there," Professor Warner said, shaking his head. "I was working on my doctorate at the time and with both my wife and child. Neither of them made it."

I blinked. "Christ, I had no idea."

Professor Warner grimaced at the mention of Christ, which was one of those things I'd noticed but never asked about. He struck me as one of those people who'd probably been religious at one point in their life before going the opposite direction as only someone really pissed off at God can.

"We were not alone down there," Professor Warner said, shaking his head. "The tunnels had been made as a challenge by the city fathers to the ghouls below, a way to channel the ley lines and steal their power. The ghouls took this personally and made an example of us. They hadn't expected so many of us to survive, though. There was much debate among them about what to do with us. They spoke English among themselves, you see, and we could hear them and their twisted debate as they dragged off the dead and dying. I can still hear the whispers and *crunching* of our dead."

What the professor was describing was madness, worse than madness, but I found myself entranced as I absolutely knew he was describing the truth as he remembered it. "There was cannibalism on the train?"

"It's not cannibalism when a ghoul eats a human, any more than when a shark eats a minnow. They can breed with our kind, because they can adopt our form and transform our DNA to their needs, but it is no more a mixing of the races than a cuckoo leaving their egg in another's nest," Professor Warner said, his face wrinkled in disgust. "But yes, the cannibalism came in time. For all their pretensions of being a superior species, they were squeamish at the prospect of murdering us individually, but we knew too many of their secrets to be allowed to walk away."

I would regret my next question for the rest of my life. "What happened?"

"A dark compact was struck, forged of shared loathing and shame, as well as the desperate needs of survival," Professor Warner said. "Those who were willing to eat of their fellow human beings would be allowed to live, while those who refused would die. I was desperate to save my daughter and willing to do anything. She was only eight and we were already hunger and thirst ravaged."

"You did it," I said.

"Yes," Professor Warner said. "I fed the horrific strips of my fellow passengers to my daughter myself. My wife refused, disgusted, and tried to stop me. It was my fellow passengers who fell upon her and the other dissenters and ended her. In the end, it was resolved in a night and the rescue team found us the next day, lowering cleaner food down to us in baskets afterward. The authorities covered up what happened, and much was attributed to oxygen deprivation and trauma, but I know the truth."

"What happened to your daughter?" I asked, knowing it couldn't have been my mother.

"She was changed by the experience, but not in the way you'd think," Professor Warner said. "The flesh seemed to trigger some sort of metamorphosis, or perhaps it was the dark blessings the ghouls worked over the meat. Her skin grew pale as alabaster, her hair white like an old woman's, and she began to fear the light as though she had developed porphyria. By the time she was fourteen, I knew I'd lost her, and she vanished. The police didn't even bother to investigate me, and I sometimes wish they'd arrested me for killing her. I would feel less guilt."

My conscious mind was already weaving together the deranged story and trying to come up with a rational alternative to what he was saying. After being traumatized in a cave-in, possibly resorting to desperate means to survive, he'd woven an elaborate justification about monsters to cope with events. Maybe his daughter had suffered from a condition related to the accident, either chemical or mental. Maybe he'd killed her and was covering it up. Maybe she had just run away or died of her condition. Seeking some way to make sense of it all, he'd become obsessed with the occult and pseudo-science, with Miskatonic University not wanting to fire him due to his history. No. That didn't make any sense. It was close, maybe, but wrong.

"How does my mother fit into all this?" I asked, knowing I was just feeding into his delusions but desperate to know.

Professor Warner barely seemed to acknowledge me. "I spent years researching the occult and seeking answers to the kind of horrors below us. I thought I'd find a sympathetic ear with the board of Miskatonic but was rebuffed. They knew of the ghouls, of course. Had known about them for a century, in fact, but considered them better left undisturbed. They only feed on the dead. *They do not hunt our kind.* Bah! Your mother brought me the journal that proved otherwise."

"Journal?" I asked.

"Sawney Bean's journal, dictated by his wife since he was functionally illiterate. It detailed all the gruesome things that he and his cult did for their evil masters. The pagan murder rites and human sacrifices that accompanied their foul banquets of the dead. The ghouls did not wait for the dead to be in the ground to begin their feasts, but hunted the living. It was proof of the malevolence of the ghouls, a race so much more advanced than our own, being every bit the degenerate savages I thought they were."

That was the missing piece and I felt sick about it. My mother was an artist and a bit of a con woman. She'd obviously forged some kind of artifact for the professor to find, and he'd taken it at face value. He probably knew, at least on some level, it was a phony too or he would have presented it to the world, but as long as it existed, it was proof his fancies had a basis in reality. I had to give it to Mom; she'd managed to keep me in college despite everything. Unfortunately, it had been at the cost of manipulating a poor madman.

"What do you hope to find?" I asked, knowing that the only way to break him out of this delusion would eventually be to head down.

Maybe not even then.

"Evidence," Professor Warner said, sadly. "More evidence. Enough to present, not just to the Miskatonic Board but their allies, that we can't just keep covering all this up. We'd never win against them in a direct conflict. They knew about atomic theory when we were still banging rocks together in the Stone Age, but we can prepare."

I took a deep breath. "I'll get a flashlight. Do you want to get Lisa and Karl?"

"No," Professor Warner said, taking a deep breath. "They've grown too close to this."

I nodded and stared down into the void. I really, really hoped that I was just going to find a flooded cavern down there.

Chapter Four

I had made a horrible mistake.

I'd expected to find the steps leading right down into the caverns and a flooded entrance, which would have cut our trip short and brought an end to the insanity. I didn't know if Professor Warner was genuinely ill or just the victim of a bunch of conspiracy theories that had piled up in what might have once been a brilliant mind, but the result was the same—he was no longer a harmless old kook talking about aliens and mole people but now bringing people deeper into his delusions.

In my case, literally, because we were going deeper and what was around me had to be a delusion. The staircase had just kept going and going, deeper into the ground, opening into passages that were far larger and more twisting than the geology of Bean could possibly have made real.

For the first twenty minutes or so, I came up with excuse after excuse, telling myself that this was a trick of the light, or that was just my mind playing tricks on me. The walls had hideous shapes carved into them that I kept insisting were just natural formations that happened to take the appearance of ghastly, inhuman faces. Except geometry and my own senses betrayed me, as I found myself walking over a perfectly smooth stone bridge across a seemingly bottomless cavern, the source of the wind I'd felt before. The walls here were also riddled with the carvings, so many that it would have taken a thriving civilization several decades to engrave, even with modern technology.

"This isn't happening," I muttered, shaking my head as I kept the flashlight in my hands pushed forwards. "This isn't happening."

"This is just the antechamber," Professor Warner said, his voice disturbingly calm, as if seeing all of this was laying his mind's torments to rest rather than enflaming them as it was mine. "We have barely begun to probe the edges of the ghoul's kingdom."

I stopped and turned the flashlight on him. He covered his face. "Professor, this is real!"

"Yes, obviously," Professor Warner said, chuckling as if it was all a sick joke. "If any of this were allowed to come out in public, we could prove the truth of the Hyborian Age, and older civilizations still. These rocks are but the newest creations of Earth's oldest inhabitants."

I was close to panic now. "What do you mean 'if any of this were allowed to come out in public?' You're talking like, what, the Men in Black?"

Professor Warner shook his head. "If only it were mere human conspiracy that held the truth back, Mr. Jameson. No, I fear the issue is a far more elemental one. It is evolution itself that works against us as academics."

"Evolution?" I asked, finally opening myself to the madness I'd previously dismissed.

Professor Warner pulled out a pack of cigarettes that looked older than me, and lit up. "Five years clean. Disgusting habit, but if I'm ever going to go back, it might as well be now. Yes, evolution. The most blessed gift that humanity ever received from the raw forces of nature—though I have some suspicions it was husbanded in—was the inability to collate the truth of the cosmos."

"I don't understand," I said, feeling a chill despite the inexplicably hot air.

"We are cattle, Mr. Jameson," Professor Warner said. "Bred with blinders and ear plugs that prevent us from seeing the truth of the horrors around us. The world is not composed of four dimensions but an ever-expanding deck of layers that each contain their own unique manifestations of hostility. String Theory, multiverses, aliens, gods, demons, Heaven, and Hell are perhaps the closest the human mind can come to appreciating the various things around us. Evolution benefited us, though, by ensuring we only see in a tiny spectrum and simply ignore the truth around us. The herd of humanity moves forward, losing only a handful of members each year, and we do not panic. This allows us to keep breeding new generations to be prey animals for our masters."

I stared at him. "That's…insane."

"Insane are those handfuls of humans born with an extra sense, perhaps because of ancestry not of this Earth, or a mutation that lets them pierce what is around us. They, we, are a threat to the herd. We show them things they cannot possibly live with and thus we must be ostracized or destroyed," Professor Warner said, almost sadly.

"I don't understand," I said, lying. I could understand what he was saying, and it terrified me. I was scared shitless, and all I'd seen so far were some impossible examples of geology and construction.

"If you carved into the side of the cliff face of Bennane Head, dug a mile deep, you would never find this cavern. It exists on another layer of the deck which other races can shuffle as easily as you and I can walk through a door." Professor Warner took a long drag off his cigarette. "I never expected to find an actual entrance to one of the ghoul doors or, if I did, I never expected to be able to go through. From that, I believe we shall not be allowed to leave. I am content with that decision, to be reunited with my family in what worlds may exist beyond, or in peaceful oblivion, but I regret that you have come with me on this."

I stared at him, letting his words sink in and almost pushed him into the abyss out of fury. Instead, I decided I would leave immediately and pretend this strange journey had never happened. If he wanted to die in some strange alien cave surrounded by hideous statues, then let him. This would be something I'd dismiss as a dream in the morning and never think of again. I'd buy a fucking ticket outward and get the hell out of the country, Armitage Award or not.

Except, that wasn't an option.

There were noises coming from the way we'd come. Noises that were like scratching on a blackboard mixed with the skittering of rats. Noises that triggered long repressed and deeply buried instincts, that made me think of deer running from a fire in the woods. Every instinct in my body screamed at me to run, so I did. I turned around and started running deeper into the twisted tunnels of the cavern, despite it being against all reason. My flashlight fell from my hands as I stumbled, yet I kept running.

Voices whispered in my ear that did not sound entirely human, more like a throat approximation of English that could be heard from all directions around me.

RUN.

RUN.

RUN.

COME HOME. The last set of words caused me to fall over completely as I entered another chamber and fell down a flight of stairs. I felt bones crack, and I hit my head as I rolled to the base and found myself in some sort of chamber that I would have called a temple if it had been built with human hands. There was a nasty crunching as I rolled around on the ground, trying and failing to get up as the room started spinning around me. It was a tall, cylindrical chamber filled with more statues. There was no source of light within, but I could see as brightly as in daytime even as my consciousness was fading.

The most telling of the statues, the one that drew my attention most, was familiar from my time at Miskatonic University. A bulbous, squid-like, humanoid thing that had been sketched many times over in various blasphemous texts, and things I'd dismissed previously as badly-done mythology or monster drawings: K'Tullu. Its tentacled mouth was open wide as if to swallow me, and its four eyes each contained a kind of multicolored gem that provided light throughout the chamber. I ran my hands through the crunching material I could feel biting into my back and picked up the pieces, cutting my hand as I did so.

I stared at the handful.

Bone fragments.

Skull fragments.

Human teeth.

I remember laughing, before screaming until I passed out.

Chapter Five

I woke up with blood in my eyes.

I reached up to wipe it away and felt it leaking still from my forehead where I had a huge gash. Cleaning my face with my sleeve, I found myself still in the horrifying temple, the ground covered in heaps of dried human bones like a waste pit for a barbecue. It was not that sight that horrified me, though. No, my mind had already processed that I was in a whole new terrifying nightmare I was unable to escape. The smell of fresh meat, blood, and other, nastier fluids wafted over from a stone table where two familiar figures were having a ghastly feast.

Karl and Lisa were standing there, their fingers and mouths covered in viscera as they pawed like wild animals at the corpse of Professor Warner. He'd had his head smashed in and they were using stolen kitchen knives and weird stone tools I could only assume had been stolen from among the artifacts at Miskatonic University. The two had deranged expressions on their faces, mixtures of joy and rapture crossed with some small, suppressed sense of disgust.

The sight sickened me before I began to crawl away, or tried to, at least. The crunching noise of my movement against the bones beneath me drew their attention.

"Hey Rick," Karl said, turning as he continued to chew on his cannibalistic feast. I didn't know how he could stand there, not throwing up what was in his mouth but just chewing. I wanted to throw up from twenty feet away.

I asked what was, at that time, a very reasonable question. "What the ever-loving *fuck*?"

"It's real," Lisa said, managing to force herself to swallow whatever it was she was eating from our late professor. "All of it. The Ultraterrestials, Great K'tullu, the gods of our ancestors, and the coming apocalypse. All of it is real."

Karl looked at me like he was trying to explain a new phone app or show off his new car. He gestured up to the statue. "They came with him, don't you see? The K'nyanians! That's what the ghouls call themselves! They weren't human, not at first! But they came down with him and can shift their forms to resemble whatever the reigning species of the time is! They bred our ancestors to be food! Food! Unintelligent cattle and pigs! Meat! But we grew minds! The spark of life!"

"The true gods have blessed us," Lisa said, clasping her hands in prayer. "Yog-Sothoth, Cthulhu, and Shub-Niggurath! All true religion is about the body! The consumption of the blood and flesh! Because it was the gods showing us how to become like them! To be immortal and eternal, free from all the bullshit!"

Karl stared at me as if trying to see something inside me. "My family has worshiped the Old Ones for as long as the white man has been in our country, Rick. But it's all nonsense. Stupid robes and chants, when the real magic is here in the Old Country. Down here in the dark places. I saw how you were disgusted by the professor's idiocy. His stupid theories and speculation, like a cow wondering why his friends kept vanishing when they go off to slaughter! The books show the rituals, Rick! The rituals to become like ghouls! We can become wild, and free, and immortal!"

I finally managed to climb to my feet and overcome my terror. This place was the gathering place of the Bean clan, a temple shrine to the Great Old Ones they'd decided to worship with their foul rituals. It wasn't a sacred place to the ghouls, though. This horrible mess was just the product of the Bean clan themselves. I didn't know how I knew it, but I knew it. It was a cargo cult, like the islanders who had created replicas of airfields and airplanes during World War II because they didn't have the context for understanding what the hell they were seeing. Both my friends were completely off their gourds, trying to comprehend something beyond their understanding and aping the behavior of beings they could never hope to equal.

"You killed our teacher and ate him," I said, very slowly. "You two are *goddamn nutjobs.*"

Karl stared at me with the kind of look you'd give someone who'd metamorphized into a bug before your eyes. Lisa just looked disappointed even as she choked, clearly having a bit of difficulty keeping down raw human meat. Because you know, reality.

"You've always had a small mind, Rick," Karl said, shaking his head and walking toward me with one of the stone knives in his right hand. "If you don't understand what worshiping the ghouls could accomplish, then you're just meat."

"You are not worshiping the ghouls, Mr. Butcher," Annie Devlin's voice echoed throughout the chamber. "You are worshiping the *sluagh.*"

"What?" I asked, looking around for the source of it.

"Sluagh, redcaps, troglodytes, Morlocks," Annie said, repeating the various names of underground monsters. "Their names don't matter, and one is as good as any other. But the sluagh are not the ghoul race. *We* are the People, and *they* are the Husbanded."

Karl looked up to see our tour guide descending the steps I'd fallen down. He had a feral, animalistic expression on his face and lifted his knife as if to threaten her. Unfortunately for him, she was carrying an old Lee-Enfield rifle left over from the Great War. Annie lifted it and fired, striking Karl in the chest with the sound of a thunderclap. Karl dropped his knife on the ground and started bleeding profusely, filling the chamber even more with the scent of blood.

"No, no, no," Lisa said, stepping back. "I'm supposed to be immortal."

Annie reloaded the rifle and aimed it at Lisa. "You're not even one of the Husbanded, dear."

A second thunderclap filled the room and I saw the girl I'd had a crush on for weeks fall to the ground, her face struck by the round, forcing me to look away. In the span of a few minutes, I'd become the sole survivor of this expedition that I'd dismissed as nothing more than a free vacation chasing fairy stories.

"Please don't kill me!" I said, covering my face. "I didn't see anything!"

It was a bold-faced lie and we both knew it. I would have done anything in that moment to take back everything I'd seen. Investigating the ghouls and the Legend of Sawney Bean had resulted in our doom. I just wanted to be back home, safe in my father's garage, working on his old Corvette, the Blue Meanie, like I'd used to do on weekends before college.

"Why would I want to kill you, Richard?" Annie spoke.

I looked up, confused. She was descending the stairs now and I saw her shimmer and shake as if I was seeing past an illusion. What I saw underneath the glamour was not a human woman at all but a kind of dog-like humanoid, like something out of a horror movie. Yet, in a way I couldn't put into words, she was still beautiful. The rifle was very real, though, and fit perfectly into her all-too-human hands.

"What's going on?" I asked, staring forward.

"Your friend was right, Richard," Annie spoke, her voice soothing. "The People did breed the Husbanded from the primates of this world as food. We cultivated food we could digest from the primordial soup across a hundred million years. The last and most nourishing of our livestock we trained to take care of itself, to build little villages and feed themselves, but that made them too ghoul-like for many of us. So we gave them their freedom and often ate from their dead. Some of us could not tolerate that, though, and dismissed claims they were feeling creatures. They bred particularly nasty and hungry variants that many of the people above are now descended from. Sadly, they have ever tried to rise above their station. To wear clothes and worship our gods in hopes of being like us. To eat the flesh of others like them. They believed they could become like the K'nyanians, but they can't be. Only a rare few human bloodlines carry any of our line and we do our best to bring them back to the People."

"The creatures outside looked from pig to man, and from man to pig, and from pig to man again; but already it was impossible to say which was which," I said, reciting the final line of *Animal Farm*. It seemed almost hilarious in retrospect. Or maybe I was laughing so I didn't scream.

"Yes," Annie said. "You are not one of them. Your mother is a lost one of our kind. You know that now, don't you?"

"Yes," I whispered. Somehow, I did. Ever since I'd been here and experienced the dream, I'd felt like I was falling deeper and deeper into a dark new world I would never escape. Now, I knew there was no escape, and I was destined to spend the rest of my life here in the darkness. As Nietzsche would say, I had stared into the abyss and now it was staring back at me.

"Your mother knew what you were," Annie whispered. "How could she not? She arranged for you to become the professor's student and come here, a place that would awaken your long-buried side. She knew, just as I did, that you would be able to enter the gateways meant for ghouls and other creatures of our gods. It was important we bring you here now."

"Why now?" I said, my throat dry and my stomach aching.

"It is almost time," Annie said. "The humans have boiled the Earth's oceans and awakened the sleepers. This is not the first time they have stirred, but it may well be the last. We must recall our children and hide below in our warrens where we will survive the Rising. Only then can we exit into what brave new world we might find."

I would have cried, but I already felt myself changing into something that held no tears. Something *hungry*. Everything around me suddenly smelled so delicious, overwhelming any disgust or lingering humanity I possessed; humanity I'd never possessed, it turned out. "I need to eat. Please."

Annie stroked my face, and I felt the fur on her hand "Then let us eat. It would be wrong to let it go to waste."

And God help me, I did.

Prisoner 191

By Philip Hemplow

Detention Site COBALT, Kabul 19th District, 2003

King sighed as the last sliver of red sun vanished behind the rubble-strewn hill to his south, and returned his attention to the road.

They were late. It was ninety minutes since he'd received notification of the Blackhawk touching down at Bagram, and the airbase was less than an hour's drive away. It was a straight road with little opportunity for getting lost, so where the hell were they?

He lit another cigarette and flicked the lid of his Zippo back and forth. He'd only taken the damned coffin nails back up since arriving in Kabul and knew he'd have to quit again before going home, or Marcie would give him hell. She'd be right. He ought to know better, especially after watching lung cancer take his old man, but Afghanistan seemed to have that effect on people: resurrecting old vices, ruining good intentions, reopening old wounds. At least it wasn't an opiate habit, which more than a few US personnel of his acquaintance would be taking home with them.

Finally, two pairs of headlights appeared briefly in the distance before disappearing into a dip in the road. Moments later, they reappeared. King could tell from their height and spacing they belonged to Humvees: one prisoner transport, one escort. Tugging his radio from its holster he signalled the bored sentries at the checkpoint, a hundred yards from the gate.

"Let them through."

The two transports slowed, to give the guards time to move the stinger barring their way, then gunned their engines and roared towards the perimeter gate, which opened at their approach. King pitched his cigarette and went to meet them.

"Took your fucking time, boys," he said, approaching the driver's window of the ambulance. The private behind the wheel shot him a withering look.

"Yeah? Well, have fun with this one. He's a real fucking freak."

He jerked his head backwards, in the direction of the passenger compartment, from which muffled yelling could be heard. King grimaced and went to see what the fuss was about.

The Humvee's rear doors flew open as he approached and a marine corporal jumped down, wiping his face and cursing.

"Filthy little fucker!"

"What's wrong, Marine?"

"Fucking animal spat at me! Sir…" added the man hesitantly, taking in King's civilian garb and unsure of his rank or service.

"Lively, is he?" King peered into the vehicle's interior, where two other marines were struggling with a stretcher.

"Most of the time he just stares at us like a fucking psycho, but trust me, you don't wanna get too close. You're gonna want to take care of his nails, too, they're like goddamn scythes."

"He saying anything?"

"Negative. Not so much as a word since we picked him up. Sir, no disrespect, but I'd appreciate it if we could get out of here soonest. My C.O. wants us back at the firebase before sun-up, and my men could really use a shower and some chow."

"Okay, let's get him inside. We'll do the paperwork, and you can hit the road."

He stood aside as the marines slid the stretcher out of the Humvee and slammed the doors. As they passed into the glare of the other vehicle's headlights, King saw the prisoner was strapped down and covered with a thin blanket. He glared around at all of them, teeth bared, cracked lips curled back, a furious sneer on his emaciated face.

"Got a name for him?" asked King, as the corporal ordered his men to fall in and follow them.

"Negative, sir. No clue who he is, but those hills are thick with jihadis. Found him in a cave overlooking FOB Crimson, sitting on the body of a local policeman—or what was left of him."

"He kill the cop?"

"Don't think so. Dude had been executed: pistol shot to the head, point-blank, but we didn't find any weapon at the scene. I think he might be cracked, sir—like, psychotic. Clawed the fuck out of one of my guys before we subdued him. Not sure you're gonna get any useful intel out of him."

"We'll see. You been through SERE training, Marine?"

"Yes, sir—in the classroom, at least."

"Then you know: they all spill eventually. In here."

He held the front door of the former brick factory open and ushered them into its reception area. "Welcome to the Salt Pit, gentlemen."

"For now, he's Prisoner 191."

King and the corporal were completing their respective pieces of paperwork, the marine blinking hard and squinting through exhausted eyes at his clipboard.

"Status?"

"Enemy combatant, of course."

"Okay...I don't have coordinates for where we picked him up. That matter?"

"Nah, don't worry about it. Just put what you can: nearest village, even just the province."

"Right...okay. Reckon that's everything. Can I get a scrimshaw?"

King signed the corporal's paper with an elaborate flourish—not the signature he used in daily life, back home: the indecipherable one he'd developed for documents he might, one day, wish to disavow.

The prisoner had already been conveyed into the bowels of the Salt Pit by two burly contractors from CACI International. While King dealt with the red tape, he would be undergoing fingerprinting, a thorough physical examination and cavity search, delousing, and testing for infectious diseases. Blood samples would be taken and shipped to the CIA's Office of Medical Services for genetic sequencing, to establish his ethnicity and likely place of origin—though the results would take weeks to come back. He would also be photographed, and his picture checked against databases of known Taliban and Al-Qaeda members. As soon as this processing was complete, he would begin his stay in what detainees knew only as 'the Darkness.'

"Well, safe travels," said King, walking the corporal and his men to the door. "Keep your head on a swivel."

"Affirmative, wilco," agreed the corporal, putting his helmet on. "If we pick up any more of these goatfuckers, we'll let you know."

"Appreciate that."

The marine saluted and led his fire team back towards the idling Humvees.

King closed the door and shivered. The Salt Pit was always cold, doubly so once night fell. The cells, in particular, were freezing—intentionally so, the most basic form of coercion. Detainees were kept naked in the cold and dark, to reinforce their feelings of helplessness and vulnerability. After his initial interrogation, Prisoner 191 would be joining them there.

Resisting the urge to light another cigarette, King locked the door and went to welcome their latest guest.

"His b.p. and pulse are dangerously low. Mild photophobia, but no other signs of meningitis, so I think we can rule that out. His dentition is terrible, but TFA. I put it all down to borderline starvation."

"TFA?"

"Typical for Afghan."

Griffin smiled as he replied, a thin-lipped smirk which only compounded King's irritation.

"Does it mean we can't interrogate him?" he demanded to know.

"Oh heavens, no," Griffin assured him, as if shocked at the suggestion. "However, I do recommend rectal feeding, to ensure adequate nutrition—quite *intensive* rectal feeding, in fact."

He grinned again, his face expressing disquieting relish at the prospect. A civilian psychologist contracted to the CIA, Griffin's avidity for the techniques he'd helped develop was frequently troubling. King could only suspect it stemmed from some deep interior dysfunction.

"As well as rectifying his malnutrition, this will, of course, help bring him to the desired state of dependence and cooperation," concluded the psychologist.

"Great, I'll get the rubber hose," muttered King, without enthusiasm. "Has he said anything?"

"Er, no." Griffin checked his notes. "The subject remains entirely non-verbal but, ah, aggressive. We had to keep him restrained during examination and, well, I must admit my inspection of his oral cavity was somewhat perfunctory—quite apart from his tendency to bite, he has the most appalling halitosis. Given his highly resistive and non-compliant state, I recommend assertive measures from the jump."

"Fine. I'll give him the once-over now, then we can start the programme."

"One point of interest is that he's heterochromic, which might help with identification."

"He's what?"

"He has two different-coloured eyes, one brown and one blue," explained Griffin, smiling indulgently. "Dan Aykroyd has it, and Jane Seymour—my sister's cat does, too. It's a harmless condition, but fewer than one percent of the population has it, so he ought to stand out on any list of suspects."

"I'll be sure to bear your sister's cat in mind, doctor," said King, snidely. "You may as well go and eat."

He left the psychologist's office and walked a short way down the crumbling corridor until he came to the black site's medical room, in which Prisoner 191 sat zip-tied to a chair, under the watchful eye of two of the Agency's private military contractors, and Bis, the Salt Pit's translator.

"Any trouble?"

The three men shook their heads.

"Well, well, well, who have we here?" began King, turning to the detainee.

Prisoner 191 stared back at him, a manic look of hungry fascination in his eyes. Now he was properly lit, King could see the discrepancy between them, one brown and one blue, as the doctor had described. He was the most emaciated detainee King had ever seen, his skeleton clearly visible beneath his skin. That skin was blotchy and discoloured, and looked like it belonged on a nonagenarian, not a guerilla. He was almost hairless, a few lank strands dangling from parts of his scalp and, as the marine corporal had warned, his nails were inches long and filthy.

A vile smell rose from him, and King could understand why the mercs on guard had their shemaghs pulled up over their noses. It wasn't body odour—not normal body odour, at least—it was something sickly and rotten which triggered a primal revulsion deep in King's brain.

"You are one aromatic sonofabitch," he commented, forcing himself to ignore the stench and inspect the prisoner's face more closely. 191 leered back at him without blinking, baring jagged, yellow teeth. Foaming saliva ran from the corners of his mouth, glistening under the lights. Behind him, Bis translated King's words into Dari as he spoke.

"You don't have to tell me your name," said King, standing straight again. "Sooner or later, you will tell me, but I'm not interested right now. To me, you're just another body: a body which, as of now, is under my control. You have no rights. You have no leverage. Nobody knows you're here. The only thing you have to offer is information and, until you give me all the information I want, here is where you'll stay. There will be no respite. There will be no mercy. It will not end. Do you understand?"

Prisoner 191 threw back his head and made a rasping sound, deep in his throat, his jaws champing as he strained at his bonds.

"Fight all you want. Eventually, you'll realise it's useless. How long that takes will tell me just how dumb you really are."

191's head came forward again. He was smiling now, but there was no humour in it, only malice. King still hadn't seen him blink. Slowly, deliberately, the prisoner began grinding his teeth, hard enough to make his captors wince.

"That'll do for now," said King, clearing his throat. "Put him in fifteen and forget about him."

"Yes, sir."

The two mercs cut the ties shackling 191 to his chair, but not the ones binding his wrists, and yanked him to his feet. Immediately, the naked prisoner lashed out a leg, with surprising speed and force, kicking one of them in the hip and sending him to the ground. The other guard promptly drove an elbow into the prisoner's face and began raining baton blows on his upper body, while Bis yelped with alarm and pressed himself against the wall.

191 cowered and shielded his head, then lunged towards the door. King stuck out his own leg and hooked his feet from under him as he ran, sending him crashing to the floor. Before he could get up, the two contractors had leapt on him and were pinning him down, eliciting maddened howls of frustration.

"Get him outta here!" shouted King, infuriated by the display of resistance. "Make him secure!"

"Yes, sir!"

Still fighting to control the struggling wretch, the two men carried him bodily from the room.

"Jesus Christ!"

King slumped into a chair and let out an exasperated sigh. "Why can't these skinny fucks get it into their heads when they're beaten?"

Bis could only offer him a sympathetic smile.

The Salt Pit had twenty cells, each about seven feet wide and ten feet long, fourteen of which were presently occupied. Only sixteen of them were regular cells, in which prisoners were shackled to the wall and subjected to continuous sensory isolation. The other four were designed for sleep deprivation, to break inmates who proved unusually recalcitrant.

King strode down the door-lined corridor, lighting the way with a flashlight. The cell block was kept in pitch darkness, all its lights controlled from a single switch, and the air was fuzzy with the dense buzz of white noise, played continually and at distracting volume. Even King began to feel disorientated after spending too long in there.

Prisoner 191 had been in Cell 15 for two days since his arrival. It was time to see how he was getting on. Reports were that he had thrashed like an eel while his captors administered his nutrient enemas, resulting in one of the guards sustaining a nasty gash to his forehead. They had taken to calling him 'Gollum', and King could see the resemblance.

Reaching the fifteenth door, he slid its observation panel open and shone his flashlight through the aperture. A low growl rose from within.

"Evening, beautiful!"

191's aberrant eyes glinted like a cat's in the light. He was crouched at the far end of the cell. His wrists were secured to a restraining belt, from which a chain ran to a sturdy, metal ring on the wall. King marvelled again at his wasted condition. He was as gaunt and fleshless as a famine victim, though without the distended belly that came with severe protein deficiency. He was also filthy, having clearly eschewed the bucket provided in lieu of a toilet. The floor and walls all around him were splattered with watery excrement, the smell of which now wafted into the corridor. King made a mental note to have him diapered.

Unlocking and opening the heavy door, King stood in the entrance, reluctant to enter and risk getting shit on his clothes. Prisoner 191 just watched him, his eyes calculating but unafraid, a string of slaver dangling from his chin. King couldn't help but be impressed. Most detainees were weeping by this point, but 191's resolve hadn't wavered a bit.

Maintaining eye contact, King took a bar of chocolate from his pocket and slowly peeled off the wrapper, letting it fall to the floor at his feet. Raising the candy to his nose, he closed his eyes and inhaled its scent, as if it were a fine cigar. Checking that 191 was still gazing at him, fascinated, he took a large bite and sighed with exaggerated pleasure.

He took his time chewing and swallowing. 191's eyes didn't stray to the chocolate in his hand but remained locked on his face instead, as if willing King to come within reach.

"You know," King said, taking another, smaller, bite, "you could do yourself some good here. How about you give us your name, for starters?"

191 bared his teeth, a warning growl bubbling in his throat. King gave him a moment to consider, then shrugged and popped the last of the chocolate into his mouth.

"Suit yourself," he said, stepping back into the passageway and preparing to close the door.

191 leapt forward, like a kitten seeing a length of yarn disappear from view, but was brought up short by the belt tethering him to the wall. His feet scrabbled for balance on the shit-smeared floor while his teeth gnashed in murderous rage.

King slammed and locked the door, then stalked back the way he'd come, annoyed with the lack of progress. He had, too, the nagging feeling he'd missed something, that something he'd seen in the cell had been 'off' in some way he'd failed to recognise. He'd reached Griffin's office before he managed to place it: 191 hadn't trembled. All the other inmates shivered constantly, if not from fear then from the subzero temperatures in their cells, but 191 hadn't so much as twitched.

"I think that guy's psychotic, for real," said King, walking in on Griffin. "Has to be. What's the point in interrogating a fucking lunatic?"

Griffin looked up from his laptop and treated him to a condescending smile. "Tempting to think so, isn't it? Not the case, however; I'm sure he's as sane as you or I. In fact, we know AQ have been giving their fighters resistance training—a prisoner at ORANGE was forced to confess as much only last week—and that's what we're seeing here. He's been taught to withstand our techniques. We need to constantly adapt, constantly refine, constantly improve our methods; we can't afford to sit on our laurels. I've drawn up an escalation plan that should challenge his conditioning quite nicely, though."

The psychologist slid a memo across the desk towards King, who took it and skimmed through its recommendations.

"Fine," he said, on reaching the end. "Seems good. Get it done. Tomorrow, we'll tackle him together."

Griffin nodded dismissively. "By all means."

"I want results, Griffin," said King, taking a step forward and allowing an edge of menace to creep into his voice. "I want him talking training camps, disposition of forces, enemy commanders—actionable intel!"

"Once the enhanced measures have broken his conditioning, I'm sure he'll sing like a canary," said Griffin, soothingly, taking off his reading glasses. "Now, I don't know about you, but I'm about ready for dinner."

"Listen to me, you son of a whore, either you spill your guts or I spill them for you! You think anyone's coming to save you? No one even knows you're here! You belong to me, now, and I will *end* you before I let you go!"

Prisoner 191's stubborn silence had finally gotten to King. It had been a week, during which the detainee had endured sleep deprivation, stress positions, and hours of merciless waterboarding. Through it all, he had presented nothing but rage; spitting, clawing, and lashing out at every opportunity. At King's insistence, Griffin had tried drugging the prisoner with various cocktails of antipsychotics, psychedelics, and classified research chemicals, none of which had effected a change in his behaviour. It was unclear whether he had slept at all, though the regular dousings with ice cold water had at least improved the smell of him somewhat.

"Last chance, asshole! From here out, things get real ugly, real fast!"

King waited impatiently for Bis to translate his threats. The only response from 191 was a feline hiss of hate and defiance.

"At this stage, it's best not to display emotion," murmured Griffin in King's ear.

"Fuck that! If he wants it tough, he can have it tough! Bring in the dogs!"

The guard at the door nodded and withdrew to the corridor.

They were in one of the sleep deprivation cells, where inmates were suspended from metal bars near the ceiling. 191 was suspended by his feet, upside-down, writhing like a caterpillar in the centre of the room. For King, the most infuriating aspect of the whole affair was that, so far, the idiot had shown no sign of knowing where he was, or why. He just kept pointlessly struggling, with seemingly no understanding of the hopelessness of his predicament, like a fly endlessly butting against a windowpane.

King fought the urge to light a cigarette, wishing the tiny cell allowed him enough room to pace. As it was, with himself, Griffin, and Bis in there, it was already claustrophobic—and it was about to get more crowded still.

A fusillade of excited barks and the slamming of a large door echoed down the corridor above the constant fizzle of white noise. The dogs were coming. King smiled, and glanced to see whether 191 had any reaction to their approach. He was certainly listening intently, and had fallen still, swaying gently in his bonds. It was difficult to read his expression though, especially upside-down.

Even the boldest Afghans became putty when confronted by the dogs. The year before, a prisoner had died of lacerations inflicted by a Belgian Malinois when an interrogation got out of control, but the value of the animals in breaking down resistance remained undiminished in the eyes of the CIA.

The two beasts now at the cell door were German Shepherds, pulling at their leashes and thrashing their tails in their enthusiasm to enter the room. The interrogators stood back to give them space, and Bis, who was terrified of them, put his hands over his ears to shut out their clamour.

"Say 'hi' to Donnie and Condoleezza," gloated King, raising his voice to be heard as the hounds squeezed through the doorway with a volley of furious barks. "Oh, but be careful—they do bite!"

Prisoner 191 remained unflinching as the two dogs reared up towards his face, baying and snapping. The sound was deafening in the confined space, a thunderous, atavistic barrage guaranteed to intimidate.

King could see uncertainty and confusion descend on the animals as 191 stared them down. Condoleezza fell silent and turned to her handler for reassurance, while Donnie's barks become more yapping and intermittent. They were not used to being ignored—but 191 did not ignore them for long.

A low, reverberating growl brewed in the prisoner's throat. The two dogs began to whine, their ears flattened, bodies low to the ground. Condoleezza tried to hide behind her handler's legs as King looked on in disbelief.

"Stop that!" he snapped, as 191's growl became an unceasing, full-throated roar, of a timbre and volume that seemed incredible given his anorexic build. The dogs' mewling grew louder, and the guard let out an exclamation of disgust as Condoleezza started pissing on his shoes.

"I said, 'stop that!'" shouted King, incensed.

He delivered a swift, powerful jab to 191's solar plexus, driving the wind out of him and setting him swinging like a piñata. He travelled backwards, towards Griffin, who was slow to notice or react to his approach.

Time in the cell seemed to slow, becoming elastic as 191 reached the highest point of his pendulous arc and turned his head—and *kept* turning his head, through nearly 180 degrees, until he was facing Griffin, behind him. Astonished, and doubting his eyes, King's jaw fell open at the same moment the prisoner's did—right before 191 fastened his teeth deep in the psychologist's neck and bit down, hard.

All hell broke loose. Griffin howled with agony as the decaying fangs pierced his skin. The two dogs bolted from the room and fled down the corridor, yowling, followed by Bis. King froze, rooted to the spot by the sight of 191 worrying at the psychologist's neck like a wolf. Only the guard had the presence of mind to react, yanking the stun gun from his belt holster and jamming it against the prisoner's chest.

Both 191 and Griffin convulsed and screamed as the electricity coursed through them. 191's teeth lost their purchase on Griffin's flesh, slipping free in a spurt of blood and saliva. The psychologist dropped to the cell floor like a broken marionette while the prisoner jerked uncontrollably in his restraints.

"Again!" yelled King, shoving the swinging inmate towards the guard and rushing to help Griffin. There was another loud crackle and a yowl of bestial fury as the guard obligingly shocked 191 again.

"Again! Give him more!"

Blood was pouring from Griffin's neck, leaking between his fingers as he clutched the wound, but King was relieved to see from the colour that it wasn't arterial. He would live.

"Come on. Let's get you out of here."

The CIA man hauled the psychologist to his feet and helped him stumble from the cell, leaving a trail of spattered blood as they went. Griffin had turned deathly pale, and King knew he was going into shock. He led him back toward the medical unit so he could dress the wound, 191's roars of rage chasing them down the corridor.

"How the hell could you let that happen?" King spat, kicking open the door to the triage room and pushing Griffin through it.

The psychologist moaned feebly in response.

"You're gonna need stitches. I'll have to send you to Bagram. You've really let the side down today, Griffin. You can't afford to lower your guard in the cells, even for a second—you know that."

King was making the most of Griffin's inability to answer back. In fact, the wound in his neck didn't look too bad. It was deep, sure, and gory, but with a bit of suturing it would heal. At least the psychologist would have a battle scar to take home.

King rooted through one of the cupboards until he found the antiseptic, eventually producing it with a flourish and a wolfish grin.

"This might sting a little…"

Griffin returned from the airbase the following morning, after wound closure, a tetanus shot, and a fistful of painkillers. He was unable to turn his head, and winced when he spoke. Once the novelty of tormenting him had worn off, King dismissed him for the day, telling him to rest until he was able to usefully contribute.

For the next two weeks, King redoubled his efforts to break Prisoner 191. Even as other detainees broke, begged, gave up the goods, and were shipped off to Guantanamo Bay or Site GREEN, in Thailand, 191 refused to play ball. He proved resilient to freezing temperatures, starvation, beatings, electric shocks, and concentrations of tear gas that could have felled a rhinoceros. Through it all, he affected an angry bewilderment at his captive status, trying relentlessly to squirm free of his bonds.

King had even tried putting him in a cell with one of the other inmates, to see if he would let his guard down in the presence of an ally, but to no avail. The flickery, black-and-white footage from the cell's camera had just shown 191 staring intensely at his guest, all night long, while the other man shrank away from him and pleaded to be released.

"I think he might just be too dumb to interrogate," said King, finally, reviewing footage of the previous evening's failed questioning. "Mentally subnormal, brain-damaged...I dunno. That boy ain't right."

"It's not like you to give up so easily," croaked Griffin, massaging his neck. The injury was still bothering him, alternately numb and tingling as it healed. He looked clammy and pale, and had been maxing out on painkillers for what he claimed was a persistent headache.

"Who said anything about giving up?" snapped King, needled. "I just think we need a new strategy. *Your* one isn't working."

Griffin shrugged. "What do you suggest?"

"I dunno...we could try the sexual humiliation stuff again."

Griffin shuddered. "No, thank you! I'm still having nightmares about last time."

King couldn't muster much enthusiasm for it, either. "Yeah. He didn't really seem to 'get' it, did he... Same with the religious stuff. I tried desecrating a Koran in front of him, and it was like he didn't even know what a book was. I even dangled a slice of raw bacon in front of him—fucker just ate it, one swallow, didn't even think about it."

He got up from his seat and paced the small office, frustrated. "If we had his name, we could go after his family, but we don't even have that! Weeks, we've been working on him, and not even a god damned name! What? What's up, now?"

"You hear that?" Griffin was scanning the ceiling with a wild look in his eyes.

"Huh? What are you—"

"Shhh!"

King stopped talking and strained his ears. He could just about detect the wash of white noise from the cell block, the distant yapping of stray dogs outside, the whine of a transport vectoring towards a landing at Bagram—nothing out of the ordinary.

"The voice of the waste!" breathed Griffin, rising slowly to his feet. "Do you hear it?"

"Uh, I don't hear a damned thing," said King, sceptically.

Griffin began to scream.

"Hear you're having problems," said the grim-faced air force medic sent from Bagram.

"Yeah, well, life in the sandbox, am I right?" replied King, beckoning him and his companion in.

"You look fine to me."

"Not me—a civilian: gone nuts, off his head. I think he's hallucinating."

"Okay. Where?"

"I'll show you."

King led them towards Griffin's bedroom, in which the psychologist had been locked for nearly 24 hours. After his screaming fit, he had run from the room, babbling and crying. When King caught up with him he had been taking his clothes off, lashing out at anyone who approached. King had ordered him confined to quarters, and assigned a guard to keep an eye on him.

"Any other symptoms?" asked the medic.

"He's been complaining of headaches for, I dunno, at least a week. He's pretty sweaty, too. I tried to take his temperature, but he won't let anything go near his mouth."

"He a user?"

"Drugs? Nah, he's Mormon, doesn't go in for that shit. He's in here."

There was no noise coming from Griffin's room. King opened the door and peeked round it.

The patient was on his bed, staring at the ceiling, muttering under his breath. His guard looked relieved and rose expectantly to his feet. While the two medics snapped on latex gloves and set about examining their patient, King drew him to one side.

"How's he been?"

"Well, quieter. Says he can't move his legs, so no running around at least. Still talking a lot of creepy shit."

King nodded and clapped the man on the shoulder. "Okay. Take a breather. Be back in ten."

The guard didn't need to be told twice, and gratefully vacated the room.

King stood and watched while the medics checked Griffin's vital signs. The psychologist didn't resist, continuing to burble distractedly as they checked his pupillary reflexes and made their notes. King moved closer and tried to catch his words.

"...sterile things...erosion...desolation...the beauty! Ruins of deep time...sunsets and starvation dreams..."

"Griffin?" King prompted him cautiously. The psychologist's eyes gave a brief flicker of recognition. "Who are you talking to?"

"the   Lilû...Pazuzu...Hecate-Ereshkigal...Ithaqua...Ghoth...vultures from below, the creeping jackals of Gehinnom—all here! Listen to their endless lament, the communion of desiccation..."

His voice was little more than a hoarse croak, and his cracked lips were gummy with dried saliva.

"You thirsty, buddy? You want a drink?"

"*No!*" Griffin's eyes opened wide, and he raised his hands defensively, as if ready to claw.

"Okay, okay! Just an idea."

"We're taking him," interrupted the senior medic. "Back to the airbase. Gonna need to run some tests."

"Is he going to be okay?" King wanted to know.

The medic grimaced. "Not soon, but it depends on what it is. We'll know more when we get results, but, meantime, he probably needs repatriating. We don't have facilities for this."

King stood up and beckoned him out of Griffin's earshot.

"It's that bad?"

"I think he's caught something, but without testing it's hard to say what. Don't suppose you know if he's been vaccinated against polio, do you?"

"*Polio*? Are you serious? No—I mean, I've no idea. I thought everyone was vaxxed for that."

"Not everyone—and this is the last place on Earth it's still endemic. Just one possibility, it could be lots of things. That wound on his neck: that a bite?"

"Yeah. One of the detainees took a chunk out of him, couple of weeks back. He got antibiotics and stuff for that, though."

"All right. Okay. Well, we'll take him with us, but don't expect him back any time soon. He's probably gonna be on the next plane to Ramstein."

King looked again at the delirious figure on the bed. He wasn't exactly sad to be losing the pompous little schmuck—he'd lost better men, in worse circumstances, and had been less than impressed by the psychologist's insights, anyway—but it would be one less person to talk to around the place.

"You hear that, Griffin? You're going home, my man. How about that?"

"When the battle is over, the solemn feast begins…reverently, they devour…purifying the unclean…"

"Sure, man, sure. You get some rest. These guys are gonna take you to Bagram. You'll be okay."

King moved out of the way to let one of the medics run a line into Griffin's wrist and hook him to a bag of saline, while the other went to fetch a stretcher. Feeling conspicuously useless, he hovered at hand, fidgeting with the cigarette lighter in his pocket.

"Keep me posted, okay?" he said, trying to sound nonchalant. "Let me know how he gets on."

"Yeah. I'll get them to call you when they know what's up," said the medic. "Probably be a few days."

"*Ghul-e biyaban!*"

Griffin hissed the words, raising his head from the pillow and freezing in place. All colour had drained from his face. As King watched, his eyes rolled back in his head, he fell back, and a convulsion ran through his body.

"Shit! Seizure!"

The medic stood back and checked his watch as the bed began to judder, its metal feet clattering against the cracked tile floor. White foam erupted between Griffin's clenched teeth, and his back arched, thrusting his chest towards the ceiling.

"No! No, that ain't good," muttered the medic, rooting through his kit, eventually producing a syringe and a small phial.

"What? What's not good?" demanded King, his voice cracking with tension.

"See how he's arching his back?" The medic snapped open the phial and filled the syringe while he spoke. "Either means he's faking—and I don't think he's faking—or he's got some kind of basal brain damage: brain stem inflammation, maybe. Whatever, it's a real bad sign."

He caught Griffin's flapping hand and plugged the syringe into the line they'd inserted. "Lorazepam," he explained as he depressed the plunger. "Should help. All I've got with me."

For long seconds, nothing seemed to happen—then, gradually, the seizure seemed to subside. Griffin collapsed against the bed with a final creak of springs, a few residual tremors still quaking through his unconscious body.

"Forty-nine seconds," said the medic, checking his watch again. "He needs a hospital. This is not manageable in the field."

As he spoke, his attendant returned bearing a collapsible stretcher. Between them, they transferred Griffin onto it and prepared to leave.

"Here, I've got that," said King, picking up the medic's bag and hurrying ahead of them to get the door. "I'll walk you out."

"If he's got people, you should call 'em," advised the medic, struggling to steer the stretcher into the corridor.

"Yeah, we'll do that. I'll tell Langley."

As they made their way back towards the reception area and the medics' waiting transport, a feral howl followed them from the direction of the cell block.

King ground the butt of his last cigarette under his heel and crushed the packet in his fist. *That was it.* He was done. No more cigarettes—

and no more Mister Nice Guy, either. It was time for Prisoner 191 to start talking. Resolute, he marched towards the cells, hitting the switch to turn on the lights and drawing his Beretta M9 as he went.

Griffin had refused to sign off on mock executions, but he wasn't there, now. Besides, the Justice Department had concluded they were only illegal if they resulted in lasting mental harm — and it was hard to imagine 191's mental condition getting any worse.

King slapped an empty magazine into the gun and checked that the chamber was empty, then took a few seconds to get into character at the cell door. Would 191 react best to an angry, unhinged performance or a cold, calculated one? It seemed impossible to know. When they'd used the mock execution technique on Abd al Rahim al Nashiri, one of the planners of the USS Cole bombing, at Site GREEN, they'd already broken him. 191 was a much tougher customer.

At GREEN, they'd threatened to use a power drill, as well as a handgun, but to King that seemed like gilding the lily. The Beretta would say everything he needed to. The prisoner could feign ignorance of English, Dari, and Pashto, but anyone could understand a gun pointed at their head. Taking a last deep breath of uncorrupted air, he opened the door to 191's festering cell.

He was greeted with a snarl that cut through the ambient white noise. The prisoner, slumped in his chains against the far wall, raised his head and bared his teeth. His eyes locked on King's in a perfect Kubrick stare, hate burning behind them. King stared back, unflinching, and racked the slide of his pistol.

"Last chance, bucko," he said, raising the weapon and pointing it at 191's head. "Got no use for a prisoner who won't talk. Any more of this, I'd have to charge you room and board."

191 hissed, but a look of wary recognition had entered his eyes, which had shifted focus to the gun. His grey tongue emerged, for an instant, to moisten his lips.

King had seen enough fear to recognise the signs, and pressed his advantage, walking towards the prisoner, keeping the gun trained on his face.

"It's check-out time, asshole. Either you give me your name, or I give you a lead injection to the head. Now, what's it gonna be? Tick, tock, motherfucker!"

191 visibly flinched as King jabbed the gun closer to his temple. It was, unmistakably, fright, the first sign of it since they'd captured him. King felt a warm flush of exultation at finally having found a chink in the bastard's armour.

"Yeah, you know what one of these does, don't you?" he gloated, as the prisoner shrank away from it, trying to duck his head around the gun's barrel. "One squeeze, just a bit more pressure, and you eat a bullet. Oh, I'll do it! No one cares what happens to you here—you got that? No one gives a shit. I can shoot you, dump you in the desert, and get a medal for doing it. Now—for the last time—what's your *fucking* name?"

He touched the Beretta to the cowering prisoner's temple. 191 recoiled and angrily snapped his jaws. He glared at King, and King finally saw what he'd been seeking in the prisoner's eyes: what Griffin would have called 'thanatopic uncertainty,' otherwise known as 'dread.' He had won.

"That's right—memento mori, motherfucker. How old are you, anyway?" he wondered aloud, staring back into his captive's variegated, blood-shot eyes. "I guess we'll find out, now."

The radio on his belt crackled abruptly, and a voice broke through.

"Boss?"

King lowered his gun, annoyed at the interruption. It was his fault, he supposed; he hadn't told the guards he would be interrogating. He unclipped the handset and brought it to his chin.

"What?"

"Sorry, boss, phone call. They said it was urgent."

"Be right there. Lucky reprieve for you," he continued to the prisoner as he returned the radio and pistol to his belt. "I'm coming back though, and, when I do, you'd better have some answers for me. Otherwise…"

He pointed his fingers at 191's face, and mimed a gunshot.

"Dead? Seriously? Dead? Jeez. How? When?"

King sank into Griffin's vacant—now, permanently vacant—chair, and tried in vain to feel something more profound than surprise.

"He died on the plane to Germany." The voice from Bagram faded in and out of the static on the line. "Terminal seizure. Nothing they could do."

"Damn...that's sad," said King, still trying to reach the part of himself that cared. "So, what was it? Polio?"

"Rabies."

"You're fucking kidding!"

"Nope. Real nasty way to go. You have dogs there, right? Guard dogs?"

"Yeah, we have guard dogs, but they aren't *rabid*! It was a detainee that bit him. Can you catch rabies like that, off other people? Oh, shit—does my prisoner have it?"

"Uh, no. He'd be dead, by now, if he did. Your guy must have caught it off an animal. Unfortunately, by the time we got the test results, it was too late. Anyway, look, I gotta go, things are hectic here. I promised I'd update you and, well, that's the update. I'm sorry for your loss."

"Yeah. Thanks. If you—"

The line was already dead.

King let out a long sigh. *Goddamn rabies...* It didn't seem right, in that day and age, for an American, of all people, to die of rabies. There was a vaccine for rabies, right? He wondered whether he should get it. He'd had a headache earlier. Had that been a symptom? Was 191 infected with rabies? Could that explain his aggression, his confusion, his refusal to eat or drink? If so, why wasn't he dead, as well?

Too many questions piling up, too many thoughts. King shook his head like an Etch-A-Sketch in an effort to clear it. Everything had been simple until 191 turned up. They'd refined their interrogation methods and legal justifications, intel had been effortlessly collected and passed on, and secrecy had been maintained. Now, Griffin was dead, and questions would be asked about that, eventually. When they were, King knew, he would need to have at least superficial answers to give.

He decided to leave 191 to stew until nightfall. His reaction to the sight of a firearm had been the first sign of weakness he'd betrayed, and King didn't want to squander that by following it up too soon. He had been neglecting his other prisoners anyway, some of whom were overdue a session of maintenance waterboarding. He would get to 191 in due course—and ensure Griffin hadn't died for nothing.

"What is it, what's the matter? What's he done now?"

King panted the words, out of breath after running the few hundred yards from the gate. He *really* needed to give up the cigarettes.

The guard gestured mutely to the open door of 191's cell and stood back. His face was deathly white, his manner fidgety and unnerved. The cataract roar of white noise reached a crescendo as King leaned warily around the door frame to see for himself.

At worst, he expected to find the inmate dead. That had happened before, and always caused a furore at Langley. Sometimes prisoners killed themselves. Others succumbed to hypothermia, or to internal injuries from beatings. What had never happened before, and would cause an absolute *shitstorm* at Langley, was what confronted him in that cell.

191 was missing.

King stared, open-mouthed, unable to comprehend what he was seeing. He had left the detainee secured to the wall by his wrists; he knew that for a fact. Now, the restraints dangled limply, one busted open, and one—*oh God, no*...one still fastened around 191's severed wrist.

"What the *fuck*...?"

"He must've got out down there, sir," stammered the guard, drawing King's attention away from the dribbling stump of forearm.

He pointed to a hole at the base of the wall, no more than ten inches by five, a tunnel bored through the brickwork which hadn't been there a few hours before.

King looked at the guard, incredulous. His head swam, brimming with astonishment and dismay. Feeling sure he must be dreaming, he knelt to peer through the hole. He could feel the breeze flowing through it about his ankles, and, sure enough, could see out across the courtyard, where the guards sometimes played desultory games of basketball, to the shed used as a kennel for the dogs, and the whispering scrubland beyond.

The concrete bricks around the mouth of the opening were pitted and crumbling, ready to disintegrate on contact. There was a strong smell of puke, and, drawing closer, King could see traces of vomitus amid the powder and rubble on the floor. A semi-circular series of indentations in the surviving bricks looked like nothing so much as bite marks, as if 191 had gnawed his way to freedom. There were shards of black plastic littering the ground, too—the remains of the cell's camera, King realised, which had been torn down and presumably used as a digging implement.

It was impossible! The whole thing was insane! He *must* have been broken out by his Taliban allies. It would have taken days to dig through the wall unaided, even with tools, even without undergoing weeks of starvation and sleep deprivation.

Especially with only one hand... Reluctantly, King stood up and surveyed the grisly, oozing relic hanging from the wall. It was 191's, without a doubt, as atrophied and cadaverous as the rest of him. What little flesh there was around the wrist was worried and torn, the radius brutally splintered and displaced. Embedded in the bone was a dislodged tooth. *Had he chewed off his own arm?*

"Find him," mumbled King, the words clotting in his throat. He repeated it. "Find him! He can't have gone far, he's losing blood. Get the dogs, get the cars, check the security cameras, get a fucking drone down here if you have to, and fucking find him!"

"Yes, sir!" The guard snapped to attention and left in a hurry.

"I want everyone out looking for him," King called after him. "Everyone! This is our mess! We've gotta clean it up!"

Left alone in the cell, King lit a cigarette to calm his nerves. Langley would be furious. It would be best if they didn't find out about the escape until 191 was safely back in custody. In all likelihood, he had bled out within a couple of hundred yards, probably still within COBALT's perimeter—unless his allies had brought a competent field medic with them. How could they have infiltrated the facility, though? How could they have known where he was?

The white noise in the cell was getting on his nerves, now, preventing him from thinking coherently—as it was designed to do. Pitching the cigarette into the corner, he left, slamming the door behind him. As he did so, his radio squawked and began to crackle.

"Sir? This is Jackson. I've got movement on thermal, one klick, east-southeast, following the base of the hill. Looks like your boy."

King snatched the handset from his belt and barked into it. "Outstanding! Keep eyes on! I'm heading out. Steadman, Morell, Kozlowsky—meet me at the Humvees, double-time!"

Breaking into a lumbering jog, he headed towards the vehicle shed. Passing his office, he stopped to grab his Interceptor tactical vest and put it on as he ran. After several abortive attempts to fasten it over his paunch while moving, he gave up and concentrated on getting to the transport as quickly as he could.

The contractors were waiting with the engine running. The outside of the vehicle sported the Red Cross emblem, which was a contravention of the Geneva Convention but would hopefully dissuade insurgents from attacking it.

"Let's go!" he yelled, as Morell revved the engine and flipped his NODs into place. "Let's get this fucker!"

He felt a childish sense of glee as the Humvee rumbled forwards, gathering speed. It was the joy of the hunt, the thrill of the chase, the elation only big guns and big engines could impart. It had been too long since he'd last felt it.

They slowed briefly to allow the Salt Pit's gates time to open for them, then roared between them and veered abruptly off-road, into the scrub, heading east.

"I see him," shouted Morell, above the thunder of the 6.5-litre turbo-V8. "Two hundred metres, dead ahead."

"Is he alone?" yelled back King, beginning to wonder if he should have brought more men.

"Yes—no…looks like he's surrounded by dogs."

"Did you say 'dogs?'"

"Yes, sir. I count eight…nine dogs."

"Our dogs?"

"Don't see how they can be our dogs, sir. One hundred metres."

"Okay, get ready! Let's take him!"

The bolts of Kozlowsky and Steadman's rifles clunked as they both chambered rounds. Not wanting to be left out, King racked the slide of his M9 and leaned forwards, straining to catch a glimpse of their quarry in the darkness ahead. Morell pivoted his night-vision optics out of the way and turned on the headlights, and, moments later, the scrawny, limping figure of Prisoner 191 came into view, only to be lost in a cloud of dust as the Humvee slid to a halt.

"Yes! We've got him! Go, go, go!" whooped King as the contractors tumbled from the Humvee. Following their lead, he chased the shouts, footfalls, and swinging lights of the other men until he almost tripped over one who had dropped into a crouch, rifle raised and ready to fire.

A dozen yards ahead, 191 hissed and snarled in the glare of rifle-mounted flashlights as the men spread out, encircling him. He cradled the stump of his missing hand, from which, to King's surprise, no blood seemed to flow. The men were shouting at him, telling him to get on the ground in English and Dari, as he growled at one of them after another.

"I've got dogs!" shouted Kozlowsky, abruptly transferring his sights to a new target. King followed his aim and saw yellow eyes gleaming at the edge of the flashlight's range.

"They're just hyenas," yelled back Steadman. "Probably tracking this dude, waiting for him to die."

"I'll clear 'em out," hollered King, firing his pistol into the air. "Go on, g'it!" He fired again, a couple of times, enjoying the thump of recoil, before forcing himself to stop.

The circling eyes winked out and withdrew. King laughed with the sheer exhilaration of it all. This backwards, shithole country could kiss his fucking ass! They were lucky he was in a good mood! They were lucky he was a nice guy! They were lucky he lived by a code!

191 had fallen to his knees. The soldiers closed in on him cautiously, weapons trained. King did, too, almost willing the bastard to make a break for it. He could see the fugitive's lips moving soundlessly, as if in prayer. *So, the motherfucker could speak when he wanted to!* As they closed the last few yards towards him, he raised his head and grabbed a fistful of dry, sandy earth, lifting it to his lips.

Time seemed to slow to a crawl as he made eye contact with King, his expression sagacious and calm, eyes shrewd with the wisdom of centuries. Then, he was gone, lost in a cloud of dust as he blew and scattered the soil into the air, blinding his captors with a sudden blizzard of grit.

King ducked and shielded his eyes, squinting to make out anything through a fog of churning muck. It didn't seem to be subsiding, the dirt not falling to the ground as it should but growing thicker instead, as more dust was swept into the air by gusts of wind which seemed to come from everywhere. In moments, they were completely engulfed by a swirling vortex of loose grass and desiccated soil, so dense that visibility dropped to almost zero.

Trapped by the abrupt cyclone, King could hear the shouts of his colleagues as they sought each other, their flashlights darting in the gloom. He staggered towards the nearest and was close enough to make out his silhouette when, without warning, the serrated shadows of half a dozen hyenas bore it to the ground with a chorus of screaming yelps.

The man's rifle stuttered a handful of bullets uselessly into the ground before tumbling from his hands. He rolled away, still tussling with the snarling, yipping beasts, and King lost sight of him amid the maelstrom. Eyes streaming with tears, hopelessly disorientated and struggling to breathe, he blundered forwards with his hands in front of his face.

He heard more yells, followed by more gunfire flashing in the murk, and dropped to his hands and knees, scared of catching a stray bullet. *What the hell was going on?* Everything had been under control, they'd had 191 cornered, then suddenly *this?* It made no sense.

Somewhere nearby, a shout of alarm was cut short by the sharp *crack* of a detonating frag grenade. The pressure wave from the explosion rippled outwards, adding thousands of steel splinters and a fine mist of blood to the swirling debris. King cringed lower still, praying for it all to end.

Suddenly, a fist burst from the earth beneath him. Before he could recoil or turn away, it clamped onto his throat, choking him. Eyes bulging, he tried to pull back, but couldn't—tried to break its vicelike grip, but failed. The ground continued to shift and crumble, draining away into some subterranean sinkhole and giving birth to 191's leering, triumphant face.

King whimpered with terror as his foe's gloating countenance closed to within inches of his own. He could hear the rasp of the prisoner's breath, could smell nothing but the foul reek of it, could only watch as he bared his carious teeth. Unable even to beg for mercy, he closed his eyes.

Nothing happened. Still, he kept his eyes shut. The fingers clutching his windpipe relaxed, just for a moment, enough for him to seize one quick breath. As he did so, 191 sniffed: a long, careful inhalation, inhaling his escaping breath.

191 began to laugh, a slow, nightmarish chuckle that froze the blood in King's veins. The grip on his throat relaxed again—and then was gone. The roar of the wind fell away to nothing and was replaced

by the patter of falling dirt. King risked peeking with one eye, just in time to see Prisoner 191 swallowed by the earth once more.

He never saw him in the flesh again.

King residence, Reston, Fairfax County, VA

Alone in the bathroom, King cried, muffling the sound with a towel so Marcie wouldn't hear. He did this three or four times a day, until the coughing subsided, all the tears were used up, and only numb horror remained. Of course, she could tell, and kept the kids away from him at those moments, but she put it down to PTSD and assumed he would talk about it when he was ready.

It wasn't PTSD.

He gazed, dumbly, at the bright red flecks on the towel, before shoving it to the bottom of the laundry basket. The coughing had started only days after 191's escape: intense, racking fits of it, culminating in blood. He didn't need a doctor to tell him the cause. He knew. It was how it had started for his old man: a few weeks of coughing up blood, then the endless scans and biopsies, the drugs, the radiation, the pain…

The Agency had been more than happy to transfer him back to the States after 191's escape. In his report, he'd ascribed Kozlowski's animal bites to the grenade that had ended Steadman's life. Kozlowski and Morrell weren't going to contradict him. None of them could explain what had happened, so King had confabulated a shootout with Taliban insurgents, interrupted by a localised sandstorm, as an explanation that suited everyone.

Downstairs, the doorbell chimed, and he heard Marcie letting someone in. There was a murmur of voices—hers and a man's—and then she called up the stairs:

"Tom? Someone here to see you!"

"Coming!" he called back.

He spent a minute dabbing at his red eyes with toilet paper, doing his best to erase the evidence of tears, before flushing the toilet and watching the water swirl, willing it to carry away his terror and grief.

Entering the living room, he didn't recognise the flint-eyed man on the sofa, but could tell at once that he was, or had been, Special Forces. Marcie started guiltily at the sound of the door, turning round with a too-bright "here he is!" and hurrying to make introductions.

"Tom! John says he's from the office! He needs you to look at some pictures! I'll leave you alone. Would lemonade be good? Or beer? I'll get you some beer."

"Lemonade would be fine, thank you, Mrs King," drawled 'John', getting to his feet and offering King his hand to shake. He continued smiling until the door closed behind her.

"She's worried about you," he said, once it had.

"Yeah, well, she needn't be," lied King, gesturing to his guest to resume his seat. "What's this about?"

"There are details I can't give you, but I'm with SAC. I'm here about a missing asset of ours, codename Halberd."

He passed King a Marine Corps graduation photo of a beaming, muscular lunk with the build of a quarterback. It had faded with age, and King could tell from the lapels of Halberd's Dress Blues and the size of the emblem on his cap that it had been taken a long time ago. After glancing at it, he passed it back.

"Right?"

"Halberd was first deployed to Afghanistan in eighty-five, to liaise with the Mujahideen in their fight against the Soviets. He was a first-rate operator with intense personal charisma, capable of blending into the local population and winning their trust. As a result of his many accomplishments in that theatre of operations, and others, he was asked to redeploy there two years ago, as part of Operation Infinite Justice."

"Admirable," nodded King. "I still don't see what it has to do with me."

"Our last contact with Halberd was on December first, 2001," persisted 'John.' "He missed multiple check-ins. I sent drones looking for him, even flew out there myself to track him down. The local sources we had told me he'd been living like a mujahid, up in the hills, scavenging and raiding, waging a one-man war against the Taliban. They said the Talibs had given him a nickname—*Jalawar*—and had diverted sizeable resources to hunting him down."

He stared at King for a moment, looking for any flicker of recognition, before continuing.

"Rumours about his activities were abundant. They said he could speak to animals, could disappear in the blink of an eye, that he never slept. They said he was a jinn."

"A jinn? Like a genie?"

"Like a devil, a shape-shifter. The old man I spoke to said Halberd had been claimed by the spirits of the waste, that he had given his soul to the desert."

"Sounds like something the PSYOPS boys cooked up, you ask me," said King, dismissively. "Spooky stories for the yokels; Operation Wandering Soul, all over again. That shit never really works. Nothing to do with my command though, if that's what you're thinking. We just interrogated the fuckers."

"Four weeks after his last contact, he was declared overdue. His current status is M.I.A."

"Rip." King shrugged. "I'm sorry, I still—"

"Tom—can I call you Tom?"

"You can call me what you like, so long as you get to the point."

"Tom, I believe a month ago you submitted *this* request for a genetic ancestry test to OMS. The sample you sent has been re-tested three times. Each test resulted in a one hundred percent match with the DNA on file for Halberd. So, Mr King, my question for you is: where did you find my friend, and where is he now?"

King looked again at the photograph in his hand. When he held it close, it was just about possible to make out Halberd's eyes, in the shadow cast by the visor of his Barracks Cover.

He was laughing uncontrollably before his guest gave up asking questions, and continued long after he had left.

Rare Meat

A Harry Stubbs Adventure

By David Hambling

"He said Pickman repelled him more and more every day, and almost frightened him toward the last—that the fellow's features and expression were slowly developing in a way he didn't like; in a way that wasn't human. He had a lot of talk about diet, and said Pickman must be abnormal and eccentric to the last degree."

• H.P. Lovecraft, Pickman's Model

"Tell me what you eat and I will tell you what you are."
• *Jean Anthelme Brillat-Savarin, "The Physiology of Taste: or, Meditations on Transcendental Gastronomy" (1791)*

London 1928

*K*illing Ingram was a liberation. It was not just that Wilson's pent-up anger and frustration at the world that had been building for so long finally found release in a great cathartic sweep of rage. More than that, it marked the moment that he broke through the bonds of law, of morality, of common decency, the chains that had fettered him. After the murder Wilson was changed forever, not just morally but physically. He realized afterwards that the first murder was the opening of the gate.

Wilson shared his rooms with Ingram, a fussy little man, a dealer in headache pills and suchlike. Ingram was short, prematurely balding, and viewed the world through thick glasses. He had the larger of the two bedrooms and so paid a higher share of the rent, but Wilson could only stand Ingram after a few drinks. The rest of the time he was unbearable. The nagging was incessant.

"I've told you before you need to open a window when you smoke those stinking cheap cigars"

"You've finished the last of the tea, again, haven't you?"

"Don't leave your dirty socks there."

It never stopped.

"I suppose you were drunk again last night and that's why you left the front door unlocked."

"Why do you read those filthy magazines?"

"I'm not talking to that debt collector again. You shouldn't buy things if you can't pay for them."

It was worse than being married.

It was all right for Ingram. The pills business was booming. Everyone wanted a good stock of them in case there was another shortage, and Ingram could give good discounts. Wilson, who was in razor blades and did not have such latitude to make reductions, was having a harder time of it. There was too much competition, the margins were too tight, and some idiot had started a fashion for beards.

Some days there was no point in going out selling. No wonder he ended up going on benders around the local pubs for as long as the money lasted. That was a release, but a temporary one. Daylight always found him again, wrapped him in a hangover, and sent Ingram to knock on his door.

"Aren't you up yet? It's eight o' clock, and I've got customers to see. Don't forget to get the bread rolls for this evening."

Ingram was a man of habit. Every evening, as soon as he came in, he would have a cup of tea and two bread rolls thinly spread with margarine and meat paste. The little prig always said grace first, mumbling to himself at unnecessary length, and filled in his daily sales book while he ate. Wilson had fallen into the practice of eating with him, and now he was liable for buying fresh rolls on alternate evenings.

That day Wilson had spent what felt like hours waiting for a client to come out of a meeting. When the man did eventually emerge, he told Wilson it was too late to talk to him, and he should arrange something next week — or the one after, it was all the same to him.

Wilson had returned home via the pub but, lacking the money to stay for long, he had come back to find Ingram sitting accusingly at the dining table, the teapot, plates and cutlery laid out in front of him.

"About time too," said Ingram. "Now, where are those bread rolls?"

"Blowed if I know," said Wilson, and laughed at his own wit.

"You've been drinking. And now we've nothing to eat."

"There's this," said Wilson, sticking his finger into the jar of meat paste and extracting a smear which he licked off.

Ingram was dumbfounded. Wilson was so amused by this reaction he took the waxed cardboard box of margarine, opened the flap and licked it like a dog lapping water. "Yum."

Ingram looked on in horror.

"You animal. You … degenerate!"

"You should try some," said Wilson, wiping the oily stuff from his lips.

"I'm not touching it now! You'll pay for that."

"Oho!" laughed Wilson, "You're going to make me, are you?"

Ingram was out of his chair with surprising speed, his face reddening.

"Yes, as a matter of fact I am," he said, coming so close that Wilson momentarily shied away from him.

"Get off," he said contemptuously, and shoved the little man away.

Ingram balled his fists and went for Wilson. A second later the two of them were rolling around on the floor like scrapping schoolboys. Wilson had the advantage in size and strength but Ingram was all anger and aggression. It occurred to Wilson for the first time that his flat mate had also been bottling up anger for some time, and he was amazed to see it coming out. He never knew Ingram had it in him to be angry.

"Animal! Filthy animal!" Ingram was shouting, "You degenerate!"

Wilson's size and experience from his schoolyard days — he could not imagine the swotty young Ingram had ever been in a tussle — soon won out. Wilson was on top of Ingram and had hold of both of his arms. He grinned down at his victim, now without glasses.

"Going to make me pay, eh?"

Ingram, angrier than ever, helpless to do anything else, bit Wilson on the wrist.

Wilson jerked his arm away, feeling the teeth dragging through his skin as he did so, and seeing bright red blood welling up from the wound.

Ingram seemed to stop for a second, perhaps horrified by what he had done, but now it was Wilson's turn to see red. It was not the biting, it was the bloodstain on the cuff. That was his only good white set of cuffs, it was the sheer aggravation of this horrible little person constantly nagging at him. And the sight of blood aroused a curious passion that mingled with his anger and accentuated it. The animal in Wilson's soul stirred.

Wilson snarled and bit back, snapping his teeth in front of the startled Ingram's face. He only did it to terrify Ingram, but something took over, and with the next bite he sank his teeth into Ingram's nose. Then he bit his cheek, grabbing hold and shaking like a terrier until he tore loose a flap of skin.

"Help!" said Ingram, hurt, horrified and panicking. "He-elp!"

That cry for help fully awoke the thing that had stirred at the sight of blood. The passion took over completely. He had his prey at his mercy and he went into a frenzy, biting and tearing.

Ingram kept trying to say something, as though he was trying to order Wilson off him, but he could not get three words out before Wilson was on his throat, crunching through the windpipe until the cries abruptly ceased and Ingram stopped his ineffectual struggles.

Some time later Wilson surfaced again, his ferocity finally spent. He sat up and looked about the room, and drew a deep satisfied breath.

He felt better than he had for a long time, as though he had just stepped out of an invigorating cold bath. It was better than being with a woman. The anger was gone and he was perfectly calm. But he was hungry, ravenously hungry, as he had never been before.

Wilson licked his lips, and now he actually tasted the delicious blood on his lips, a warm sticky gravy, the original and tastiest of meat sauces.

"'We've nothing to eat'," he said, mimicking Ingram. "Nothing to eat, eh? Nothing to eat? We'll see about that. God, I'm famished."

Standing up a little unsteadily, Wilson found his sample case and extracted an old cut-throat razor. Not a popular line, but you had to offer a complete range, and there were still some traditionalists about. He found a dinner plate and, kneeling next to the body, set about slicing off thin strips of succulent pink meat, his mouth watering.

One

My arrangement with the other occupants of my working-space is an entirely informal one; my room is sub-let to me, or rather to the notional entity of 'Lantern Insurance', by their employer. The girls who pack china into parcels for mail-order delivery have in principle nothing to do with me, nor I with them, but in practice we are the best of neighbours. Lacking a kettle of my own, I get regular brews from next door, in exchange for the odd bit of heavy lifting and the service of discouraging unduly persistent male callers.

Sometimes I also entertain them with what they call 'ghost stories', edited accounts of some of my cases which are suitable for public consumption, and most of which are rooted in comic misunderstanding rather than uncanny apparitions.

Occasionally I am called upon for a more serious task.

Kitty, the overseer of the packing operation, lingered just long enough after delivering a most welcome cup of tea for me to detect that there was something on her mind.

"Mr. Stubbs," she said, repositioning a strand of chestnut hair. "You know as how I wouldn't bother you with anything trivial."

"Miss Edwards," I said, as it seemed we were being formal, "I would never think such a thing."

"It's just … it's Betty's admirer," she said. "You do know Betty has had an admirer?"

Overhearing conversations about the packer's relationships with men was unavoidable, as Kitty well knew. I did not deliberately eavesdrop but the chatter as they called across the room was often hard to ignore. And I think I had passed the man waiting outside once. He had not made much of an impression, from his suit I judged him to be an ordinary young man of the commercial type who might be considered the finest gradation above me on the social scale.

"I had gathered something to that effect," I said.

I also knew from what I had overheard that Betty was expecting, or at least hoping, for a marriage proposal in the very near future, that he was generous with money when he had it, he was considered good-looking when he could be bothered to dress up properly, and no slouch on the dance floor. I had my doubts about that last one. Men who are good dancers are not always to be trusted with women.

"Betty hasn't heard from him in some time," she said. "Six days, to be exact."

"There's been a tiff then," I said, though that length of time was pushing it. The longest Sally had gone without talking to me had been twenty-four hours after I had stood her up on a date without sending any explanation. (That one had been a matter of life or death, and I was forgiven after a suitably lavish floral apology had been delivered).

"No," she said. "No disagreement at all. He just—" she made a chopping gesture—"cut her off. Hasn't written to her, hasn't replied to any of her letters. And before, not a day would go by that she wouldn't at least hear from him."

"He lives in the borough, does he?" I asked.

"He does," she said. "He works long hours, and he has other engagements, but six days ..."

"She's worried that something has happened to him?" I asked. "An accident."

"She's been by his flat," she said. "There's never any reply. And no light in the window at night. Not him nor his flatmate."

"Strange," I said.

"Yes," she said, giving me a look.

Reporting this to the police as a missing person would clearly be premature. The constabulary would likely conclude that cutting off contact with a paramour was not of itself evidence of foul play. This left Betty in a difficult situation.

"You feel the matter warrants further investigation," I said.

"I couldn't have put it better myself, Mr. Stubbs," she said. "And with you being an experienced investigator and being right next door, well, you seemed like the obvious person to ask."

It was not an appealing case. For one thing, it did not have any of the hallmarks of the uncanny which I had become attuned to. For another, it would put me in the unenviable situation of standing between two ex-lovers and taking fire from both sides.

"You understand that my role is strictly investigative as regards the putative disappearance," I said. "If I can establish that the man in question is in fact safe and well, I will do so. And if I find that he is indisposed for some reason, I will report that fact. But I'm not undertaking to carry any messages between the two parties, nor give any details beyond a bald statement of whether or not he is present and correct."

Kitty bit her lip. She had questions she wanted answered, but she understood my reticence.

I could envision any number of scenarios, ranging from his being in the clink to having run off with another lady, which he would not wish to communicate back to Betty, and I surely would not be the bearer of such news.

"That would be ever so good of you," said Kitty. "I'm sure you have methods to find these things out far better than we could."

Her smile was pure flattery. But show me the man who does not enjoy being flattered by an attentive woman.

"You should warn Betty that whatever it is, it won't be good news."

"I suppose not," she said. "But it's always better to know, isn't it?"

That was a questionable statement if ever I heard one. And by the time the case was over, Betty may have wished she had remained in blissful ignorance of the awful fate of her lover.

Consciousness washed over Wilson over the next few days, ebbing and flowing. Sometimes it seemed to him that he was dreaming when he was wide awake.

More often he imagined he had been going about his normal daily life when he had woken up with a start and found himself curled up in a ball, one of Ingram's half-chewed ribs in his mouth.

Fear at what would happen to him and revulsion at what he had done gradually receded as he ate his way through Ingram's corpse. Those feelings were giving way to a growing sense of elation and sheer delight. Wilson was a free man at last.

At first he had been thinking mainly about the money. Ingram kept a cash box under his bed. Wilson had broken it open with a hammer and chisel, spilling out a treasure trove of notes and coins, more than enough to settle all Wilson's outstanding debts. Far better though was Ingram's account book and the cheque book in his bedside drawer. All the statements were kept punctiliously up to date, and the savings account contained more money than Wilson would have dreamed possible. This, when Ingram had steadfastly refused to lend him so much as a shilling. Money was wasted on his type. Wilson would put it to better use.

Ingram, with his steady income and his frugal habits, never splashed out on meals out or even a decent suit. No fear that he would blow money just to impress a woman. No doubt he was planning to marry someone equally colourless and buy a house, to breed more dull, workaday little Ingrams. Well, Wilson had put a stop to that.

He envisaged a shopping spree in the West End. Some suits from Saville Row, shirts from Jermyn Street, for the first time he would be able to afford the best of everything. Proper handmade shoes, not the ready-made sort he was forced to wear, but works of art crafted to his feet. And jewelry: a diamond tie-pin of course, monogrammed cufflinks, maybe a fine gold signet ring. The very latest wristwatch, rather than an old pocket-watch, and perhaps a gold Dunhill lighter, the sort you could work one-handed. Then he would be able to step out as he was always meant to, as a proper man of fashion.

And, when he was suitably attired, take a trip to Europe, travelling First Class. To Cannes and Monte Carlo, of course, that was the place. He would see the sights and swagger about a bit. And while he was there he would try his luck at the gambling tables and see if he could spin out his fortune—or, better, find an even wealthier victim and keep his run of luck going.

Wilson spent his days sleeping, his nights gorging and planning, prowling the apartment and taking furtive looks out of the window. He could see people walking past on the street below, people who had no idea of what he was or what he had done. Little people. Little, edible people.

Ingram's body was disappearing at an alarming rate. As the days went on the flesh had become more tender, more flavorsome, and richer, like well-hung game. Wilson realized now that it had been a mistake to start eating so much so soon. But his craving was so intense he could not have stopped himself.

Wilson ate prodigious quantities, savoring every morsel, chewing the tripe, scooping out the mushy brains and cracking open the bones for the soft marrow. He had never known what it was to be truly hungry before, and the joy of feeding that hunger.

Eating the raw meat had become so much easier. Wilson's jaws and teeth had developed to chew and tear, and now he had no need of cutlery. Also he was starting to think less of the fine clothes he would buy and the sights of Monte Carlo and more about the next victim he would find there. Or maybe he would do that before he set out; Ingram was disappearing fast and in a very few days he would be entirely gone.

He looked out the window again, and stretched his elongated arms. As a man walked by under the street light, Wilson wondered how difficult it would be to follow him, wait until the chap reached some dark and deserted spot, then strangle him. It would be done quickly and quietly—no biting this time, that would leave too much blood and no time to lick it up—and then he could carry the precious meat back to the flat.

Not back here. There were too many people looking in from across the street, too many creaking on the staircase next door. An overcoat and a hat would disguise Wilson's appearance but one look in the mirror told him that his days of passing as human were over.

He laughed at his reflection, which laughed back with jagged teeth and a wicked look in its eye.

He would find somewhere quieter, and somewhere darker where the damned sunlight was not so infernally bright in the daytime. Somewhere that he could feast and sleep in peace and contentment, some cool, dark, damp spot. He had been dreaming of desert caves, of dells deep in the forest ... but even in London there were plenty of underground spaces waiting to be claimed.

Before, he had only been aware of the above-ground world, the streets and bars and shops. Now his mind was seeping downwards, and all the places he had ignored before — the sewers and culverts and cellars, the crypt in the cemetery, the forgotten caverns — these places started to emerge into his consciousness.

Soon, when he had finished the last of Ingram, except perhaps for a souvenir bone or two, he would move on. He would find somewhere better. And he would find better eating.

Wilson reached up and swung from the doorframe like an ape. He felt so powerful, so invigorated … Before the murder he had been a wage-slave, chained to the Monday-to-Friday drudgery of having to beg and fawn for sales. That was all behind him. Now he was a predator, the king of the jungle.

Wilson grinned when he thought of his former customers. Wouldn't they be surprised to see him now? That would be a real jape! Twice as good as grabbing some stranger, to get one of those pompous asses, strangle them slowly and devour them, piece by piece. It seemed to him now that all of his customers were big, fat men with plenty of surplus meat on them, juicier morsels by far than the anemic Ingram. He wanted to go out and hunt, but the evenings were still too light and they would be tucked up in their beds at night. But maybe, he thought, swinging by his arms again, he could do a little night-burglary.

Wilson was still thinking about how he might hunt down one of his customers when a visitor came knocking at the door.

Two

A church pew is not my natural habitat, even on a Sunday morning, but Sally likes to go along and I like to accompany her. She says we could both do with a bit of respectability, and I dare say she is right.

This Sunday I had an ulterior motive, and the square item in my coat pocket distracted me several times during the service and the altogether too extended sermon.

Looking about the church, I quickly caught sight of Miss Frey with her aunt in their pew two rows in front of us. Miss Frey was a fifteen-year-old with something of a grudge against the world. She was one of the least feminine girls I ever met, but while she did not abide by the normal rules of good behavior she was a better person than most. And extremely talented in her particular field.

She spent the service fidgeting. When her aunt chided her, Miss Frey started looking through the hymn book, as though it held the answer to some question of vital and urgent import to her. It looked to me as though she was checking the numbers of the hymns, her lips moving as she did so. Counting the number of times a particular letter occurred in each one, or dividing the hymn numbers by the number of verses to find a pattern, knowing her.

At last the blessing was given, the last hymn was sung and, fortified by the Host, refreshed by the blood of the Lamb and cleansed of our sins, we emerged fresh into the world. I daresay most of us were looking forward more to a good Sunday roast than the resurrection and the life everlasting.

I left it to Sally to make contact with the Freys. She is more adept in these matters than I.

"Good morning Mrs Frey."

"Good morning," said the aunt, polite but not quite polite enough to address Sally by name. Christian charity only goes so far with some people.

"And Miss Frey, how are you? That dress looks very nice. The colour suits you."

"Thank you," said Miss Frey, who had no more interest in women's clothing than I did, but who Sally was tutoring in such things. "So does yours."

I appeared behind Sally and beamed, amiably I hoped, at her aunt. Before I could frame a greeting the aunt was talking to a woman in a hat.

But Miss Frey, who could hardly have missed my appearance, made a bee-line for me.

"What is it?" she asked. "What's the case?"

Miss Frey is the most direct person I know. Sally is teaching her the ways of polite society, something her aunt gave up on long ago. She has improved greatly since our first meeting when she attacked me with a pair of scissors. She handles frustration better, and carries out the meaningless rituals required by our society with little irritation. But there is an understanding that with me she can dispense with small talk.

"A missing person," I said, producing the notebook from my pocket. "I'm hoping that this holds the key."

She flicked through the pages, eyes widening with delight. The whole thing was written in cipher, and had defeated my amateurish attempts at applying the standard methods. Some sections also included a sprinkling of what I recognized to be astrological symbols, which to me made the whole thing even more ominous.

"Oh, that's good," she said. "He's coded everything. It is a 'he,' I take it?"

She ran her eyes over the lines of text, looking for patterns and correspondences. Sometimes Miss Frey can read code as easily as handwriting, others take a bit more time and elbow grease.

"A young man," said Sally. "And a very intriguing case. Completely vanished!"

Miss Frey dragged her eyes from the notebook and, with a glance towards her aunt, stuffed it into her handbag and held it tightly.

"You've got to tell me all about it," she said.

"I don't want to plant any preconceptions," I said. "Anything I say might sway you to subconsciously look for things that aren't there. However, in recognition of your services, I will sketch the outline."

She was only a young girl and this was hardly a matter suitable for one of her years. But Miss Frey was as bloodthirsty as any seasoned grandmother who pores over the pages of the Police Gazette in search of juicy murder stories and there was little point in my holding back. Especially as she might well identify the relevancy of details which had escaped me.

"I approached the premises at approximately seven P.M.," I said, formal reportage being her preferred form of communication. "A time of day selected to ensure that the individual would have returned from work but would not yet have set out for his evening's entertainment. I quickly ascertained by ringing the doorbell and knocking at the door that nobody was in residence who wished to answer. Also, that there were no lights burning in the entire apartment.

"At the same time I noted that there was a 'To Let' sign displayed prominently in the window of the downstairs flat, and the room beyond was devoid of furniture. That was a pity in one way; downstairs neighbors are often an excellent source of information about the coming and goings of those in the flat above, and would soon be able to tell me if my man was still in residence. On the other hand, there was nobody to alert the upstairs about a doubtful character seen snooping about.

"There remained a slight suspicion that somebody might be present but who did not wish to be known. In my capacity as a debt collector I have often seen this type of behavior exhibited."

"What did you do? You must have broken in, or you wouldn't have the notebook."

"I waited outside the door for a few minutes, listening and looking for signs of movement inside. It then struck me that there was a slight crack around where the front door met the frame, a sign perhaps that it has not been properly closed. On trying the door, I found it to have been left unlocked."

Breaking and entering is a serious offence. However, entering through an unlocked door is more of the nature of trespass and treated more leniently by the law. Given that I could claim reasonable grounds for concern about the occupant's health and had been sent on an errand of mercy by Betty, I felt I was on good legal ground when I stepped over the threshold.

I recounted the rest of the incident to Miss Frey in detail, from the moment I murmured "Meredith, we're in." It is a line from a music-hall sketch, and reciting it has become a nervous habit or perhaps a ritual of personal protection.

I closed the door behind me and cleared my throat.

"Hullo there," I said. "Is anybody in? Just wanted to let you know you left your door unlocked."

It was silent as the tomb. At my feet was a drift of post, an accretion of several days at least.

I located the hall light switch. A side door led to the coal cellar and a flight of stairs up to the flat itself. I clumped my way up the staircase, loud enough to ensure that anyone would hear, and repeated my greeting before going through the door at the top.

In my early days as a butcher's boy in my Pa's shop I was faced with many of the less appealing jobs, which often included the cleaning up of dried blood after a day's work. On a summer's day, the yard behind a butcher's carried a smell that is as vile as it is distinctive, and attracts clouds of buzzing flies. That self-same aroma greeted me here.

I paused and strained my ears to catch the sound of a breath, a creaking floorboard, the slightest motion. Whoever was inside must know I was here, and would be ready for me.

I stepped inside and smartly flicked the light switch. The room, which combined dining and sitting room in one, with a galley kitchen off to one side, was empty. I stalked round the rest of the place, wary of ambush, and found nothing.

A short inspection revealed that it was a two-bedroom apartment, evidently occupied by two young gentlemen. There were dirty plates in the sink, clothes in the wardrobes, and every other sign that both of them were still in residence. But judging by the staleness of everything in the larder, as well as the post downstairs, nobody had been here for some time.

Most significantly though, one corner of the dining room rug was covered in a single spreading dark stain with the unmistakable smell of old blood. There might well be other explanations, but it was hard not to conclude that a man had bled to death here. Closer examination showed that someone had tried to sponge the blood off, and the floor around showed signs of abrasion as though it has been scrubbed with a hard brush. It was a poor job; disposing of the carpet would have hidden the evidence. But maybe they just wanted to stop it leaking through and had not finished clearing up here yet.

Perhaps I was being melodramatic, but I was struck by the conviction that I was the first on the scene of a horrendous crime, and I had better tread very carefully if I did not want to get any more involved than I already was.

I found a laundry basket full of bloodstained clothes. There had been so much blood and it had so seeped that it was not easy to tell which clothes, other than a shirt and a jacket, might have been the ones worn by the victim. But I judged that the killer had stripped the victim naked before disposing of the body.

Examination of the kitchen area did not turn up an obvious murder weapon. There was a carving knife vicious enough for the job, but if it had been used for such a purpose it had been well cleaned and returned to the bottom of the drawer.

I also found a case of razors, including two decent open razors. I fancied that the edge of one of them showed some discoloration, but it was hard to tell. Again, if it had been used, it had been cleaned afterwards and would not give up its story.

I was excited to discover the wallet of one of the men, which I assumed meant he was the victim, the other was the attacker. But then I found a second wallet in the other man's bedroom, as well as a watch and other personal effects. Both of them, it seemed, had left behind everything a man would normally take with him, down to a pair of spectacles on the dining table, bent somewhat out of shape.

Had both men then been killed, and their bodies abstracted, by some third party? This was spinning theories far beyond the facts. I needed evidence.

Twenty minutes of searching did not turn up anything material. The presence of two wallets, one containing notes, and a broken cash box still full of money and a cheque book, plus sundry minor valuable items, indicated that if there had been a crime, robbery was not its purpose.

I was about to give up when, wedged under the mattress of one bed, I found a notebook. It was neatly handwritten but seemingly composed in gibberish. The characters were all familiar, the sequence in which they appeared was not English nor any other actual language. The text was also sprinkled with symbols emphatically not from our alphabet, which I believed to be astrological.

A number of small jars stashed in the same location proved to be empty meat paste jars, well cleaned out, with the lids attached. I was at a loss to see the connection or why they might be hidden, and I took the trouble to check that they really were empty.

There was no particular reason to think that the book or the jars might be connected to the disappearances. On the other hand, it was the only thing in the entire apartment that suggested mystery and concealment.

"It's quite a mystery," Sally said when I had finished. "And the only clue is that book there. Do you think you can do anything with it?"

"It's Sunday now," said Miss Frey, squinting. "But I can work tonight …and I can snatch a few hours on Monday … hmm. I'll have something for you on Wednesday afternoon. You can visit when Aunt's at her sewing circle between three and five."

"You'll crack it in three days?" I asked. I doubt whether many professionals would have given that sort of assurance on so brief an examination.

"Or less," she said. "If this is from one of your superhuman beings or ancient civilizations it might take the whole time. But if it's someone normal it should not take that long."

"I will see you on Wednesday then."

"Absolutely," she said, holding her handbag in a death grip.

"She lives for this sort of thing," Sally said fondly as Miss Frey and her aunt made their way through the post-church crowd. "She's lucky she met you."

"So long as it doesn't lead her to any harm."

I had seen on many occasions how an interest in mysteries had turned into a life-devouring obsession. By now I could count several cases where that obsession had ended in death, or worse. I had a profound responsibility to ensure I did not accidentally lead her into spiritual and physical danger.

Wilson's second victim was a disappointment.

His stalking technique had been, he felt, flawless, especially for one inexperienced in it.

She had hammered on the door as though she meant to break it down, and he could hear her muttering at him through the letterbox downstairs. The word 'money' was mentioned several times. She wanted her money. That was odd. Wilson's memory of life before was becoming vague, but Ingram was never short of money, and all the people coming round after unpaid debts had been pursuing Wilson.

He also noticed that it was quite dark. It must be night now. Why would someone come and visit Ingram at this time of night? He was vaguely aware it was Friday night, a time when Wilson would usually be out at the pub. Did Ingram have assignations when Wilson was not there?

By craning his neck by the front window and looking down, he could just see the shabby old woman at the front door. No, he did not recognize her, and he could not imagine that Ingram would have anything to do with anyone like that.

He caught a glimpse of one of her hands, and that made his mouth water. There was a whole new body waiting for him just downstairs, asking to come in. What better opportunity could he ask for?

Wilson stood up to go down and open the door, but he had not taken two steps before he knew that it would be a mistake. Even in this light she would see him, she would never come in, she would run away screaming.

He went to the window and looked up and down the street. It was deserted. Maybe it was later than he thought. But conditions looked perfect for a hunt.

He waited for her to finish knocking and calling, and when she had finally had enough, he hurried down the stairs. He did not close the front door fully behind him, but set out down the dark street after her. He moved as quickly as he could on his bare feet, leaning forward using his long arms as extra legs to give him speed.

He could see her ahead of him and he judged his pace so he would catch her between streetlights, where it was darkest.

She had only looked around at the last moment, when he was almost on top of her. Her eyes widened and her mouth opened but she did not let out a sound. Then Wilson's fingers closed around her neck, and she had lost her chance to scream forever.

Wilson congratulated himself on the utmost restraint. He had not bitten her, no, he had not taken even a tiny nip of that flesh. He just wrapped his hands around that neck and squeezed, and squeezed, until the kicking stopped entirely and she was quite dead.

He marveled at how he was able to pick up the body and tuck it under one arm like a parcel as he loped back. The whole thing had gone off perfectly and there was nothing at all, not even a spot of blood on the pavement, to tell anyone what had happened.

He did not take her back to the flat but to a new lair he had remembered the day before. This place was more to his taste, dark and quiet and secret, though not so far away from people as he would have liked.

Disappointment followed quickly though.

He had reduced his former flat mate to a few well-gnawed bones and the hunger had been growing.

Ingram has been a lean man, sure enough, and although the flesh was the tastiest thing he had ever eaten, Wilson has been looking forward to something a bit plumper and juicier. The hunger in him seemed to grow the more he ate, and he had eaten far more than he would have thought possible.

But when he unwrapped his new prize, it was like discovering a lump of coal in his Christmas stocking.

There was layer after layer of clothing, all of it giving the false impression of substance. She was an old chicken with fluffed-up feathers who, once plucked, was just a scrawny, insubstantial creature with nothing to her. The woman was nothing but skin and bone with hardly a decent bite of meat anywhere on her.

In his first enthusiasm, Wilson had stripped off one arm and chewed down all the stringy flesh before he fully realized what he was doing, swallowing it before he had a chance to enjoy the meat.

It was also beginning to strike Wilson how much bigger he had grown. With the addition of Ingram's substance to his own he was, he joked to himself, twice the man he was before. And his appetite had outpaced his own growth, like a fire which becomes hotter the more it grows.

Wilson ground his teeth, holding back from the next bite. It was frustrating to have made such an audacious move, to have gone outside for the first time in his new form, to have hunted prey, brought it down, and carried it back, only to find that the whole game had hardly been worth a candle. Wilson had risked discovery, risked everything—in his imagination he saw his enemies as a hue and cry of men with pitchforks and shotguns and dogs—for a scant few mouthfuls of sustenance.

But there was something else. The old woman had a small parcel with her, from which an appetizing aroma wafted. Wilson had been intrigued to find some tasty little morsels inside.

That was a bonus. And her carcass would keep Wilson going for a few more days while he worked out a foolproof plan for his next capture.

And, if there was not much of her, the fresh meat was still delicious.

Three

Like many people, I owe the direction of my life to an accident of birth. Rather than being born with the proverbial silver spoon in my mouth though, I was born gnawing on chop bones—just the thing for teething babies, according to family lore. Having a butcher for a father, I was fed on a diet rich in beef, lamb, pork and other meats. I do not say that any of my schoolmates suffered from malnutrition, but the fact that both my brother and I grew into such a strapping pair of young hooligans suggests the value of protein for building young bodies.

Would I have become a boxer without the advantage of a beef-fed physique? Certainly there are plenty of pugilists with less muscle on them, but it is fair to say that I was chosen in the army as a contender for the ring on the basis of the width of my shoulders rather than aptitude. I picked up the art of the gloves quickly enough though, and the progress of my career from boxing to debt collecting to legal work and my current investigatory pursuit is documented elsewhere.

My size is also a disadvantage. For example, I had to approach Miss Frey's aunt's house with the greatest circumspection, so that my arrival at the back door while the aunt was at her sewing circle would not be noticed. At best, my presence would spark rumours among the neighbours; at worst, someone would call the police and report an intruder, resulting in red faces all around.

The aunt kept both front and back doors locked in her absence, supposedly for Miss Frey's own safety, but more likely to keep her out of trouble. The enterprising young lady had learned the art of picking the back door lock. It was open when I arrived.

She was waiting at the kitchen table, the notebook propped open in front of her with marmalade jars, surrounded by sheets and sheets of writing, a pen clutched in her hand.

"I gather then that you were successful," I said.

"Pretty much finished," said Miss Frey.

"I think I owe you something for all that paper you've used."

"Oh, Aunt's used to me using a lot of paper," she said offhandedly. "It wasn't that difficult once I saw it was a Della Porta cipher from this crib sheet, then it was just a matter of transcribing it all."

She slid out a loose sheet from the notebook on which there was a grid of letters, with twenty-six copies of the alphabet, each displaced by one letter from the one above.

The general idea of a Della Porta code is familiar enough to cipher aficionados. Each letter in a specific piece of text is used to encipher your message. So if the first word in the text is A, the first letter of the message is shifted by one place, if it is B it is shifted by two places and so on.

"But deciphering a cipher you need to have the key in question," I said

"Well, yes," she said. "But if you look at the crib sheet, you can see little dots where he rested his pen most often while he was looking up."

I looked closely, and I could see that the coder must have accidentally touched his pen to the paper while looking up rows and columns. They appeared to me at first to be randomly distributed, but on closer inspection they only appeared in certain columns, such as the C, I, O, S and V.

"It stands to reason," she said, "that he was only using one word over and over as the basis for his cipher, as he only needed to hide what he was writing from casual observers, not from Military Intelligence."

"Good thinking," I said.

"So it was just a matter of finding a word that had all the letters which he had used and none of the others. And testing it against a few lines of text I soon saw it was the word 'victorious'."

I am sure she did. I am equally sure I would not have found the word in a month of Sundays.

"I see," I said. I had questions but Miss Frey had earned the right to tell the story her own way and I determined that I would give her free rein to do so.

"After that it was just a matter of transcribing it into plain text. It's a diary, a rather peculiar one. Right from this first line he writes here at the top."

She underlined with her finger where she had deciphered: "To the one who is victorious, I will give the right to eat from the tree of life."

"The Bible?"

"Revelation 2:7. Always a bad sign when they start quoting from the Book of Revelation," she said knowingly. "It attracts lunatics like moths to a flame."

I did not know where she had acquired this particular nugget of wisdom but it chimed rather well with my own findings. Maybe they should not go teaching the Book of Revelation in Sunday School.

"It is followed by a line I do not recognize: 'The king, who has ruled for longer than any man remembers, presides over these feasts'—it says it's from the 'Regnum Congo,'—that's Latin for the Kingdom of Congo."

"That is in Africa."

"The first few entries concentrate on a person, a man called W, who is in close contact with the diary writer," Miss Frey went on. "He doesn't like W at all! He says he's 'morally deformed', 'depraved,' 'an ethical imbecile' and 'prone to every vice'. But he also says he is 'quite suitable'."

She paused and gave me a meaningful look.

"Ideally fitted for what, I wonder?" I duly asked.

"After a week or so of personal insults and observations, they are interspersed with dietary notes. 'breakfast 2 rashers of bacon, 2 eggs, 2 slices toast', 'tinned steak and kidney pudding, bottle of Bass', 'tea with milk, 3 ginger nuts', 'tinned corned beef hash', 'bag of caramels from sweetshop', '2 slices bread with jam and margarine'. All with dates and times."

"And he felt it was worth putting all of this in code," I said.

"The diary is very concerned with W's diet, with what he eats and when, and where he gets his food. The writer is particularly keen on noting what W drinks after a night's 'debauchery'. What do you think he means by that?"

"Debauchery is excessive indulgence of one's appetites," I said. "I assume it means he came back from the pub after a few too many."

"Oh," she said, as if she had been hoping for something more exciting. "Well, it notes that W is prone to bringing back fried potatoes, which he sometimes finishes the next morning. He also eats bread rolls and takes leftovers from the larder. Even if they're not his. Can't resist a bread roll."

"Very reprehensible I'm sure," I said, but it seemed quite petty to go to the trouble of writing them down. Even if he was going to present the other man with a list of the things he had wrongfully consumed, it would be laughed off.

"There's about two weeks of that," she said, turning over pages. "And after that, he starts with the symbols. Did you recognize them?"

"Astrological signs, I believe," I said, feeling only slightly patronized. I had been in this business for considerably longer than Miss Frey who was, after all, just a schoolgirl.

"Specifically the planets, plus the sun and moon, which aren't actually planets. So we have '3 grains of Jupiter in meat paste. Taken'. The next day. '4 grains Sol in leftover scrambled egg. Not Taken'. '2 grains Venus in milk—W commented on bad taste, but taken'."

"But what are Sol and Venus? Was he poisoning W?" I said.

"Not exactly, I don't think. He always records the effects the next day: 'Weds 6th—W out of sorts but probably hangover'. 'Fri 9th—W sorry for self, and off-color'. 'Monday 12th W sick in bed. Reduce dose of Jupiter, or balance with more Mercury?? Unclear'. Later on he settles for meat paste to administer it every time."

"So - he was poisoning W," I concluded.

"I think he was trying *not* to poison him," she said. "There are calculations with all the astrological signs where he works out all the doses for a given time period. Whenever W gets too sick he gives up and starts again."

You could write the sum total of my knowledge of the pharmacopoeia on the back of a postcard and still have space for the address. But I have spent some time perusing the works of the great alchemist and physician Paracelsus. On the matter of poisons he once noted that the dose makes the poison: according to him, all medicines are poisons given in the wrong dose, and likewise all poisons are medicines if administered correctly.

"So this was in the nature of a medical experiment," I said. "Although in this case this patient does not appear to have anything much wrong with him—there's no note of symptoms or their improving, is there?"

Miss Frey shook her head.

"He is more concerned with W's moral well-being, or his lack of it," she said. "At one point W says he will go to church, and he writes 'why now? He will wreck the whole thing'. But W oversleeps anyway and doesn't go."

That tickled a memory somewhere.

"This reminds me of a book," I started. "About medicine and moral character—"

"*Strange Case of Dr Jekyll and Mr. Hyde*," she said. "The doctor is looking for a drug which purges evil from the body. Or at least separates it from the good."

"It's a wonderful tale," I said. "But not one to be taken seriously … surely?"

"But it has to be something like that," she said. "Also, I don't think he's very good at it. He keeps making mistakes in his calculations—he has trouble doing them in code and he sometimes transposes wrongly. In a couple of them he doesn't even bother coding and he still gets it wrong."

She wanted to show me some of the calculations, and I nodded and agreed with her while she explained. Miss Frey has magical eyes which can see mistakes in a row of numbers as easily as a hawk picks out a vole.

"He ends up administering four times as much Mars as he means to. That's where it stops, so that might be something to do with it."

"Not necessarily. The world is full of happenstance and coincidence."

She made a sound that might have been a harrumph and gave me a look before going on. It seemed we were agreeing to disagree.

"At back of the book there are addresses—three of them—along with the same symbols with dates and amounts."

"Aha. Now, would those be his suppliers of the mysterious materials, do you think?"

"Well, obviously," she said. "And then, finally, right at the back on the last page, there's this one sentence in big capital letters. And it's not in code ... but it is in gibberish. There are other bits of gibberish in the main text, but this one is definitely the important one."

She showed me the words, a tongue-twisting conglomeration of unlikely consonants with a few vowels sprinkled in.

"How do you know it's not code?"

"Trust me on this matter, Mr. Stubbs," she said, in the manner of one older than her years. "What I can say is that it is in a foreign language, but not one of the usual ones. Or one of the unusual ones." She cocked her head. "More like your 'Ia Cthulhu' abracadabra, wouldn't you say?"

I had to admit it did look very much like one of those languages which were not originally spoken by human tongues, passed down in works like the infamous Necronomicon from one generation of wizards to the next.

"A key phrase to activate a magic spell," she said. "Or deactivate it, would you say?"

"Well that's another little cherry of a riddle on the icing of a cake of enigmas," I said.

"You have an idea, don't you?" she said. "About what happened to the two of them. And it's something to do with the occult, some dark business?"

"I don't know if I have an actual idea," I said. "But I'm formulating some impressions."

"One of them killed the other and ran away," she said. The evidence I had seen in the flat was certainly suggestive of murder.

"Either the final dose poisoned W and he died of it, and the diarist had disposed of the body so the coroner wouldn't do a test and find all the poisons in it. Or else—W found out he was being poisoned and killed the other one, and disposed of the body and went on the run."

"Both good theories," I said.

"Or else a third person found out and killed both of them."

"'The investigation is continuing'," I said, quoting the line always trotted out by the police when they failed to catch a murderer. "But I do believe your excellent work will help us find out. Now, may I see those addresses?"

Wilson's second expedition had been one of reconnaissance.

He had found an overcoat, and when he judged the time to be about two in the morning, he had gone out into the street to see what he could find.

Wilson's night vision was greatly improved. It was not as clear as day, but the darkness was more like a light fog which he would see through with his new eyes. The streetlights burned like electric arc lamps, throwing shockingly bright discs of light onto the pavement, which Wilson scurried around where he could, or hurried through quickly.

Occasional cars swished past, their headlights throwing twin bright lances ahead of them, and one or two motor-bikes. Wilson wondered about the motorcyclists but decided that even though he probably could grab one, it would make far too much noise. The street was deserted, but the racket of a machine crashing and spinning would bring faces to those curtained windows on all sides, and it would come to nothing.

Everything was closed, shuttered, blinds pulled down. Wilson checked the doorways to see if there was anyone sleeping in them, but found nothing. That was probably the doing of the police, moving on any who tried to sleep rough in these parts. The police! Wilson looked about him as he remembered them, the sticks, the iron handcuffs. He would keep an eye out for the police.

The Electric Café was still open, an all-night place whose front was a rectangle of pure light. He did not dare look in but could hear the jangle of cutlery and a murmur of subdued conversation. The café was the haunt of men who worked the late shift, the night owls, and others who worked anti-social hours.

Wilson waited in a doorway to see if anyone would leave, but when they did it was a group of four workmen together, all carrying toolboxes.

He dared not stay any longer. He did not know how long it would be between police patrols, but he felt that staying too long in one place was pushing his luck. There was always the chance that a motorist might see him lurking there and say something to someone.

He sniffed around the Salvation Army hostel, hoping to catch some latecomer arriving, or maybe a man who suddenly found the atmosphere oppressive and needed a drink, but without any luck.

Wilson climbed over the iron railings around Tivoli Park as easily as a monkey, leaping down onto the grass and crouching on all fours. Two cats who had been sniffing at each other bolted in different directions at the sight of him.

He grinned to himself, amused at their terror. Cat-meat had no appeal. What he wanted went on two legs and tasted so much better.

He was getting to know the place. Next time he would find a vantage point where he could watch a street and an alley or two, somewhere he could stay undisturbed while he waited for his next meal.

Wilson was learning patience. This was a long game.

Four

Two of the addresses in the back of Ingram's notebook were duds, but the third took me to an undertaker, a small concern located down a side street under the name Brown. The window display of urns, blank headstones and dried flowers looked dusty and outdated even to my untutored eyes. The place had seen better days. I was met by a middle-aged woman whose countenance suggested that her habitual air of woe might have been more than just a professional mask. It did not take a genius to deduce that she was running her late husband's business and finding it a struggle.

When I handed her my business card and explained that I was not a prospective client but wished to make some professional enquiries of her employee Mrs Verse, she started trembling. For once it was not my size and appearance that troubled her but the air of officialdom and perhaps the word Investigator on my card.

"She's gone. Have mercy on me, please!" she said, putting a hand on my arm. "I'm just a poor widow! I didn't know anything about what that horrible woman has been up to!"

This outburst seemed to catch both of us by surprise and she withdrew her hand and put it over her mouth, giving me a suspicious look.

I am an unskilled and unconvincing liar. Some of us just do not have the knack for it, or any other kind of fast talking. But sometimes the truth, suitably rearranged, will do just as well.

"Mrs Brown," I said. "Compose yourself. I have not shared any of my findings with the law, and I have no reason to suspect you of any wrongdoing."

I placed my closed notepad on the desk, and my pencil on top of it.

"I will not take down anything you say. But if you tell me about Mrs Verse, I will be able to focus my investigation narrowly on her."

"I don't know where she's gone," said Mrs Brown. "I swear it to heaven. I knew as soon as she did not show up for work yesterday it was the end. She's gone, fled—and left me to answer for her sins."

I nodded with the gravity appropriate to a conversation with an undertaker.

"And you haven't seen her since … Tuesday evening?"

"She left here as normal. She had been a bit tetchy during the day, but not much more than usual. When she did not come in the day after I sent a note, then I went round."

"You were anxious about her?"

"She never missed a day here. After she first came, five years ago. When my old assistant had to leave to care for her aunt, Mrs Verse turned up. She had references, and she had so much experience with handling and preparing the dear departed … I didn't like her face the moment I saw her, but what could I do?"

"So your relationship with your employee was strained?"

"Strained?" She let out a long breath, shaking her head. "If I didn't know there was no such thing as witches, I would have said she was one. She's a dark, bitter woman, is Mrs Verse. Unctuous with the clients, you know, bowing and nodding too much, but as soon as they've gone—all sneery."

I have no idea what goes on behind the scenes at an undertaker's, nor do I wish to know. As with the butcher's business, what the eye does not see, the heart does not grieve over. Some things are better kept away from the public gaze.

"But she was always dropping hints and giving knowing looks to me, saying as how wasn't it a pity we made so little money and wouldn't I like to make a bit extra on the side. I always said I didn't know what she was suggesting and she just laughed in that sly way of hers and said maybe it was better that way."

"But you had your suspicions."

"I did," she said, wringing her hands. "From the start. She had the keys and sometimes I'd find signs that someone had been in here during the night. Always when there was a lying in. And only when it was a female loved one who was lying in. When I confronted Mrs Verse about it, she said it was a pity to be lying in here all on your own and maybe the dear departed wanted some company. I did not know what to say to that, but I did see that the next week she had a new black lace shawl—much better than anything I could afford."

"That's suggestive," I said.

"She said she'd come into a bit of cash, and if the business was struggling it did not matter if her wages were delayed that month. Well, the rent had gone up, and … her wages have been in arrears."

I could guess just how far they were in arrears. It sounded as though Mrs Brown had her unwelcome assistant for free. It was the sort of pact with the devil that people who are in financial straits all too easily fall into.

"And once or twice men came round and asked to talk to her—I always told them they could ask me, I'm the proprietor, but they left in a hurry. "

"What sort of men?"

"Decent men," she said, a little huffily. "A better class. Except maybe for a bit of a look in their eye. Not the sort of thing we usually see in this type of establishment. This place usually has a dampening effect on people's demeanor rather than … exciting them."

Mrs Brown might not have suspected much at first, but her suspicions must have grown over time, and I'm sure she came to realize the kind of trade Mrs Verse was engaged in.

"But of course you had no real evidence and no grounds to suspect anything was wrong," I said reassuringly.

"None at all," she said. "On one occasion though, when she was going out, I saw her take out a letter from her bag for the postbox down the street. She stopped to look at something, and I saw the address. It was for the classified advertisement office of a gentleman's magazine."

The classified sections of those magazines are, as a rule, strictly respectable as far as outer form goes. The advertisements are always couched in a language of code-words understood only by the initiated. The publishers could never be accused of knowingly acting in the capacity of procurers, but it is said that some of the most exalted of them, read by the highest in the land, also cater to the most depraved tastes. But only in code, and only via Post Office Box numbers which could not be traced.

Clearly it had been a profitable trade for Mrs Verse, and I suspected it would have taken serious jeopardy to drive her away.

I could tell though that Mrs Brown had still more to unburden herself of.

"Mrs Verse always said that so long as the face and the hands were presentable for the funeral, it did not matter what happened to a loved one when they were with us. But there are things … " She gave a slight shudder and stopped speaking.

Silently, she led me through to a back room, the main feature of which was a bier for a dead body which was thankfully empty. She folded back the hanging edge of a tablecloth to reveal a row of drawers, and indicated the lowest of them, as though she could not bear to touch it herself.

"That's Mrs Verse's drawer," she said, looking away. "I looked in it by accident one day. See for yourself."

I opened it gingerly. In among what I took to be the usual accessories of the undertaking field—cotton wool and putty and jars of makeup and colorings of various sorts to make the deceased more presentable to their relatives—there was a roll of tools which I would most associate with my previous trade. There was a stained apron and a couple of small filleting knives, a hacksaw, longer blades, serrated knives, and a number of bloody cloths. As well as two small empty jars of meat paste.

Mutilation of a corpse is a serious offence. And while perhaps some of her customers might have been medical men desperate for samples they could not get through the usual channels, this looked like a more ancient and less honorable trade.

Shakespeare speaks of witch's recipes which involve the liver of a hanged man or the heart of a murderer and suchlike. And I had read of alchemists and others who believed that certain human organs contained special powers which could be chemically extracted and reduced to their essences or salts. I could easily see how certain organs might be cut out and blended into a paste so they could be surreptitiously included in a victim's diet.

It all made a certain horrible kind of sense. I closed the drawer, and she replaced the cloth which hid it.

Mrs Brown, in my estimation, was not a bad woman, but rather the victim of an unscrupulous schemer.

"None of this is direct evidence of a crime," I said. "But maybe you would be well advised to dispose of this material before someone else comes looking."

She nodded once.

"Thank you, Mrs Brown," I said. "This has been most enlightening."

"Thank *you*, Mr. Stubbs," she said.

I had encountered the idea of medicinal cannibalism before; it was not uncommon in previous centuries, and Paracelsus mentions the beneficial properties of human blood. No less a person than King Charles II himself ingested a brew made with powdered skull. It seems possible that Ingram, who was something in the pharmaceutical trade, might be dabbling in this field.

As usual though, my personal speculations were made irrelevant by some correspondence from someone far better-informed, as my associate Captain Cross, a dealer in occult books was able to explain the matter fully.

Item: A letter to H. Stubbs Esq., from Captain Cross.
Stubbs —
Re — your enquiries of the 14th.
'Regnum Congo' — 16th century Portuguese book describing interior of Africa, including cannibalism by aristocracy with supposedly beneficial effects.

Obvious link to formula, which is from 18ᵗʰ Cent. French 'The Ghoul Cults' (Cultes des Ghoules in original Fr), derived from Alhazred's infamous work.

Formula is alchemic necrophagy, i.e. consumption of human body parts—Jupiter = Liver, Sol = Heart etc... Cult believes human flesh was the forbidden 'fruit of tree of life' and weaning onto it can exchange spiritual immortality for bodily immortality. The angelic self is displaced by bestial etc. etc. Weaning is complex and involves verbal formulae, etc. Getting wrong means death. Getting right means becoming a ghoul.

One copy of 'The Cults of Ghouls' now at British Library is known as 'Ingram Copy', belonged to noted 1860's pharmacist of that name, may be relation to your Ingram.

VERY bad show if someone trying out recipe. Dangerous at best.

Word to the wise—AVOID GHOULS—have met—violent, unpredictable and very tenacious.

If you want to raise a hunting party, free all next weekend if convenient. Will bring suitable ammunition.

Sorry for shortness, things a bit hectic.

Yrs,

Capt. X

Now it was all making sense, in a horrible sort of way.

The Bible tells us that humans tasted the fruit of the tree of knowledge; this has made us thinking beings and separated us from the animals. Previously we ate only of the tree of life, with the presumption that in Eden we were immortal. Ingram had sought to reverse that transformation and exchange intelligence, moral judgment and mortality for the mind of an animal and immortality.

And he had been testing ghoul-formula, aided by funerary ingredients from Mrs Verse, on his unfortunate flatmate.

It seemed more than likely that Ingram met with success shortly followed by death. The rug I had inspected had been stained with his blood as the ghoul feasted on his body.

And the ghoul was still out there, looking for victims.

Wilson's life was changed. The world above was now only interesting for the food it harbored. Wilson slumbered for long hours, perhaps sleeping through entire days, waking only to drowse and eat and contemplate his next foray.

Sometimes he found rats, pounced on them and devoured them quickly. Rather tasteless snacks they were, but he enjoyed the little spurt of blood and crunch of bones under his teeth. Other creatures, little wriggling earwigs, long-legged craneflies and woodlice were more amusement than nourishment. What he craved in the deepest pit of his being was the taste of human meat.

He had been to the cemetery and sniffed around but he could find no recent burials. They were buried too deep, inside sealed boxes, and none of that aroma escaped. A few of the graves had flowers on them, but they did not seem any more recent than the rest.

He prowled around several times, pausing in the moon-shadow of a mausoleum, reaching out to touch the faces of the stone angels. What he needed to find was a grave that had just been dug but not yet used, one that would soon be filled. His brain worried at the puzzle; graves were dug the day before they were used, or so he seemed to remember. But how long in between burials? How many thousand people were there in Norwood, and how many died each year, each month and each week? It was too difficult for him to work out.

What he did work out though was that if someone died soon—say tonight—they would be buried in a few days at most. If someone from one of the houses around here was found dead, he would not have long to wait before the cemetery was restocked with fresh fare.

He would need to stretch out his meals, adapt to a slower pace of life. Like the crocodile in the Nile, he could laze away the days and weeks, eating his prey a bit at a time, digesting it gradually.

He patrolled the night streets, thinking of runaway children, or drunken revellers passed out on park benches, but his fantasies always deceived him. Every possible meal turned out to be a trick of the shadows or a discarded piece of sacking.

Once he peered in an uncurtained window and saw an old man darning socks. He ducked away before the man could look up, but he had looked so tasty … but he was not desperate enough to risk anything. His intelligence may have been blunted but a kind of animal cunning had grown in him. He had a sixth sense for when people were coming and an instinctive knowledge that any discovery would be a disaster. He had to be completely silent, a ghost passing unseen through the night world. He would get his chance soon enough, though the pangs of hunger were growing worse.

The idea had come to him in a dream. In it he had relived part of his previous life, going dancing with a young woman. At the time, his eyes had played all over her body with lascivious interest; in the dream he now saw her in a very different light, but he woke before he could take a bite.

Wilson cursed his luck, but then he recalled that the girl, Betty, was still his. All he needed to do to get her to come to the flat was write a letter. In the letter he could entreat her to silence, make sure that she did not tell anyone where she was going. Her disappearance would be a complete mystery.

He rubbed his dry hands together. Back in his old life he had always been able to write a persuasive letter, win a girl round however badly he had behaved. His hands were big and powerful now, but Wilson had no doubt that he could counterfeit his old handwriting. The sharp edge of intelligence may have faded, but his cunning had grown and he had a lifetime of smooth phrases he could reuse.

It was just a matter now of counting the hours before she came to the door with the key he had enclosed in the letter, all unsuspecting.

A sound brought him out of his daydream. Someone entering the house; a heavier footfall than usual. Not Betty. He had best lie low.

But anticipation started to get hold of him. His mouth began to water, drool running from the corner. He could not hear the weight of that tread *without thinking how much good meat there was, just a few feet away. A whole carcass, a walking feast of flesh.*

Then the aroma hit him. It was like every roast beef dinner he had ever enjoyed, every juicy pork chop, every sizzling sausage, every crisp rasher of bacon all in one. He had not long since eaten, but the thought of letting it get away was more than he could bear.

Without thinking, Wilson leaped up and scrambled up the cellar stairs on all fours.

Five

I did not need Cross to tell me ghouls were dangerous and that I should be wary of tangling with them. Perusal of the *Arabian Nights* tell us that in the days when everyone carried a sword, ghouls were known to be difficult to kill. This was a fair warning that they were not as mortal as we humans and not to be tackled casually. But I had a secret weapon.

In the tales of the *Arabian Nights* and other pieces of folklore, the way to stop a ghoul was not by force of arms but with words. Specifically, a verse or two from the Holy Quran.

It may be that, backed with the force of true belief, such verses would be efficacious. But I had a different theory. Pious Moslems might well consider that only their own holy book would do, but it seemed to me that the way to stop a ghoul was to employ the same magic that had brought it into being. Any religious man, Moslem, Christian, or Jew, might be appalled by the idea of using pagan magic. But, like Paracelsus, I tended to the view that the words themselves were neutral, merely part of the structure of the world. They could be used or misused according to the moral principles of the speaker.

It therefore seemed to me that anyone who knew the process for creating a ghoul also knew how to uncreate it, or at least keep it at bay. Anyone experimenting with the dark arts will be familiar with the wise maxim that one should not call forth that which one cannot dismiss, and would keep the recipe for dismissal close at hand.

I concluded, then, that the verbal formula in the back of the notebook was that dismissal. Ingram must have the phrase memorised, but having it there in big letters would allow him to refresh his memory easily. If I was right though, he had not been able to utter it at the crucial moment. I made a copy for my own use. The line was oddly difficult to memorise—each time I tried I got several syllables wrong—and I concluded it would need to be read out. Preferably from a safe distance.

My return to the flat was perhaps optimistic, but from the information that Miss Frey and Captain Cross had supplied I believed I had an idea of what had happened, with the only question being where Wilson was now—and whether his disappearance was, as I suspected, linked to the sudden departure of Mrs Verse. Now I knew what I was looking for, I had an idea where the missing man might be found.

I suspected he might still be concealed on the premises, and I meant to find out.

As it turned out, I did not need to do much looking.

I had barely gone two steps up to the flat when the cellar door opened behind me and I looked around into a nightmarish visage of living horror, gazing hungrily up at me from the shadows beyond.

I had anticipated that there would be some alteration of features and perhaps a modification of form. But, naively, I was still thinking in terms of the more natural processes of growth and change. If a boxer wants to put on weight and bulk, it is a slow, arduous process. Building muscle takes time and effort. I was not thinking of the more mysterious transformations that nature can work, which take place on much shorter timescales and which are more drastic in nature.

He hesitated for a moment after opening the door, squinting as though dazzled by the dull light of a cloudy day indoors.

He was half naked and crouched rather than standing upright. My first and abiding thought was of a human hyena: his long-fingered hand sported claws which looked adapted for burrowing, for excavation and, no doubt, digging up bodies. His face had elongated into an animal muzzle and his mouth was filled with curved dagger-like teeth, dentition of a carnivore.

And he was big. Being hunched over concealed some of his size, but he was definitely in the heavyweight class. If he continued growing at that rate he would soon attain cyclopean proportions, and become an unstoppable cave-dwelling, man-eating Polyphemus.

In a moment, he had overcome his aversion to the light and came bounding towards me.

At an earlier stage in my career I would have been paralysed with fright and that would have been the end of Harry Stubbs. But I am somewhat hardened to these things now, and had some idea of what to expect, so I was able to respond as a fighter and not as prey.

He was coming at me from below, and practically on all fours, giving me a good advantage in height, so I pivoted and raised a foot to meet his charge. Planting my boot on his chest high above his center of gravity, I sent him toppling backwards into the cellar. It was more of a shove than an actual kick, intended mainly to keep him at bay. Even so, the shock of impact was considerable, his weight and forward momentum having been greater than I had expected and I was also pushed backwards.

This first impact forced me to make a rather rapid reappraisal of my entire approach to this encounter.

Roughly two seconds ago I had understood that ghouls were, like hyenas, mainly scavengers which fed on prey already dead, and that when they did attack they did so by ambush. The folktales suggest they rely on deception and trickery, luring travellers to separate from their party so they can be taken. It did not seem to me that they were particularly fearsome predators along the lines of a big cat, and I had assumed that, given what I at that point understood to be my physical superiority, I would be able to subdue this individual.

In my days as a doorman I had often been required to restrain rambunctious characters who had the ferocity of those whom alcohol made combative, and I had learned some useful techniques for doing so without inflicting much harm.

Given his size and aspect, restraint no longer looked like a practical option. On the other hand my assailant was now falling downstairs and that should give me time to do the necessary.

I withdrew the notepaper from my right-hand pocket with the words I must speak. I suspected it might take me several efforts to deliver it correctly. It would stop him from approaching though, and hopefully enable me to start some kind of dialogue, assuming he retained some vestige of human intellect.

Unfortunately, my assumption was again proven incorrect, and I had barely got the paper out of my pocket before the ghoul had caught itself on the banister and came bounding up the stairs again towards me. He might have been made out of rubber, and his energy was undiminished.

There was little room in the small hallway to adopt a fighting stance, so I backed off towards the front door. The ghoul tried to grab at my hands, and I evaded his swipes and jabbed back. He had a good reach but made poor use of it, and I caught him on the nose without difficulty.

A punch in the face is a sobering experience to one who is not accustomed to it. Receiving one often jars badly-behaved types sufficiently for them to reconsider their course of action. You can tell a lot about a fighter by how they react to a blow to the head.

This one barely blinked. He was not about to quiet down and behave himself.

He lunged for me. In the normal course of events I would have evaded him easily, but boxed in as I was with the walls on either side of me and the door at my back, I had no room to maneuver and no way to get away. His wide-open jaws with those terrifying teeth hurtled towards my neck, so I took the easiest defence available and thrust my forearm into his mouth.

This was not so careless as you might think. I have some acquaintances who are in the line of burglary and it's not unknown for them to enter houses where a guard dog, often of the mastiff variety, is known to reside. Obviously they prefer to avoid encounters with such beasts but, if the worse comes to the worst, they say the best defence is to put something in the beast's jaws—ideally a stick, but sometimes a limb will do.

This is because of the way leverage is exerted by the jaw muscles. At the widest extent of gape, these have little closing power. So long as you keep those jaws forced open they have little biting strength, and my forearm was big enough to prevent him closing his jaws in the slightest—though I felt those teeth going through my coat, jacket and shirt.

He tried to open wide to disengage, tried to turn his head, and failed in both. There followed a short dance with him trying to back away from me and get his jaws loose and me pressing forward and trying to pin his head against the wall with my arm, leaving him effectively de-fanged.

Of course these tactics would work better with a dog. Though inhuman, my opponent had hands and had hold of my arm in both of them. Concerned that his next move would be to break my wrist like a dry stick, I hit him where I felt it would do most good with my free right hand.

The solar plexus is a point in the abdomen, below the rib cage and behind the stomach. Anatomically, it is a meeting point of several lines of nerves, but mainly it is known as a highly vulnerable spot to aim a strike. Boxers are trained to tense their stomach muscles so such blows have little effect, but anyone who is unaware or caught off guard is vulnerable.

A good blow to the solar plexus will knock the wind right out of a fighter, usually causing them to double over. It gives the exact sensation of being unable to breathe. I cannot say whether this is genuine paralysis but the feeling is certainly real.

As I said, both his hands were on my left arm, so he had no defence and I hit him as hard as I liked, a good upward-driving blow right on the button.

There is another effect of a blow to this region which I have often observed, but never in the ring. Boxers, obviously, do not eat a heavy meal before a fight. But in affrays outside public houses with men who have several pints of ale in their bellies, a blow to the solar plexus will often have the effect of causing the subject to eject the contents of his stomach in short order. This, like a blow to the face, is an excellent sober-upper. In the aftermath, having thoroughly ruined his shoes, the recipient of such a blow may change his manners.

The target in this case had not been drinking, but he had been eating. As I was to discover, he had recently eaten the equivalent of several heavy meals. Rugged as his constitution was, the outrage of a heavy punch to the solar plexus drew a volcanic response and he heaved mightily.

At this point of course my forearm was wedged squarely across his open mouth, and the process of freely vomiting was severely impeded. Jets of disgusting material spurted from the sides of his mouth and his nose, but the majority of the material was contained or diverted.

I should have pressed my advantage but I involuntarily drew back and my arm left his mouth at the second heave. I delivered a couple more good blows to his head but he was too busy ridding himself of gut contents to even notice.

Again I thought of the scrap of paper, now balled up in my right hand, and whether I might now have enough time to unfold it and speak the words. I backed away, keeping my eyes firmly on the choking man-beast. He did seem to be suffocating in his own effusions.

I might mention at this point that there were considerable quantities of vomit across the arm of my suit. Afterwards it left a pale mark as though the sleeve had been dipped in bleach. I assume that the digestive juices of the ghoul are far more powerful than those of a human, with the power to rapidly break down organic material. Quantities of this corrosive semi-liquid had been diverted into the ghoul's windpipe and organs of breathing, and one can only guess at the level of pain and the amount of damage it inflicted there.

For some long seconds I thought he was going to die on the spot, and I was more concerned about how one could administer first aid to one who was technically more undead than alive in the first place.

But, just as I thought he was going to succumb, he suddenly drew a jagged breath and, with a resilience which was more than human, he again threw himself at me like a wild thing, jaws agape.

My mental processes were working at fighting speed, and another idea had occurred to me. After seeing the way he had been choking, it struck me that, invulnerable as he might be to blows, he had certainly not enjoyed having his air supply cut off. And the sight of those teeth put me in mind of another story about a burglar who had stuck his hand down a dog's throat and choked it to death.

It seemed worth a try, having already established that my adversary's jaws lacked force when they were at full gape, and his defence was not existent.

His eyes appeared to pop as my fist entered his mouth and lodged somewhere inside.

He tried to bite down, but again the sheer size of my fist and wrist prevented him. The instinct to bite and gnaw was strong, but it was not doing him a bit of good, and after a moment he must also have begun to appreciate that he could no longer breathe.

I pressed the advantage, again shoving him violently backwards, catching one arm by the bicep to improve my grip while he took hold of my wrist.

He was working his jaws the whole time. Whether he was trying to spit my hand out, or whether he was trying to chew and swallow, was not clear. His strength was far more than the usual, though, and if I had not had the advantage of position he would have forced me off.

I heaved him around, slamming him into the walls to prevent him from getting a proper footing. This made a fair amount of noise but he did not emit any of the sounds of distress that a human would have done subjected to the same treatment.

As I was forcing him back there was, though, a most unwelcome noise, a burbling gasp indicating that he was succeeding in breathing despite the obstruction to his airway. I was causing him discomfort, no doubt, but I was not going to finish the fight that way.

I had barely begun to appreciate the significance of this change to the combat before he had raised one leg and, with impressive flexibility, used it to shove me backwards.

I felt his teeth tear down my forearm and rake the back of my hand as I drew it away from those recurved fangs. He rolled back, away from me, and I stepped back, thinking again of the paper with that spell and whether I could keep him down and kneel on his neck long enough to recite it.

Except that I was no longer holding the paper.

He rolled and came up in a crouch, panting and glaring daggers at me.

I think we both realized where that scrap of paper was at the same time. It had been in my fist and I must have lost it somewhere in his throat.

As a general matter of principle, magical invocations must be spoken to be effective. But there are some notable counter examples from various sources, in which the written word itself is considered to have potency. For example, those of the Jewish faith habitually protect the entrances to their houses with tiny scrolls of holy words affixed to the door frames, and may carry similar scrolls about their person for similar effect. In the traditional practice of sorcery, words—supposedly the names of demons, but in truth who can say what they really signify—are inscribed around a magic circle to activate it.

The virtue apparently lies in the words themselves, and they do not necessarily need to be spoken aloud. I can only surmise this from the effect that the scrap of paper had on the ghoul.

He opened his mouth and gaped. If he had not already exhausted the entire contents of his digestive system he might have been able to eject it. But he merely heaved. And then, involuntarily I am sure, he swallowed. His teeth had left deep scratches down the back of my hand, and the blood he would have tasted must have been irresistible. He was nothing if not a slave to his appetites.

After he swallowed he swayed, dropping to all fours.

This might have been my cue to make good my escape. He looked as though he might be incapacitated for more than a few moments, and I had no weapons left to fight him. I backed away, but did not attempt to flee.

He tore at his throat, first casually and then with increasing violence. Those big, blunt claws might not be meant for rending flesh, but he quickly lacerated himself, with the sort of injuries that would appear fatal on a mortal human, before he took a step that no ordinary human would do, thrusting one of his own hands down his throat in a vain attempt to reach the paper—which must by now surely have disintegrated.

The paper had gone but the words remained, and those, it seemed were having their effect.

Metamorphosis is a perilous process when one is transitioning between two forms which are not compatible with each other. This, I suspect, is why becoming a ghoul is not a straightforward matter. If the transformation is not carried out in the proper manner, the human and ghoul elements of the body fight against each other. The human part attempts to reject and eject the ghoul; the ghoul attempts to devour and digest the human. One cannot survive in a mid-way stage between the two, and that was where the thing in front of me now found itself.

There was a horrible wrenching sound; if you have ever heard a shoulder being dislocated in a fight you will have some idea of it, except that the sound was repeated with lesser noise and popping, as though every part of his body was being crushed, contracted, from his snout-like face to his lanky arms. He did not go into convulsions so much as crumple up, with a ghastly exhalation that can only have been a death rattle.

The body lying in front of me was recognizably human, but distorted as though his bones were made of wax that had melted in the heat. His face was collapsed on one side, and blistered as though burned with acid.

I stood there for some time, breathing heavily, reassuring myself that the fight was over. I did not propose to touch that body to check for a pulse, but the longer I stood there the more obvious it was that he was deceased.

I would have been interested to know what a coroner would have found as the cause of death, and whether there was any way of connecting it with the traces of paper lodged in the ex-ghoul's gullet. But I was certainly not sufficiently interested that I would allow any chance of a coroner ever seeing this body.

"Well then Harry," I said to myself. "This is a right mess, isn't it?"

The dead body, the acrid vomit spattered about, the blood, and the damage to the walls and bannisters amounted to a charge of murder, one that would be squarely directed at H. Stubbs.

The main thing was not to act hastily. Most likely nobody had seen me enter and, if I managed the thing correctly, nobody would see me depart either. Any connection with me would be completely erased.

The plan was simple enough, but required me to stay on the premises until well after nightfall. Ideally I would stay until the late hours of the evening.

In the meantime, I would keep myself busy.

I collected a bedsheet from the flat above and wrapped the body to transport it upstairs. I employed blankets to mop up the worst of the mess as best I could without touching it.

I went down into the cellar. There was no electric light—there never is in coal cellars—but I had matches and I was not surprised to find human remains. Not very much by the way of human remains, though two skulls were placed prominently on a lower step like trophies. A number of bones were arranged more haphazardly about the place, and I collected these along with some more grisly remnants in another sheet.

Remnants of articles of clothing indicated the second victim had been a woman. When I discovered a fancy black lace shawl, I recalled what Mrs Brown had said. Either it was quite a coincidence, or the second victim was the baleful Mrs Verse. Of course she would have had to visit Ingram—he would never have come to the undertaker's and she could hardly send human remains by parcel post.

Working in a butcher's shop can be a useful preparation in certain lines of work, and meat and bones are just meat and bones so long as you do not think too much about where they came from.

I needed to create a scene. I placed the shrunken body of the ghoul on one bed, and arranged a number of empty bottles from the kitchen around it. I placed a selection of other bones in the second bed and the larger skull on the pillow. The smaller skull, with some trepidation, I put in a brown paper bag to take with me.

I poured two bottles of methylated spirits around, carefully trailing it behind me as I retreated towards the stairs. Then I lit it with a single match, which I carefully retained in my gloved hand, and made my way out of the back door and through a small yard into a back alley. I was then able to make my way back out on to the street and watch from a discreet distance as the interior windows started to flicker with orange firelight. I had left the kitchen window open to ensure ventilation—I did not want the fire to smother itself—and smoke began to leak out. Nobody would notice it unless they were looking for it, and smoke from a kitchen window is hardly a rare occurrence.

House fires break out for a number of causes, among the commonest being the careless use of candles and indoor fires, and poorly-installed electrical systems. There is also a significant sub-class of those in which a man—it always seems to be the male sex—is smoking in bed after drinking and sets fire to the bed clothes, burning himself to death. That was the scenario which I was trying to suggest in this case, with the additional implication that his flat mate, sleeping, had been overcome by fumes and perished in the blaze.

Of course there were all sorts of glaring contradictions in the evidence, not least the fact that one of the victims was only present in the form of charred bones and these would not go unremarked. But experience has taught me that people by and large see what they expect to see, and interpret everything in the light of the known. When you hear clip-clopping outside the door you assume someone is riding by on a horse, not a zebra. Unless there is reason to expect an explanation that is out of the ordinary, people usually reject it out of hand and assume the mundane.

It is easy enough to set up a death scene in this way. But I had been at pains to leave various valuables such as watches and wallets in plain sight, to rule out any possibility of a burglary. A suspicious investigator might raise the theory that an assassin had broken in, killed both men and set the fire to conceal the crime. His superiors, however, would not be too happy to accept the idea that two seemingly blameless and respectable men would be murdered in this way. And when the investigator suggested that one man had been stripped to bones first, and that maybe even some of the bones were not his, eyebrows would definitely be raised.

Sherlock Holmes might solve the whole thing in one go, but any sensible observer would conclude that it was nothing more than a fire. The eager investigator might keep his eye out for any similar cases, in case there was a gang at work. As the ghoul and its creator were now both accounted for, there would be no such recurrence for him to investigate.

I headed down the street, walking half a mile before I reached a bus stop to take me home. The bus was pulling up when I saw a fire engine, bells ringing, hurtling in the other direction. The firemen would find the house thoroughly ablaze. The ground-floor flat was obviously untenanted, and there was no possibility that anyone on the upper storey could have survived, so they would concentrate on bringing the blaze under control and ensuring it did not spread to any of the adjoining premises.

I do not say I slept soundly that night, and I opened the morning papers with some nervous anticipation. The newspapermen had done their job, and there was a brisk, three-paragraph story about the fire. Cases where lives are lost always merit a piece in the news. Much of my careful staging was wasted: the building had so devoured itself, burning itself up from the inside, that any evidence of what had occurred had surely gone forever. The story reported that the roof had partially collapsed, but the bodies of two men, presumed to be the flat's usual occupants, had been recovered. The names had not yet been released.

I puzzled over how the conflagration could have been quite so severe for some time. It finally dawned on me that Ingram must have had a plan of how to dispose of his experiment once it was complete, and fire was an easy way to remove all traces of a monstrous body. The loft spaces I had not inspected must have been packed with enough flammable material to ensure that everything inside the house was burned to ashes.

The newspaper story lifted from me any responsibility for relaying what I had found to Kitty. The address of the fire was given, and the chances were that the first person who read it would have asked if that was the house number of Betty's male admirer. Under the circumstances it seemed wiser to say no more about it. Betty would certainly be no happier for anything I could tell her, even if she believed me, and any tale I told her would incriminate me in at least one suspicious death.

However, I did feel a need to share my experience with somebody. Of course I told Sally everything, and as usual she chided me for being headstrong. She cleaned the wounds on my arms — puncture marks on the left forearm, long gashes down the right wrist and hand — with salt water and then again with iodine, and they both stung like blazes. All the while she told me I would be lucky if I did not get tetanus at least, and I should have waited until the Captain could come to assist me, and he would have ensured that the business was done properly. This is regardless of the fact that the Captain is a deal less cautious than I, and the outcome would have been similar.

But she also seemed to be just a little pleased with me, especially after I discovered the letter that Betty had received from Wilson.

"Just think," she said. "She would have come, wouldn't she, all unknowing? It doesn't bear thinking about. But Harry, do take the Captain, or someone, with you next time."

I gave an edited version to Miss Frey, who deserved something for the invaluable assistance she had supplied. She was particularly interested in the effects of the written word. I had some slight hesitation in sharing this sort of thing with her. Miss Frey is young, but mighty oaks from little acorns grow, and it seemed to me that she was learning the rudiments of sorcery. I suspect that if she were to wish to experiment, she might do it with better result than poor Ingram.

"It's an evil business," I concluded, to leave her in no doubt about my views. "But I suspect the sad fact is that inside all of us dwells a primeval, carnivorous beast, hungering to extend its life at the expense of others."

"But still," she said thoughtfully, as though not convinced it was a bad idea.

"Still?" I said, keen to dissuade her. "Eating human flesh is a ghastly thing. And adopting a more carnal state can only improve the physical at the expense of the spiritual."

I recalled that Miss Frey liked to take constitutionals around West Norwood cemetery at odd hours, as she found the place peaceful. I did not like the turn this conversation was taking at all.

I was about to demand that Miss Frey hand over all of her notes from the case, just in case she was ever tempted to misuse the information they contained and cause another disaster. But this might alienate her. Further, she could probably recreate them all from memory.

I hope and believe that the matter is now firmly closed. I am keeping an eye on Miss Frey. As far as I can tell, she is interested in deciphering, making sense of hieroglyphics and other strange texts, and similar matters, and her interest in the occult is purely incidental.

And Betty, I am pleased to report, did not mourn her lost admirer for long. The collective wisdom of the china packers had indicated that he had only written to her after a long break because he had been with another woman, one who must have seen right through him. Nobody wants to speak ill of the dead, but it turned out that one of the other girls had a friend who happened to know Wilson by reputation, and now she was able to speak freely. In short, Betty has an engagement to go to the greyhound racing with a young man who works in a drapers. She has borrowed some shoes and a bracelet which goes with her good dress.

The lad is called Walter, and he can afford to be free with his money because he lives with his parents. His only quirk is that he is a vegetarian, a habit of life which a confirmed meat-eater like myself will never understand. But perhaps sometimes it is better to err on the side of caution.

Andrew Doran and the Genesis of the Ghouls

By Matthew Davenport

ARKHAM 1943

Chapter 1

Antiquities sales were, unfortunately, commonplace among the high-society types in Arkham. I would have thought that such practices would be dying out, but the invitation in my hand was proof to the opposite.

This one was at one of the more opulent houses in Arkham's Hornsby Hill area.

As a professor of archaeology, I erred on preserving the history over the preservation of the artifact itself. Mine was not an interest in fortune or glory but expanding the knowledge of the world. When an artifact ended up at an antiquities sale, the chances of ever knowing for certain where it came from dropped to almost zero. Yes, the person selling it could tell you where they found it, or how it came into their possession, but could that be trusted? Not to mention the amount of data you lose when an artifact is pulled from the ground and that information is not recorded. How deep it was can tell you about when it came from. What it was found with could tell you who owned it. Where you found it could tell you how it was used.

One man's spoon could be another man's heirloom, and none of that was ever sold with the artifacts at antiquities sales.

Then why was I here, wearing my last good suit and climbing the marble steps toward the entrance to a house that would never let me set foot in it otherwise?

As much as I hated antiquities sales, I would rather be there, purchasing them, than let something sacred to history fall into the wrong hands.

Or rather, as was the more definitive reason that I went to these horrible things, letting an artifact of great occult power fall into the wrong hands. That was the major reason that I chose to go on these little trips. Once every ten or so of these events someone would put something radiating pure power up for auction, and it was my role, as a representative of Miskatonic University and generally nice guy just trying to save the world, to keep those types of artifacts from the hands of evil men.

Or worst: idiots.

I was not fooled, either. The other buyers were not oblivious to these powerful artifacts. Most of those that were present stalked antiquities sales for just those reasons. It wasn't enough to be wealthy enough to buy and trade cities, they wanted real power. For them, the power to melt the faces off of their rivals, transform their lovers into Adonis, and the command of reality's very nature was all worth a little damning to Hell.

"Would you stop brooding?" my former secretary and friend, Carol Berg, said to me as we took the lengthy steps up to the gothic building. "I spent a lot of money on this dress. If you are to accompany me, I require you to at least pretend to be excited to be here with me."

"I hate these things," I said. Then I gave her a quick look. Carol was a friend, nothing more, but I wouldn't deny that she had spent good money on the silver dress. She was not entirely human, and I worried that if something happened here, she would have to ruin that nice dress to transform into the beast she hid from society. I forced a smile.

"You're right, though. That dress was worth every penny. You look wonderful."

She nodded her appreciation of the compliment. "Thank you. I would return the compliment, but I have seen that suit so many times at so many different school functions that I don't believe you own anything else."

My suit was plain and brown. I would have worn a tie, but I could not find either of the two ties that I stole from my father about twenty years ago. The suit was showing wear in spots and I pretended not to notice if anyone asked.

"That is entirely fair," I said. "If you need to sit a few spots away from me to disassociate yourself, I would not be offended." I winked.

Lately my life had taken a darker turn. Friends had been dying and monsters had been getting away with more than I was known to let them. I was forcing some positivity into this experience, as much as I could muster.

"Don't be silly," Carol smirked. "If I did not sit with you, who would?"

I returned her smirk as we reached the doors to the McCallister home. It was more of a mansion than a home, in that I could not imagine anyone actually living here, but that was because my own apartment was not much more than a closet with a window.

A butler stood at the doors, waiting to accept our invitations before we entered.

These invitations came to the campus Anthropology Department every year. This year two came, and giving Carol the second was an easy decision.

My annoyance must have been evident as I approached Craig Templeton, the McCallister House butler. This time, the annoyance was that I had to give him anything. He knew I would be here, I was always here. Yet, here we were, once again doing this ridiculous transaction of entry in exchange for the invitation.

Craig took mine, wrinkled from inside my suit jacket, and said nothing until he turned to Carol.

"And you, madame?"

Without hesitation, Carol proffered her, undamaged, invitation. Craig seemed more animated as he gently took the paper from the University secretary.

"Thank you," he said to her. She winked, touched his hand and returned her own thanks before moving on into the house with me.

I couldn't hide my smile. "What was that?"

Carol, cursed with Ithaqua's magic to be paler than most, even when in her human form, was turning redder than I had ever seen her without blood on her face.

"I might be an ancient monster, but I am not dead, Andy," she answered. "Besides being moderately attractive, Mr. Templeton is an excellent cook."

My smile only grew bigger. I was not trying to tease her so much as I was genuinely happy to find out she had something outside of the monsters and magic we had to face so regularly.

Alright, I was teasing her a little.

"So, you have had dinner with him?"

Carol stopped, turned to me and gave a tight-lipped smile. "I do have a life outside of begging professors of archaeology to step out of their dreary apartments once in a while." Her smile turned malicious. "And no, we haven't had dinner, yet. I was speaking of his breakfast skills."

It was my turn to blush, but my smile didn't fade.

"Good for you," I said. "I hope it continues to go well."

Carol's mirth vanished entirely. In its place was a carefully-controlled blank look. I knew that face. She was upset and covering it.

"We both know that fate has chosen a much different path for me."

She was right, and I felt guilty for hoping for better for her. Being what she was, a creature commonly—and sometimes incorrectly— referred to as a Wendigo, meant that she had a beastly nature that was not entirely under her control. Any normal people that she associated with for lengthy periods of time had a chance of living in danger. She was completely in control, but even recently we had seen things try to take advantage of her nature. It just wasn't safe.

"My apologies," I nodded and offered her my arm. "Would you like to continue inside?"

We walked through several different rooms, following a roped-off path toward the parlor that would house the auction. The opulence was incredible. The drawing room had chairs that looked to be of Chinese origin, while a library that we passed seemed to be built to mirror the look of the Parthenon, with books in place of where the statues would be along the walls. This was an exercise in power, demonstrating what they were capable of with what they had.

As beautiful as the rooms were, I noticed several artifacts of occult origin in some of them. Tablets for summoning calmer seas were mixed in with heirloom cookbooks. I began to wonder if this path was chosen for demonstrating the financial standing of the McCallisters, or if this was a tour of their accumulated occult power.

It was likely both.

I failed to have enough class to know what the room was called that the auction would take place in. It was probably something simple, such as the "show room." It was a large space, about the size of a baseball diamond, filled with chairs aimed toward the front where space had been cleared and a podium had been set to host the antiquities sale.

"There's the Marsh heiress," Carol nodded as we entered the room and began navigating toward a seat. The woman she pointed at was veiled in all black and barely moved. "Clara Olmstead. Poor woman wanted nothing to do with the family and now she's the only one left who can make any decisions regarding the estate."

"The only one left on land," I amended. "I don't seem to recognize anyone here," I said.

Carol shook her head. "You wouldn't. When you were the dean, I was forced to mingle more with the board and the donors, seeing as you wouldn't. Doing so requires a general idea of who the main players are. Even if you had been a more ..." she searched for the word, "present dean, you would have hated that part."

I appreciated her way of saying I was horrible at the job. I had never wanted it in the first place but hated the way I lost it even more. Still, I was glad that Carol still had her position where she could more or less run the school by proxy.

"Is there anyone else here that maybe I should be aware of?" If she knew the players, then my friend, once again, was showing to be a valuable resource.

"Oh," Carol's mischievous grin from before returned and I did not understand why, "at least one more."

Carol pointed, but before I could turn to see who she meant, someone was gently touching my elbow.

I was shocked into silence by the radiance that stood before me.

Wearing a shimmering blue dress and standing almost a head taller than me was an angel of dark hair and glasses with deep red lenses. Perhaps not an angel, so much as a snake in the Garden of Eden.

"Andrew, if you don't close your mouth a fly might get in," Bethany Coombs said in her sultry manner.

"I'm sorry," I said. "It isn't every day that someone you're more familiar with seeing eviscerating the devil himself shows the angels how it's done."

Bethany Coombs was my part-time associate on many artifact hunts. Throughout the years we had battled monsters, saved civilizations, and flirted on more than one occasion. There was more to this Amazonian woman than met the eye, that is, unless you looked her in the eyes. She was a princess of the Yig, a species and religion of people who worshiped the snake god, Yig. Unfortunately, as princess, she looked too human and was forced out of her role as queen. She preferred it that way, though. Instead of being tied down to her people she was able to travel the world and build a life for herself, all while her people footed the bill. She might not be allowed to be queen, but they would be damned if their royal lineage was going to starve.

She might be only a princess, but she was queen of flirting, and on more than one occasion I had wondered if Bethany and I might have a future together. That was another relationship that likely wasn't in the cards. Bethany had promised to provide an heir to the throne as part of her exile and was forbidden from mating with anyone who was not of Yig ancestry.

"If your face was any redder, Andrew, I would be wondering if I left the hotel naked." She leaned in, closer to my ear and said, "Wouldn't that have been a sight?"

I clapped my hands and pulled away before I lost complete control of my senses to the seductress. "Should we get seats?"

We gravitated toward the middle and all sat, with Carol between me and Bethany. That was for the better, as I needed a moment to cool down.

"So," Carol was smirking, "no invitation, I assume?"

Bethany laughed. "American royalty tends to ignore the royal family of Yig." Her gaze fell on Clara Olmstead. "In favor of the Dagon line, it would seem." She turned her face back to me. "Andrew, through the flushed excitement of your endorphins, you still look sour. Relax, please. You haven't lost the auction, yet."

In truth I felt better than I had previously, now with the surprise arrival of a new friend. This was the first of these McCallister auctions that I had seen her at. Bethany Coombs did not waste her time on hopes and rumors, like the school required me to. She was here for something specific. The auction list was kept private, but the House of Yig was resourceful.

I leaned in. "What do you know?"

Bethany rolled her eyes and leaned back in her seat.

"Wonderful, Andrew. Thank you for asking. The dress? No, just an old thing I had lying around. You look ..." she paused a little too long, "nice, too. How is my favorite boring professor?"

"He is rude," Carol said, "and as direct as ever, but you know we aren't dumb. What do we need to know? Are we in any danger?"

Bethany smiled at Carol. "I have missed you, Carol, but when are we not in danger?" She sighed. "Grumpy or not, it is good to see you, Andrew. Truth be told, I don't know exactly what it is. A stone tablet with minimal description. Supposedly something of great power." She leaned in and let her tongue dart between her lips as she said, "Or so a little ssserpent told me."

I chose not to push her. We had worked together long enough that I knew Bethany's tells. When she said that a serpent had told her, it meant that her loyalists in her Yig family had provided the information for her to investigate. That information was unquestionably reliable.

Carol frowned at me. "All of your connections and you never get that kind of information. Imagine how many of these things we could have avoided."

"Quiet you," I returned. Then I smiled and nodded toward where the McCallister butler had just entered the room. "Think of what you would have missed if we hadn't gone to these."

Bethany followed my nod and smirked. She didn't see the glare that Carol was sending my direction.

At that moment, and led by Craig Templeton, a dark-skinned man with a large scar and a tight suit stepped to the podium at the front of the room. It wasn't until that moment that I realized how the room had filled up. The event seemed ready to start.

Bethany leaned toward Carol, not taking her eyes off the man at the podium. "Carol, the butler is yours…"

The man at the front cleared his throat and spoke once the room settled down.

"Ladies and gentlemen," he said. "My name is Robert Dashel. I have been given the honor of welcoming you to the McCallister's Annual Antiquities Auction. They have graciously offered their home and several artifacts from their personal collection for this event. Many of you do not know of me." He cast his eyes across the crowd. They stopped on me for a moment longer than the rest before he continued. "I believe that I, unfortunately, only recognize a handful of you. I am a specialist in occult antiquities. In that role, I have traveled the world in search of ancient secrets that might make the modern day simpler, more fruitful, for all of mankind. These auctions provide an equal opportunity for all who attend to benefit from my labors." He paused for a breath and looked across the crowd again. "Now that we are introduced, let the auction begin." From somewhere on the podium that I could not see, he produced a gavel, hit the podium twice, and stepped off to the side to watch the proceedings.

Chapter 2

Carol smirked at Bethany. "I wondered what your type was."

"Type?" I asked, finally catching up with the conversation. Was I the only person not there to socialize?

Bethany nodded up toward where Robert was beginning to parade the items up for auction.

"Tall, dark, and all mine." Her eyebrow went up. "His eyes seemed to linger on you. Do you know him?"

"They didn't linger on me," I explained. "They lingered on both of us."

"What?" Bethany's lust turned to concerned curiosity. Contrary to her outward actions, she disliked scrutiny of any kind. She had no interest in being anyone's pawn toward getting closer to her people. "Both of us?"

"Don't you recognize him?" I asked with genuine surprise. How could she have forgotten Robert Dashel? If not his name, then at least his face.

Bethany was getting annoyed with me. "I'm sorry, Andrew, but I left my mind-reading hat in my other pants."

I sighed. "Perth. About seven years ago."

Her mood dropped considerably. "That was him?" She was whispering now. "That piece of—"

"What happened in Perth?" Carol cut her off.

Bethany sighed and provided an explanation while I continued to watch the auction for any items of interest.

"It didn't start in Perth, but that is where we ended up," she explained. "At that point, we were being hunted and needed to find a way out of Australia as soon as possible. Entirely because of that man's," she pointed subtly at Dashel, "stupidity."

"I wouldn't call what he did stupid, so much as duplicitous. He got what he wanted." I countered.

Bethany rolled her eyes, but otherwise ignored me. "A little serpent told me that some of the farming locals in the hills not far from Perth had been listed as suspects in multiple grave robberies. One or two robbed graves wouldn't have been a problem, but this was quickly escalating. When we arrived, 31 bodies had disappeared. The local law had gone out to the farms to investigate. They found several small families that were more than happy to let them search the farm. They found no evidence, no corpses, nothing. When they didn't turn anything up, they had to leave. They, and my serpents, weren't convinced though, so I called Andrew and together we conducted our own search."

Carol was no longer paying attention to the auction, instead drawn into one of my past hunts. "What did you find?"

Bethany shrugged, "Nothing at first. Then Andrew made some off-handed comment about the occult under his breath and they heard it. Suddenly, they knew we weren't with the law, even if Andrew's horrible fake Australian accent hadn't given it away, yet."

Craig the Butler was handing the smaller artifacts to Robert, who gave some sort of story as to the provenance of them. Well, it was less about where they were found and instead embellished stories about how he acquired them. I knew of at least three of those stories to be fabrications, as I had collected the actual artifacts and they were currently nestled in the University Armory.

We really had nothing that we wanted to bid on. There was no list provided in advance, so we had to sit through it all. Our goal was to make certain that any real artifacts didn't go anywhere too dangerous. A rich idiot wanting to bid on the Hand of Glory that Dashel paraded around was more than welcome to any negative side-effects that might come with it. Not that there necessarily would be, but sometimes those things were as cursed as they were powerful.

Which was the entire reason I was here.

"Not being the authorities isn't a crime," Carol pointed out with a knowing look.

Bethany smiled. "No, but when they knew we were asking questions to suss out an occult connection, they were onto us. That's when they went feral."

"Feral? What were they?"

"They weren't human. Well, they were as human as you and I are." There was no need for it, but Bethany lowered her lenses to wink with her snake-eyes. "They were ghouls. Andrew called them 'Day Runners,' because they were the members of ghoul society who were tasked with wearing illusions to live among the humans to gather food and resources."

This seemed to sadden Carol and her features fell, only a bit. "Most do not have it as simple as you and I do."

Bethany nodded. "No, they do not. You and I are lucky to have an easier time at hiding." She elbowed me. "It's nice to have friends who can help with that." She sighed. "Ghouls eat corpses, so it was not difficult to figure out what was going on. We were more on their side than not. People need to eat and I have never understood the human need to revere the corpses of the dead. Unfortunately for us, they had no reason to trust anyone. We were captured and put into a cage underneath their barn. The floor was wood, but that was to hide multiple entrances to a series of caves that they had dug under a large part of the surrounding area."

"They didn't know what to do with us and would not be able to decide until they could meet with their Elders. So, they left us alone, likely with the hope that we would die and they could skip a week or two of robbing graves. Andrew was still a low-power wizard back in those days, so—"

"No," I hated being described like that, "I was not." Bethany and I ignored each other as she continued telling the story. A lot of what I once was capable of had labeled me as a wizard, but that term bothered me. It either conjured up mental images of Merlin casting spells to protect the kingdom, or it brought to mind, in those who knew, the vile nature of what a wizard truly was. Every wizard traded something for their power. Sometimes it was their free will to a creature that liked convincing humans it was a god. On other occasions, it was a trade of physical well-being, the wizard's very self, for powers to manipulate our small slice of reality for selfish needs. The cost was always more than the power you received.

To that point I was, in the smallest of ways, similar to a wizard. I had traded my own mental faculties, fracturing my psyche for a grasp at small amounts of power to keep myself safe. That was until my fractured mind decided to attack me back. I bartered away that fractured spirit I had unknowingly created from my own spiritual flesh to the god of chaos, Nyarlathotep. It had left me stripped of all power, but I was given a second chance at life.

I was still trying to figure out who had won on that trade.

Bethany continued.

"He knew some kind of magic and was working on a spell to veil us into looking like we were dead on the floor. His idea was that when someone looked into the cage, they might decide to come in and try to eat us, or at least check on us, and we could make our escape. Except, he couldn't get it to work, for whatever reason." She straightened up, "I, on the other hand, knew they would want us a little bit rotten first, for flavor, of course. So, I ignored him and went to work fashioning a crude knife from stones that I found in our cell."

Bethany's face turned sour. "It was him, wasn't it?" It was a rhetorical question, but it was aimed at me.

"Without a doubt," I answered.

She sighed before continuing. "In the end, neither plan worked." She nodded toward the front of the room, where Robert was walking around with an amulet. I had seen versions of it before. It was made from a piece of meteor that Dashel claimed had been broken from a dying alien world. He was wrong in where it came from, but that was not a new thing for him. I knew it to be an amulet of stone commonly referred to as a 'piece of the void.' They were capable of granting odd powers, creating a focus on the person who held it. Many of those attending likely thought they could use it to manipulate events, but mostly, I had seen these things give visions of horrific futures that were either caused by the stone's properties or mind-shatteringly complex. "That was when he showed up. Dashel had heard the same rumor that Andrew and I were there to investigate, but Dashel was there for a different reason. He somehow figured out that this was an extension of a ghoul nest and had shown up to hunt for their Genesis Tablet."

"I am unfamiliar with that term. What is a Genesis Tablet?" Carol pressed.

"Most people are unfamiliar with it," the princess explained. "I had to explain it to Andrew. Until that day, I had assumed they were a myth. A Genesis Tablet serves two purposes, the first of which is to generate a ghoul nest, which is different from a nest of any other kind of creature. They are a species whose home straddles two worlds. They live partially on our world and the Genesis Tablet creates a soft space between worlds that allows the ghouls to cross over to the rest of their nest, held in the pathways between here and the Dream Lands. The spells on the tablet, passed down for generations of ghouls, create that weak point and always connect back to the pathways. Taking a Genesis Tablet from a ghoul nest stops the ghouls from being able to return home, provide resources for their people, or feed them."

"Mr. Dashel wanted to have a tool that would provide access to the Dream Lands to whoever bought it." Carol pieced together.

Bethany smiled, acknowledging that Carol was right.

"Why can't they just make another tablet?" Carol asked.

Bethany shrugged. "Andrew and I don't know if they can. As far as our research has taken us since Perth, these are generational tablets, held by tribes and passed down from nest to nest."

It was Carol's turn to smile, and she turned it on me. "You don't know? That must bother the hell out of you."

I smiled, entertained by Carol's barb. "More than you know."

She turned her attention back to Bethany. "You said that the tablet had two purposes. What was the second?"

"A Genesis Tablet houses the unknown origin of the ghoul race," Bethany explained.

"Something that the ghouls prize over almost anything else," I added.

Bethany leaned back in her seat and eyed the man in question as she continued her story. "Dashel took it and we had no idea. He upset them more than … well, I haven't seen any group that upset since the war my people threw over whether or not I was to be dethroned." She went quiet at the memory.

I was starting to lose what little interest I had in the auction and picked up the story from there. "He stole the tablet, but he could not remember how to get back out of the ghoul-made caverns. He got lost and ended up next to us, which was lucky for him in a handful of ways, the first of which being we were right next to the exit."

Bethany let out a scoffing noise. "The second way he was lucky was that we made for great patsies. Without knowing what he had done, we appreciated that the thief released us from our cage. At that moment, ghouls caught up to him and a fight broke out. During that fight, our rescuer vanished from sight. Ghouls aren't mindless creatures. On top of being formidable in strength and vicious killers, they also have opposable thumbs and know how to use guns." Bethany said the last bit as if it was a neat fact in a soap commercial. "Andrew and I held them off for a while, and even managed to hear them accuse us of taking the Genesis Tablet, but we couldn't do anything about it while we fought. The pieces began to fall into place just as Andrew pushed us into a pocket universe with some Yithian—"

"Cthonian…" I corrected.

I felt Bethany roll her eyes. "Cthonian space magic thing."

"Cthonian Territorial Charm," I sighed. "You're just embarrassing."

She waved me away. "Whatever. Like most of your spells at that time, you messed it up, too. Time displacement or something. I mean, it worked exactly as he had intended, in that we were no longer visible to the ghouls, and we were close enough to our home reality that we could wait and watch for when the coast was clear, but whatever went wrong with the spell made time inside our pocket dimension move at a crawl. We hid in there for only an hour, but for Andrew and I something closer to an entire month went by. We watched the ghouls slowly search for us before the coast was clear enough for us to return.

Empty-handed and hunted by ghouls, we took our time getting back to Perth and even there we recognized several of them searching the docks for us."

"I have been intrigued by ghoul culture since first learning of their existence," Carol said after taking a moment to process Bethany's story. "Many, including myself upon occasion, have referred to me as a Wendigo, an Algonquin word that tends to reference a very specifically different kind of creature. When looked at from the facts, I have all of the characteristics of a ghoul without the canine features." She rolled an idea around in her head. "I am what I think a ghoul would be if they had been creatures of Hyperborea, and touched by the cold magics of Ithaqua."

Bethany let those ideas bounce around in her head before adding, "Well, and the diet."

"How do you mean?" Carol asked.

"Ghouls feed entirely on the dead with a preference for older, rotted things. Yes, they eat human flesh, but that is their sole diet. You, on the other hand, only became what you are by eating flesh to survive, and I can only assume that you don't prefer it … um… aged."

Carol nodded. "That is factually accurate, but seems more like preferences. Perhaps ghouls and myself are distant relations, separated by the magics of our creation."

Bethany smiled. "If only we had the Genesis Tablet, maybe that would tell us."

"Well, shit," I was staring up at Robert and his newest piece for auction. "There it is."

He held above his head the Genesis Tablet of the ghouls.

Chapter 3

I had been watching the butler and the artifact dealer for all of Bethany's story. Mentally, I cataloged anything worth noting and continued to keep my eye on Dashel. He was a snake, and yes, I was only judging that based on my one meeting with him prior to this.

It came as a complete surprise to me when the tablet was finally presented.

I watched as Craig gently walked over with a box that was large enough that it needed to be held with both hands. Robert turned to take it from him, but Craig did something that I had not seen him do with any of the other artifacts. He held up his hand.

While I never suspected the box to contain the tablet, it was obvious that this box held some sort of reverence to at least the butler.

Robert stopped, frozen in place, obviously curious but also not wanting to disrupt the auction to ask what was going on.

Slowly, the butler's hand lowered and lifted the lid on the box. There was something in his eyes that I could not read. It was a mix of excitement at what he saw, and something else.

Just as slowly as he had lifted the lid, Craig reached down and parted a cloth before withdrawing the tablet and handing it to Robert. As the tablet left Craig's hands, his face fell back into the blank mask of the butler, but his eyes never left the tablet.

That was when I directed the ladies' attention to the stage.

"There it is."

"There I was," Robert began his sales-pitch, "surrounded by ghouls—" he held up his hand to silence the two gasps that escaped the audience. "Yes, ghouls. Beasts that live on the cusp of life and death, born of petulance and living on the edge of our very reality. They surrounded me, upset that I had entered their domain." His smile lit up, erasing the look of gloom from his face and his story at the same time. "But who could hate this face?" He let the few chuckles die out before continuing. "As much as we know about the ghouls and what they are today, the carrion-eaters of the human race, it is eclipsed by everything that we do not." He thrust the tablet into the air and I saw Craig tense. "This is one of their rare Genesis Tablets!" He brought it back to his chest and held it tight while he spoke. "They circled me with murder in their eyes, until I offered them something they wanted more. It was an amulet of Nyogtha, the 'thing that should not be,' and spawn of Tsathoggua. To the ghouls, a god. Once they saw that I held an amulet of their deity, they demanded it in trade."

Still holding the tablet, Dashel shrugged and smirked. "Who am I to refuse such a kind offer? That is how I came into possession of the Genesis Tablet. The only relic in all of history that holds the true story, as shared by the ghouls and passed down for generations, of the origins of the ghoul race!"

"Ghouls everywhere will be able to sense that," I said as fear lanced through me. "I don't know how he kept it hidden for seven years, but we are in grave danger right now."

Bethany smiled. "Was that a pun, Dr. Doran?"

I rolled my eyes, "Now is not the time."

Carol's features seemed to mirror my upset. "How did he hide it for so long? Is it possible that he still has protections on it?"

Shaking my head, I said, "I don't know. There's nothing I can think of that can hide something like the Genesis Tablet from its people, but I don't know everything. Hopefully, whatever spells or wards he put on it are still there."

Bethany reached past Carol and touched my leg, nodding toward the tablet.

Not the tablet. She was directing my attention to Craig.

He looked angry.

Carol sniffed the air, and I would not have noticed if she hadn't followed it up with three, much deeper, sniffs. She eyed Bethany and then Bethany did something I hadn't seen her do in, well, probably seven years.

She darted her tongue in and out.

That is how snakes, and snake-people, 'smelled' by tasting the air.

"Shit," I vocalized as they continued this behavior for a few more seconds.

If Carol was sniffing, that meant something was up. If she wanted Bethany's confirmation, then I was desperately wondering why I had failed to bring my pistol.

I returned my attention to the stage. It was split between the Genesis Tablet and Carol's boyfriend. There was something about him that...

There! His anger was becoming more powerful than his attention span and I saw a flicker of something in only a brief moment.

"Good news, Carol," I said. "I don't think your boyfriend is human. He's wearing a veil."

Bethany was already looking around at the entire audience around us when she commented, "He's not the only one."

Carol nodded in agreement. "We are surrounded."

"Surrounded?" My hand ached for a gun. "By what?" I asked as if I didn't already know the answer.

"You said it yourself," Bethany was suddenly cat-like and leaning back in her chair as she ran her hand down the thigh of her dress, "there's nothing more precious to the ghouls than their Genesis Tablet."

No, not cat-like. Snake-like. She was doing something.

"Ghouls? In the open?" I was shocked that they were among people and in the lights, but not surprised that they had come for what was theirs. "This is very bad. Are any of them human?"

"About half," Carol answered.

I had been only moderately on alert for the dangerous artifacts, but now my mind was nothing but alarm bells and sirens. "If the ghouls reveal themselves, everyone here will be dead. Ghouls survive through secrecy, they keep that secrecy by never leaving witnesses."

Bethany's sensual stretching suddenly made sense as she shoved a pistol into my hand. It was a Colt 1911 and while not a large gun, it was not small either. "You cannot tell me that you were hiding this underneath your dress."

She leaned over Carol and looked at me over her glasses with those oddly enticing snake-eyes. "Not in the least. While you, and anyone else who was watching, were watching my hand slide against the curves of my leg, my other hand reached under the chair and pulled this pistol up from where I had taped it underneath before the auction began."

With the secrecy of years of practice, I leaned over to cover up the gun and inspected the magazine. There were seven rounds.

"You wouldn't happen to have any more bullets on you, would you?" I asked my friend.

Bethany rolled her eyes again. "You're never happy, are you? I'm sorry, Andrew, but I left the bullets in my other folding chair."

This would have to be enough.

Bethany leaned over again, but not to me. "Carol, my dear, I have heard the stories but am unfortunately unfamiliar with your skills. I assume that you're more dangerous than a pistol?"

Carol gave a half-grin as her skin began to pale beyond shades safe for human flesh. "Ms. Coombs, I am more dangerous than most militias."

My eyes had returned to the stage and I saw as Robert began to stutter over his words. His eyes were darting all over the audience. He was noticing what we had sniffed out. Craig was not the only veiled ghoul who was getting agitated.

In that moment, his eyes met mine. They looked confused and searched mine for meaning before his mind registered that I was no longer comfortably watching the auction. His eyes went wide when he realized that I was readying myself for a fight.

"Carol?" I didn't take my eyes from Robert's. "Permission to shoot your beau?"

Carol's voice was barely human, escaping her mouth as a low growl. "I suppose. Try not to kill him, though."

As if on cue (and with the canine-like hearing of ghouls, perhaps it was), Craig stepped forward. In a single movement his veil dropped, he grabbed the tablet from Robert Dashel, and swiped a clawed hand across the artifact dealer's throat.

I leaped to my feet, but the crowd was already standing and screaming. My ability to fire my weapon was hindered by their movements. Somehow, over the noise, the butler-turned-ghoul could be heard by everyone.

"The ghoul people are proud and will not be trespassed against."

The crowd parted and I fired one shot. I hit the ghoul in the leg and he dropped.

Carol had turned fully into her monstrous form. She stood almost a head taller than her previous almost six feet, was gaunt in a way that most people would find unhealthy, and her fingers had lengthened and grown claws. Even her face had changed, gaining sallow cheeks, teeth too big for her mouth and her eyes turning red. She was terrifyingly beautiful.

Over the sudden commotion—more over all the people being attacked by what they thought were other people than my firing the pistol—I heard Craig's voice shout, "Get the doors!"

People from the auction that seemed to be wrestling with other people suddenly broke from their fights and moved toward the two room doors on opposite sides of the auction. The doors slammed shut and shotguns appeared in the hands of the ghouls masquerading as people.

"Protect the people," I shouted over the screams. I looked to my companions and indicated the guards at the doors. "We will need those guns."

Bethany grabbed my arm as I started to move, halting me.

"Andrew," her look was earnest and filled with concern, "are we in the right here? They are reclaiming what Dashel took."

I pointed at an old lady running down the aisle between the chairs who was screaming and crying.

"None of these people are Dashel."

Bethany frowned but nodded. "You're right."

It was at that moment that I realized I might have a serious problem during this fight.

"How am I supposed to know who's human and who isn't?"

Bethany raised an eyebrow. "Aside from the fact that only half of them are trying to kill the other half?"

Carol, now fully transformed, turned and faced me. Fear tore through my stomach before I reminded it that she was on our side. "We will have to tell you," she growled.

Then she grabbed a nearby man and ripped his head off his shoulders.

"He was a ghoul," she supplied, before bounding off after her next victim.

As she landed, a man leaped from the back of the room and soared over three meters before landing and jumping again at Carol, another almost three meters away.

I fired the pistol once and he fell to the ground.

"Alright," I said, "I think that I have it figured out now."

Chapter 4

Both of my friends were right. Even with veils still disguising their inhuman nature, it was easy enough for me to tell the difference between humans and ghouls. To put it simply, the ghouls were fighting like inhuman monsters which, if you ever needed an example, Carol was demonstrating as well. Ghouls and Carol were moving through the crowd and tossing bodies, slashing with claws, and showing other feats of incredible strength and speed.

They were beings with animalistic prowess and they were using it.

To our credit, only three humans had died so far. That I could see, anyway. There was a lot going on and I was more focused on the living.

A ghoul was chasing after an older woman wearing furs. I kicked out to stop him as he ran by, but he leaped over my foot quicker than I could adjust. Turning, I shot him in the back.

Then a hand with red nail polish slapped me in the chest. I looked down and then almost-forgotten muscle memory returned, and I relaxed.

There were years, good years, between my graduation and my coming to work for Miskatonic University, where I traveled the world learning as much as I could and getting into more fights than any one person deserved. During that time I traveled with Bethany. She was angry and violent and out to prove that while her people might not want her visibly on the throne, she still had something to offer the world. During that time, we got into fights together and learned to work together with an almost musical grace.

The hand on my chest was one of those moves and while we had done it enough times that I wouldn't need a moment to understand what was going on, I appreciated her hesitating, even for that brief moment, so that I could remember what was going on.

With my body relaxed, I let Bethany's hand guide me, with force and speed, back and toward the ground, and I bent my knees for the return. Her hand was holding the front of my shirt and the strength given to her by her royal lineage made me weightless in her grip.

I felt the air as a clawed hand swiped where my face had been.

Looking down, which was formerly forward, I shot the ghoul in the head. As I went back, I tipped my head up to look across the room.

Bethany pulled me back up and was gone and fighting another before I could thank her.

Which I wouldn't, because we had been saving each other's asses for so long that our appreciation was already well known.

The problem was trying to fight so many assailants without using up all of my ammunition. I became a mix of punches and backhanded swings with the occasional bullet being fired.

I pulled two more ghouls away from people before I realized that the veils were starting to slip. A magical disguise is a simple enough spell but, like all magic, concentration helps.

A punch to the chest drove me back and into a wall. The hit knocked the wind out of me and I was gasping for air while I started rolling along the wall away from my attacker. He looked like a man in his early seventies but he clearly was anything but. I stopped rolling and squared off against him. The gun was tight in my grip but the ghoul did not seem to care. A scuffle behind me pulled my attention. Something was coming at me from that direction as well. When my attention split, my first attacker lunged.

As previously implied, I am no stranger to a brawl. I expected my divided attention to get me into trouble and as soon as I realized my mistake at looking behind me, I spun to my right, stepped back, tried to split my focus. The second assailant could not correct his course quickly enough and landed where I had been standing. The first one was more prepared. He leaped over the first, landing and twisting to launch again at me with an open hand. Those hands, veiled as they were, hid claws meant for tearing meat.

I brought my gun up and killed him with a bullet between his eyes. Then I stepped forward and attempted to do the same with the second attacker still on the ground. Unfortunately, that was when the gun ran dry. Two quick stomps stopped him from being an issue any longer.

Looking around, I attempted to assess the situation. The guards on the side of the room opposite myself were helping Craig out the door. I quickly spotted Bethany and indicated that he was on the move.

She was beside me quickly enough. "What's the plan?"

"There isn't much of one," I said. "The ghouls are going to kill everyone here."

"Not once they get the tablet," Bethany shrugged. "If we continue to defend, they will leave once Carol's boyfriend escapes with the Genesis Tablet."

I shook my head at Bethany, grabbed an old lady and slammed her head into the nearest wall, and saw her disguise begin to fail. I pointed at it for Bethany.

"Ghouls live in secrecy," I explained. "They have kept that secret for thousands of years by eliminating all witnesses during larger events." Spreading my hands, I indicated the auction. "This would count as a larger event."

"So," Bethany kicked a ghoul in the chest and her incredible strength sent him flying through several of the foldable chairs, "if their disguises fail, they will still kill everyone here?"

I shook my head. "It won't be an 'if' so much as a 'when' if we don't end this fast." Then a thought struck me and I shook my head. "That won't work either. The stink of the tablet. No matter where they get to, the ghouls will always be able to find them. We are going to need to negotiate."

Bethany laughed. "Negotiating with ghouls? You just like setting impossible tasks for yourself, don't you?"

"I wouldn't call it impossible," I shrugged. "I've negotiated with plenty of less agreeable beings before. I have even negotiated with Yig, through one of his avatars."

Bethany patted my arm gently. "Sure you did, sport. I'm sure that's exactly what happened and not you remaining mildly entertaining enough for the Great Serpent to decide to spare your life."

My eyes were flitting about the room, trying to take stock of who was fighting who, how close we all were to dying, and where best to place my allies. Then my eyes rested back upon the auction stage.

Turning back to Bethany, I spoke quickly. "I have a plan. Work with Carol and get the guns away from the guards. We need the exits cleared."

Bethany took off with incredible speed. By the time that I reached the stage, she had already dispatched the first two ghouls with guns and had begun working her way across the room toward the other two.

Artifacts of various degrees of fakery rested between me and my goal. I just started tossing them. This wasn't me disrespecting history or my profession, so much as disregarding the fraudulent waste of everyone's time that most of this auction was. I am an archaeologist first, most days, and chose to gently handle the one or two legitimate pieces or any piece that I could not be certain of.

I stomped down on the amulet of Nyogtha I found nestled in the large case that the box with the tablet was pulled from. It was carved with the right symbols, but in the wrong order. Dashel had probably been keeping it with the tablet in order to better tell his story.

My hands came across the slick surface of the Hand of Glory and it spoke volumes to my habits that I did not recoil at the grotesque nature of the hand. It was slick from whatever oil or wax was used in its construction. Historically, a Hand of Glory is a powerful magical item made by amputating and drying the hand of a hanged man. Oddly enough, the one in my own hand had the rare privilege of being the owner's right hand. Traditionally, it was always the left hand unless the hand of the offender belonged to a murderer. In that case, the offending hand would be chosen. It didn't matter, or if it did, it worked in our favor, as the power radiating from the hand was likely felt by almost everyone in the room. This murderer's hand was about to be put to work saving lives.

I fished a lighter out of my pocket and took my time lighting every fingertip.

The effect was immediate. Once the last finger was lit, everyone in the room froze where they were and in the middle of whatever they were doing. The speed with which the room went from a wild frenzy to a complete standstill was a shock on its own.

The silence and lack of movement made me want to move slowly. That would be stupid, though. I knew what the hand had done. It makes everyone in the nearby area immobile unless I did not want them to be. That and the fact that Craig the not-butler was limping away with the Genesis Tablet meant that our time was limited.

I ran to Carol and pushed some of my will into the Hand of Glory as I touched her transformed shoulder. A shudder ran through my friend as the spell released her and I moved to free Bethany next.

"Wonderful," Carol said as we gathered on the stage. "Now, we can kill them all and remove the humans without much issue."

I shook my head. "We can't kill them."

Carol frowned down at me with her monster face. "What do you mean? It would be easy with them like this."

"I'm not saying it's physically impossible. I'm saying that we need them alive." I nodded toward Bethany. "I was just explaining to Bethany that we need to negotiate for their safety, otherwise everyone here will be hunted for the rest of their lives."

Bethany handed me one of the shotguns she had pulled from the dead guards and enough ammunition to fill my pockets. I handed Carol the still-lit Hand of Glory.

"I am going to need you to stay here," I explained. "This thing won't stay lit forever." I gave her my lighter. "If a finger goes out, light it back up. As long as the hand stays lit and you stay here with it, they cannot move." I showed her how to free people so that she could start getting them out of the auction.

At least the survivors would have a head start if the negotiations failed.

"You're going after the tablet?" Bethany asked.

"No," I said, "we're going after Craig. If we can catch him before he hands off the tablet, it would be easier to convince the ghoul hierarchy of what we want to do if we have a ghoul on our side."

"And if he's already passed it on?" Carol asked.

"Then we will have our work cut out for us," I said. "The Genesis Tablet is no good to the ghouls in our world. They will want it in the hands of their elders, and that means that they will need to push it into their pathways between here and the Dream Lands."

Seeing that the door that Craig had run through was still locked, I searched the frozen ghouls for the keys and couldn't find them.

"Would you mind?" I asked Bethany while nodding toward the door.

"You," she sighed, "are a useless human."

Chapter 5

Bethany's evaluation of my personal worth aside, she burst through the door with a single kick.

With friends like her, how useful do I need to be?

Following Craig was not difficult. Even without Bethany's heightened sense of smell, the blood trail was plainly visible.

Unfortunately, getting to the tablet was not going to be a simple task. We had only made it down the first hall off of the auditorium when a group of three ghouls, without magical disguises, turned and fired at us with more shotguns.

Bethany and I dove back around the corner to the previous hall. Plaster and mortar exploded at head height.

"When I say to," Bethany hissed, "shoot at them."

I nodded and Bethany leaped out from behind the corner and toward our attackers. She darted into the hall and jumped at the far wall.

"Now," she shouted.

I stepped out from behind the cover and lowered the shotgun at the ghouls. They were suddenly torn on what decision to make. Who should they hit first?

As I fired, I didn't even concern myself with whether or not Bethany would be hit. She was a princess by birth, but as she slid down the hall with grace and speed, leaping off of the first wall to the next before dropping to the floor and then back to the far wall, it was obvious that she was born to be a queen of her species.

I managed to kill one ghoul and wound the one at the center of the group before Bethany, avoiding every bullet, landed on them. In a spray of blood that somehow missed her dress, they were dead.

This was how we tracked Craig. We would make it deeper into the house, we would run into more ghouls and have to kill them, and then we would continue.

"This many dead ghouls is not going to look good during the negotiation," Bethany smirked after the third group of ghouls that tried to stop us.

I reloaded the shotgun, noticing that my pockets were already half emptied.

"Ghouls don't look at death like you and I do. Survival is the most sacrosanct tenet of their mostly non-existent religion." We turned the next corner and found stairs to what I was already assuming had to be the first of multiple cellars. "Death to them is how we see farming. It's a means of food production. Now, if we burned the bodies, that would be a problem."

We had reached about halfway down the unlit stairwell when Bethany's hand touched my sternum. In the dim light I saw her point above and just in front of us, in the darkness of the ceiling.

She mouthed, "Shoot."

So, I did.

The gunshot lit up the space briefly, and I saw that the ceiling was much higher than I had expected. Above us had been Craig, latched onto it to either ambush us or wait for us to pass.

Now he was laying on the stairs with Bethany's knee on his chest. I stood above him so when he spoke to me, he had to look up.

His veil had dropped, but I knew that it was Craig because he was the only ghoul who was actually wearing the outfit of their disguise. His leg and stomach were bleeding all over a nice suit befitting his station.

A ghoul in a suit.

"You dare?" he spat up at me. "First, you steal from us our nest's most sacred object, then you try to keep us from retrieving it? You fool humans!"

Bethany slapped him with her inhuman strength. He grunted with the hit. "You damned idiot," she said. "We don't want your tablet. We want you to not kill the humans back there."

He spit blood as he spoke. "They are no less foul than you. Taking the significant cultural heritage of others to increase their already significant station and impress their friends. The blood of innocent ghouls was spilled in our home and you seek to save those who bathe in it."

I shook my head. "You are kicking the rock that caused the avalanche. Those are the heads of powerful Arkham families. Families that know different magics than you do. Families that will come after all ghouls for this. We can stop this now, before a war starts." I sighed. "This will never end unless we force a conversation right now."

"The benefit of no witnesses," Craig's canine face twisted into a semblance of a smile, "is that they will not know that it was the ghouls."

Something about how he said that triggered a connection in my head.

"Dashel never hid the tablet from the ghouls," I said.

"What?" Bethany looked up at me, "Then how did they not find him?"

"They did," I said. "A long time ago, too." I returned my attention to the ghoul. "When did you realize that he worked for the McCallisters?"

"As soon as we learned his name." He was gloating.

"Andrew," Bethany still sounded confused, "what is going on?"

I sighed. "Carol has been seeing Craig." I looked at Craig, "Did you veil your scent, too?" I didn't wait for his answer and returned to explaining to Bethany. "She doesn't mingle easily, so they have been seeing each other for maybe a month or two, and the invitations for the auction went out about a month ago as well. He's been here for at least that long." I frowned. "The McCallisters wouldn't hire a butler without a proven work history. Did you kill them, too?"

The ghoul gave us his ugly smile again.

"So, for a while then."

"What do you mean?" Bethany asked. "This was planned? For how long?"

"I said it earlier. It would be nearly impossible to hide something like the Genesis Tablet, and our pal Bob didn't even try. They've known where Dashel was the entire time," I said. "They used the veil magic to replace the main family and waited until Dashel wanted more cash. Then they asked him to supply the event."

"How did you get all that?" Bethany asked.

"All the ghouls in attendance, Carol's dating history, and the way he said that they won't leave witnesses. He's going to destroy the house, I think."

"What? Why?" She asked. "That will only draw attention. Police, fire department, everyone will want to know what happened."

"In any other city, yes. Not in Arkham, though." The ghoul's eyes were fluttering but he kept talking. "The families will pay to keep the auction quiet and the McCallisters have long since stopped caring for this house." He began making a noise. I couldn't decide if it was a laugh or a cough. "Their sins shall hide ours."

I turned to Bethany. "I don't know that this is a negotiation anymore. They planned all of this. Everyone here will die unless we stop them."

Bethany's face twisted in disgust. "We can't just kill them all," she shook her head. "What do we do now? We can't let them kill the guests and we can't just murder an entire nest of ghouls who are clearly in the right on most of their points, if not the murder." She took a deep breath. "Should we just leave?"

That felt wrong to me, but I wasn't certain that she was wrong.

"We can't, though," I said instead, "can we? We are part of this now, too. They knew what they were doing when they invited us. We're as marked for death as the rest of them." I was scrambling and trying to come up with a new plan but was hitting more dead ends than solutions. "We still need to get the tablet. It's a bargaining piece, at least. Perhaps if I am holding it, I can convince them to leave."

"The ghouls will not be manipulated," Craig wheezed.

Bethany smacked him to shut him up, and then grabbed his long chin in her hand and forced his eyes to meet hers. "Where is the Genesis Tablet?"

"You will never find it," was all the ghoul would offer as a response.

"Can you smell it?" I asked my friend.

Her tongue darted in and out a few times as she turned her head from side to side.

Bethany nodded.

I returned her nod and Bethany leaned in and held his mouth and nose shut, choosing the classic style of Burke and Hare to execute this already-dying ghoul.

"I can smell it, even follow it, but it doesn't smell like it is anywhere close," Bethany said. "It seems to be fading."

"That's because it isn't here anymore," I explained. "He took it to the pathways between worlds. His people likely have it now."

"We can't take on an entire ghoul nest, Andrew. We couldn't seven years ago, and we certainly cannot now."

"As long as you can still smell the tablet, the pathway remains open."

"There are still too many ghouls for two well-meaning auction-goers," Bethany repeated her point.

I held up my hand. "Just get us to the pathway while it is still open and I'll figure something out." I didn't have to add the obvious 'I hope,' as Bethany had known me long enough to understand that most of my plans were of the hopeful variety.

Without the olfactory senses of my companions, I had to be content with deductive reasoning aiding me in the search for the pathway. As I followed Bethany, I tried to take into account how much time Craig would have had to open the gate, do the hand-off, and then get back to the stairs and hide. The hiding spot seemed last-second, so he'd heard us coming and then hid.

We exited the stairs into a poorly lit, and large, room with an expanse of wine racks lining every wall. Across the room from us was another stairwell.

I started for it when Bethany grabbed my arm and spun me around. Her tongue was out and she wasn't focused on me.

Instead, her attention was focused on one of the wine racks about ten feet from the stairs.

I knew it wouldn't be far.

Something stuck to my shoe. I looked down to see that the ground was covered in a red stain. I didn't need any other confirmation to know that Craig must have stood here, bleeding out, as he handed the Genesis Tablet off to one of his kin.

Bethany pulled her tongue back into her mouth and made a sour face. Stepping past her, I reached toward a bottle covered in about half an inch of dust.

My hand didn't touch it. An invisible wall stopped me, pressing against my fingers and halting my progress toward the bottle.

"This is it," I voiced what we already knew. "He used the Genesis Tablet to create the portal to the pathway here."

"Very well." Bethany reached forward and pressed against the invisible wall. "How does one traverse this portal?"

Well, this was awkward.

"Uh," I gave as an answer.

"You don't know how to get through there?" I could see the look of 'useless human' had returned to her face. "Do you even have a plan?"

"One bite at a time," I said. "That's my plan."

"What does that mean?" She leaned in and looked over her glasses at me in that way she loved to use as a tease. "Bite you? Here? This is hardly the time, Andrew."

"No," I sighed. "That's my plan. How does one attempt to eat an elephant? The answer is, 'one bite at a time.' That's what I am doing. The first bite was to find Craig. The second was to find the portal. Now we need to figure out how to get past this portal."

"I think that I hate you," Bethany said with a grin on her face.

I grabbed a bottle from beyond the edge of the portal and pressed it against the invisible surface, my hands pushing against the butt of the bottle, trying to pierce the veil with the spout.

"Are you really going to make me do this?" Bethany suddenly seemed annoyed.

"Do what?"

"You're going to try and be the one who uses cunning and force and I am left being the one who uses the magic? We cannot reverse roles at this age, Andrew. We are too set in our ways."

She was admitting that she could get us in there, but she was going to make me pay for it with this show.

"No, you're right," I said. "I'll use this bottle's pressure to create a magical piercing device. You can't see it, but I am mouthing the spells and incantations of Appalachian shamans."

"Very well," she ignored me completely. "I will save us with not only my strength, my charm, my ruthless heart, and my venomous wit, but also with my inherent gift of magic, as bestowed upon me by my god."

"You forgot to mention your alluring physique," I added to the bribe.

"Andrew, my body speaks for itself. Now stand back." Bethany stepped forward and pressed both hands against the invisible portal. Her mouth began to move and I heard words I had only ever heard once before.

When I had ventured into a temple of Yig and fought one of his proxies.

"Go," Bethany grunted. "Now."

I bent to step under her arms and pressed into the barrier.

Lights exploded in my vision and for the briefest of moments, I felt as though I was falling in each direction. It felt as if the very cells of my body were trying to escape my center mass and only my strength of will kept me in one piece.

Just as quickly it was over and I stepped onto solid ground. The darkness was impenetrable and until a bright light quickly marked Bethany's arrival, I could see nothing.

When the darkness returned, I touched Bethany's arm for reassurance.

"Andrew, I understand that you think you might be comforting me, but may I remind you of my darker nature?"

"Right," I remembered, but left my hand on her arm. "Snakes, caves, and darkness. I'm the only one who can't see, right?"

"Darling," Bethany laughed out loud, "between the effort needed to traverse the portal and this situation with the lighting, you had better work very hard not to lose me while we go in search of this 'next bite' of your elephant."

Chapter 6

My vision may have been limited, but my sense of smell wasn't.

I shushed Bethany. "Do you smell that?"

"Rot," Bethany whispered into the dark.

"Is there anything we can do about the lights in here?" I asked.

"Do I really need to remind you that you had a lighter earlier today?" Bethany huffed.

"Do I need to remind you that I tasked Carol with keeping the Hand of Glory lit?" I am willing to admit that without Bethany most of this evening's rescue efforts would have been for naught, but I am also not going to sit here and be accused of being inept as well.

"Fair point," Bethany agreed. "Well, I don't see, wait," she paused and moved. There was a lot of movement.

Feet on stone.

Clothes rustling.

Several things snapped, like a stick or bone.

A sharp crack and the sound of stones sliding over each other.

"Here," Bethany's hands found mine and pressed something into them. "That's flint and sticks and dried vegetation. Assuming that physics works here, and that you know how, this should help you start a fire."

"What, no fire magic?" I teased.

"Sorry, I left my fire spells in my other dress," she laughed.

I hadn't really been expecting Bethany to provide any sort of magical light. I was more hopeful that she had a lighter secreted away under a curve somewhere. Bethany might be the princess of an ancient race of snake people with access to powers far beyond those of mortal man, but those powers were something she was granted by a lineage that told her she wasn't good enough to remain among her people. To that point, she has never enjoyed employing their use, opting instead to fight things that didn't require her to tap into the well of power provided by her people.

Taking the rocks and adding some fabric from my own clothes to the mix, I began working on striking up a fire. After a few minutes, I had a good enough flame to start working on turning those sticks into a torch.

Once that was done, we kicked over the fire and began our hunt for the ghoul nest.

Ghouls are an odd species in that they, unlike the majority of the other races on our planet, do their best to not mingle with us. The other species here like to use us for their own purposes, even in innocent ways. Yes, ghouls eat human corpses, but that's the extent of it. If they could be done with us entirely and move into the pathways between our world and the Dream Lands, they would do it without hesitation.

To that point, I had no idea if this particular nest would have a name, or even what the hierarchical structure could be. I was planning to negotiate with, or at least distract, a nest of ghouls. I had more information on ghouls than just about any other human, but even that was so minimal as to make this a very dangerous undertaking.

As with everything that tended to put me in dangerous situations, I wouldn't be doing it if there weren't lives at stake.

The portal had opened up into a series of caves, all with higher ceilings than I had expected to find. Ghouls like tight and dark places, but the ceilings were about forty feet above us while the width of the cave went back and forth between a few feet to as wide as fifteen feet.

The archaeologist within me was desperate for a camera just to take a picture of the walls. Whatever was going on in this geology, it wasn't the usual stratigraphy you would find on Earth. The lines between stone and soil types were not lines at all and in some cases swirled to the point of almost complete circles.

I had never seen anything like it.

The floor was somehow smooth except for places where the ground broke. Any gaps in the stone flooring were minimal and we stepped over them with ease.

Whenever we came to a path, I let Bethany sniff out the best direction. I might be a useless human, but I knew when I was outmatched. Until we walked into a fight or a meeting with the elders of the ghoul nest, I would mostly be useless.

To the credit of Bethany's sense of smell, our migration through the tunnels was getting to levels of stink that even I couldn't ignore. We were getting close.

A grunting hoot noise sounded from behind where we had come from and I touched Bethany's arm to stop her advance.

"What the hell was that?" she demanded. A rare look of fear flashed across her face.

"What do you know about gugs?" I asked.

More gugs. I had run into these things before. They were terrifying and I was hoping to never come across them again.

"Little things with face tentacles, about the size of cats, that like to eat flesh. A horde of them would be bad." She turned her head away from the sound and looked me in the eyes. "Are you saying that was a gug? I don't know if we can fight more than a handful of them and survive."

I nodded. "You're almost right. The gugs that wander from their caves, where they choose to feast upon lost travelers and ghouls tend to be the smaller ones. They run in packs like that to stay alive and feast quickly on large corpses, but that isn't their normal size. When they get older they can grow as large as a car."

"We definitely cannot fight something like that," Bethany's eyes were wide.

"No, we cannot and while I am no outdoorsman, I have to imagine that that sound means that they found something to track and are telling the others in the area."

"Us," Bethany agreed. "They smell us and it doesn't help that we've been busy fighting their favorite food for the last hour." She paused before adding, "It won't help our negotiations to lead car-sized predators to the nest of the people we are trying to negotiate with."

"No," I agreed, "it won't."

"What do we do, then?"

Damn, I wished she hadn't asked that question.

I held up the shotgun. "If there's only one, we should be fine…"

"You are stupid and I hate you," she said.

"Noted." I looked around us, taking in our surroundings, possible cover and defenses. "If we go back a bit, we might be able to set up an ambush. They will smell that we are in the area, but not where we are."

"Do you know how they hunt? Because I do not." She crossed her arms. "If they only hunt by smell, then, yes, we might be able to confuse them. If they use echolocation, have a heightened sense of sight, or senses beyond the understanding of us poor Earthlings, then we are damned."

Bethany's tongue darted out again before she slapped her hand over my mouth with enough force to make my teeth hurt.

"We're too late," she hissed.

I listened as her hand lowered and could hear the slow shuffling of something as it squeezed between cave walls.

We were exposed. We had just been about to head down a corridor toward where Bethany believed the nest to be. The area around us was fairly wide, similar in size to that of the campus cafeteria. Out of three of the caves that met up with this opening, gugs squeezed through and into it, their tongues darting out ahead of them and tasting the air much like Bethany did with her own.

I didn't think putting out the torch would be much help at this point and decided against it.

The last time that I had witnessed a living gug was during a drug smuggling operation at a similar portal path to the Dream Lands. Those had been the size of cats, the gug's mortal enemies, and I had been saved by the presence of many cats coming to my aid.

These gugs looked almost identical to those, except much larger. All three of them looked similar to cats in their shape, with black fur and bodies that seemed to flow over their environment as they walked.

Outside of that comparison, there was nothing else cat-like about them. Their eyes protruded from either side of their head and their mouth, vertical in their face instead of horizontal, was filled with ridiculously large fangs. None of these larger gugs had the tentacles that I had seen on the smaller ones previously. Their limbs, though cat-like, ended in paws, two each, at the end of every leg, allowing for them to better climb and grasp in otherwise treacherous cave environments.

Or to grasp my neck as they tore the flesh from my face.

Each gug had the ability to stand up on its hind legs and use its forelegs like arms and hands in a bipedal way. The only coherent thought aside from hoping that they didn't notice us was my desperate and silent plea for these horrific things not to stand up fully. I was not certain that even my well-armed psyche could handle that much fear at once.

I realized that Bethany was already moving. She stepped away from me and the light and her rose-colored glasses finally disappeared. She was preparing for combat.

"Stay there," she whispered to me. "Keep their focus. I will move into position."

"How long do I stay here?" I asked, but Bethany was already gone.

That was when I heard the breathing behind me.

Turning my head slowly, I looked over my shoulder and was only mildly relieved to not see a gug standing there.

Instead, a ghoul was behind me. Not just any ghoul, either, but one adorned in a makeshift bone armor from the skeletons of many humans. His face was painted and had a more canine look to it. Behind him were many more ghouls, mostly hidden by the darkness.

They were not looking at me.

"Do you speak English?" I asked.

The ghoul nodded. "You have brought the gugs to our home."

I saw a moment of opportunity. "No," I said. "We raced them here, to warn you."

He raised an eyebrow, sniffed, and then smirked. "You are one of those who stole the Genesis Tablet from our nest."

I shook my head. "No, I am one of those who was there when that thief tried to sell it, but who wants to see no more people killed."

If I was curious before whether or not the ghouls knew I was here, all doubt left my mind as they began moving toward me.

"Those who hurt ghouls face their judgment."

"And they have." I spoke quickly, never taking my eyes off the ghouls. "The only person who stole from you was the first to die and several more have died already, including several of your own people as those others defended themselves. There is no reason to continue killing the humans."

"No reason?" His voice rose to a snarl. I had not seen the object in his huge hand which he now held out for me to see. "Look what your people have done!"

The Genesis Tablet had looked intact at the auction. But up close I could see that while the characters in the upper section were clear and distinct, the last two lines were blurred as though they had worn away.

"Some of the power has been drained from it," said Bethany. "Someone tried to tap its energy."

"Your people did this," said the ghoul, flexing his claws. "Your meddling has destroyed our tablet, doomed our nest."

It was obvious to me now that Dashel had been trying to use the tablet for his own purposes. He had only tried to sell the useless remains when that failed.

"It's not broken, it can be restored."

They both stared at me as though I was mad.

"You lie. Nobody knows the secret of the Genesis Tablets," said the ghoul.

"No archaeologist has ever had a chance to look at one."

Was I bluffing? Not exactly. I had the germ of an idea from what Carol had said.

I ran my finger down the tablet, trying to understand the logic of it to restore the missing characters. I had assumed it would be in a language I recognized, but the text was a bizarre mix of Sumerian cuneiform, Egyptian hieroglyphics, ancient Hebrew and others I did not know. It was jumbled together in a way that made sense only in the crazy logic of dreams. It was a lexicographer's nightmare.

Of course.

I put on my Ancient Civilizations 101 voice and tried not to sound as though I was working it out as I spoke.

"It's quite obvious that the ghouls' dual existence across the Dream Lands and the waking world, along with their symbiotic relationship to humans, are fundamental to their origin. The only reason why you can't see it is because you're too close. You see ghouls as perfectly normal, but to humans you are nightmarish. That's literally what ghouls are: walking nightmares that have gained access to our world from the Dream Lands. That's why there are many tablets as each civilization creates its own type of ghoul, from Africa to the Arctic. Each tablet is simply the account of a nightmare that opens the way between the worlds."

"That makes sense," said Bethany. "Nightmares are a powerful phenomenon unique to your species."

"So, all you need to do is to top up the tablet with some nightmare juice." That was as far as I had got, but the next step came to me in an instant. "And I don't like to boast, but I've got as big a stock of nightmares as anyone alive."

At least I was confident about that part.

"But how does that help us?" asked the ghoul. He was skeptical, but there was hope in his voice. This poor crazy human might just be able to save the day for his people.

"Simple. Just use magic to channel some of my nightmares into the tablet. To a wizard like you that's as easy as siphoning gas from one car to another." I was right, but they needed to trust me. "Right, Bethany?"

She gave me an eye roll.

"Andrew, only you could make the most powerful art in the universe sound like roadside assistance. The energies involved could rip apart the thin fabric of your human mind."

"That's a 'yes' from you then."

"It is not right," the ghoul said. "You should not touch it, but it has already been defiled."

He was on the edge, trying to decide if breaking a small rule for the betterment of his people was worth it.

In the end, he made the right choice and likely saved mine and Bethany's lives in the process.

"What do you need to do?" he asked me, knowing full well that it was not much.

"I will need to touch the tablet," I explained. "The rest is up to you. You will need to connect my mind to whatever power you pull from the Dream Lands and the pathways. Once that connection is made, the Genesis Tablet should do the rest."

He nodded and stretched his hand forward, offering the tablet.

Hesitancy stopped me from just grabbing the tablet, but when I did touch it, nothing happened. I don't know what I was expecting aside from some sort of unpleasantness, but—

Fire lanced through my mind as the ghoul connected my dreams, my nightmares, to the Genesis Tablet.

I could feel every misstep, embarrassing moment, and more being pulled from my mind. The real value of me holding this tablet was in that 'more.'

Cats with their own civilization, conqueror worms sleeping beneath the crust of the moon, bug scientists from Venus, the oily blackness of life flittering between the spaces of our moments, the arm of a dead man replacing my own, my death and the darkness and silence that ensued for millennium before an Eldritch Horror reached into the blackness and demanded an audience…

The nightmares left my mind in such a way that I remembered them, but it felt as though they would no longer be waiting for me on the other side of sleep.

My concentration had been entirely on the nightmares leaving my mind, so I was lost in confusion when I returned to myself and found Bethany struggling to restrain me. From behind, she had wrapped her arms around me and was forcibly holding me in place.

"What happened?" I rasped.

Seeing that I was in control again, she slowly let me go. In front of me the ghouls stood cowering. All except the one in the bone armor.

He held the Genesis Tablet still, and I could see that the words that had faded had returned.

At least that worked.

"You touched the tablet and started to scream," she explained. "You were still screaming as you started lashing out, fighting and swinging at everything that wasn't there."

"It was there," I said. I was reacting to the nightmares. That's why we dream in our sleep. If we were awake and thought those nightmares were real, we would be trying to fight or run from them.

I took a deep breath before stepping slowly toward the lead ghoul.

"So, we're all buddies again now," I said. "And no more humans will be killed."

"Not by us," said the ghoul. "We owe you that. All is settled between us." He was not happy, especially at the thought that humans now knew their secret, but ghouls have a strict code of ethics and I knew they could not harm us. "The gugs, though, may have other ideas."

That still gave us plenty of opportunities to die. But we had a fighting chance.

As quickly as they appeared behind me, the ghouls were gone.

The nearest gug leaped at me.

With one hand, I swung the torch back and forth at its face to slow it down. With the other, I fired a shotgun shell into its face. Blood splashed over me, but the roar that the monster sent my direction let me know that it wasn't done with me yet. Standing at the mouth of the tunnel to the ghoul nest, the other two gugs couldn't get to me, but at least one of them had just discovered where Bethany was.

The gug facing me was so close that I worried I would lose my torch and then my visibility. That would be fatal. I fired the gun again, and then once more, pushing the creature back until I found a place on the wall of the cave where I could jam the torch and advance.

Shadows danced across the rock walls as I prepared for what would likely be my last monster fight.

How many bullets the gun had remaining was not at the top of my mind. I needed to push this thing back so that I could get myself to a more agreeable position. I fired again, counting them as they left the gun. The gug let out a whimper that I was proud of.

My pride was short-lived, though, as one of the gug's two pawed arms reached forward and grasped the shotgun. In just as fast a move, it was out of my hands and across the room faster than I could say 'defenseless.'

Gladly, that was still within the parameters of the small parts of a plan that I had. The previous shots had bought me enough space for momentum. I took one step back and ran forward and toward the gug. It reared up, giving me that terrifying view of a gug in its bipedal form. It roared and ran at me like that, reaching with its massive paws.

While only a few feet, I gained enough momentum to drop to my knees and slide past and under it. My stop was not graceful, as I rolled over and came up in the middle of the cavern, suddenly surrounded by all three gugs, and a flipping snake-lady as she tried to get onto one of their backs.

Bethany was fighting the gug to my right while the one behind me was spinning to come at me. The third seemed more intrigued by where I came from, and I could only assume that it still smelled the ghouls and wanted only their flesh.

As it turned its head to face this new morsel just a few feet away from it, the gug decided that perhaps the human would be a tasty treat as well.

The shotgun was a few feet away from me, closer to Bethany and the gug that she was fighting.

Bethany was amazing. In my brief glimpses at her own fight, she was using feats of incredible strength and agility to bound over and around the creature at speeds that it could not keep up with. Gugs are fast, but Bethany was faster.

I scrambled for the gun as the first gug turned around to face me and my newest adversary started toward me. Bethany ignored the gun completely, opting instead to punch the gug she was fighting in the eye over and over again with all of her force.

The second gug made it to me just as I made it to the shotgun and backhanded me, twice, technically, into Bethany's gug.

It was too busy trying to get her off of it for it to notice me, but I noticed the blood pouring down. Whatever Bethany was doing, I hoped it wasn't hers.

Backhand or not, I still had the shotgun and I twisted around and fired again. The second gug let out a roar of pain and clutched at its own neck. My first gug was almost to me, I turned the gun and fired again.

Only to discover that the shotgun was empty. I had a few shells still in my pocket but did not know how I was going to retrieve them and load the weapon before the gug killed me.

The gug coming at me had a mess remaining of its face. Where my multiple shots had hit it, in the face and throat, blood poured out. While obviously pained, the gug was not slowed in its quest to end my life.

The beast returned to all four legs and galloped toward me. The room was not that big and in two big bounds it was already to me and Bethany.

Rolling, I went under the legs of the creature Bethany was fighting and managed to shove two shells into the gun before the creature slumped to the ground, dead and with a gaping hole in the side of its head. Bethany had literally punched a hole into it.

Her arm was covered in the gug's blood as she landed on the ground facing away from me and toward my two enemies.

"Do I need to kill yours too?" she asked.

"I would not be upset by that outcome," I answered.

Both gugs looked at Bethany, the warrior princess with blood dripping down her arm. This little thing had just shoved its arm into the head of one of their own.

They both turned their attention back to me.

"No, don't worry about it," I said through heaving breaths. "I've got this."

Bethany smiled, crossed her arms and stepped toward one of the vacated tunnels.

I had a plan that would only work once, and if it worked I was going to need a new plan very quickly.

The first gug, whose face was now a mass of gore, reached for me. I let it grab me with all four of its furry paws on those two arms. These things were fast but I was hoping that, at least in this moment, I could be faster.

The monster's vertical mouth opened and it lunged to bite me in half. I fired once into the thing's mouth as it prepared to bite me. Whatever the gug had in its head exited through the back of its skull and we fell to the ground.

I had one shell remaining in the gun and didn't know how many were still in my pocket. The final gug was on top of me and tossing the body of its friend away, where it collided with a rock wall with a meaty thunk.

It slammed one double paw down at the ground, I thought to grab me, but I rolled away and heard as the pads of the arm slammed into the rock flooring.

Rolling to my feet, I picked up the gun by the barrel like a club and swung it at the thing's face. It bit down and snapped the shotgun in half. I didn't let go of the jagged piece of the barrel that broke off. Instead, I stepped forward and jammed it into the gug's mouth sideways, propping the thing's mouth open.

The gug still had hand-things, so I was not expecting this to work for long, but I only needed a moment.

Bethany leaped up onto the creature's back and put her hands on either side of its gaping maw and pulled.

When the tearing sound had ended, the gug laid mostly in one piece on the ground, dead. Its head was split open where Bethany had torn it in half.

Covered in the blood and sweat of our battle, we turned back toward the path.

To their credit, the ghouls in the McCallister house kept their veils on after they were ordered to stand down.

We were able to convince the families that Dashel had been using the auction to rob them with fake trinkets he had made up and when his companion, posing as the McCallisters' butler, had discovered that Dashel intended to double-cross him, the entire plan fell apart.

The resulting battle amongst the patrons was part of the confusion in the wake of Robert Dashel's murder. The families agreed it would be in everyone's best interest if all acts of violence were attributed to Dashel and the butler, Craig.

When the police came on site and saw what families had been involved, they were more than happy, in a financial sense, to ignore whatever bits of the fiasco we needed them to.

It was convenient, if a little disturbing how easily we were able to get the police to ignore what should have been a grisly crime scene.

Carol, still holding the now unlit Hand of Glory, met us at the campus truck we had borrowed for the night.

"Exciting?" she asked.

I shrugged while Bethany nodded.

"Exciting is a word for it," I said. I was still surprised by how willing the police were to ignore mine and Bethany's being covered in the brackish gug blood.

"Sorry about your boyfriend," Bethany added with sincerity.

Carol shrugged this time. "It is for the best. His ideology was likely going to become a problem."

"That sounds like a common issue with the men we know," Bethany smirked and sent a wink at me.

"And where is the glamorous Ms. Coombs headed now?" I asked.

Bethany shrugged and pulled her rose-colored glasses back out. Putting them on, she flashed a smile that could send men to war.

"You two seem to find all the fun," she said. "I'll be around."

The Urge

By C. T. Phipps

Chapter One

"So, you want me to kill your son, huh?" I asked, taking my hands out of the pockets of my waistcoat to adjust the fedora on my head. A lot of folks didn't much care for a woman wearing man's clothing in the Dreaming City. The Dreamlands liked everything anachronistic, but I was a private dick and I sure as shit wasn't going to be running after targets in high heels or tight dresses.

Across from me in the apothecary shop were my two potential suckers, er, I mean customers, who were bald-headed with large ears as well as visible canines whenever they opened their mouth. Just inhuman enough to let people know they weren't your typical Dreamlander humans. I could see past the glamours they wore to the canine horrors beneath, just like they could see past my visage, but we all preferred to wear masks when living topside.

The shop was a typical one in that it catered to the superstitious, dabblers, and alternative medicine types far more than it did the serious professionals. In the Dreaming City, everyone could wield magic if they set their minds to it, but most of us preferred to keep it at arm's length. The price for real sorcery was your sanity and most people preferred frog legs tea and fake rhino horn for their remedies over the actual juju powered by the Old Ones.

Walter Crait, the husband, was wearing a pair of black slacks and a plain white t-shirt with an apron over it. "No, we don't want our son killed, Ms. Howard. We want Martin taken back alive if possible."

"Call me Jackie," I said. "It's the at all possible part that I wanted to clarify on. If your son has gone feral, then there's not necessarily much that I can do about that."

Feral ghouls were something of an ugly stereotype among our people, but it was something that still had a basis in reality. For all the hate groups' propaganda that every ghoul was a ticking time bomb to cannibalistic berserker rages, it only happened to a few troubled souls. Usually, they were changelings that couldn't handle the transformation from humanity to ghouldom and retreated into a savage animalistic predator state.

Mrs. Linda Crait put on a pair of bifocals. She wore a plain blouse and floor-length blue dress. "It's not that he's gone feral. It's more complicated than that."

"Uncomplicate it then," I said, dryly. "Because every minute we talk here is another one I could be looking for him or you could be finding a new shamus, because I won't take a case where my clients hold out on me."

"Please, you're the only one we can trust," Walter said.

"That remains to be seen," I said, crossing my arms. "I may be furry underneath this red hair and white skin, but don't try and pull any of this 'we're all in this together' bull crap. I was raised on the surface of the Earth by humans."

There was a sharp divide in the Dreaming City among the ghouls who could be called "orthodox" and "secular," if you needed to put labels on it. The orthodox ghouls were the ones who had been raised underground or in the Dreaming City's vast warrens. The secular, mostly changelings but some half-breeds like myself, were as often as not people who had been brought up among the people we later learned to eat. I'd been lucky to grow up with parents who didn't care I was a monster, mostly because they were monsters themselves, but that left me distinctly isolated from what was supposed to be a big extended family.

Bullcrap.

"It's the Urge," Linda said, finally admitting what they'd been holding out on.

"Ah," I said, as if that explained everything. And it did. The Urge was a primal instinct among the ghouls, as much as our need to eat the flesh of sentient beings. It was the urge to reproduce. Not the urge to have sex, which ghouls roughly had at the same level as humans. No, it was instead a kind of primordial need to either sire an heir or carry one to term that started as an unpleasant itch before gradually dominating your thoughts. The term "biological clock is ticking" didn't work as a metaphor unless the biological clock was a time bomb. "So, he needs to find a mate, put a bun in the oven, and hunt for a few byakhee eggs to impress the lucky lady's parents. What's the problem? Is he gay? Commitment phobic? Bad breath?"

According to legend, the Urge had been placed into the ghoul species by Tsathoggua to guarantee the immortal species kept reproducing. Why he/she/it thought this would be a problem with ghouls unlike virtually every other species in the cosmos was anyone's guess, but there it was.

The Urge was nondiscriminatory and a major source of upheaval among the secular ghouls. Couples were routinely broken up, families destroyed, and religious vows violated when the Urge struck an individual that needed to find the most suitable mate possible in short order. Thankfully, it only happened about every hundred years but meant that it could add up; some ghouls I knew were old enough to remember when the oceans drank Atlantis.

"Martin is a self-hating ghoul," Walter said, softly. "He is the product of one of my dalliances in the mortal world during my own Urge period."

"Your wife is very understanding," I said, sarcastically.

"I took him as my own once he became part of our household." Linda shrugged. "I conceived a daughter later during my Urge. These things happen."

"He grew up among human parents until I was able to rescue him from them at age twenty," Walter said, pausing. "It was very traumatic to find out his true nature and took many years for him to adjust."

"Uh huh," I said, getting bored. "Could you jump to the part about why he's going insane?"

"He promised he would never pass along his cursed blood," Walter said, gesturing to the apothecary shelves. "So, Martin took the Milk of Ghataskhi and destroyed his ability to sire. The Urge remains, though."

I stared at them. "You're telling me that your son disappeared, has probably lost his mind, may start attacking people soon, and is almost certainly going to contribute to more people in the Dreaming City hating us, all because he gave himself an alchemical vasectomy?"

"Yes," Walter said, nodding. "He must be brought back so the Ritual of Tayah'nal'oo can be performed."

I nodded. "Which I clearly know."

"It will spawn a child from his blood," Linda said. "A homunculus that will satisfy the Urge for the next century."

I looked between them. "And I take it he didn't like this option when it was explained to him the first time?"

Homunculi were little, tiny wizard and priestly servants that barely had any sentience. They were the kind of thing that got out into the city at large and ended up scurrying in the shadows after their masters died, living off blood and vermin. Knowing they were the product of someone's own blood but denied any chance at a real life made my skin crawl. Why was it there didn't seem to be any magic that wasn't inherently vile?

"He refused," Linda said. "Now he has no choice."

I didn't want to point out he very much had a choice. It was a choice between becoming a monster in mind as well as body, a choice between creating a monster, or a merciful death as a man.

"Alright, I'll take the case," I said, knowing I was going to regret it. "Now we just have to discuss my fee."

Thankfully, it turned out selling exotic animal parts and powdered flowers to suckers paid well and I had a small black ruby from Leng with the promise of another one should I bring him back alive. Killing

Martin was something they absolutely wanted to avoid but I got the impression both parents considered it to be preferable to his succumbing to madness. The rest of the ghoul community would come down on them and the Dreaming City's authorities on ghouldom if he ended up murdering humans in his madness. Feral ghouls threatened the fragile peace between all the peoples in the Dreamlands, and the Craits had a few hundred other children from their millennia of life to worry about.

Unfortunately, when I arrived at my office I found another complication waiting for me. He was trouble, I could tell with his sharp dress sense, nice shoes, black jacket, black tie, blond hair, and pretty boy features. Late twenties to early thirties and from money. Worse, I could tell he was one of the most dangerous things a human could be in the Dreaming City: an academic. The little golden Greek letter pin on his lapel told me he was from the University.

"Ms. Howard?" the man spoke in the kind of generic New England accent the upper crust tended to speak around here despite the fact New England hadn't existed for centuries, at least the one I was from. But I was hardly the one to complain about anachronism.

My office was a study in contrasts and stereotypes. It had a desk covered in files, a bookshelf of bad detective fiction, a coatrack with a hidden gun in the spare trench coat I kept there, and a window showing the Dreaming City outside. The Dreaming City was a composite of just about everyone's dreams, at least among humans, of what a bustling metropolis should be.

It was a refuge for some people, a prison for others. In an infinite multiverse of worlds all doomed to die at the hands of the Great Old Ones when they rose, it was a waystation for those refusing to die just yet. The way I perceived it was something around the 1940s due to all the old comic books I'd used to read during my mortal years: Batman, Superman, and Dick Tracy. Other people? Well, the city was in the eye of the beholder. I imagined some people saw it as more akin to ancient Sumner or Tenochtitlan.

"That's what it says on my door," I said, walking toward my desk. "I see you just let yourself in?"

"The super says you haven't paid your rent in two months and agreed to show me the place," the man said, calmly.

Being a detective in the Dreaming City should have been easy given all the secrets everyone was hiding, but the problem was that most people were more interested in keeping them covered up than paying to discover them. It also didn't help that the demihuman peoples like ghouls and Deep Ones preferred to solve things in-house. The fact I'd been hired by the Craits was something of a minor miracle and I had to wonder if that meant the elders of the local clan had advised them on a more extreme solution regarding Martin. But what could be more extreme than killing him? I was missing something.

I frowned before flopping myself down in the swivel chair behind my desk. "Yeah, well, I'll be dealing with that soon. May I ask who the hell you are and what you want with me?"

"My name is Percival Madison," the man said, giving a name that positively oozed class. "I'm a graduate student at the University."

"Nice to meet you, Percy," I said, putting my hands behind my head and leaning back. "How can I help you?"

"I want to help you find Martin," Percy said, looking down at my chest as I stretched before flicking his eyes back up to my face. Men were men, easily fooled by appearances. I wondered just what he would think if he could see the real me. Then again, many men of my acquaintance didn't care if they didn't have to. That was the key to a successful relationship, in my opinion: dishonesty.

"News travels fast," I said, pausing. "No offense, you don't strike me as the kind of person the Craits would tell their business to."

"On the contrary, I'm an old friend of the family," Percy said, adjusting his tie. "My area of special concern is human-ghoul relations. I'm the author of *On the Origins and Culture of Ghouls*. That was my thesis and a project Martin helped on."

"Get out," I said, gesturing to the door. "I'm not a science experiment or something for you to study."

"I know where Martin is and what he's up to," Percy said. "And it could be the answer to something I've been working on for years."

I paused, sighing. "Alright, you have five minutes, Pretty Boy. You realize that your friend did something stupid and is probably going to get so horny now that he gnaws someone's face off, right?"

The Urge was one of two ways that ghouls tended to end up going feral. If you didn't have a child in a century, then it would take over. The other was refusing to eat the flesh or brains of sentient people. A ghoul who didn't indulge in cannibalism, if you considered eating humans or other thinking creatures that, was one who would also lose his mind. We had to spread our existence and be the boogeymen or other races' dead if we didn't want to become the monsters that others feared us to be.

"Yes," Percy said, shaking his head. "I encouraged Martin to not feel disgust toward who he was and simply do what was necessary. Instead, he rejected that and now seeks an alternative means to cure himself of what he views as a disease."

I found myself annoyed by Percy almost instantly. There was only one kind of person more annoying than someone who hated ghouls for what they were born as: someone who was intrigued by us as something exotic and alluring. I didn't want to have to deal with any werewolf fanboys or cannibal enthusiasts.

"You said you knew where he is and what he's doing," I said, dryly. "Get to it."

Percy nodded. "Our studies extensively examined the idea that ghouls were the products of the Great Old Ones modifying one of the races they encountered on their long journey to Earth from Vhoorl, in the Twenty-third Nebula. Possibly Xoth where Cthulhu mated with Idh-yaa. It is there they developed their ability to shapeshift and mate with any—"

"Speak English, Doc," I said, having absolutely no care about the places and planets humans speculated the supernatural came from. Some things were beyond mortal comprehension and nothing good ever came from trying to figure them out. A surprising thing for a private detective to claim, but life was just full of little ironies.

"I'm only a Master of Anthropology," Percy said, sheepishly. "He wants to summon Azathoth, Sultan of All Demons, to make him pure."

Chapter Two

The hairs on the back of my neck stood up, which was damn impressive if you knew how many I had underneath my glamour.

"Azathoth?" I asked, staring at him. "Isn't that like summoning God to change a flat tire?"

I wasn't a witch or occult scholar, but I'd heard enough crazy talk from cultists as well as my fellow demihumans to get the basic gist. There were the Great Old Ones, the Other Gods, Yog-Sothoth, and above even that was Azathoth. Azathoth was the supreme being in the multiverse, existing in the heart of creation and destruction as the entity that bound all living things. Unlike most creator deities, though, it was pointless to worship him because he was both blind and dumb. Also insane. Which explained a lot about the universe once you thought about it.

"The madness of Martin's plot is known to me," Percy said, pulling out a pair of spectacles and starting to clean them with an honest-to-God silk handkerchief. Seriously, he was way too posh for my office. "Unfortunately, that doesn't mean he's not capable of doing what he intends to do."

"Explain to me what you mean by that as if my formal education is this much." I lifted two fingers and pressed them together. I'd not even been born in the City, but in a dead world village where the height of technology had been a windmill-powered generator and a gas-guzzling Corvette left over from before the world ended.

Percy put on his glasses and looked damn good in them. "The University has many relics acquired from the waking world, even places no longer in existence or away from the various permutations of the Earth. One of these is an alleged relic of the Xothian ancestor race of the ghoul species, the one Martin and I dubbed the Efreet, after the—"

"Yes, genies," I said, knowing that much.

"Err, not quite but close enough for the layman," Percy said, having that kind of 'I want to lecture on this subject but am not going to' that a lot of male intellectuals just loved. I hated that it turned me on. "Either way, the Pipes of the Demon Sultan—"

"Did you name it that?" I asked, raising an eyebrow.

"Maybe," Percy said, abashed. "Either way, the Pipes of the Demon Sultan were said to be something used by the Xothian Efreet to summon manifestations of Azathoth during the cosmic alignments. The Xothian Efreet would then bind the blind idiot god's avatars and force them to grant wishes."

"So, it summons genies who grant wishes," I said, nodding. It wasn't the weirdest shit I'd encountered in my time as a gumshoe, not by far. "Maybe we should let him do it. If he hates being a ghoul that much, becoming a human might not be the worst thing. Mind you, I bet his parents would just consider that a death sentence by other means. What? Thirty or forty more years of life? Barely an eyeblink in a ghoul's life."

Percy's expression told me I was missing something. "I'm afraid it isn't that simple."

"It never is," I said, sighing. "So, Pretty Boy, what is the downside that I'm missing for him tooting his own horn?"

"Pipes," Percy corrected. "The Xothian Efreet were a space capable people that rode byakhee to uninhabited systems across the galaxy to perform their summonings. That is because each of the systems would subsequently develop a black hole."

I blinked slowly. "That seems bad."

"You could say that," Percy said.

"That sounds city-destroying bad," I repeated.

"Yes," Percy said. "It's difficult to speculate on what exactly a gravity singularity would do in a reality formed from consciousness, but yes, the City and all surrounding lands for as far as the mind can conceive."

Something wasn't adding up. "So, why the hell would Martin want to summon the Big Bad Demon God? It doesn't seem like being human would be worth it if it meant dragging the entirety of the world down with him."

Percy frowned. "I don't know. He should know better."

I nodded. "Well, thank you for your tip, Percy. Did you tell the authorities?"

Percy narrowed his eyes. "The only people I trust less with the Pipes of the Demon Sultan than Martin would be the police. If they somehow did manage to stop him, a miracle, then the Pipes would end up on sale to some rich dabbler with more money than knowledge. Then the world would certainly be doomed."

It was a surprisingly sensible decision from someone who clearly came from money and didn't have the kind of experience with cops I did. "Smart move. Still, I think this is where we part ways."

"I need to come with you," Percy said, simply. "Only I can possibly talk Martin down and the Pipes must be retrieved for safekeeping. They are vital evidence in proving my thesis on ghoul origins."

He was smart not to trust me even if I didn't want a planet-destroying magic wish-granting device. You could never be too careful in the big city. "Sorry, Pretty Boy, I work alone."

"I can tell you where Martin's apartment is."

"His parents already gave me the address," I said.

"His real apartment."

Percy owned a 1930 Rolls Royce Phantom that he gave me a lift in toward the nice part of town. He was packing a Colt Detective Special in a holster under his jacket as well. We were near a set of art deco apartments that were in a nearly completed building, all glass and weird angles. It was not yet for sale but still being shown to the public. Apparently, Martin had been using the basement for his research after bribing the owners.

"Why have a separate apartment?" I asked, sitting across from him as we found a parking place.

"The University is riddled with cultists and wannabe wizards," Percy replied. "When we discovered the nature of the Pipes, we decided to continue our research into the origins of ghouldom and their connection to the Xothian artifacts we'd found in private."

I could have asked him why he thought Martin was any better hands for this weird world-destroying magic. Or him for that matter. Anyone having weird world-destroying magic. Instead, I asked something personal. "So, why are you interested in ghoul history?"

"Why not ghoul history?" Percy asked, surprised.

"Most humans who study us just want to figure out how to kill us easier," I said, shrugging. "It's the immortal shape-changing cannibal werewolf thing. It's a real turn off to most people."

If Percy found my joke funny or even noticed it was a joke, he didn't give any indication. "I believe history is the key to learning how to understand one another. Humans, Deep Ones, Yigians, and perhaps even other more inhuman species. The truth will set us free."

His naiveté was touching. "The only two species that get along in the Dreamlands are humans and cats. That's because humans are enslaved by felines and happily so."

Stepping out of the car, I headed to the bulkhead entrance to the apartments. I had my Colt single action army revolver drawn. The single greatest handgun ever invented. I didn't expect Martin to have succumbed to feraldom yet, but I wasn't discounting the Urge was already affecting his sanity. That might have been the reason for his cockamamie plan to summon Azathoth and become a real boy. The only thing was the Urge usually made you want to gnaw people's faces off rather than practice black magic. I needed more information on what was going on.

Reaching the door, I tested the knob and found it to be unlocked. Which was a good sign as it indicated Martin might have been home. Kicking the door open, I found myself in a place less like a proper bachelor apartment and more like some paranoiac's mind prison. There were papers taped up against the walls, scattered across the floor, a literal drawing board filled with illustrations, and a collection of stone artifacts scattered about that had probably been lifted from the University. On one side of the wall, there was a set of star charts for a corner of the Milky Way I wasn't unfamiliar with, and the word

FREEDOM written across it in red paint. It was right next to a map of downtown. Near the open door to the bathroom was a large two-door wardrobe. The place smelled of stale coffee, cigarettes, incense, and blood—which was never a good combination. No sign of Martin himself.

"Your friend needs to hire a cleaning lady," I said, putting away my gun. "Does he normally decorate in crazy?"

Percy followed me in, showing he was at least willing to follow my lead in dangerous situations. Good, doing otherwise would have gotten him killed. "No, I can definitely say this is new. Normally, Martin is extremely tidy."

"Is it possible someone tossed the place?" I asked, looking around.

"Perhaps," Percy said, picking up some of the papers on the ground. "This is definitely our research, though. Except he's gone off on a large number of tangents that seem extremely speculatory."

"Define speculatory," I said, wondering if this was a case of an academic having gone off his gourd because he'd seen things man was not meant to know. I'd never heard of it happening to a ghoul before, but it wasn't *impossible*.

"Martin and I had some luck translating fragments of the Xoth tablets recovered by some Leng traders," Percy replied. "The tablets are older than anything other than Elder Thing writing or the text on the walls of R'lyeh itself. They spoke of the society that existed on Xoth and what may have happened to it. The Efreet's, I mean."

"No offense, but that was like a billion years ago," I said, confused. "Who gives a shit?"

Surprisingly, Percy didn't correct my estimate of how long ago it probably was. "The dinosaurs were not yet even evolved, let alone humanity by this time. Still, he was particularly interested in the legends of the Old Ones bringing the ghoul race with them and, more precisely, how they had uplifted them."

"Uplifted?" I asked.

"Granted immortality, shape-changing, and sapience," Percy rattled off the facts. "Supposedly, the Xothians were nothing more than savage animals before they were blessed by the travelers from the stars.

The Great Old Ones named their race as the K'nyanians and made them chief among their servitors. Ghoul creation legends are transmitted orally by tradition, but enough of them have been written down to give a sense of how their religion functions to even an inquisitive outsider."

"Ah, it's a religion thing," I said, regretting bringing it up. "That explains it. People get really antsy when you start poking holes in their creation myth. I knew one Deep One fisherman who took a harpoon to his brother's head when he suggested that, maybe, Cthulhu didn't consider the fishmen to be his holy heirs but just vermin setting up in his tomb while he slept."

"Hmm," Percy said, clearly not listening as he continued to examine the documents. "He's cross referenced the Elder Things civilization and Great Race as well as lack of fossil record regarding anything other than those two periods before the Hyborian Age. I don't understand what his point is, though."

"Yeah, well a fossil record is hard to verify in the Dreamlands. Maybe we evolved here." I turned to him before realizing I was distracted by his presence. So much so, I'd wanted him to ramble on about this nonsense rather than shut up as I'd normally want.

Dammit.

Not now.

I had my own problems to deal with.

"Unlikely," Percy replied. "The Dreamlands is immaterial and immortal. Ghouls can leave and enter physically but the life processes of the mortal world don't happen naturally. Traditional bioscience and alchemy show that ghouls had to have evolved in the Waking World originally before migrating here. Same as humans."

"It sounds like you both need a girlfriend," I said, pausing. "Or boyfriend, I'm not judgy."

Percy looked up from the papers, annoyed. I hoped he wasn't one of those weirdos who were fine with ghouls but got bigoted about his own kind. "Martin's issues with sex are part of the reason we're here. As for me, I don't lack for female attention. I was married until recently to a Jewish woman named Sonia. Sadly, it didn't work out. I was too much of a homebody for her."

Good, then I wouldn't have to kill her. Dammit, of all the ironies. Now I was dealing with it. "So, any luck on finding out where he is?"

Percy walked up to the star chart on the wall. "Unfortunately, about the only thing I can confirm is that he's worked on reconstructing the original Efreet ritual to summon Azathoth and definitely plans to perform it somewhere here in the city. Specifically, the downtown area."

"So somewhere among a million or so residents, great," I muttered. "Any idea when this world-destroying ritual is supposed to happen?"

"Tomorrow night," Percy said.

"Of course it is," I muttered. "It's never in three thousand years or last month but you missed it."

"Much experience in world-ending disasters?" Percy asked.

"No, but I know every cult in the city looks forward to the end of the world," I replied. "They always think that they'll either be spared or are crazy enough not to care. One thing that puzzles me, though."

"One thing?" Percy asked, sarcastically.

Okay, he had a point there. "One of the things that puzzles me is why Martin is going so hard on all this ghoul stuff if he hates being one."

Percy looked confused. "Martin doesn't hate being a ghoul."

I blinked. "What?"

"He hates being part-human," Percy said. "Being a ghoul is something that makes him feel immensely proud. He despises that his father mated with a woman in the Waking World. All our work together was accompanied by things like, 'you are a credit to your race', and 'if only you'd been born better.'"

I believed him. "The Craits have been lying to me. Either that or they have no idea what their child has been up to."

There was a banging noise in the wardrobe. I wasn't sure what the hell I might find inside. Approaching as I gestured for Percy to stand back, the doors to the wardrobe burst open and a fur-faced ghoul in a cap, linen shirt, and pants burst out. It wasn't attempting to attack, though, but bowl past us. Rather than shoot him in the back, I holstered my weapon before running after him.

"Stop!" I shouted, not exactly having time to be eloquent as I went after the furry bastard.

I managed to catch up quickly while he went up the stairs, tackling him to the ground.

"Don't hurt me!" the ghoul said, sounding all too human. This was probably not one of the older members of our race. They tended to be less of, well, a wimp.

I lifted back my fist. "Who the hell are you and where is Martin?"

"My name is L-Leonard," the ghoul said. "I d-don't know where Martin is."

"What's your relationship to him?" I asked.

"I w-work at the funeral home, Restful Hearts," the ghoul said. "I get him the parts he needs."

"You're his dealer?" I asked, shaking my head.

As mentioned, ghouls needed the flesh of sentient beings to keep our heads on straight. For the ghouls who belong to the orthodox sects, they tunneled through the Dreamlands into the various mortal worlds to steal the bodies of the buried dead. Hopefully ones without all the nasty formaldehyde and other chemicals that ruined the taste. For those of us who lived a more secular life, well, we had to find our own bodies to munch on. I'll be honest, you didn't want to know what happened to the bodies of the guys I had to polish off during my private detective work. I mean, I didn't set out to do it. I wasn't a serial killer, just the regular kind. For money and usually in self-defense. The other guys were assholes. Okay, I was making myself sound like a monster even to myself. Oh well, waste not want not.

"Yeah," Leonard said, frowning. "He stiffed me on the last batch too! I can't even afford a good glamour anymore! I can't do my job looking like this! I'm going to have to move back to my clan."

I got up off him. "You poor thing. Well, we need to find him or we're all going to have a helluva lot more problems than unpaid bills."

"I think I may have a way of finding him," Percy said, heading up the stairs. In his hand was a clump of fur, Martin's I presumed.

"Let me guess," I said, sighing. "Magic."

"Magic," Percy said.

Chapter Three

"I hate magic," I muttered, keeping my hands in my pockets as we walked down the streets of downtown.

"It's just a tool. Neither good nor evil," Percy said, holding up an ornate bronze compass that had an elaborately etched star on the bottom that made me uncomfortable just looking at it. Inside the compass was stuffed with bits of Martin's fur, a piece of paper containing his true name, and a bunch of doodles that I didn't understand the meaning of.

Percy was apparently an amateur thaumaturge and while a rare skill on Earth among humans, it was common as dirt among the educated classes of the city. It was the same as most places in the Dreamlands: every priest, king, and advisor depended on sorcery to survive against the real powers of the universe. At least the ones humans could even conceive of opposing.

Which wasn't many.

I rolled my eyes before pulling out one of my hands and sticking a thumb out that I aimed at my heart. "See, that's what humans say and they're always wrong. My mother was a witch, and my father was a dabbler. Every time they used sorcery, it made them worse people. No matter the reason, good, bad, or indifferent. They both said, come on, Jackie, everyone uses magic. Well, not me. I may need a shoeshine and am back on my rent, but no one has a lien on my soul. I own it free and clear."

I did know a bit of magic myself. My mother had taught me how to edit memories and how to lull most men as well as some women into loving you. Neither of which were things that I particularly wanted to demonstrate. Magic wasn't inherently evil, according to the people I knew, but it always seemed to end up being used for the basest, most selfish reasons.

"Is that from a movie?" Percy asked, still staring at the compass. We'd been walking around downtown for hours, and I was starting to think this had been an enormously bad idea. And by starting, I meant I'd started thinking that and was about ready to hurl the goddamn compass into the bay. Just as soon as I bummed a lift off Percy to the docks.

I grimaced, turning away. "I may be paraphrasing 1991's *Cast a Deadly Spell*. They showed it here at the movie theatre last year, or was it twenty years ago? Eh, time runs weird around here. I remembered the speech, at least."

"Mmm hmm," Percy said, not looking up. "By your parents, I assume you mean your adoptive parents?"

"Yeah," I muttered. "My birth mother didn't survive birthing me. How did you know?"

"You are very human for a ghoul," Percy said. "Even a hybrid."

"Is that an insult or a compliment?" I asked, curious.

"Yes," Percy said, looking up. "We're here."

"You're kidding," I said, looking up. We were now just outside the Randolph Carter History Museum, devoted to trying to make some sort of narrative from the imagination of Earth's greatest dreamer. It was a big blocky building that dominated a large chunk of the area despite the fact its real estate would have been more valuable given over to a skyscraper or bank. None of the city council would touch the place, though, due to the fear of offending its subject.

At least among humans, Randolph Carter had created the Dreaming City from his longing for New England during his quest to find Unknown Kadath. Apparently, he had done such a good job the gods of Kadath had taken up residency here for a few years and populated the place with their spawn. I didn't take that kind of thinking too seriously, since every mythology seemed to want to make its people the children of gods.

"The compass doesn't lie," Percy said. "He's inside."

"Martin? Inside? Right now?" I asked, honestly surprised this had worked.

"That is what I mean," Percy said, frowning. "This is a very good place for him to do the ritual."

"How is that?" I asked, confused. "Seems pretty public."

"Not when it's closed," Percy said. "Which happened a few minutes ago. The best ritual rooms cost upward of $200,000 in Republic dollars or an equivalent in gold. The Carter History Museum has its own on display that could be easily repurposed. It also wouldn't require Martin to involve any of the local lodges or fraternities."

"So, he's doing the End of the World on the cheap," I said, sarcastically.

"World-ending magic is expensive. Far more so than a professor can afford, even tenured," Percy said in such a deadpan tone I didn't know if he was joking or not.

"So, we just go in there, beat the living crap out of him, take the Pipes, and the world is saved?" I said, pounding my fist into my palm. "I like this plan."

"That's not a plan," Percy said. "Especially if Martin brought along his henchmen."

"His what now?" I asked, doing a double take. "He has *henchmen* now?"

"Henchpersons. Henchthings. Students," Percy replied, frowning. "Ones taken advantage of by Martin's charisma and belief that he is onto something glorious about the origins of the ghoul race. Ones that believe he might be able to share the immortality of the ghoul race and perhaps induce transformations."

I stared at Percy. "That's not describing students. That's describing a cult. You didn't think a cult was worth mentioning?"

"I'm mentioning it now," Percy said. "Albeit, I probably should have mentioned it earlier."

"You think?" I asked. "Maybe we should have brought that Leonard guy. An extra pair of hands in getting Martin to cough up what he owes might have been helpful."

"Assuming he was telling the truth," Percy said, frowning. "There's something very strange going on here."

"You mean aside from a guy who wants to destroy the world so he can get wishes," I replied. "Which seems to be a dumb action since the world is kind of necessary to enjoy the wishes. Assuming you're wishing for anything normal."

Which was a big if.

"Yes, aside from that," Percy said, frowning.

"You may be right," I said, frowning. "In any case, I can see everyone already leaving through the front door. If we're going to get into this place, I suggest we take the back."

"If we're doing the rush him plan."

"So, yes."

Percy put away his compass and nodded.

Breaking into the museum was easy for someone who had been breaking into buildings for the better part of decades. Private detectives weren't supposed to break the law as part of their job, but the laws in the Dreaming City were more suggestions than hard rules. Technically, I was pretty sure liquor was still illegal because it had been when Randolph Carter had dreamed the place into existence. The people who hired me as their private dick did so because they knew I'd be going the extra mile.

Now, I was going the extra mile to save the world or, at least, the city. Allegedly. I was presently hoping Percy was full of crap and he was confusing some conch shell or old ghoul relic as something that could summon the God of Gods. Even in the Dreamlands, the kind of magic that could do that was rare as a night-gaunt's teeth.

The interior of the museum looked pretty much as you'd expect a place like it would: full of trinkets and bones left over from the remains of what people alleged to be Randolph Carter's adventures. He was an interesting character even if you didn't buy into his mythology, and one of the few humans that even orthodox ghouls spoke of with reverence. There were relics of Ulthar, a gallery of Pickman originals, historical artifacts from Celephaïs, and rebuilt temples to Nyarlathotep as well as Nodens.

Unfortunately, what we didn't find was any sign of Martin or his so-called cult. We managed to avoid the underpaid rent-a-cops that oversaw protecting the museum, which frankly was not difficult because they were trying very hard not to see us or anything else that might end up killing them messily and without great difficulty. Eventually, Percy's compass led us to an empty exhibit room with no sign of the man. There was just a bare tile floor and white brick walls with a mirror covering one of them.

"Well, if the world ends because we can't find the guy, I will laugh," I muttered, not actually finding it funny at all.

"I don't understand," Percy said, looking at the compass.

"It doesn't work, what's to understand?" I replied. "Maybe Martin has worked up some juju to protect himself from being found."

"If he was that good a magician, then he wouldn't need a stolen artifact to make himself pure," Percy said, walking around in a circle.

"By pure, you mean—" I still wasn't getting this. Being distracted by the beginnings of the Urge wasn't helping matters.

"A ghoul with no human blood," Percy replied.

That was the part I didn't get. "Yeah, but ghouls with human blood and without it are the same, aren't they? They wouldn't be able to mate otherwise."

"That was always a question of our research," Percy replied. "The closest answer we were ever able to get from ghouls or doctors was, 'it's magic. Don't question it.'"

I got the impression that answer didn't fully satisfy Percy, even if it worked for me. "Yeah, well, Pretty Boy, you…" That was when I smelled something very familiar: blood.

"What?" Percy asked.

"Here," I said, going up to the mirror. "It's coming from inside here."

Percy walked up to the mirror, which just showed our reflections. The glass was unusually dark, though, and I could feel the smell of blood wafting from within. There were other smells as well, fire and incense.

"I see," Percy said, reaching into the mirror and causing it to ripple like a pool of water.

"This is gonna suck," I muttered.

"Probably," Percy said, pulling out his gun before stepping through the mirror.

I followed him.

The sight that greeted us on the other side of the looking glass was pretty much straight out of one of the Pulps I occasionally indulged in when bored out of my skull. There was a big pentagram made from red paint on the ground, an enormous altar in the center, and torches standing at strategic places throughout the large stone chamber which had ghastly statues spread throughout.

The thing that really gave the place its ambience, though, was the five black-robed guys standing at the points of the star and the sixth looming over the altar. The only thing missing was a nubile young sacrifice on the altar, a shame really, and there was a weird, twisted horn with three ends instead. If you were to need an image for 'alien musical instrument', you could probably have done no worse taking a picture of this thing.

There was a sky above us that depicted alien constellations I didn't recognize as well as stars that were different colors from the ones that normally hung over the Dreaming City. Red, yellow, magenta, and colors only ghoul eyes had words for were present. I didn't know if we'd been transported into another dimension or if we were just in another part of the Dreamlands.

"The Xoth Exhibit," Percy said, pistol drawn. "It's not supposed to open for another month. You covered it up with a glamour."

Ah, more illusions. I pulled out my pistol as well and took aim.

"Yes," the central robed guy said, whom I presumed to be Martin Crait. I couldn't tell at this angle and with the fact he was wearing a particularly hideous wax mask of an eight-eyed thing. His voice was muffled under the mask, but still understandable. "It is a shame no one will ever be able to see the research we did together, Percival, but a greater calling demands this reproduction of a long dead race's religion. I take it you are the woman that my so-called parents have hired to thwart me?"

"Jackie Howard, PI," I introduced myself. "Thwart is a strong word, they wanted me to bring you back to them before you did something stupid. They think you're going feral because you can't put a bun in some ghoul girl's oven. I'm getting the impression something much bigger is going on."

That was one thing I'd figured out when dealing with wizards, businessmen, and gangsters: they all loved to hear themselves talk. "Yes. You were not hired to retrieve me but to silence me. They hired you because you are an outsider, and the truth that I hold in my heart is dangerous to all of those who are of ghoul blood."

I was very stupid with my next question. I should have just shot the guy and his goons, then taken the Pipes. I would have gotten paid either way. "What truth?"

"Ghouls are human," Martin said, his voice full of absolute loathing and disgust.

"Martin, we've talked about this," said Percy.

"They're human!"

"Okay, and?" I asked.

Martin pulled back as if I'd said something ludicrous. "The teachings of the ghoul race are that we came with the Great Old Ones from Xoth. That we were modified in their image and turned into their chosen servitors. Instead, this is all lies propagated by the priests and elders. The Great Old Ones came with no servitors resembling us! The original Xothian race were the flying polyps! Ghouls are just yet another offshoot of the infantile hominids the Elder Things experimented on. Warped by the dreams of the Sleeping Ones and no more their holy children than any other puerile mammal. The whole history of the ghoul race is falsehood based on superstition!"

"Okay, and?" I asked, not getting it.

"Fascinating," Percy said, clearly more interested in this than I was.

"Silence!" Martin shouted, balling his fists. "You do not understand, Ms. Howard." Men told me that a lot, usually in connection with who else they had been caught sleeping with. This time he might be telling me the truth. "You could not comprehend the burden of knowing that ghouldom is not the center of the universe! That we are but insignificant specks of nothing that have no role in the favored plans of the true masters of the cosmos!"

"No," I replied, honestly. "I can't say that I can. To have that illusion stripped away means I would have to have believed I was the center of everything to begin with. I don't get why you intend to blow the horn of judgement, though. You going to summon up God just so you can spit in his face? If you are, respect for ambition, but I can't let you do that."

"I am going to make the ghoul race pure," Martin said, coldly. "To destroy this wretched half-existence and every other ghoul in the Dreamlands before rebirthing us as a new species! One that will—"

That was when I shot him. I emptied my revolver into the mad academic in what was probably murder but I considered to be justified because 'plotting to destroy the world and become a god' was basic grounds for execution in my opinion. A couple of his cultists ran to stop me, one of them drawing a sacrificial knife, but both went down in a hail of Percy's bullets. One day those guys are going to learn to carry guns, but this was not that day.

The others ran for the right side of the room where they opened a fire exit that had been covered up by the set design around us. Moonlight streamed in as the door burst open, before closing behind the fleeing grad students.

"Well, that was suspiciously easy," I said, walking over to Martin's body on the ground.

"Don't jinx us," Percy said, lowering his pistol and looking at the bodies of the two cultists he'd killed. "This is going to be hard to explain to the police."

"For twenty bucks each, I know five Micks who will swear you were playing poker with them all night," I said, looking down at Martin's body. He was still, one of the shots having gone through his heart. "Assuming you don't want to say you were with me instead. Which is an option."

"Excuse me?" Percy asked.

I reached down and removed Martin's mask, exposing the human-like furry face of a hybrid who hadn't completed the transformation between ghoul and man. It was less like the canine face of a true ghoul and more like the Wolfman played by Lon Chaney Junior. It was the face of a man who had been confronted with his humanity every time he looked in a mirror and undermined his sense of divine destiny.

"Yeah, I'm not getting paid, am I?" I muttered, wondering how I was going to explain this to his parents.

That was when someone hit me over the back of the head with a pistol grip.

Chapter Four

I admit, I was fully expecting to awaken to Percy standing over me with a smug expression on his face that said, 'Oh, ho, ho, ho, private detective lady, you fell for my trap. I used your attraction to me to manipulate you before betraying you in a way that should have been obvious from the start. Look at me being so rich, pretty, and smug.'

Okay, yeah, I had issues.

Blame the father of my first son, whom I haven't mentioned for a reason. Instead, much to my surprise, I saw Percy was battered and blue next to me. He was tied up to one of the torch posts with his hands bound in rope. That wouldn't have kept him tied up, but I suspected he wasn't going anywhere from the beating he'd received. I, by contrast, felt unharmed but was presently tied to the altar where the Pipes of the Demon Sultan had been on display. Oh, and someone had taken my clothes.

Great.

Thanks for that.

I wondered if we'd missed some of Martin's followers, but the answer to who was holding us prisoner came moments later when I saw the face of Mrs. Crait, wearing a plain summer dress but staring at me with empty, soulless eyes. Mr. Crait was sharpening knives nearby, whistling a little Irish ditty.

Well, that was ominous.

I struggled in the ropes binding me. "I can understand how you might be upset at how my encounter with your son went. Given the unpleasantness involved, I'm willing to waive my fee and—"

"Those aren't the Craits," Percy said, looking up with one side of his glasses smashed in.

"Pardon?" I asked, looking down at him, then at Linda and Walt.

"They're wearing their skins," Percy replied.

Linda just smiled, and I saw her face twist and contort in a way not even a talented shapeshifter could pull off.

I blinked, processing that. "Huh. Just what the hell are you then? No, wait, let me guess. Great Race of Yith?"

"Very clever, Ms. Howard," said not-Walt.

Not that clever. When the perp was displacing someone else's mind so they could occupy the body, the most likely suspect was a race which had that as their standard MO.

"Yith?" said Percy, baffled. "What possible interest could you have in the origin of the ghouls?"

Non-Linda just looked at us with increasingly inhuman eyes.

"They're prospecting," I said. "Looking for a new territory to take over. A new species they can parasitize. The entire Yith population migrates together through time and space, taking over one species after another."

"Your work was very useful," said the fake Mrs. Crait. "You discovered the Children of Xoth, whom we have only heard whispered of in legend. And Martin, with his obsession with ghoul lore, was able to find the Pipes which for so long had escaped us."

"And you just don't care about this world being destroyed," I said. "Because you'll all psychically teleport somewhere else before it happens. Leaving some other suckers in your bodies to get disintegrated. Like you always do."

"We will claim the bodies of the Xoth in the Cretaceous Period and move on when we are done with them," said non-Linda with a shrug. "We will survive all things."

Bizarrely, that meant that the Yith that existed sixty-five or sixty-seven million years ago were inhabiting the bodies of the Xoth. Except, this was a group of Yith from before then, who were now going back in time to take the Xoth's bodies, which they already had in my timeline, which would lead to the Xoth's extinction, which would lead to the ghouls claiming their origin story, which would lead to Percy here making a paper on them that the Yith would find, that would encourage them to steal the Xoth's bodies in the past that—Great Tsathoggua, I hated time travel.

"The human will tell us how to bring forth Azathoth, and we will sing the song that ends this diseased illusion and get the information we need to carry out our next Great Migration. We have not yet begun to torment him to bring out his secrets."

"Yeah, well, Percy is not nearly stupid enough—" I started to say, wanting the cops to show up for the first time in my life.

"Please don't hurt her," Percy said, speaking up. "I'll do what you say."

"Pretty Boy, what are you doing?" I asked, confused. "If you help these people, then we'll all die."

"I love her," Percy said, speaking up. He was either suffering a concussion, or had lost all sanity. "If you promise to let her go, I'll tell you how to perform the ritual."

Martin and Linda exchanged a look.

"Agreed," Martin said, before I could point out that this would only get me an extra minute or so of life before the black hole swallowed everything.

Percy began reciting a spell of some kind that was clearly never meant for human tongues and sounded like he was clearing his throat. It would have been humorous if not for the fact that I could hear scratching at the air like someone was starting to claw through an invisible wall. *"Ach'tang gh'tagh Azathoth. Ach'tang g'tagh Nyarlathotep. Gul'tum'ack Yog-Sothoth. Shakal'un'zabaalm!"*

The Yithians began repeating his words, speaking them far faster as well as like a choir.

"Maahch'tuul! Maahch'tuul! Naka Azathoth! Naka Azathoth!" Percy continued speaking. "Blow the horn that ends worlds! Release the Lord of All Djinn!"

"Stop this, Percy!" I shouted. "You can't want this to happen! Stop!"

A single frightening note was blown upon the horn, and I would have done anything to make my ears burst at its presence. I could hear it joining a chorus of a hundred other awful instruments. The Yithians let forth a cheer, each speaking joyous praise to gods that felt nothing for them or any other being in the cosmos. Not even themselves.

Then silence.

The silence lasted a minute. "Percy?"

"I'm here," Percy said.

I opened my eyes and saw we were still in the room, but the flying polyps were gone. A trail of blood was coming from each of Percy's closed eyes, and I suspected he would never see again.

"What the hell just happened?" I asked. "The world didn't end. I think."

"*The Pipes of the Demon Sultan* are not limited to summoning Azathoth," Percy said, coughing. "They can also send you to his court at the center of the universe, or, well, galaxy. The translation is a bit iffy. Either way, I don't think we'll be seeing either of those two individuals again."

"Couldn't have happened to a nicer pair of people." I started gnawing on the ropes binding me with inhuman teeth, disrupting my glamour and revealing the hideous dog-like thing beneath. Once my arms were free, I ripped the ropes binding my legs away and went to Percy's side. I hated what I looked like and knowing that Percy would look upon my animalistic furred form with revulsion, especially since the Urge made it clearer with every moment that he was the one I wanted as my mate.

"I'm sorry. Maybe there's something we can do for your eyes."

"I doubt it," Percy said. "Even closed, my eyes witnessed things that burned away Sodom and Gomorrah."

"And that love stuff?" I asked.

"A trick," he said. "I'm sorry."

"It's fine," I said, feeling the side of his face with the tips of my fingers. "But I need something from you."

Percy didn't respond.

"Step away from the human," another voice spoke behind me.

There, Leonard was standing with a shotgun. Gone was the petrified-looking drug dealer and in his place was a cold-blooded lupine with a face human enough to show off his inherent thuggishness.

"Oh, you've got to be kidding me," I said, turning my head. "What the hell do you want?"

"To silence the blasphemer," Leonard said, scowling. "I appreciate you finding Martin and his cult. I managed to get the three students who fled when they practically ran to my car. I'll deliver their bodies to the butcher, and they'll join the ranks of the city's missing soon enough. Martin, being one of us, will be burned."

I noticed his body was still off to one side, slowly rotting from where he'd died earlier. Like most men, he'd emptied his bowels upon death. Which, to ghouls, wasn't inherently disgusting to smell but certainly noticeable. There was no sign of the Pipes of the Demon Sultan and I hoped they'd gone with the Not-Craits to meet their god.

"Yeah, well, he's dead and I'm not getting paid," I said, keeping myself between him and Percy.

"He means me," Percy said, breathing softly but shallowly. "Don't you?"

"Yes," Leonard snarled, a look of disgust in his all-too-human eyes. "The Elders have demanded his death as well."

Great, so Leonard actually was working for the orthodox ghouls. "He just helped save the world, jackass."

"He knows too much," Leonard said, growling. "The secrets of Xoth can never be shared."

I stared at him. "Seriously? This is all about the fact ghouls didn't come from another planet? Who cares?"

"*I do,*" Leonard said, growling. "Our society is kept together by the knowledge we are the Children of the Great Old Ones and that they are our mother, father, and masters. Without their power and judgment looming over us, our society would rip itself apart. People would lose all hope and become wild as the animals we truly descend from. That cannot be allowed."

I had to wonder about anyone who was only kept from going on a killing spree by the idea they'd be smacked down by a bunch of alien gods. "Listen, if it's not true then things like the Urge and feraldom can be treated. They're not some divine curse—"

Leonard lifted his shotgun. "Step aside, Jackie Howard. The only reason I am sparing your life is because you are kin to us. You may not acknowledge the bonds of blood that bind us all together, but I do."

"Let him do it," Percy said, coughing. "The burden of the knowledge I carry can only cause more misery."

He sounded broken and I couldn't help but wonder if it was because we'd killed his friend, his life's work almost destroyed the world, or he'd gazed into the heart of the cosmos only to see a monster rather than a divinity.

"Alright," I said, slowly getting up. "I guess this has to end only one way."

"Good call," Leonard said, gesturing with his shotgun. "Get out of the way."

I responded by ripping his throat out with my teeth.

No one was going to harm my mate.

The steamer ship leaving the Dreaming City would head to Ulthar next and from there, we would seek out a fairy tunnel to take us to one of the many Earths that lay beyond the Dreamlands. The 1920s, 1940s, or 2000s were all time periods that were appropriate for living and well before the era when the Great Old Ones usually rose.

I stood on the deck, once more covered in a glamour and visibly pregnant with my second child. I was dressed as a proper lady, now, and while I hated it, it was a small sacrifice to make for my family. The Urge was satisfied and there was no need to continue the charade of being Percy's wife, but I'd grown accustomed, addicted you might say, to being his human consort. Like the fairy queens of old, I was playing the role of a housewife until the time that he passed away.

It would not be long.

Seeing the sight of Azathoth and his court, even through closed eyes, had stripped my husband of his health as well as his sight. He had only a few years left in him even with the magics I'd done to remove his memory of everything related to ghouldom, our history, the origins of the species, and the larger reality above us.

Percy had never held being a ghoul against me and I knew that he'd accepted me as I was. Yet, it was easier to believe the lie that I was a human woman once my magics got into his psyche.

Easier for his family, easier for society, and easier to keep him alive when the orthodox ghouls still wanted his head. All of Martin's papers had been burned and the University had repudiated their work once it had become clear they'd stolen artifacts like the *Pipes of the Demon Sultan*. I suspected there were also human wizards who despised the notion that the races capable of interbreeding with mankind were closer to cousins than cuckoos.

When we reached Earth, probably New England, I intended to take away the rest of Percy's memories of the Dreaming City so he could enjoy his remaining years in peace. With any luck, he would forget his wife and child were monsters. There was no end of reasons for why a man might have lost his sight and memory after all. It was a violation of his free will and his magic, but I understood, now, why my mother did such things to her lovers. Why my own father had been troubled by his own terrible burden of knowledge.

Because sometimes, ignorance was bliss.

The Black Echo

By Philip Hemplow

"Rabbit! Get your ass over here!"

Lieutenant Calf yelled the words over the mutter of the jeep's idling engine. Across the clearing, a shirtless soldier detached himself from his squad and loped towards them. He was short—of course—no more than five foot two, with the wiry torso of a bantamweight fighter. A torn playing card, the knave of hearts, jutted from the scrim band of his helmet.

"Congratulations, Rabbit," said Calf as the dirt-streaked soldier approached. "I got you a replacement for Bennett, from fourth. He's green, but he's pint-sized and he was moronic enough to volunteer. Try not to break this one. Alysson, this is Sergeant White. Follow his lead, do what he says, and you might just live long enough to regret your dumbass decision."

"How's Bennett doing, sir?" asked Sergeant White, with barely a glance at Alysson.

"From what I hear, he's crazy as a crawdad: gibbering on 'bout gooks watching him from the bath taps or some shit. You and Charlie sure did a number on that guy."

"Section Eight?"

"That'd be my guess. Anyway, good luck, kid," concluded Calf, turning to Alysson. "Now, grab your shit and get the fuck outta my breezer."

Alysson did as he was told. The lieutenant gunned the engine as soon as he was clear, and skidded the vehicle through a tight 180 turn, throwing up a shower of mud. "Do your job, maggots!" he bellowed as he stomped on the accelerator. "See you in hell!"

He rocketed off in the direction they'd arrived from, the bounding jeep rapidly becoming indistinct, before the rain and encroaching darkness swallowed it altogether.

"Sir, I just want to say—" began Alysson, falling in behind White as he stalked back towards his unit.

"Forget it." White cut him off. "No one's interested in what you want to say, PFC Alysson. Just tell me why you volunteered for this detail."

"Because I want to kill commies, sir," said Alysson, puffing out his chest.

"Now, why the fuck would you wanna do that?" muttered the sergeant.

"Sir?"

"Where you from, Alysson?"

"Oxford, Mississippi, sir."

"Any Vietnamese boys ever cut up rough in Oxford? You get a lot of communist insurgencies down there in Mississippi?"

"I just want to serve my country, sir."

"Then you really are as dumb as you look. You smoke, private?"

"No, sir."

"Drink?"

"Not since I got in-country."

"Well, that's something at least. Keep it that way—no matter what any of these dumb assholes up ahead offers you. If Charlie smells that funk on you while we're downstairs, you'll get us both killed, fast as shit."

"Understood, sir. Sir, can I ask: what happened here? To the trees, I mean."

Alysson gestured at the rotting woodland all around them, the bare trees and the black mulch underfoot.

"Ah, they sprayed that chemical shit all round here last month. They say it's to stop Charlie hidin' in the trees—only, Charlie don't hide in no fucking trees, now, do he?"

They had reached White's squad of unshaven, tired-looking troops. Each sported a playing card on their helmet, like their sergeant. Two were keeping watch, rifles up, scanning the dripping woods for movement. The rest sat or sprawled, sheltering from the rain beneath the branches of a tree that had somehow escaped the worst of the defoliant attack.

"This is the new guy, from fourth platoon," said White, waving a hand in Alysson's direction. "What was your name, kid?"

"Alysson, sir."

The squad muttered and chuckled:

"Oh, man."

"How old is she? Fifteen?"

"Nice daisy chain, Alysson," scoffed one of them, pointing at the garland of oxeyes around Alysson's neck. "Boyfriend give you that?"

"No, your momma did." retorted Alysson, well used to jokes about his name and height.

"This here bunch of yahoos is second squad," continued White. "Introductions can wait. Mariano, give him the six."

"What about Bennett, Sarge?"

"Bennett ain't coming back."

"Ah, shit."

The rifleman, Mariano, pulled a deck of playing cards from his pocket and leafed through it until he found the six of hearts, which he skimmed to Alysson. "For luck," he said, as Alysson examined it.

"Right on."

"You'll need it."

"These boys will have our backs while we're down there. Mariano works the comms. It's him you'll be talking to."

"When do we start, Sarge?"

"Now! We've been locking it down, waiting for you to get here. These lummoxes are all too big, and protocol says no one goes in alone. You got a silencer for that 1911?" White nodded towards the pistol on Alysson's belt.

"A suppressor? No, Sarge."

"You fire that downstairs, you'll deafen yourself—and me. Give him Bennett's piece."

One of the men stirred with a sigh, and handed Alysson a stubby .38 revolver with a bulky suppressor screwed to the barrel. Alysson regarded it dubiously.

"This can even work worth a damn?" he asked.

"More or less. Means you won't blind yourself with your first shot, at least. Remember: when we're down there, you don't ever fire more than three shots from that thing before reloading. You got that? Three. Just three." White held up three fingers for emphasis.

"Three rounds only, okay. Why?"

"Cos if Charlie reckons you need to reload, he'll rush you. Don't let it get to that. I'll be ahead of you; if I pass my piece back, you take it and give me yours, on the double, while you reload mine. Here—dump those mags and pocket some shells. Somebody give him a flashlight. You keep the flashlight in one hand, gun in the other, and your knife where you can get to it fast, all the time. Now, you sure you're ready for this, kid?"

"Ready as hell, Sarge," asserted Alysson, taking a perpendicular flashlight from Mariano.

"Is this guy for real?" scoffed one of the squad, behind him.

"I don't see you volunteering, Crossman," snapped White. "If he says he's ready, well, I guess that's ready as anyone gets. We're gonna take it slow, give you time to adjust, but if you run into problems, *do not panic.* Okay? Panic'll get you killed. We go careful, we go quiet, we take our time. Got all that?"

"I've got it, Sarge."

"Good. Then I reckon it's time to jump in the river and learn to swim. Let's move up. On your feet, gentlemen—with me."

The entire squad moved off, deeper into the woods and the gathering dusk. Despite his bravado, Alysson's heart hammered like a woodpecker and his mouth was dry. His hearing seemed suddenly hyper-acute, registering everything: every twig snapping beneath a Vibram-soled combat boot; every raindrop pattering on slimy, deliquescent leaf litter; every puff of breath from the men around him, and, behind it all, the distant, monotonous *crump* of outgoing artillery.

One of the riflemen behind prodded him with the butt of an M16 as they walked.

"Hey, new guy—you know I think we're alone now?"

"Sure, if you say so."

"The song, moron! Do you know the song, *I Think We're Alone Now*? Come on, Tommy James, man, the fucking Shondells!"

"Yeah, okay, yeah! I know it! Tommy James. That's some real teenybopper shit."

"Yeah? Well, when you come out the ground, you make sure you holler that teenybopper shit at the top of your fucking lungs. Got that?"

"What the fuck for, man? Why?"

"So we don't perforate your ass, that's why. You're gonna be covered in shit, head to toe, right? You might come out some other exit. It's gonna be dark. For all *we* know, it's Charlie coming at us, so you sing the fucking song, clear as a bell. That way, we know it's you. Dig?"

"Yeah, okay. Got it. Sing the song…thanks."

"That's if you even make it back…dumb motherfucker…"

Ahead of them, White stopped and crouched, signalling for the others to do the same.

"Entrance is just up there, in the roots of that tree. It's about two feet by one. There's probably a ton of other ways in and out, but this is all we've found so far. Lose the shirt, kid, it'll be hot down there. Mariano: hook him up."

"Stay still," said Mariano, behind them, as Alysson obediently pulled his olive drab shirt off over his head. He felt something heavy being attached to the back of his cotton webbing belt and tried to look over his shoulder.

"Relax, hero—just commo wire," said Mariano. "It'll unspool as you go. Means I'll be able to listen in on you down there. Also, you get lost—just follow the wire back, like a fucking breadcrumb trail, yeah? Here, find somewhere to strap this." He handed Alysson a small microphone and a strip of tape. "Put it where it won't catch on shit."

After a moment of indecision, Alysson slapped the mic under his clavicle, guessing it would be the most secure place. "What about headphones?" he asked.

Mariano shook his head. "One way only, bucko," he said. "You need to be listening to what's occurring down there, not Harrison and Lewis jerking each other off up here." He held one cup of a headset to his own ear. "Push the transmit button so I can check it's working."

Alysson found the switch and depressed it, drawing a satisfied thumbs-up from the comms man.

"Good enough," he said. "Remember, noise travels down there, so you wanna stay quiet. Just pump that squawk switch twice to send 'all clear, moving on.' Okay?"

"Roger that."

They fell quiet as an F-105 Thunderchief roared overhead, going north, its shape shifting and insubstantial in the mist, engine glowing angrily through the murk.

"Okay, let's get in there," said White, once it had passed. "Stay behind me. Only move if I move. Don't make unnecessary noise—and don't get killed, kid."

"I'll try, Sarge."

"Cos I don't want to have to haul your skinny ass back outta there. Let's go."

Keeping low, Alysson and White crept on bent legs towards the entrance.

Alysson lunged forwards, following White's feet into the tunnel's mouth. It was as tight a fit as the sergeant had described, forcing him to twist his shoulders to squeeze through the tiny aperture. As soon as his head was inside he wanted to gag on the cloying air within, thick with geosmin, rhizomes, and mildew. Ahead of him, White flicked on his flashlight, so Alysson did the same. Their bulbs, intended to preserve scotopic vision, flooded the tunnel with hellish red light, revealing walls of wet slime festooned with tangled roots, protruding rocks, and the tails of writhing worms. It felt like slithering through a diseased intestine. Appropriate, thought Alysson, since there was undoubtedly much shit ahead.

"You okay back there, kid?" hissed White, turning his beam back towards him. The whites of his eyes glowed pink in the red light.

"All good, Sarge."

"Don't call me that. Not down here. No ranks in the Black Echo."

"The 'Black Echo?'"

"Down here. Underground. You know the Army: everything's gotta have a nickname."

"Okay. So, what's yours?"

"I don't care. The guys usually call me 'Rabbit.'"

"Rabbit. Huh."

"On the move."

White swung his light back around and continued shuffling forwards. Alysson followed, pulling himself along with his elbows, careful to keep his revolver's suppressed muzzle out of the mud. Despite his best efforts to keep up, White's feet receded into the distance ahead of him, quickly passing beyond the feeble range of his dim flashlight. Alysson forced himself to go faster, ignoring the abrasions and knocks he suffered as a result.

The tunnel went straight for some way, then dipped suddenly down; so suddenly that Alysson had no time to think about stopping himself before he was sliding uncontrollably down the muddy incline, on his stomach. The spool attached to his belt started to whir faster as it paid out commo wire behind him. Just as he had accelerated to an alarming speed, he tumbled out of the chute, landing in a heap of sticks and dry leaves, and the fall was over.

The chamber he'd arrived in was appreciably larger than their route in. It was perhaps only four and a half feet high and not much bigger laterally, but it felt like a cathedral after the claustrophobia of the shaft. White was crouched nearby, peering into another crawlspace which seemed to be the only other exit.

"You hurt?" he asked, without looking.

"Not a bit," Alysson assured him, getting to his hands and knees.

"Ventilation shaft," said White, gesturing towards their point of ingress with his revolver. "Don't see us getting back up there. Need to find another way out."

"Okay," agreed Alysson.

"See that stick of bamboo up ahead?"

White pointed the gun down the passage in front of him. It took Alysson a moment to make it out in the red gloom, but then he saw it: a hollow bamboo tube, protruding from the wall, camouflaged by a thick coat of mud.

"Yeah. What is it?"

"Go under it. Don't touch it. Boobie trap."

"A trap?"

"They put a two-stepper inside, on a noose. You dislodge the tube, the noose comes loose, you get fucked."

"What the hell's a 'two-stepper?'"

"Snake. Pit viper. It bites you, you're dead before you take two steps."

"Fuck!"

"Keep your knife ready, in case. It'll be all right. Come on."

White shuffled into the passageway. This one was high enough to allow for locomotion on hands-and-knees, but he pressed himself flat when he reached the bamboo tube, and shimmied underneath it. Alysson copied him, holding his breath, suddenly aware he was sweating profusely, expecting at any moment to feel a seething, scaly weight land on his back. Was it his imagination, or did he hear a hiss as he wriggled past the bamboo deathtrap?

"Send an 'all clear,'" prompted White once they were both safely past. "Let them know we're doing okay."

Alysson obediently pumped the transmit button taped to his chest, twice, sending the agreed signal, then made haste to catch up with the sergeant, who was scuttling away on all fours.

Ahead, the tunnel curved sharply to the right. To the left was a niche, in the roof of which was a wooden hatch, wide enough to admit a person.

"Cover the corner," murmured White. Alysson nodded and trained his weapon on the bend ahead, while White inched towards the niche, leaning to see as much of the opening as possible. Alysson held his breath as his partner edged into the space and, slowly, carefully, stood up, raising the hatch with the barrel of his gun.

For a tense moment, nothing happened as he played his flashlight around whatever room lay above. Eventually he sank back to his knees and gestured for Alysson to follow him through the hatch.

They pulled themselves up into a roughly rectangular clay chamber, perhaps twelve feet by six. Hammocks were strung across it, three deep, from wooden stakes hammered into the walls. The room stank of unwashed men and dirty laundry, but was deserted. A few piles of clothes and a metal ammo box were the only other signs anyone had been there.

"They sleep down here?" marvelled Alysson.

"Oh yeah, for months," White assured him, turning over some of the discarded clothes with the barrel of his revolver.

"That's nuts! How do they stand it?"

"They're tough as a motherfucker, that's how. Some of these sons of bitches have been fighting since '46. Hell, some of 'em were fighting the Japanese before that. They've been through war, occupation, famine…never known a single damned one of them surrender. They kicked the French's ass and now they're kicking ours. See, Alysson, unlike you and me, they *want* to be here—don't touch that!"

Alysson had been about to reach for the ammo box, but withdrew his hand.

"Don't touch anything. Open that box, could be a live grenade inside waiting for you. I told you, they love them some traps."

"Jeez. Anything else I should know?"

"Yeah. Lots. Come on, this is a dead end. Let's go back down."

They dropped back into the tunnel and continued to edge around the snaking bend. Alysson's nerves had settled somewhat now. He trusted White, he realised. The sergeant had a quiet authority that inspired confidence, even in the breathless dark of the tunnel complex. That was more than he could say for some of the squad leaders in 4th platoon, including his own. Somehow, Alysson felt safer in that tunnel, with White, than he had walking patrol under his assigned sergeant.

That soon changed.

"Damn it."

In the red light of their torches, the scummy water looked like blood.

"Is it flooded?" asked Alysson.

"No," replied White. "You can swim, right?"

"Swim? In that?"

They had been underground for an hour now, passing through another makeshift dormitory, a small storeroom filled with scavenged bits of metal—bomb shrapnel, discarded brass, even empty soda cans—and a brutal spike trap comprising two log rollers studded with punji sticks, in a small pit beneath a breakaway floor.

Now, the tunnel seemed to end in a small pool of stagnant water.

"It's a U-bend. Seals off the rest of the network in case we try to gas them out. Only way on is through. Shouldn't be far. You'd better go first."

"Me?" Alysson was alarmed.

"You've got the wire. When you get to the other side, tug it, and I'll follow you through."

"I dunno, man," said Alysson doubtfully. "What if it's a dead end?"

"I told you, it's just a gas barrier. If you do hit a dead end though, turn around, come back."

Unless the pool widened out substantially underwater, it didn't look like there would be enough room to turn round. Alysson tried to imagine swimming backwards, and couldn't.

"Won't the water fuck up our guns?" he suggested, desperately.

"Nope. I'll need to scrounge some WD-40 from somewhere when we get topside, but they'll be fine for now. Your light's waterproof, too, so use it. Be careful when you break surface," White continued, "in case Charlie's waiting for you with a garrotte. Hey," he added, seeing the uncertainty on Alysson's face, "this is what you volunteered for, guy. This is what it means to be a tunnel rat. Go on. You'll be fine. Take a deep breath and just go for it."

Alysson had run out of excuses. Kneeling at the edge of the pool, he began to hyperventilate, oxygenating his blood as much as he could, until he became dizzy and a strange kind of euphoria settled on his brain. He thought briefly of his parents, wondering what they imagined he was doing at that moment and how far from the truth it was. What would the military tell them if he simply drowned, head-down, in a pitch-black tunnel, forty feet beneath the forest floor?

He found himself pitching forwards, taking the decision without meaning to, plunging head-first into the pool. His face broke through a surface layer of algal slime into depths that were disconcertingly warm, like swimming through a lake of tears. Panicking, he stretched forwards with his torch and forced his eyes open, revealing only red-lit silt and swirling mud. As his feet followed him down he fought the urge to retreat, kicking out with his legs and hitting the rough walls around him, banging his head on the low roof and involuntarily releasing a stream of bubbles from his nose.

He fluttered his feet again, seeking the bottom of the channel with his fingertips to pull himself along.

Gruesome insects swam about him, attracted by the flashlight as he reached the tunnel's lowest point. He scudded a few more feet, then rolled onto his back, the better to navigate its upwards turn, tangling his legs in the trailing commo wire as he did so. It didn't matter. The buoyancy of the air in his lungs was pushing him upwards now, with gathering speed.

Too late, he remembered White's warning about garrottes, breaching like a whale, with a vast gasp and snort of relief. In a panic, he swung the flashlight left and right looking for any sign of hostiles, but found none.

The U-bend had only been five or six yards long, he realised, but had felt much longer. If asked, he could have sworn he'd spent a full minute underwater. Giving the commo wire a couple of sharp tugs and slamming the squawk button twice, he clambered out of the duct into a new tunnel, which was slightly wider and higher than the one he'd left behind.

It took him a moment to notice the smell. Sweet, pungent, and unmistakably organic, at first he wondered if it was coming from him, perhaps from the water he'd just swum through—but, no, it was in the air all around him and seemed to be coming from somewhere up ahead.

"Told ya it'd be fine."

Alysson jumped at the sound of White's voice. The sergeant's head had emerged noiselessly from the pool behind him.

"Jesus, Sarge! Rabbit, I mean..."

White heaved himself out and shook the water from his pistol while Alysson peered off into the gloom.

"Rabbit...what's that smell?"

White sniffed the air and grimaced. "That, buddy, is death."

They crouch-walked down the uneven, veering corridor, guns at the ready. The stench of decomposition grew stronger the further they went. Alysson suppressed the urge to gag, not wanting to make any noise that might alert a skulking enemy.

The reek had become overpowering by the time White leaned carefully around the next corner, keeping his flashlight away from his body, ready to duck back should bullets greet him. When nothing happened, he stepped out of cover, beckoning Alysson on.

Another twenty yards of tunnel stretched ahead, but the walls here had been messily excavated; lumps of clay, soil, and rock littered the floor where someone had dug into them on either side. For a moment White and Alysson continued their advance, but once the light from their torches revealed the contents of those untidy cavities, they came to a halt.

"Jesus Christ..." muttered White, playing his light over the scene.

A thicket of decaying body parts protruded from the exposed clay: limp arms, dangling legs, and more than one putrefying human head.

Alysson felt his gorge inexorably rising and backed away fast, cracking his head on the roof as he did so and falling over backwards. Trying to get up again, he lost control and puked in the corner they had just turned.

"Hey—hey, Alysson, it's okay. They can't harm you. Come on, get it together."

"What—what happened here?" was all Alysson could manage as White helped him to his feet.

"They stow their dead in the walls down here. Stops us being able to estimate their casualties. Looks like someone decided to dig 'em out again."

"Why?" asked Alysson, more plaintively than he would have liked.

"Fucked if I know."

Alysson stared at the carnage, unable to tear his eyes away. A blackened, slime-coated face stared back, frozen in a moment of terrified sorrow. It was the closest Alysson had been to the enemy, alive or dead, since arriving in-country. He couldn't help trying to undo the corrosion in his mind's eye, to picture the man—the boy—as he would have looked in life: plump-lipped, flat-nosed, wide-eyed...not all that different to Alysson's own face, he realised.

"Sooner we're past 'em, sooner the air'll clear," declared White, and grabbed Alysson by the chin. "Let's look alive."

"Roger that," nodded Alysson, composing himself.

"Good man."

He tried to avoid looking at the disinterred remains as they sidled past, but the flashlight's carmine glow still showed him things he didn't wish to see: amputations, gouged flesh, torn viscera.

"Rabbit," he whispered, hesitantly. "They—they look like they've been *eaten*."

White looked over his shoulder. "Rats big as dogs down here, kid," he said, before moving on. "Keep your cool."

"'*Rats as big as dogs*.' I know what fucking rat bites look like," muttered Alysson unhappily, following him.

"Holy shit, they got *lights* down here?" breathed Alysson, gazing open-mouthed at the dead bulbs daisy-chained from the ceiling at the crossroads they had reached.

"Sometimes," said White, pausing to check his compass. "There'll be a bicycle-powered genny somewhere. Guess it makes for good exercise when you're stuck down here."

"I'll be goddamned... Wait, they're moving. See that? They're swaying."

"Breeze from a ventilation point, maybe. Maybe just the air cooling now it's night. Starting to think Charlie bugged out of here in a big hurry," said White, looking down each of the three tunnels leading off from the junction.

"How you figure that?"

"No one around. They'd have heard us coming by now. Left their stuff behind, didn't set any new traps for us...dunno. Don't like it."

"I thought you said they never surrendered."

"They don't."

"So..."

"Dunno. Stay sharp. Watch our six. Let's follow these lights."

The chain of light bulbs led straight on, down a slight incline. At intervals, hatches hidden in the floor indicated the existence of another level, below. They carefully lifted each one, checking for ambushers, but found only empty chambers and another tunnel, running perpendicular to the one they were in.

"Rabbit, what's that?" said Alysson after they closed the third such hatch, squinting at something right at the limit of their lights' range. "Something moved up there."

They both directed their beams ahead, revealing a torn sheet of material, flapping from the entrance to a side-chamber into which the swaying string of bulbs disappeared. It rippled and undulated silently, flowing like a chiffon scarf in the faint breeze. In the red light from their torches, it looked ink-black, reflecting nothing.

"If I know Charlie, that's a field hospital," said White, moving towards it. "They line 'em with our parachutes, try and keep things sterile."

"No shit? Clever little bastards."

"They find a use for everything. You drop a deuce, they'll probably pick it up. Explains the blood, too."

"Blood?"

Rabbit pointed at the floor ahead. Unmistakeable, bloody drag marks emerged from the entrance beyond the billowing fabric, leading away from them, deeper into the tunnels.

"Watch that corner," cautioned White as they approached, keeping his own gun trained on the side-chamber. Alysson did so, his mouth dry, his flesh creeping with tension. The blood on the ground had long-since dried and darkened, but it gleamed like rubies in the complementary red rays of their lights. Pints of it had been spilled. Whoever had been dragged had either been dead or very nearly so.

They edged around until they could see into the makeshift hospital. White had been right: its roof, walls, and floor had been covered with sagging parachute nylon, making Alysson think of Bedouin tents and *The Arabian Nights*. In a couple of places, the 'chutes had been ripped away, torn down like shower curtains to expose the hard clay behind. Blood had sprayed, run, and dripped everywhere, as if the interior had been redecorated by a homicidal Jackson Pollock. A sticky pool of it had collected in the centre of the room, where a toppled chair and broken crutch lay in it.

"Jeez Louise," breathed Alysson.

"Ain't that some shit?" agreed White. He nodded at the nylon ceiling. "That's arterial spray. Some poor dope got wasted here."

"And not by us."

"Maybe he was one of ours."

"Fuck...Hey, what you doing?"

White had dipped his fingers into a large cracked jar that lay overturned on the floor, oozing some kind of gel. Alysson winced as he brought them up to his nose, then put them in his mouth.

"Ugh, Rabbit! What is that?"

"Honey. It's good! Want some?"

"No, thanks. Why the fuck is there a jar of honey?"

"They don't got disinfectants or antibiotics, any of that shit, so they use honey to kill germs. Some real shit must've gone down here. No way they'd leave all this behind."

They scanned the room, taking in the improvised dressings scattered about the floor, the crude stretcher, now snapped in half against the wall, the makeshift operating table with its suggestive rope straps.

They both saw it at the same moment.

"There's a guy!"

"Contact!"

White dropped into a shooting crouch, arms extended, revolver and flashlight both aimed at the slender foot protruding from beneath the torn down parachute in the corner. Alysson copied him, going down on one knee on the gory floor.

"Cover the door, man!" snapped White, his tone frustrated.

"Sorry!"

Alysson pivoted to aim his gun into the corridor instead. Behind him, he heard White gingerly creep towards the prostrate figure they had glimpsed. There was a rustle of nylon, then a sigh.

"Relax, kid. Already dead."

Instantly, the tension drained away. Alysson, too, let out a sigh of relief. He glanced over his shoulder and saw White nudging the dead body with the toe of his boot. Checking the entrance one last time, he backed towards the sergeant.

"It's a girl!" he exclaimed, looking down.

"Never seen a girl before?"

The girl wore the black pyjamas of a Viet Cong guerrilla. A large gash on her forehead had been neatly stitched, and the stumps of two missing fingers were crudely bandaged.

"No...just wasn't expecting it, you know?" said Alysson, feeling stupid.

"Yeah, well get used to it. These VC broads'll fuck you up. Third lost seven guys to one bitch with an M-14 a few months back. Shot with our own fucking guns." White solemnly shook his head. "This one's been dead a while—infection, maybe. Well, saves us having to drag her ass back upstairs, I g—"

There was a loud splintering sound from the body. Alysson jumped as though stung, while White took a measured pace backwards and aimed his gun once more.

"The fuck was that?"

The sound came again, and the dead body's lip curled as though caught on an invisible fishing hook, one cheek swelling and distending.

"What the fuck, man?"

Alysson had his own gun trained on the corpse now, his hand shaking wildly. One of the dead woman's eyes began to bulge from her face, canting as it protruded. Two gouts of congealing blood erupted from her nostrils. Her mouth began to open.

"You said she was dead!"

"She *is* dead! Keep your fucking voice down, kid! Back up!"

They backed up, keeping their guns and lights on the twitching cadaver as its jaw yawned like a python's. A faint glow could be discerned behind the dead girl's teeth. It brightened rapidly as her jaw dislocated with a loud *crack* and—horribly, impossibly—a claw-tipped, luminescent arm emerged from her mouth and clamped viciously onto her face.

"Rabbit, what the FUCK?"

Another arm followed it and cast about for something to grip, dripping with blood and brain matter. They were tiny, a doll's arms, lean and skeletal but powerfully strong, glowing with unholy phosphorescence.

The corpse's skull buckled yet more as something monstrous began twisting into view, its obscene gestation complete. There was a creak of straining bone and cartilage. Alysson could see the sharp little talons cut into dead flesh as the cadaver-born *thing* tried to pull itself free. He wanted to run but couldn't remember how—couldn't remember how to do anything but stare in mute, uncomprehending terror.

The woman's throat bulged hideously as something chewed and fought its way through the foramen magnum. Finally, it emerged, like a lizard from an egg: a pale and luciferous homunculus, flecked with gore. Its tiny, elongated head reminded Alysson of a chimpanzee skull he had once seen in a museum. There was something canine, too, about its long snout and grinning jaws. Its eyes were large and lidless, exophthalmic, clearly designed for life underground, in what little light came from the creature's own body.

Still retreating, Alysson's heel caught the broken crutch in the middle of the room, sending it skittering across the floor. Instantly, the vile parasite's head swivelled towards the source of the noise. Its bulbous, unblinking eyes fixed on Alysson, and its doglike mouth opened, revealing tiny, fang-like incisors.

Moments later, a high-pitched, keening shriek filled the cave. The sound seemed to overwhelm Alysson's nervous system like an electric shock, sending him to his knees. From the corner of his eye, he saw White stagger sideways and fall, like a boxer whose legs had gone. Without meaning to, Alysson jerked the trigger of his gun.

The sudden explosion blinded and deafened him, as White had warned it would. There was a terrifying zip of ricochets as the 130 grain .38 Special careened around the room like a trapped bird, making Alysson flinch and cower.

The screeching had stopped. Alysson could move again, his ears still ringing. He looked up in time to see the newborn scavenger scuttle from the room, bounding on all fours. It looked back for a second, bared its teeth in a snarl, and was gone.

"Jesus, *fuck!* Rabbit, you okay?"

Alysson tried to help the sergeant up, but was slapped away.

"You are one stupid motherfucker," said Rabbit, angrily, getting to his feet. "You're goddamned lucky that bullet didn't kill me, or you. If you're gonna shoot, make sure you fucking hit!"

"I didn't mean to! It was an accident."

"You think that makes it better?"

"Rabbit—what the fuck was that? What was that *thing*?"

White shook his head. "Man, I don't know…mongoose or something."

"A *mongoose*? Come on, man, that was no fucking mongoose! It was in her *head*, man!"

"How do you know? You ever see a mongoose? Shit, maybe it was a bearcat."

"Wasn't no fucking cat, man! It was…"

"What? What was it, then?" demanded White, rounding on him. "What do you think you fucking saw?"

"A Martian?"

"Jesus fucking Christ, man, a *Martian*?"

Alysson could picture the rest of the unit, listening over the microphone on his chest and laughing at him. He didn't care.

"Look, I don't fucking know, all right? Some kind of fucking cave monster! It climbed out her fucking *mouth*! It glowed in the dark, man!"

White grabbed Alysson by the shoulders and shoved him back against the nylon-draped wall. "Get it together! Keep your fucking voice down! You forget where we fucking are? Listen—listen to me," he continued, his voice barely more than a hoarse murmur. "Whatever that thing was, we're gonna come back down here with a flamethrower and barbecue its fucking ass, okay? Then, we're gonna lay demo charges and blow this whole place to hell. That sound good? That sound like a plan you can get behind? Nod your fucking head!"

Alysson nodded, slowly at first, then more vigorously.

"Okay, good! Now...Charlie's bugged out—time we did the same. We're gonna look for an exit. Reload your gun, square your head away, and let's do it. Oh, and if we see that thing running around out there again, shoot like you mean it, next time."

"Okay," said Alysson, starting to feel calmer, glad to know they would soon be topside again. "I'll blow its fucking head off!"

"Attaboy. Look lively, now."

White took the lead again. Rather than returning the way they had come, he kept following the corridor they had been in, still creeping stealthily, gun at the ready. Alysson kept behind him and concentrated on copying his movements, occasionally casting a nervous glance behind.

The tunnel snaked up and down, twisting through switchbacks and hairpins as they went along. It's muddy floor recorded scores of sets of footprints, some shod, some barefoot, some long, narrow and...clawed.

"Rabbit, you see these footprints?"

"I see 'em."

"What the fuck made those?"

"Don't know; don't want to know. Keep moving."

They made cursory inspections of a couple of hatches in the roof, which led only to dead-end chambers. Then, the roof became so low they were forced onto hands and knees again, crawling another thirty yards before reaching the end, where they were able to slither down to a comparatively large, uneven hollow, some twenty feet across.

Two other dark hallways led off from this nexus, about which shovels, picks, rope, and buckets were carelessly strewn. An overturned wheelbarrow had spilled its cargo of rock and clay nearby, and in the centre of the chamber was a gaping hole surrounded by banked earth. White leaned cautiously over the edge and shone his flashlight into it.

"Straight down," he said, and hocked phlegm into the shaft.

"Were they mining something down here?" wondered Alysson, aloud. After the electric lights and makeshift hospital, he would not have been surprised to discover the complex also contained a fully-functioning quarry.

"Nah. Charlie's been digging himself a well."

"Busy little bastards…"

Alysson joined White at the lip of the shaft. "Don't see no water," he commented, supplementing White's feeble flashlight beam with his own.

"Nah. Looks like they ran into a cave system before they hit water. See that fissure, there?"

Alysson saw it, right at the bottom of the well, maybe thirty feet down, at the limit of their lights' range: a jagged, horizontal crack, perhaps cut over aeons by the water the diggers had been seeking. Something next to it caught Alysson's attention: pale and straight, it stood out against the jagged outlines of debris. It took him a moment to identify it.

"Rabbit—is that a fucking *bone* down there?"

"Where?"

"Right by that cave hole. Looks like a bone."

"Yeah…looks like it."

"Where'd it come from?"

"A leg. You can see the joint."

Alysson shuddered involuntarily, feeling suddenly cold despite the airless heat of the tunnels. First, whatever that freakish, glowing creature had been, now stripped human bones—he wanted out.

"Rabbit—"

"I know. Let's head that way. It goes up." White indicated one of the two possible unexplored tunnels. Alysson agreed and circled around the half-dug well in that direction, then stopped and frowned. Were his eyes playing tricks on him? Had being underground, staring into the red light for over an hour, done something to them?

"Is that daylight?" he said, with mounting excitement.

There was unmistakably a glow of light coming from the tunnel they were approaching. Behind him, Rabbit reached forward and lay a hand on his shoulder.

"Shhh!"

Alysson froze. They had only seen one other source of light down there and this one was growing brighter. There was a noise coming from the tunnel, too: the faint sound of something dragging along the floor. He trained his gun on the entrance, ready to shoot the scampering gremlin should it reappear.

It definitely wasn't daylight. It had the same sickly quality as the phosphorescence emitted by the monster—the alien—whatever it had been. Was it radioactive? Some kind of nuclear mutant secret weapon, released on the battlefield by the communists to poison them?

The noise coming from the tunnel stopped. Alysson heard the click of White turning off his flashlight and did the same. White's hand clamped onto his shoulder and gently drew him backwards, then pressed down until he was on the ground, the banked earth around the well against his cheek.

The darkness was almost total, only the faint, flickering lambency of whatever approached them providing any point of reference. Alysson stared at it until his vision swam, ready to duck down behind cover once it appeared, but needing to know what it was. It resumed its approach and, moments later, skulked into full view.

It moved on all fours, wolf-like. A spindly, hunchbacked monstrosity, it could only be the progenitor of the hatchling they had encountered in the infirmary. Were it to stand upright, it would be as tall as Alysson himself. Its teeth were an inch or more long, and between them it gripped the wrist of the corpse it was dragging: the decaying, black-clad body of a Viet Cong fighter. A rancid aroma of decomposition came with it, and Alysson could only believe this cadaver, too, had been dug out of the tunnel walls.

The loathsome thing paused and turned its head from side to side, sniffing. A low growl escaped its throat, then rapidly became something very like...laughter: a coarse, baritone chuckle which turned Alysson's blood to ice. The sound of it echoed down the well shaft, eerie and unmistakably malevolent.

Alysson dared not move, dared not so much as breathe, as the ghoul pushed the corpse it had claimed up the small embankment opposite him and toppled it into the well. After a moment in which they anticipated it, it hit the bottom with a crunch of breaking bone. The ghoul sighed with what seemed like satisfaction. Its long tongue flickered out, tasting the air like a snake's, and with another growl it began to stalk around the well's perimeter.

Alysson felt White's hand slap his shoulder, and a moment later was blasted by hot ejecta from the cylinder gap of the sergeant's revolver. The gun roared in his ear, deafening him, and the ghoulish thing tumbled backwards, rolling onto its back.

A second later, it was up again, keeping low to the ground on all fours. Whatever bioluminscence it was emitting faded to almost nothing in an instant, reducing the thing to little more than a faint grey outline, a mere trick of the light. White fired again, but the horror scuttled sideways, crablike, and seemed unhurt.

Remembering his own gun, Alysson tried to aim but had lost the target. Was that it—or that? Or were they just after-images, ghostly impressions swirling on his retinas?

Not wanting to hit White, he flicked on his flashlight at the same moment White turned on his. For a second, there was no sign of the creature—but then he saw it, flattened against the ceiling, clinging like a spider and stealthily advancing towards them. Before either of them could draw a bead on it, it sprang forward with a snarl, landing in a crouch at Alysson's feet.

The next thing Alysson knew, his flashlight was spinning through the air as the thing batted it from his hand and closed its long, strong fingers about his throat, abruptly choking him. Its touch was cold and dry, and burned like bleach. It was blazing with light again now, like a creature from the blackest ocean deeps, lifting him into the air with ease. The expression on its hound-like face was cruel and triumphant, its breath a rancid gust of decay. Its bulging, white eyes moved independently, like a chameleon's, one swivelling to keep track of White while the other bored into Alysson with cold, alien hate.

Alysson could feel his larynx crumpling in the thing's fist. Its skull jerked towards him, quick as lightning, easily evading White's point-blank gunshot before seizing the sergeant's wrist with its free hand. White responded by leaping onto the monster's back and locking his arm around its neck, trying to use his weight to drag it to the ground.

The ghoul staggered, sputtering foul gobbets of putrid flesh, and Alysson felt its grip on his throat loosen. He lashed out with his feet and was suddenly released, falling painfully to the ground as the beast turned its full attention on White, both of them tumbling to the floor and rolling, locked together like fighting mink.

Gasping for breath, he got unsteadily to his feet, trying in vain to aim his gun at the growling monster without endangering White. The sergeant was on top of it now, pinning it to the ground and trying to keep out of reach of its snapping jaws.

"Fuck you!"

He headbutted the ghoul, hard enough to splinter its front teeth. The thing threw back its head and bayed like a wolf, the sound seeming to communicate excitement more than alarm. It echoed through the deserted warren—and was answered.

The answering call came from below, from the depths of the well shaft, shivering on the air like a summons from hell. Alysson leaned over to look, and saw two more glowing, cadaverous beasts scampering up the pit's uneven walls towards him.

"Rabbit!" he yelled. "Two more! Let's book!"

"Get outta here, kid!" shouted back White, bellowing in pain as the ghoul scrabbled at his midriff with its clawed feet, fighting like a cat. His bellow became an unending scream as the thing eviscerated him, blood deluging from his shredded abdomen as the monster cackled beneath him.

"Run!" screamed White, throwing himself to the side with the last of his strength, pulling the ghoul with him, rolling them both over the lip of the well.

Alysson gasped with horror as they plunged out of sight, leaving him alone in the darkness, both roaring in fury. Their bellows lasted only a moment, terminating in an abrupt and sickening thud. In the frozen seconds that followed, only agitated hissing rose from the darkness below.

Not wanting to know, not wanting to see, Alysson forced himself to look. His own flashlight had died when it hit the ground. He couldn't see where it had gone and didn't know if it would still work. White's had gone into the pit with him. Now, the darkness was total, instantly disorientating. He could feel it pressing in around him, almost hungry for him, eager to claim him forever. Groping blindly on hands and knees, he felt his way to the edge of the well and leaned over.

Two white, subtly glowing forms prowled the darkness in front of him. Distracted by the falling bodies, they had descended to the bottom of the shaft once more, where they seemed to be sniffing and pulling at something—presumably the shattered bodies of White and his foe.

Alysson could see little by the light of their faint incandescence until, suddenly, one of them grew brighter. White tongues of angelic light rippled across its body, revealing the sergeant's bent and broken remains in front of it. An unbearable pang of grief overcame Alysson at the sight, and tears welled in his eyes. White's determined, youthful face stared vacantly back, his own light extinguished forever.

The glimmering ghoul shifted, squatting over the dead man and hiding his face from view, settling on his head like a chicken on an egg. It burned even brighter, shining like a beacon now as it desecrated White's corpse.

Without warning, the loose clay under Alysson's hand gave way, and his hand shot out into empty space. A shower of soil and rock dust fell into the pit while he fought to regain his balance. The two ghouls looked up, and he knew they had seen him. They flared like white phosphorous, filling the well with light as they raised their heads and growled.

The one perched on White's head stayed where it was. The other sprang onto the wall and began climbing swiftly towards him, baring its teeth in an excited, imbecilic leer. Alysson leapt to his feet in a panic and ran blindly into the shadows, consumed by the need to escape. He had no hope of climbing back out the way they had entered before it was on him, but his mind's eye seized on the two other exits they had seen, and led his feet in the direction he remembered the nearest one having been. His outstretched arms met the chamber wall, and he felt his way along it until he found the opening. With a last, terrified glance behind him, at the rapidly-brightening aurora shining from the well's mouth, he hared into the tunnel, stumbling and sobbing in a wild funk of terror.

This tunnel was narrower and higher than the others they had traversed, with only a few inches clearance between his shoulders and the walls on either side. He careened off them, staggering as the passage zig-zagged left and right, before treading on a loose pebble that sent him sprawling to the ground.

The shock of hitting the floor made him freeze in place, pain breaking through his adrenaline rush. He was suddenly aware how much noise he had been making and how quiet it now was. Was the thing following him? Did it know where he had gone? Perhaps staying still and silent would be safer than racing through the maze of tunnels in the dark.

"Gibb'l'eh Nyogtha y'hah Pnath..."

The voice sent an involuntary shudder through Alysson's body. Burbling, plosive, and freighted with threat, the sound of it filled his mind with images of decay: dying flowers, swarming flies, crumbling bones, sprouting mold—a barrage of morbid impressions, startling in their vividity. Alone in the blackness, he could see nothing else, could think nothing else, and for a moment became nothing more than he was: a confused and terrified mammal, clinging pathetically to the surface of a doomed and whirling rock.

It was hunting him, he knew. The snuffling, croaking noises it made grew louder, and now a faint, white glow impinged on the perfect dark, rapidly growing brighter. The thing was in the tunnel with him, following his scent. He needed to escape but had forgotten how to move. His mind refused to focus on anything other than his abject horror and despair.

It lurched into view around the corner, no more than twenty feet away, forced onto its hind legs by the narrow confines of the tunnel, and fixed Alysson with its vacant, wall-eyed stare. In its claws it held the wire trailing from the spool at Alysson's back, leading it right to him. Its hound-like jaws parted in an ugly, triumphant sneer.

Alysson jerked the spool of wire from his belt and tore the microphone from his chest, gabbling into it and stuttering with fear.

"This is Alysson! If you can hear me, don't come down here! Rabbit's dead! Rabbit's dead, and I'm about to—there's *things*—there's things down here! Rabbit's dead, st—"

The ghoul yanked hard on the commo wire, whisking the mic from his trembling fingers, and advanced on him, rolling its shoulders as it strode forwards. Alysson retreated, still on the floor, his heels scrabbling at the tight-packed earth. It was no use. In mere moments it was looming over him, reaching for him with a festering sigh of satisfaction.

As he recoiled from the thing's groping, white claw, something dug into his lower back. He felt it stretch and snap, with a sudden *twang*. An instant later, he sensed something massive rushing towards him from above, and flinched just in time as a giant block of wood swept past, centimetres from his scalp.

The giant, swinging mace thudded into the ghoul with enough force to lift it off the ground. It would have sent the beast flying, but for the vicious stakes protruding from it. Instead, the creature was left skewered and hanging, frantically struggling to free itself from the bamboo spears now impaling its thorax and throat. It was blazing with light now, shedding clouds of glowing mould spores as it writhed, rending the air with bestial roars of pain.

Alysson's mind was swamped by the creature's anguish. His vision dissolved into stroboscopic flickering, like a fusillade of photographer's flashbulbs going off, the pain in his head amplifying until he was sure his skull would fracture. The transfixed ghoul continued glaring down at him, its grotesque face contorted by an expression of uttermost contempt.

Alysson's muscles began to spasm uncontrollably, and, with no other means of escape, his mind retreated swiftly into unconsciousness.

On your feet kid—now!

Alysson's brain spoke to him in White's voice, bringing him reluctantly back from oblivion. A ferocious migraine pounded in his head, and he felt sick. Every muscle in his body ached and twitched, as though he had run a marathon. His throat and nose felt clogged with something vile, his taste buds saturated by something unfamiliar and repulsive, making him gag and spit.

He opened his eyes, but the blackness persisted. The tunnel was still, but from somewhere nearby came the sound of steady, relentless dripping. He groped blindly in the darkness and encountered his discarded reel of commo wire. So, he hadn't moved, or been moved; he just didn't know which way he was facing, or where to go.

You got matches, don't you?

He did! In his pocket was a tube of army-issue waterproof matches, maybe twenty of them. With shaking hands he fumbled for them, opened the tube with difficulty and, at the fifth or sixth attempt, succeeded in applying one to the striker.

The match's flare blinded him instantly, forcing him to shield his eyes. Once his pupils had contracted sufficiently, he turned his head and almost yelped aloud at the sight of the dead ghoul. Even in death, its lips were curled in a malefic sneer, its lidless eyes baleful and opaque. Whatever ichor had flowed through its veins now pooled on the ground beneath it, the drips only now gradually slowing.

"Ow!"

The match burned Alysson's fingers and he quickly discarded it, rushing to strike another.

Get moving, kid. Come on! Fight or die.

"Yeah. I'm on it."

There was no way back without pushing his way past the mace trap and its dangling victim, but he knew he didn't have enough matches to light his way back to the entrance they'd used anyway. He could only press on and hope to find another way out, or another source of light. He forced himself to stand, swayed for a moment until his heart caught up with the exertion, then turned his back on the dead monster and stumbled forwards.

He went as quickly as he dared, terrified he would step on another booby-trap in the gloom, and wishing he'd been carrying the signalling flares, instead of White. At least the passage he was in seemed to be leading upwards now. He would take being captured by the VC over spending another minute underground.

As luck would have it, by the time his tenth match burned out he had found a small kitchen area, in which were the remains of a cooking fire. Amid the ashes were some pieces of unburned wood, the largest of which, with the expenditure of another few matches and a lot of gentle blowing, he managed to reignite. The flame was feeble and flickering, but brighter, at least, than his precious matches. Shielding it with his hand, and blinking away tears as the smoke stung his eyes, he continued searching for an exit.

The tunnels were eerily quiet, now. Alysson passed deserted alcoves and antechambers, climbed over abandoned defensive positions, and carefully picked his way past another tripwire, but began to despair of ever finding a way out of the subterranean maze.

When he did find it, he almost missed it: a series of wooden stakes, driven into the wall to create a makeshift ladder, leading up through a narrow chute in the roof. With his smouldering torch beginning to die, he climbed them. At the top was a heavy trapdoor that took all his strength to lift. A gust of fresh, cold air instantly extinguished the remains of his torch.

His teeth began to chatter uncontrollably as he realised he had done it—he had found a way out. The darkness above was the darkness of night, the silence now broken by the chattering of a million forest insects all around. The trapdoor had rocks and soil glued to it, fashioned to look like a small termite mound, and he was emerging from the forest floor.

Climbing out into the midnight air felt like rebirth, like baptism, like waking from a nightmare. Alysson rolled over on the ground and paused for a moment to savour the breeze, letting it flood his lungs and displace the foul miasma of the tunnels, his filthy skin bathed by the gently-falling rain.

He had done it.

He had escaped.

He was free.

He opened his mouth and began to sing, hoarsely at first, then lustily and with growing joy:

"I—think…we're alone now! *I think we're alone now! There doesn't seem to be anyone around!*"

Overcome by elation, he began to laugh hysterically, and pounded the ground with his fists.

Only then did strong fingers close around his ankles and yank him back into the Black Echo. Terror returned, and with it vertigo. He was falling—the trapdoor above him was swinging closed—a tenebrous voice echoed in his head: "*Ghulah n'ghft k'naa ngoth!*" His body was crumbling as he spun through the air, becoming powder, becoming dust. His shrieking faltered as his larynx disintegrated, his hands splintering to pieces before his eyes and floating away like wisps of burnt paper.

He woke up, screaming into the darkness of the hospital ward, fighting with the straps that kept him confined to his bed. Lights converged on him from the shadows—not ghouls this time, but orderlies wielding penlights and syringes.

He screamed as they wrestled him back onto the bed and pinned him down. "*It's in my head! Don't you understand? Get it out! There's one in my head!*"

"Shh, relax, Private Alysson. Go back to sleep," whispered one of the orderlies, gripping him by the chin as the sedatives began to take effect. Alysson's vision swam and his muscles sagged as the drug pulled him into its embrace, and within seconds he was comatose once more.

The orderlies sighed collectively and returned to their station at the end of the ward, where a dark-suited man was poring over the new patient's records by torchlight.

"How long?" he asked.

"Not long," answered one of them. "According to the X-ray, maybe two or three days."

"Good," replied the stranger, satisfied. "The deployment in Quáng Trj was a success, but the bioweapons were not retrieved. Special Actions need replacements as soon as you have them."

"Yes, sir. We'll transport it to the reproduction facility as soon as we can."

"Good." The stranger stubbed out his cigarette and rose to leave. "CORDS will arrange the …materiel. Fine work, gentlemen! It may be writing cheques to the devil, but we'll win this war yet!"

In his dreams, Alysson screamed without end.

Dangerous Dogs

By David Hambling

"The price of a changeling, I suppose—you know the old myth about how the weird people leave their spawn in cradles in exchange for the human babes they steal."

HP Lovecraft, *"Pickman's Model"*

"Homo homini lupus est" [Man is wolf to another man]
Titus Maccius Plautus, *"Asinaria"*

London, 2024

Janine raced ahead, jogging with the three Bull Terriers on taut leads like a warrior queen in a chariot pulled by war hounds, with Lydia trailing behind.

Janine was always in the lead. First on the karaoke, the first on the dance floor, first on the Espresso Martinis. She was also the first up in the morning, taking the dogs out for a run and completing a module of her animal nursing course before her flat mates crawled out of their hangovers. Janine was first to arrive at work, first to step up when anyone needed a hand. Even after a long day's work and cleaning out kennels she was full of energy, which is why she had hurried Lydia to get here on an urgent mission before the cemetery gates closed for the night.

Janine had the same appetite for life as the dogs. To them every day was a new adventure, every walk was exciting, everyone they met was a new best friend. They bounded up to meet life with happily wagging tails. Their owners rarely had half the zest for life their charges had.

"There it is!" Janine and Lydia yelled in unison as they saw the gates across the road.

West Norwood Cemetery, South London's great Necropolis, where thousands of bodies and thirteen geocaches were hidden, was waiting for them. Its wrought iron gates stood gaping open under the white arch like something from an old Hammer Horror flick.

The dogs automatically sat down in a row on the kerb and waited to cross at the light, giving Lydia time to catch up. Two Asian women in headscarves made a wide detour, darting nervous looks at the dogs. Janine smiled reassuringly at them while one-handedly extracting her phone and flicking to the geocaching app.

The crossing lights went green.

"Go, doggies!" called Janine, and they stampeded together across the road, past a war memorial and through the cemetery gates. Beyond stood an avenue of tombs like grey cottages topped with angels and crosses.

A pair of police officers stepped out from behind the gate posts. They were equipped with the Met's full array of law enforcement hardware: body armour festooned with loops and clips, earpiece trailing a tightly coiled wire, handcuffs, batons, yellow-handled Taser, pepper spray, all secured with a fetishist's dream of Velcro straps.

"Excuse me," said the male officer. He spoke with the careful neutrality of an official, as though he had not noticed the blue streaks in Janine's blonde hair, the tats, the silver lip-ring, and made his own conclusions about her lifestyle choices. But for now he seemed entirely focused on the three dogs. "Are those your dogs?"

Janine flashed a smile. "Uh-huh. It's okay to take dogs in, isn't it?"

Janine sensed Lydia's tension next to her. The dogs, who might have been made anxious by the scrutiny from oddly dressed strangers, were chill. Lydia was not. She had once told Janine, when they had called the police to deal with an irate and drunken client, that nobody in Greece called the police unless they were desperate, or rich. Ingrained distrust was difficult to shake off. Lydia needed more positive experiences with British police.

"Do you live around here?" He had not returned her smile.

"Colliers Wood. It's just a few stops on the Northern line."

She tried another smile.

"Not many people bring their dogs that far for a walk," said the PC, determinedly neutral. His colleague was looking over the Staffies, who looked back, tails wagging contentedly. Janine shortened the leads so she did not have to stand back and shout. "Have you been here before?"

Janine bit back a joke about 'do you come here often?' but tried to match the officer's tone and facial expression.

"No, first time," she said.

"Is that one an XL Bully?" The female officer asked, pointing at Pixie.

"No, they're all Staffies." Janine counted them off: "Hagrid's just a big boy. The others are Wolverine and Pixie."

Janine was used to this. The police had their own view on which dogs were legally accepted Staffordshire Bull Terriers and which were banned Pit Bulls and XL Bullies. The police had the final say on whether or not a dog was a banned breed. XL Bullies were determined by size — anything over twenty inches at the shoulder but other aspects like 'blocky head' and 'deep chest' were police judgements. Anything could be deemed dangerous, regardless of actual ancestry. Anything could be a Pit Bull if the police said it was. If they decided a dog was illegal, it was a death sentence. The main thing was not to let a dog get dragged into a legal process which it might not come out of.

"There have been some incidents with dogs in the cemetery," said the first PC. "Dangerous dogs."

"Really -- what incidents?" asked Lydia, alert when animal welfare was at stake.

"Are you the registered owner?" The first PC asked Janine.

"Yep. They all came from the charity animal hospital in Collier's Wood—we're both animal nurses there."

"Ah, right." He was fractionally more relaxed. As Janine hoped, the fact of their being nurses, even animal nurses, changed things. "We'll just need to take a few details."

The PCs took their names and addresses, without explaining why they needed the information. Janine co-operated with everything, though the questioning had an insistent tone as though they were trying to elicit some information that Janine and Lydia were concealing. After another close scrutiny of the dogs, and a reminder to dial 101 if they saw anything, and warning them that the cemetery gates would be closed in half an hour, the officers allowed them to enter. Janine maintained her poker face as they went.

"I thought he was going to make us turn out our pockets," Janine whispered to Lydia when they were out of earshot, and they both giggled. Janine's pockets were stuffed with poo bags, dog treats and tug toys.

"They didn't even ask why we were here," said Lydia.

"Just as well."

You need some front for Geocaching. It is a real-life treasure hunt with a virtual component, with millions of enthusiasts worldwide, but outside of the closed circle of devotees it is unknown. Geocachers seek out hidden containers stashed in public spaces, purely for the sake of being able to tick them off on the geocaching website. Crawling under park benches and scaling trees in public is not for the timid, and geocachers tend to prefer places where there are less people about.

Cachers are guided by a combination of GPS co-ordinates and cryptic clues. Sometimes the challenge is reaching the GZ—Ground Zero, the location—but usually the frustrating part is finding the cache. Even a metre away, a nano cache the size of a ballpoint pen cap can be hidden in a hundred places, inside hollow fence posts or between courses of bricks. Finding them is an art.

The cemetery was a great place for caching: not many people around and a million overgrown hiding places, crumbly stonework everywhere. The target was a multi-cache, with a set of clues scattered about the cemetery and a physical cache at the end of it. That was enough for Janine to "egg her comma" as the cool kids said, for her score to reach the magic one thousand caches mark.

The series of caches in the cemetery was called "Death Match," and it looked like they had all been put down by the same setter at the same time. A compass arrow on Janine's phone pointed to the first cache in the series. Fifty metres straight ahead down the path, past the Gothic cottage which housed the cemetery administration.

"The clue is 'Maximum Destruction'," Janine told Lydia.

"What does that mean?"

"Don't know, but it's only rated 1/1 so it can't be that hard. That means it's an easy clue in easy terrain."

1/1 would be a gentle introduction. 5/1 would be a fiendishly cryptic clue that was easy to reach. 1/5 could be an easy clue at the top of a tree, which was why serious cachers came with ropes and harnesses. Janine was not expecting any of that, just an outing with a helpful non-cacher.

A woman approached them pushing an empty buggy. A small child ran from behind her, heading directly for the three dogs walking in front of Janine.

"Sit, doggies," instructed Janine. All three stopped and sat obediently on their haunches as the little boy dashed up. He stopped short of them at the last moment, suddenly uncertain. Janine squatted down, eye level with the boy.

"Just stay still and let them come to you," she said softly.

The boy looked back at his mother, then stood there, arms at his side. The three dogs, understanding Janine without needing to be told, came forward, tails swishing gently from side to side.

"He loves dogs," said the woman with the buggy.

"These are Wolverine, Pixie and Hagrid," said Janine. "Stand quietly and see if they'd like to sniff you, as that's how dogs learn about you. Always let dogs come to you. You know why? It's because you're so big and scary to them and they're frightened if you rush up."

The boy laughed at being big and scary.

The dogs sniffed all around him, and Hagrid licked at the boy's hand which made him laugh again. Janine showed the boy how to pet dogs, then produced some dog treats and showed him how to scatter them in front of him so each of the dogs got some.

"Staffies are great with kids," Janine told the mother. "They're very gentle dogs, and they don't mind rough handling."

If, Janine mentally added to herself, you pick the right dog. But at the moment she was the breed's publicity agent and a bit of spin was justified, especially after all the bad press.

"I thought I might get one. For protection. 'Cos I'm on my own, y'know."

"Having a dog does make you feel safer," said Janine. "But they need a lot of walking and they're not really suitable for small flats."

"There's loads of them on the estate," said the woman. "All the boys used to have them. Now they've ended up with the mums."

After completing her small session of animal awareness training, Janine found Lydia studying her phone.

"Oh my god," Lydia said, sounding the last word with an elongated Californian 'gaaad'. "This is terrible. You know what the policeman said about incidents? There is a story in the local paper that they found human bones chewed by dogs."

"What?"

"They say the drug dealers starve their dogs for a week, then bring them here and dig up bodies which have just been buried. They say they do it to give their dogs a taste for human flesh."

"That's so sick," said Janine. No wonder the police were interested when they saw her with her three Staffies. "As in bad sick, not good sick. If it's even true, which it probably isn't."

"Well, I know Staffie owners like that," said Lydia. "Like Mr Hewitt, he's really scary."

Staffies, XL Bullies and Pit Bulls were the weapon dogs of choice for the wannabe urban gangsta, status symbols to make people respect you and keep their distance. They were kept in concrete pens, fed sporadically, and socialised badly if at all. Status dogs were bought and sold for a few hundred pounds, then dumped on girlfriends and mothers when the owner could no longer be bothered.

Janine hated to see animals treated so badly. The one good thing was that they often developed a close bond with their owner. Some of the real hard cases came over all soppy when they talked about their Killer or Tyson and would go to any length to get treatment. Mr Hewitt, rumoured to be the local drug kingpin, had been in tears over his dog's eye infection. And the dogs seemed to adore their owners, however badly they were neglected.

In fact it was all a neat illustration of the central theme of the dissertation Janine had been writing for the last few months, which had the working title 'Raised by Wolves'. She had been gathering evidence that wolves had domesticated humans rather than the other way around. One of the key pieces of evidence for this was that humans had a social structure which was much closer to a group of free-living dogs than any primate group.

Primates can work together in small family groups, but not on any larger scale. The advantage goes to the individual who has the most cunning, the most ruthless Machiavellian schemer. Violence and murder were common in pre-human hominids. Groups broke up easily, and the species had flirted with extinction as numbers dipped low. Around 900,000 years ago there had been only about 1,300 proto-humans.

At the same time there was another species which also pursued herds of elk and mammoth and other large prey. Packs of grey wolves spread across Europe, Asia, North America and North Africa, displacing big cats as the top carnivore. The wolves' secret was social organisation. Wolf packs bonded, not just for the hunt but for life. Hunters gorged themselves after a successful hunt and regurgitated food, not just to feed the young but to share with other members of the pack who had missed out. They nursed each other's cubs, and moved and worked as a group. The packs endured, spread, multiplied.

Humans started to follow in the wake of the packs, two-legged scavengers hoping for a share of the prize. Sometimes when the wolves brought their prey to bay, the human joined in with the kill with stones and sharpened sticks. The wolves started waiting for their human allies, who were such efficient killers, and it became a shared activity.

The two species fused into a super-pack of canines and hominids. In the process, they both evolved. The wolves became dogs, first tolerant of humans and then actively attached to them from birth. The mentality of the pre-humans changed too: they became pack animals. The tribe became important to them. Ideas like brotherhood and belonging dominated their thought. They forged life-long partnerships and friendships. As they became dog-like, humans learned how to love.

At least that was the argument in Janine's dissertation. She was still working on it, gathering clues, fitting in new pieces of evidence…it was well established that the process of co-evolution had brought the two species close together mentally. Dogs, unlike other wolves, could read human facial expressions and follow pointing gestures without training.

Dogs did have a civilising influence, she knew that. But it did not always work. There were dog-fighting rings, and some of the owners made half-witted attempts to train their dogs to attack. But digging up corpses for them to eat? That was disgusting. And weird.

"Aha!" said Janine, pointing at a solid oblong gravestone.

"'Hiram Maxim.' The inventor of the machine gun, I think."

"Makes sense for 'Maximum Destruction,'" said Janine.

Caches could not be left close to burials, but it must be very nearby. Janine explored a signpost next to the Maxim tomb, and, right down at ground level, found a metal cylinder the size of her finger. Inside was a rolled up piece of paper; Janine dished out a biro and added her caching name—HuntsWithHounds—to the list and the date. The cache was claimed. The electronic part was easier, but the old-fashioned way of claiming a cache was more real.

Janine flicked up the answer screen, entered MAXIM and received a satisfying electronic warble in response. The second clue was unlocked. If the rest of them were this easy, there would be time to take the dogs for another run afterwards.

They pressed on past a bench with an arrangement of empty lager cans. A colourful mix of Hells, Skol and something called Excelsior. It might have been an avant-garde comment on urban life. Janine would have taken a picture—she liked to put quirky photos of London on her Insta—but time was passing.

"The clue is 'Think inside the box'," she told Lydia as the counter rolled down to less than ten metres.

"But they're all in boxes," said Lydia.

Janine spotted it first, a pair of boxing gloves carved into a stone slab. There was a niche at one end of the grave for floral tributes, occupied by some plastic daffodils. After all these years someone still remembered him.

"A boxer," said Lydia. "Does that make sense?"

"It does to me," said Janine, already leaning forward to take the name from the gravestone and enter it into the onscreen answer box.

A man standing by some bushes seemed to be weeping, head lowered. Then Janine saw his stream of piss glittering in the evening sun. While they were writing up the cache, the man ambled towards them. Despite the mild weather he was wearing a heavy coat, and a shapeless red, yellow and black woollen hat over dreadlocks.

"Muggle alert," muttered Janine. One of the perils of geocaching was being interrupted by people who did not know what it was all about. The dogs looked up without moving. They were trained not to approach people.

"You spare a pound for a cup of tea for an old man?" He breathed stale lager and halitosis at Janine, holding out a hand with knuckles swollen with early arthritis.

"Cup of tea," said Janine, with a slight snort. "Yeah right. Comes in cans now." But she reached for the coin purse in her backpack.

"You don't know what I been drinkin," said the man loftily. "I say to you, judge not—judge not, or you be judged yourself."

She placed the pound coin in his palm. "You're quite right."

He looked down at the coin for a minute, then put his hand in his pocket. "Sin is death. Life is the gift of Jah. All these dead—death to the unrighteous...you know? All the dead underground. We all goin' underground."

"Absolutely," said Janine.

"Hah, you don't know nothin' about it," he said, turning away.

"Should you give those people money?" whispered Lydia.

"It stopped him from bothering us," said Janine. She always gave money to the homeless.

They pressed on to the next cache, passing row upon row of headstones and tombs, before going through the gates of the cemetery-within-a-cemetery that was the Greek graveyard. This was why Janine timed this trip for when Lydia could come with her.

The tombs here were large and elaborate, built for the wealthy families of London's Greek community more than a century before. They were grander and more solemn than the tombs in the other areas, and also packed more closely together. This was an affluent neighbourhood and a patch was hard to get. Enormous marble chests were crammed in with canopied structures with fish-scaled roofs and marble pillars and towering slab-sided mausoleums. Some were replicas of Greek temples, Christianised but still recognisable in their fierce pagan geometry.

Everywhere the script was Greek, with sometimes a few supplementary lines in the Roman alphabet. Janine felt she had stepped into an Aegean landscape. A classical temple dominated the site, fronted with frieze decorated with Christian angels rather than centaurs and satyrs.

"What does it say?"

"'The trumpet will sound and the dead will rise,'" Lydia translated.

"Well that's *not sinister at all*," said Janine. "Let me know if you see any walking dead."

Google Translate might have done the job, but it was not the same as having a friend along. Even with the dogs, visiting a cemetery at twilight called for some support.

A woman swathed in black passed them. Deep lines were incised in her brown face beneath a headscarf. She looked like the women you see in a thousand island villages, knitting and gossiping over endless tiny cups of coffee.

"*Kalo apogevma*," Lydia said politely nodding.

The woman did not turn to look at her, but spat one word as she walked by. Lydia's face fell.

"Oh dear. Doesn't like dogs in cemeteries?" asked Janine.

"She called me a slut," said Lydia. "Or is it a whore? I guess it can mean either. Because I'm wearing jeans, you see. Not acceptable for a woman, of course! Village women, they're the Taliban. Only not so liberal. And they bring the village here with them."

Janine knew that village life in Greece was one of the reasons that Lydia had emigrated, and quickly turned the subject to the next clue.

With a little translation from Lydia, they tracked down the cache to an urn by a tomb modelled on a temple to Athena. While Janine logged the cache, they saw the woman in black again. This time she was standing by another gravesite. She jerked her hand forward, as if tossing something over a grave.

"What's she doing?" whispered Janine.

Lydia shrugged, mouthing "I don't know."

They went over to the grave after the woman had gone, and Lydia picked up a tiny brown speck from the lettering carved into a black marble slab to show Janine.

"What...?"

"Millet seed. For the *vrykolokas*," said Lydia.

Janine gaped incomprehension like a goldfish.

"It's a Greek thing like a vampire or a werewolf. It can't leave the grave until it's counted every single seed."

"Wait a minute. Is it a vampire, though?" asked Janine. "Or a werewolf? They're a bit different, y'know. One's sparkly and sexy, the other is hairy and hot."

"Not in Greece," said Lydia, shaking her head emphatically. "*Vrykolokas* means 'wolf hair'. It looks like a man or a dog, and it comes out of its grave and eats bodies. Like a vampire. It prowls through the village, knocking on doors. But it can only knock once. That's why superstitious people don't answer the door if there's only one knock."

"Really?"

"And they come from Bulgaria."

"Uh-huh."

"Well, that's what people say in the villages." Lydia shrugged. "There is a lot of prejudice about Bulgarians. But, you know, I don't think there's been a scientific study with peer review."

The sun was on the horizon now, but Janine reckoned they still had half an hour of light left, enough for three more caches if they were lucky.

The dogs ploughed ahead. They would keep going all day and all night. Janine would have loved to have let them off the lead, but, as with many cemeteries, that was not allowed here.

They passed a man with a shaved head in a Crystal Palace strip towed by two Mastiffs, biceps bulging from the effort of holding the dogs back. Typical big dog owner, having to prove he was in charge — why couldn't he train them to walk to heel properly? But the dogs were in good condition, even if he had given them huge, spiked collars.

Janine raised a hand; Mastiff man gave her the minimal nod of dog-owner solidarity, and she noticed a deep scar creasing his chin. He looked preoccupied, as though he was trying to do a difficult calculation in his head. She did have three Staffies, which gave her some sort of dog cred, but he was not about to stop and exchange a few words as owners usually did. The Staffies seemed disappointed about the missed opportunity to socialise, but Lydia did not.

"Did you see those wolf collars? He looks like one of those difficult clients who shouts a lot," said Lydia. "And sticks his face too close to yours."

"Mastiffs looked okay though," said Janine. "Tails weren't docked."

Tail docking stopped dogs from communicating; without the friendly signal of a raised tail, an approaching dog could look hostile and that could set off a whole cycle of aggression based on a misunderstanding. That pair had been intact, healthy animals, who would have come and said hello if their owner had let them.

"You know it's getting dark," said Lydia.

"Just three more."

The ground shuddered beneath them with a rumble too low to be heard, setting all three dogs barking. The Mastiffs answered from some distance away.

The graveyard was riddled with tunnels, most of them connected to the catacombs constructed in the cemetery's early days. Back then, the lead-lined coffins were lowered from the chapel on a silent hydraulic lift, then filed away on shelves in the gigantic underground repository. Some of the other tombs extended underground too, and the old River Effra flowed under the cemetery on its way to join the Thames somewhere beyond Brixton.

The sound might have been stones grinding as they shifted on each other, but it had a resonant quality like a vast alpine horn. The odd thing was that it sounded at the exact moment the last ray of sun disappeared from the peak of a monument which had caught Janine's eye. This was the most unconventional grave marker yet, a single standing stone straight out of Avebury or Stonehenge.

"They'll shut the gates soon," said Lydia, looking at the time on her phone.

"You take the doggies back to the entrance," said Janine, unwinding the leads from her hand. "I'll just get one more cache. If I miss closing time I'll shin over the railings."

Lydia looked doubtful but knew better than to argue. The ten-foot fence topped with iron spikes would be too much for her, but nothing stopped Janine when there were geocaches involved.

As Janine passed the dogs over, there was a yowl in the distance, but she could not tell from what direction. It was hard to tell if it was human or animal. All three dogs turned toward the sound, rapt, noses quivering. Probably teenagers messing around.

As Lydia and the three dogs disappeared into the gloom between rows of headstones, Janine suddenly felt very alone. It wasn't her friend she missed so much as the Staffies, her dogs, her family.

It was dark enough now that looking at the next clue on her phone left a bright oblong shape dancing before Janine's eyes. Half-blinded, she turned down the screen brightness and rummaged for the little wind-up torch in her bag. She needed it as the path ran behind a stand of trees and the shadows were full dark.

"Dive deep for this one," was the clue. It would have been much easier in daylight, but it was only three metres away.

There was a movement down the next row of graves, and the clinking of collar chains. The shaven-headed man in the Palace strip was still around. It was funny he was still here…unless he had stayed to follow her, now she did not have the dogs. Janine had ducked down and turned off her torch without thinking. Creeping paranoia was catching up with her.

Funny that, she thought, *all it takes is being on your own in a graveyard when it's getting dark and you start getting scared.*

A minute later, after finding the deep-sea diver the clue had been guiding her to, she hurried quickly on to the location of the next cache. Janine was stopped by a sharp little cry. She swept the torch about, looking for the source of the sound which must be very close.

Her first thought was *Jesus Christ, someone's abandoned a baby in the cemetery.*

The noise had come from one of the tombs, a huge stone chest the size of a fallen wardrobe with a gabled roof topped with stone crosses. Her torch showed one slab had pivoted open about its middle, and excited little sounds came from the darkness beyond. This time, to her great relief, it sounded nothing like a human baby.

It sounded a lot like fox cubs. Or maybe puppies.

Closer up, she saw through the opening to where steps led into a cavity beneath the tomb. It was cluttered with branches and clumps of dried grass, and a dark opening beyond suggested tunnels leading further still.

"What is this?" Janine asked out loud.

The cemetery guide mentioned catacombs somewhere, but there was no access to the public. Otherwise there would definitely have been some clues down there.

One face of the skewed slab was mossy, the other was clean. That meant it must be closed most of the time. She remembered the subsonic grinding from earlier.

She felt the pull-push as curiosity struggled with apprehension. Classic approach-avoidance behaviour. But why would she avoid it? There was nothing to be afraid of here. Not for a grown-up adult woman who was capable of removing spiders from the bathtub on her own.

The smell though was odd. And there was something about those yappy, squeaky sounds which did not seem quite right.

She went forward half a step and paused again. Approach-avoidance. But she had come this far, and she did not have to actually squeeze through down into the tomb, she just needed to get close enough to shine the torch beam into it.

The walls were a mass of carvings. From here she could see the small chamber was covered in comic-book panels packed with human figures. She stopped the torch light for a second on a baffling Gothic scene, set in a graveyard.

The clamour rose sharply as Janine waved the circle of light around, and four little heads looked up.

They did look like fox cubs, but bigger. More like wolf cubs, or puppies of some large, powerfully built breed.

Janine loved puppies and cubs and all things small and helpless. But her instinct was telling her to back off, to get away from these. Something stronger than the drive to care and coo over the newborn, a repulsive force from somewhere far back in her brain. These were not friendly things.

The cubs looked at her for a moment, then went back to feeding, tearing the last shreds of meat off bloody bones, two playing tug of war with one larger one. They were surrounded by bones; what Janine had taken for branches and sticks were older, dried bones, grey or white with age. The whole lair was carpeted with them.

Janine automatically identified them as human pelvic bones, partial human ribcage, and the curved dome of a human skull, so different to any animal skull. The bone of contention in the tug-of-war was a human femur, a very fresh one. In the foreground was a little splash of colour. A woollen hat in bright red, yellow and green. Jah colours.

The lair smelled like a cross between a kennel that needed cleaning and a butchers' shop. But that was not what made Janine step back and recoil. It was not even the bones, which looked unreal. It was the other thing.

The cubs had faces that were almost like wolf cubs, though with less of a snout. But they also had little hands with little fingers holding on to the bones they gnawed so greedily. Primate hands, baby hands with nails rather than claws.

Janine took another two steps back. She could feel the gears in her brain slipping as it tried to make sense of the scene.

She had been on some wild trips. Years ago, when she had been much too young, she had a fling with a man who called himself a 'Psychonaut,' an explorer of the edges of human consciousness. There had been a lot of mushrooms and other consciousness-altering experiences for six weeks before she realised he was not an other-worldly quester but a chancer who wanted her mainly for money.

She knew what hallucinations and out-of-body experiences felt like, and the transcendent vision that cuts through the dark of a festival at 3am with the force of divine revelation. She knew what it was like to see how the walls started to move towards the end of a twenty-four hour shift. And she had known many, many people, mainly clients, who had lively conversations with completely fictitious partners. This had some of the same tinge of the dream world reaching out into reality. But it felt too real to ignore.

She sat down on a fallen stone.

It was not even the cubs, or whatever they were. Or not just them. It was the combination of those things and the carvings around them.

"'Raised by wolves,'" Janine said to herself, then stood up again and leaned into the tomb entrance. She ignored the little sounds from inside and shone the beam of her torch up and down the carvings.

They looked like stylised copies of copies, refined and simplified through many iterations into a story simple enough for the smallest children to understand. Or perhaps just to imprint on and remember. Maybe the images would come back to them in dreams which would suddenly start to make sense when they reached a certain age.

Torch in one hand and phone in the other, Janine took video of the little creatures, and the carvings on the walls around them. The video was murky but it was good enough. It was evidence that whatever madness this was, it would show up on camera. Assuming anyone else could see it.

She backed away, pocketing her phone, wondering what to do or who to report this to. She could not just post the video online without any explanation, and she could not begin to understand what she had seen.

She could put it up with the tag #WeirdThingIJustSaw but that seemed all wrong. Something told her that if nobody had ever been able to capture a picture of those things before, then something would stop her from doing it too.

She needed to share this with someone, to talk to another human being. Just as she was about to call Lydia, Janine heard a stealthy shuffling through the dark, coming closer.

Janine's first thought was that it was the Mastiff owner. But there was no click of claws or jingle of metal from the dogs, and the brief glimpse she caught of the approaching figure showed that it was hunched over and oddly proportioned. And not, in fact, shaped like a man at all.

Her reflexive response was to shine to torch on the approaching figure, to see them better and to correct the weird shape that her brain had warped them into.

Janine swung the torch beam up, and two eyes shone back at her like headlights.

Reflection from the tapetum, she thought automatically. A feature of cats, dogs and other predatory animals. But not primates. Humans don't have eyes like that.

Vrykolokas was her first thought. But not something that rose from the grave, something that lived in graveyards and used them as a source of food. Something that lurked behind the gravestones and made it unsafe to be around cemeteries after dark. The mother of the litter she had just seen. Human-like, related to humans maybe, but not human at all.

Janine's torch illuminated the face which blended human and canine features. It might once have been a person before it changed, with older age stretching out the muzzle and filling the jaw with big yellow dog teeth, powerful enough to split bone and get marrow, baboon hands with long nails. It was like seeing a Neanderthal, except this was an older and wilder branch of the family tree.

Janine responded automatically. She had faced hundreds of dogs behaving aggressively, often confused or in pain. She looked to one side; making eye contact might only provoke it to attack. She did not make any sudden moves. Screaming or waving your hands was stupid. Instead, she backed away.

Bitches can be dangerous to anything they perceive to be a threat to their puppies. Not every dog, not every time, but the main thing was to make sure she was not between the female and the litter of young in the tomb.

There was a fresh outbreak of mewling, yapping cries as the cubs sensed another presence, and Janine stepped back more rapidly. Then the ghoul lunged forwards, and she ran.

Janine was fit, and a good runner. In the dim light the grassy space between rows of graves was a pale road stretching out ahead, and she went full speed down it. She heard the thing loping behind her, fourfold sounds like a galloping horse. Running like a baboon, she thought abstractedly.

Before she could formulate the thought that any animal which is human-size runs much faster than a human, something grabbed Janine from behind. It felt like being jerked backwards during a road accident, as the seatbelt violently restrains you. The ghoul had hold of her rucksack and Janine was spun round, somehow managing to stay on her feet as she slipped the strap off her shoulder and spun free. She caught a glimpse of dark eyes before she caught herself on a gravestone and went zig-zagging off down the pale grass pathways between the graves and the overgrown bushes, ducking low as she entered a maze of mausoleums.

She sensed rather than heard that it was no longer behind her, and dropped down, trying not to breathe too loudly, willing her eyes to adjust fully to the darkness.

She needed to get out of the cemetery, and fast.

Janine was good at in crisis situations. If an emergency case came in from a road traffic accident, or if a patient's skin started to turn blue in an operation, Janine reacted promptly and efficiently. She started to crawl on all fours, scanning the skyline for any sign of movement, working out her orientation, how far it was to the nearest possible way out, and whether she should stop to call for help.

At the same time, another part of her mind was processing what she had seen. A… thing, a ghoul, a human-like but non-human being that did not exist in any biology textbook. Part-human, part-dog and part nightmare, an actual bogeyman capable of ripping a person into bloody rags. Domestication syndrome is an evolutionary effect causing domesticated species to have smaller teeth and shorter muzzles. Whatever this was, it was un-domesticated.

It made sense on a visceral level; every child knows there are monsters in the dark. It did not make sense on a logical, rational level though, not unless you believed there might be things that existed in the liminal space of human awareness, just beyond the reach of scientific instruments.

When some bands of humans and wolves formed their alliance, others were left behind in the slipstream of evolution. The bands of men and hunting dogs multiplied, driving the other humans further and further into different evolutionary niches. Maybe they retreated into the forests and tried to live on berries and nuts, or maybe they withdrew to sea-caves and survived on what they could glean from the oceans, returning to a semi-aquatic life.

Most endangered of all were those who lived in the shadow of the pack-hunters, feeding on scraps. They lived not just on the odd prey animal that was driven in their direction by the hunters, but they also lurked around the campfires, picking off stray humans and stray dogs when they could catch them.

The proto-humans fought as a band and never abandoned their injured. They won every direct confrontation with their dark cousins. If the others had just been animals, the proto-humans would have easily exterminated them, literally hounding them to death like the competing cave bears and sabre-tooths that were gradually wiped out by the hominids and their dogs.

The unhuman others were destroyed, group by group and finally one by one, hunted through woods and marshlands by bands of warriors led by hunting dogs, warriors who thought of them as supernatural terrors.

But the others were not animals. They had a dark intelligence and wild desperation. They sought to gain their enemy's strength by eating them, by absorbing the flesh of humans and wolf-dogs, by becoming their enemies. They learned stealth and cunning and disguise, getting ever closer to the ones they hated, slipping into encampments at night to steal children and dig up fresh graves. Their Shamans poured out blood and screamed prayers to the wild gods of chaos, brewed up ever-wilder concoctions of herbs and fungi to reach into the places beyond space and bring back eldritch magics too dangerous for any sane person to handle, calling into themselves the power of the wolf.

The others were never quite extinguished but became a darker hybrid of human and canine which combined the most destructive instincts of both. The last few survivors learned to escape into the cracks in reality, the narrow crevices between dream and reality where mundane hunters could not follow. They disappeared into folklore and superstition. They lurked where they could be only seen in fever dreams, or by seers in trance states and by the truly insane. They only emerged to hunt.

Even when their adults were wiped out they could remain concealed in the gene pool for generations, a disease dormant within a healthy body, and break out again.

When humanity started to settle, a few of the others lived in the shadows around the great graveyards of the early civilisations. Wherever there was dead flesh they could thrive. They followed in the way of armies, plundering battlefields by night. They had found their niche: no longer humans but ghouls, eaters of dead, haunters of lonely places where they preyed on the unwary.

Janine had to call the police. She may have dazzled the ghoul with that first flash of torchlight, but it probably had very good night vision, as well as superior hearing and sense of smell.

Those two armed officers must still be nearby. Even if she could not give them a street address, she could give them her GPS coordinates. All she needed to do was to sit tight and let them deal with the situation. Janine knew her limits, and they had sometimes had to call the police at work. This was definitely one for a team of armed police rather than an animal nurse. All she needed to do was call them; she was sure the ghoul would vanish as soon as they appeared.

She squatted down and fished out her phone.

Dial 999, then: "Which emergency service do you require?"

The voice on the phone was horribly loud. Janine thought it must be audible a hundred yards away.

"Police," she hissed, putting her hand over the speaker.

"Putting you through now," said the muffled voice.

The phone rang twice and a male operator spoke.

"Upper Norwood police station. What is your emergency please?"

"I've just been attacked," said Janine. She looked over the top of the gravestone and was face to face with the ghoul.

It lunged with two clawed hands stretched out towards her.

She half-fell backwards and the claws slashed the empty air in front of her, the gravestone blocking it from getting close enough.

She ran round a large hexagonal tomb, turned and turned again. The ghoul was big and fast, but was so massive it could not handle sharp turns. Janine, with her low centre of gravity and shorter legs, had the advantage as long as she could keep moving. She had been running dogs over agility courses for years, and adrenaline fired through her.

Nine people out of ten would not have escaped. Janine was the tenth.

She ran towards a light which marked the building by the entrance. Janine had a strong urge to head back to the gates, or at least to somewhere there might be people. The ghoul couldn't follow her where there were other people, she was sure of that. She even had an idea that it couldn't even exist where there were people. If she could just get out of the graveyard to the normal world it would vanish like a bad dream.

The nightmare was right behind her. She heard it thumping along, front legs and back, a clumsy, heavy-footed gallop but still faster than her.

Then she saw the dogs running towards her as she reached the circle of light—Hagrid and Pixie in the lead, an eruption of barking as they saw her, and the thing behind her.

Disastrously, she looked back, tripped over and fell headlong onto the turf.

The dogs passed her and stopped in a line, facing the ghoul, barking like furies, standing between her and it.

The ghoul had stopped when it saw them. Now it raised itself from a crouch to a full standing posture. In the light it looked even more of a mutant horror: it towered over the dogs, baring long, jagged fangs, and gave a feral snarl. The dogs backed off for a moment then came forward again, barking all the while, and fanning out, taking turns to make short feints at the ghoul.

Janine had never seen this behaviour before. But then she had never seen a pack of wolves facing a bear over a fresh carcass.

Get up and run, a voice said in Janine's head. *The dogs will buy you enough time that it'll never be able to catch you.*

The ghoul had weighed up the threat from these three yapping creatures. Millennia of instinct kept ghouls away from dogs, their mortal enemies, but there was helpless, juicy prey just a few feet away, and it had young ones to feed.

As the ghoul advanced Hagrid leapt up, snapping at it with eager jaws; there was a momentary struggle and the twenty-kilo dog went flying backwards through the air and hit the stone side of a tomb with a hefty thump and fell to the ground.

Staffies are tough. They are the tanks of the dog world, rugged and solidly built, armoured with muscle. It is more than a matter of physique. For centuries they had been bred for fighting, and sometimes the breed seemed to be virtually immune to pain. Once they get into a fight with another animal, Staffies are notorious for their tenacity.

They are called Bull Terriers because they were bred to fight bulls. Hagrid's ancestors had been matched against fighting bulls in a pit while baying crowds cheered them. Being kicked around, gored or tossed in the air was expected at the start of the match before the opponent had been worn down.

Hagrid bounced on the ground, flipped over and threw himself back on the ghoul without a pause. He was flanked by the other two leading with open jaws. In seconds the ghoul had a dog clinging to each arm and one on its leg. White teeth ripped into the dark hide as each dog flung its head from side to side. The ghoul's skin tore easily, more like thin fabric than normal flesh.

Long claws raked down both Hagrid's sides, but once he had a grip he would not let go. Terriers have massive jaws held fast by layers of muscle. In earlier times people believed that they had a locking mechanism like a mechanical clamp, a myth not disproven until the 1980s, and to the casual observer they certainly appear to lock. Terriers only come loose if you tear them loose, and when the thing hauled Hagrid loose he came away with jaws full of dark, rubbery stuff as though he was ripping the stuffing out of a badly-made dog toy.

The ghoul howled in rage, flinging Wolverine somersaulting over a gravestone and catching Pixie's charge mid-leap, outsized hands locking around the dog's neck. In spite of the tattered ribbons of flesh hanging down the ghoul did not seem to be badly hurt. The physical body was just an extension of the darker things that existed mainly in dreams.

It was the sight of Pixie struggling that upset Janine. Without thinking she picked up a stone the size of her fist and went for the ghoul. The ghoul released Pixie to slap at her. Janine was knocked over backwards, like the victim of a hit and run driver. Her shoulder struck something hard, but there was just numbness, not pain, and she rolled over and to her feet.

There was a jingling sound and more, louder barking. The ghoul pitched forward at Janine's feet as two enormous mastiffs leaped on it from behind. The ones they had been walking earlier.

All she could see was a rolling mass of bodies, grey and black and brown fur thrashing around. The noise was like all the worst waiting-room fights she had ever seen, rolled into one.

Janine picked up her stone and hit at the ghoul where she could, where there was a gap in the dogs: the shoulder, the chest, the knee, one good strike at its head. She was battering a punching bag, and that just made her hit harder. Dogs were still getting thrown aside, but not as far. There was a lot of blood. Wolverine had a big scratch down one side, but he rolled free with a foot in his jaws, shook it aside and went back for more.

Suddenly Janine was face to face with the ghoul. The two Mastiffs now had hold of its forearms—trained attack dogs, Janine thought—holding it back, but it still surged towards her with open jaws. She struck at its face with the rock, sending bits of broken teeth flying in all directions. As the ghoul fell forward, dogs clinging on, she backed off, ready to strike again.

The ghoul was still not cowed, and with a squealing growl it raised itself up, lifting the dogs off the ground.

As it did, it was smashed down again by a length of heavy iron pipe crashing into its head from behind.

As it lay flat, still struggling, the shaven-headed man in the Crystal Palace strip raised the pipe again in both arms and hammered down again, and again, big biceps flexing, as though he was driving a stake into the ground. At the fourth blow, the ghoul's head collapsed like a split watermelon and the creature stopped moving. The dogs continued to tear at it.

"Fuck me, that was a rough one," he said, between panted breaths, and grinned. "You alright, girl?"

Janine nodded. She put down her stone carefully.

"Stone is good," he said, holding up the pipe, showing it smeared with slimy stuff. The insides of the ghoul did not look like anything

Janine had ever seen, more like half-set jellies than internal organs. "Better than trying to shoot it. But cold iron does the job better."

He tossed the pipe aside and inspected his two dogs, patting them and checking them for injuries from both sides while muttering encouraging noises as they sniffed around him.

"We're alright aren't we? Eh? Good job you did, and you, yes, you did." The Mastiffs looked ready for another round of exercise. "Here, one of yours is bleeding."

Janine was the vet nurse at once, kneeling down to steady Wolverine and examine him.

"You've got a good team there," said the man appreciatively. "They'd have taken that bitch down alright, with your help. It's all human-dog coordination, right?"

Suddenly Lydia was by her side, panting.

"What happened?" She asked confusedly, looking from Janine to the man in the football strip. When Janine did not answer, she said, "The gates were closed already when we got there, and I couldn't find anyone to open them so I came back to look for you. But the dogs went mad and got away from me." Seeing the remains of the dead thing she added, "What is that?"

"Heh," said the man, looking from her to Janine. "What that is, is just what it is. Don't look, it's messy."

"Should... we call the police?" Lydia asked uncertainly.

"Don't be stupid," he said, reattaching the leads to his dogs' spiked collars. "What are the feds gonna do? Nah, we got to get out of here now, just in case. I'll show you the way."

None of the dogs was seriously hurt, but Hagrid and Wolverine would need attention. Janine and Lydia, dogs in tow, obediently followed the Mastiffs who both seemed cheerful after the encounter, as though ripping monsters apart was their usual exercise along with chasing a ball.

"There's a loose railing over here you can get through," he explained. "But you shouldn't be in here. You ought to know better than walking through a cemetery at night when it's a full moon. You ain't Buffy, y'know!"

The disc of the moon was now rising above the trees, shedding pale light across the cemetery.

"That thing…" Janine started. "Do you know what it was? Have you seen one before?"

He clicked his tongue and shook his head.

"You really don't want to know," he said. "You got out of this alive. Go and just keep going."

"But—"

"Good bunch of Staffies you got there," he said. "Frenchies are popular—great little dogs, lots of spirit, some of them—but that thing would have six for breakfast. Staffies are fighters. Only problem having them is the idiots who think they're Pit Bulls and give you grief. But you know that, right?"

Lydia tried to ask questions, but Janine was not ready to say anything yet. She wanted to find out more, but the man would not give them a name. He had an odd tattoo on one arm which Janine could not properly make out, but nothing else would identify him. She had not even heard him call his dogs by name.

"Great dogs," she said. "Old English Mastiffs?"

"Eotenhounds," he said with a wink. "Sort of special-purpose breed. Furry sharks when you need 'em to be, big soft idiots the rest of the time."

They talked more about dog breeds, but once they were through the railings he just nodded and disappeared fast down the street, jogging alongside his dogs.

"Are you alright?" Lydia asked. "I mean, really?"

"I'm fine. But we'd better get these back to the hospital and see if they need stitching."

Ryan was the vet on duty. He was a good friend, and didn't ask any questions when Janine brought the Staffies in with a story about being attacked by a Mastiff. He did not think stitches were needed, and Lydia helped Ryan clean the wounds then seal up the scratches with glue.

Wolverine wagged his tail contentedly as they worked, whap-whap-whap on Lydia's shoulder, as though to tell her he was a good boy and he knew it.

"Better keep them in kennels overnight. Must have been a hell of a big Mastiff," Ryan murmured to Lydia, not looking at her.

"I didn't see it."

Janine went back to the cemetery first thing next morning before work, slipping through the gap in the bars before coaxing the dogs through one by one. It was a bright, chilly morning, and the dogs did not seem worried about going back. Maybe the thing had receded like a bad dream to them, too.

There was a mark on the grass where the body of the ghoul had been, as though a million slugs had crawled over the spot. Looking more closely she found brittle grey stalks like dried plants that might have been the shrivelled remains of ancient, decalcified bones, but nothing solid.

She found her backpack behind a gravestone, but she did not recognise the place and she could not find the tomb where she had heard the yapping cubs. She walked up and down, but it was all very different in the daylight. Everything was smaller and the angles seemed to have been rotated. She checked details on her phone, giving the co-ordinates of where she had been the night before. It was the right place, but not the right place. Maybe it was the sort of place that only existed on a dark night before the full moon rose.

She would never find that tomb.

Her finger hovered over the thumbnail image of the video she had taken last night. She thought about the man with the Mastiffs, and whether she really did want to know.

She deleted the video without looking at it, then emptied the recycle bin so she would not be tempted to try and recover it.

Then Janine went to find the last three geocaches. Nothing, but nothing would stop Janine from getting her thousand when she had worked so hard for it. She did it in time to get back to work with a light heart.

Before long, with nobody to feed them the hungry little ghouls would turn on each other. They would tear apart the weakest member of the litter and eat her. This would continue until only the strongest was left. Metabolic changes would kick in; it would shed its teeth, its snout would recede to human proportions, and it would start crawling through the tunnels, surviving on worms, beetles and whatever else it could get.

In a few weeks it would emerge out into daylight and be discovered in front of an old grave, a mysterious but perfectly normal abandoned baby girl.

The foundling would soon bond to her foster family but she would always have a special affinity for graveyards and other dark, deserted spaces. She would not be unusual in having strange and sometimes nightmarish dreams. She would be quite ordinary, right up until the point in her late teens when she started having an insatiable craving to eat human flesh, and the process of metamorphosis into her adult form began.

In fact, the only thing that would make her any different to other people was a marked lifelong and incurable phobia of all types of dog.

Delicacy

By Eric Malikyte

Through the telescope, John sees his neighbor enter the living room. One that's been converted into an art studio.

His neighbor is carrying a large brown box under his arm.

John's blood pressure spikes. He can feel the heat in the collar of his plaid pajamas.

With great anticipation in his movements, his neighbor opens the box and carefully retrieves its contents.

Like a peeping Tom, John watches his neighbor place five plastic bags along his work bench. Each movement, performed with ritualistic precision. John speculates on whether this has something to do with his neighbor's culture. John licks his lips—because in his mind, he can see Indiana Jones running from naked Aztec warriors, each of them eager to eat his flesh.

When John's neighbor is done, he removes the cloth covering a large wire armature. The kind used for clay sculptures.

But his neighbor is not using clay. No.

John takes a deep breath.

The boxes…they're filled with human flesh.

Every day, it's the same. For weeks now, John has watched his neighbor, a man named Emmanuel Garcia, receive package after package. Each filled with various body parts. And use them to make all manner of abhorrent things. Things no God-fearing man would ever present to the world as "art."

John watches Emmanuel open one of the plastic bags and retrieve what appears to be a sheet of skin. Watches him stretch it out and carefully place it on the wire portion meant to represent the collar bone and shoulder. The first of many layers. Before long, there is a wing of preserved flesh glowing in the light from the lamps.

As his neighbor works, a joyous smile etches its way across his face.

A smile that makes John feel nauseous. He thinks his neighbor's teeth are…sharper than they should be.

Just thinking about it makes his blood boil. He asks himself, if the man's done *that* to his living room, what has he done to the kitchen?

"Are you spying on that poor man again?"

John's heart leaps into his chest. He turns to scold his wife.

"How many times have I told you not to sneak up on me when I'm gathering evidence!" John says in a harsh whisper.

"And I've told you not to spy on the neighbor!" His wife crosses the room, closing the curtains on his telescope. "The doctor said you're supposed to be resting while we wait for the test results."

"I'm fine. This is important. This guy's—"

"A well-respected artist with an exhibit at the Virginia Museum of Fine Arts."

Her hands are on her hips, face screwed up with her typical "I told you so" look.

"What?" he asks, though it's more of a surprised noise than an actual question.

"Didn't know that, did you?"

"He's using human flesh, I mean, where does a man get such a thing!"

"All donations."

"But, it's not normal…"

"You know what also isn't normal?"

"I swear, if you say—"

"Spying on your neighbor, John. It's creepy. And you're lucky he hasn't noticed you yet."

"Probably wants to use my skin next…"

His wife is moving away, taking the laundry from her basket and folding it. "I expect you to drop this and get some actual rest. I'd be able to see those dark circles under your eyes from the moon."

"Hyperbole."

"How do you know? Have you seen what you look like in the mirror?"

"I'm telling you, Judith, that man's up to no good. No one who makes things out of skin can be normal."

"John, there are artists who make sculptures out of poo."

"And that ain't right neither! But this…"

"Is fine. We know he's an artist. Leave it at that."

"But…"

Her face is no longer pleasant. No longer playful. She rolls her eyes and rubs her temples. "I'm getting a migraine."

"I don't see why that—"

She points to the door. "Go lay on the couch, and I'll fix you some soup."

John stares at the floor. Then his bulging stomach. "I'm not hungry…"

"The doctor said you need to eat."

"I'm just gonna throw it up, what difference does it make if I don't eat?"

"Because, the doctor said."

He sighs. There's no winning with her.

Later that week, John returns from the doctor's office.

Before the wife can say a word, he's hobbling up the stairs, itching to get to his "investigation journal."

He's breathing heavily and holding his aching gut by the time he makes it to the little writing desk in his bedroom.

He turns on the radio, and uses his phone to play his favorite podcast, *Neighborhood Watch*, through its speakers. A conspiracy program dedicated to government cover-ups, UFOs, and the paranormal happenings *"they"* don't want you to know about.

His writing hand moves swiftly across the page, scribbling with mad fury.

He writes: *"Same crap as before. They don't know what's wrong with me. Why my body refuses to accept the garbage my wife calls food. She actually suggested I do a juice cleanse! A JUICE CLEANSE! It'll be a cold day in hell before I ever do one of those!"*

John eyes the bathroom door connected to his bedroom.

His days always end one of two ways.

Either he vomits up his meals, or he spends his day making friends with the toilet.

The doctors ruled out cancer, tick bites, and several autoimmune diseases.

John goes back to writing, lamenting the fact he hasn't had a steak in eight weeks. He hardly remembers what it tastes like to have a good meal. To not be repulsed by what goes into his mouth.

Now all he knows is the pang of hunger, and the throbbing, aching, twisting pain in his gut.

He writes: *"I asked the doctor if maybe Judith's been poisoning me. She smacked me pretty hard for that one. Seemed like a good question to ask. I've seen TV. Lots of women poison their husbands. And Judith would get a fat check from the life insurance company if I died.*

"Makes me wonder if she's in league with the neighbor.

"Would explain why she wants to shut down my investigation.

"If I can't trust my own wife…

"And this artist business!

"Oh, I see right through it. I do. I did some searching on this Emmanuel Garcia, and what I found was quite enlightening. He was a doctor in Mexico. Oh, yes. A doctor. And his social media suggests something happened to him that forced him to move to my country. While his social media was not specific, a search provided some additional context.

"My dear neighbor was involved with plastic surgery. And one of his clients suffered a severe infection after an operation. The authorities wanted to question Emmanuel."

His attention is brought back to his radio. The host, Arther Moory, has gotten through his initial introduction and sponsor reads.

"Tonight, we've got a very special guest," Arther says. "He's the author of the new book, 'Uncovering the Truth Behind Ghouls in Suburban America.' Please welcome Doctor Samuel Pikeman. Doctor Pikeman, how are you?"

"I'm quite well, thank you, Arther," Samuel says.

"Now, tell me about your new book. What is a ghoul?"

"Well, now that's really quite interesting. In ancient times, people believed that ghouls stalked graveyards in the hopes of consuming fresh corpses. Some believed these creatures to be supernatural, others thought they were grave-robbing cannibals. But now, of course, we're tolerant of such abnormalities. Aren't we?"

Arther, Samuel, and John all chuckle. John makes sure to write that last bit in his journal.

"So, is this a work of fiction?" Arther asks. "Or are you saying that ghouls are real?"

"Oh, I think there's no doubt, Arther. Think about it. A cannibal, or a ghoul, would not need to stalk the graveyards. They could enjoy their preferred meals under the guise of performing services for normal folks without ever raising suspicion. After all, isn't it customary for morticians to remove the body's organs during the embalming process? What's to stop them from taking those organs home and eating them? Ask yourself, if you ate people, wouldn't you do the same?"

"I sure would!"

"Exactly!"

John scratches his chin, his face scrunched up in deep thought.

The mental image of his neighbor taking out handfuls of human flesh and shoveling them into his mouth is almost enough to calm the ever-present ache in his stomach.

"In my research for the book, I found a lot of overlap for urban legends regarding missing persons and Chupacabra sightings that suggest the old legends might not be so fantastical after all."

"Fascinating."

John's eyes find the covered telescope by the window.

He leaves his journal behind and decides it's time for him to get to work.

John watches his neighbor over the course of several podcasts. Each of them featuring Doctor Samuel Pikeman. Each of them, going deeper into the conspiracy surrounding ghouls.

Once again, John's neighbor receives a delivery. A box full of human flesh. A human skull with no jaw, several bags of skin, and hair of various colors and textures. Emmanuel holds the skull up to the light, almost as if he's admiring it, and places it on the part of the wire armature meant to represent the neck. For a long while, the man takes sheets of skin of various pigments and stretches them over the skull. Sews them to together with needle and thread.

When Emmanuel is satisfied with the front of his sculpture, he rotates it around. Gives John a full view of it.

John gasps. It's a face with no eyes and no jaw.

White and brown skin, like a Frankenstein patchwork that cuts the head in half. The way it stretches over the teeth...like dried, rotting chicken skin.

The hair, though. Somehow, that's what really disturbs him. Like some kind of voodoo doll.

John feels as though he's seen it before.

Somewhere. Maybe in his nightmares?

"We like to think that cannibals don't exist in the United States," Samuel says. *"That people like Jeffrey Dahmer and Albert Fish are once-in-a-generation phenomenon, or it only happens overseas, right? But, according to my research, it's a lot more common than we think."*

Later that night, once his neighbor has retreated from his art studio, John writes in his journal again: *"It is my belief that this Emmanuel Garcia fled the authorities and is now hiding in my country, refusing to take accountability while he makes unspeakable things in his home.*

"I think he tried to kill that patient of his so he could use them for his own purposes. Maybe he's using these sculptures as some kind of delicacy for his fellow cannibals?"

John has covered his telescope with the curtain.

Luckily, he heard his wife's footsteps on the stairs in time.

When she spots him lying in bed, reading his book on serial killer cannibals, he can tell she's suspicious.

"What, no spying this morning?" Judith asks.

"No, Dear," he says, marking his place by dog-earing the page—something that has always driven Judith insane. "I'm doing as you asked. Is that not enough?"

"And yet you're still reading about cannibals." She moves toward the bathroom attached to the master to touch up her hair. "Somehow, I don't think that really counts as letting this business with the neighbor go."

"Will nothing satisfy you? I'm not spying!"

"Unless you closed the curtain and jumped into bed when you heard me on the stairs."

He stares at her with his jaw hanging halfway open. "How dare you accuse me of—"

A knowing look. "So, you mean to tell me you *weren't* watching the neighbor?"

"...I wasn't." He points to the book.

Judith sighs and smooths out her dress, then heads to the bedroom door. "Well, I guess I'll leave you be. Just try not to do anything to provoke that poor man."

John scoffs. "Poor man!"

"Right, well, I hope you have a pleasant day, John. I have to go to work now."

"Yeah, rub that in my face, why don't you. If I weren't sick, I'd still be the bed winner, you know!"

"Bread winner, Hun, not bed winner."

"Who needs to win bread? It's bed winner. My grandpap said so! Are you calling my grandpap a liar?"

She sighs, heavily. "I'm leaving, John. I'll bring home soup for dinner."

"Not that shit from the grocery store, I hope. I was up all night hugging the toilet no thanks to that garbage last night."

"No, not from the grocery store."

Before long, she's gone, and John's out of his bed and watching from the windows for her to drive away.

He scoffs. "Bread winner. Garbage."

Taking great care not to upset his gut, John shuffles out of bed and plants himself at his telescope again.

The car is gone from the front of Emmanuel's house, and the curtains are drawn.

"Gone," John pouts. And after all the effort he just took to get out of bed, too.

But, he can't just do nothing. Now that he finally has peace and quiet, it's the perfect opportunity to continue his investigation.

Where can he get more information on ghouls and cannibals, though?

John eyes his laptop.

What about social media? His wife's always on that Reddit thing, maybe he can look through there?

It's a terrible effort, getting off of his stool and limping over to his little writing desk. By the time he's reached his chair, he's sweating, practically heaving from the effort.

He eases into the chair, the sphincter muscle in his lips constricting into an O from his bubbling, seething gut. Opens the laptop. And begins typing as the worst of the pain fades.

He finds Reddit and, seeing that there are pages for his favorite news programs, he decides to see if there's one for his favorite podcast. Sure enough, Neighborhood Watchers has a page. He clicks on the link and sees there are hundreds of links, people asking questions about UFOs, ghosts, and government mind control programs.

He doesn't see a topic on ghouls yet, so he goes through the motions of learning how to make a new post. And writes: *"I recently listened to the series with Doctor Samuel Piker, and was wondering if anyone had any more information about ghouls I could find? I suspect my neighbor might be one."*

John clicks "Post" and waits.

And waits.

And waits some more.

It's nearly noon before someone replies to his thread.

John jumps at the chance to read.

The first message reads: *"There aren't many books on them, the government keeps a watchful eye on information about them. If people knew the truth, they'd all leave the cities for the country."*

John8969: *"Well, where can I find more? My neighbor makes sculptures out of human flesh. He fled to this country to avoid the authorities in Mexico."*

SovereignCitizen1099: *"Maybe you should email Doctor Samuel Pikeman, then?"*

John kicks himself, wondering why he didn't think of that.

He tabs over to his email and writes out a similar message to Doctor Samuel Pikeman, and hits send.

John is about to spend the rest of his afternoon staring at his email inbox, waiting for a reply, when he gets a notification from Reddit. Someone else has responded to his post.

He clicks the link in the email.

GrimPatriot889: *"I believe I can help you, friend. Send me a message on here and we can discuss your options."*

It takes John a while to figure out how to send GrimPatriot889 a message, but eventually he does.

When GrimPatriot899 asks John to tell him about his neighbor, why he suspects him to be a ghoul, John furiously types all of his observations. The fact that Emmanuel makes human flesh art, the odd hours he keeps, how he never sees him with family or guests, and his questionable past.

GrimPatriot899: *"Would you be willing to meet in person to discuss these theories? It's not safe to go into too much detail about ghouls. They could be watching our conversation."*

John8969: *"I live in Henrico, Virginia, near the Richmond city limits."*

GrimPatriot899: *"I can meet you in an hour. We can choose a public meeting place. Like the library off Laburnum, if you'd like."*

He looks at the clock. It's 3:00pm in the afternoon. His wife won't be home until 6:00pm at night.

John8969: *"Never been there. But ok. I will meet you in one hour."*

GrimPatriot899: *"I look forward to it, friend."*

With a sense of great urgency, John carefully makes his way down the stairs—holding his gut and cursing with every single movement—into the kitchen. Grabs his keys, and begins the long trek to the garage to his red pickup truck. The S10 is the one thing in this life that he's still proud of.

When he slides into the seat, the pain in his gut is almost unbearable. A pain that seethes and bubbles and cripples. A pain that reaches all the way up his esophagus to the back of his throat. To a place where the pang of hunger is most intense.

He curses this mystery illness for robbing him of enjoying the ten-minute drive to the local library.

Curses it as he parks, exits the S10, and makes his way into the library. Sweats bullets as he walks down the steps instead of taking the elevator. When someone tries to help him, he shrugs them off and bites their head off, saying, "Do I look like a cripple to you?"

John does not realize that the answer to that question is yes.

He spends most of his time in the library violating their noise policy by groaning and moaning as he looks around for his new friend. After what feels like an eternity of searching, he practically collapses into a chair.

It dawns on him that he never asked what this stranger looks like.

He decides, as long as he's at the library, he might as well look for books about ghouls. The table he's at, however, is on the lower level of the library, with nothing but children's books.

John approaches a middle-aged woman with a name tag—which he does not bother reading—with blonde hair and glasses. "Where are the books on ghouls?"

The woman looks confused. "I'm sorry?"

John rolls his eyes. "I'm looking for books on ghouls. Can you help me?"

"Oh, you must be looking for horror books, the adult books are upstairs."

John hobbles off in a huff and surveys the stairs. This time, he decides it would be better to take the elevator, and is surprised to find far fewer books on the first floor.

He's about to give up and return to his truck when he finds Doctor Samuel Pikeman's book in the new releases section. He picks it up and hobbles to a table nearby.

The first few chapters are about ghouls and the legends that surround them.

One section describes the mythic ghoul as having originated in Arabic culture. Mortal monsters who spent their time eating human flesh and haunting graveyards. He heard that on the podcast too.

But what is curious is that the book describes them as targeting children and taking on the form of their most recent meal. In mythology, they sometimes make their homes in deserts and covet gold coins. This makes him wonder about his neighbor. He's pretty sure Mexico is a desert. He's certain he saw that on TV.

The Muslim Hadith suggests that ghouls are corrupted jinns or devils, who would disguise themselves as beautiful women to lure unsuspecting men to be eaten alive. John scoffs at the notion that Muslims could ever get anything right and assumes they just stole it all from the Bible. He's a God-fearing Christian man, after all.

In the West, ghouls have been described as frequenting graveyards to consume freshly-buried corpses. Their favorite meal, though, is children. Especially live ones.

John reads that Edgar Allan Poe described ghouls as being, "neither man nor woman... neither brute nor human." And he wonders if his neighbor fits this description. The man's got a slight frame, not much muscle on the body. A real artist type. The mental image of his neighbor luring unsuspecting school children to his dinner table, knife in hand, fills his mind.

Somehow, the image feels right.

It must be true. He can feel it.

But just as he thinks he's really getting somewhere, someone sets a book down in front of him.

"Are you John8969?" The voice comes from an older gentleman dressed in a double-breasted jacket. The kind that was popular when he was a boy in the 1970s.

John nods. "How did you—"

"You're reading Doctor Samuel Pikeman's book," the gentleman says, gesturing to the open book in front of him. "I've been looking for you for the last half hour. Why didn't you respond to my messages?"

John shrugs. "I left the house."

The gentleman sighs. "I suppose it doesn't matter."

The man takes a seat in front of John. He has jet-black hair, and looks like he walked off that show his wife is always going on about. What was it called again? Mad Men. That's the one. His eyes, though, there's something about his eyes. They're the kind of eyes he imagines hunters have.

"Are you well?" the man asks.

John realizes he's hunched over the table, holding his gut. His brow is drenched in sweat.

"Stomach problems," John says. "Doctors can't figure out what's wrong with me."

"And you can't keep anything down?"

John nods. "Are we going to talk about my health, or are we gonna do something about my neighbor?"

"Tell me, friend. Do you sometimes experience a pang of hunger so great, it's all you can think about?"

John blinks. "How did you know?"

"Would you care for a meal? I believe I can heal what ails you."

John's wristwatch beeps.

He's got thirty minutes to beat his wife home from work.

John curses.

"Is there a problem?" the gentleman asks.

"My wife. She's going to nag me to death if I don't get home before her."

"Then I suppose you should leave. But, perhaps we can meet tomorrow?"

"Here?"

The gentleman shakes his head. "No. At my home."

John struggles to get out of his seat.

The gentleman offers him the tattered book he brought with him. "For your research purposes."

By the time he leaves the library and crawls back into the S10, he's got less than ten minutes to get home.

John does not beat his wife home. When he limps into the kitchen, holding the tattered book his new friend gave him, she's sitting at the dining room table with her arms crossed.

He spends the next hour listening to all manner of complaints from his wife as he attempts to get back upstairs to his investigation.

The rumbling, gnawing pain in his gut makes him want to do things. Sometimes, he'd do *anything* to make it go away.

The pang of hunger in the back of his throat as she goes on and on and on. It strikes him that he hasn't eaten a real meal in so long.

She tells him his attitude sucks. That he's not taking his health seriously at all. That his obsession with the neighbor is causing people to talk. That they all think he's a conspiracy wacko. A real nut job.

He ignores her. All he can think about is that she's going to heat up that shitty goddamn soup. She'll make him eat it, even though he hates it. Even though she knows he's going to be gagging and convulsing over the toilet until midnight.

His anger.

Oh, it burns so bright.

Finally, he can't take it anymore. Finally, he does it.

Tells her to shut her whore mouth and storms up the stairs.

Back to his investigation.

John slams the door behind himself.

He spends the next three hours ignoring the sounds of his wife sobbing.

Three hours watching for his neighbor to return to his demonic sculpture.

Nothing. The man must have eaten well before starting his work, because he doesn't so much as nibble on the body parts he uses for his so-called "art."

Frustrated with the lack of evidence tonight, John covers the telescope and crawls into bed. The whole time, as sleep threatens to take him, he stares at the covered telescope.

John can't help but wonder if he's missing out on something truly damning. Something that will prove his suspicions right.

If maybe his neighbor knows...

As his eyes slowly close, he daydreams what it'd be like to finally be vindicated. To prove his neighbor is nothing more than a gross murderer. A flesh-eating deviant.

His dreams, however, do not follow this line of thought.

No.

When sleep finally takes him, he dreams of himself at his dining room table.

He thinks to himself how unusual it is to have peace and quiet.

The smell in the air. It's...positively heavenly. The smell of herbs and spices, garlic and salt and pepper. The sound and aroma of sizzling, decadent meat.

His mouth is watering. The hunger, all consuming.

He can see her in the kitchen. Young and shapely. Moving the skillet with such precision and grace.

But one thing is quite odd.

The horrible pain in his stomach is gone. In fact, he's having a feast. Eating more than he has in a long time. Like a young man again! Shoving delicious pieces of steak in his mouth. One after another. Each one juicier, bloodier than the last.

His wife must have finished cooking it ahead of time. In his excitement to finally eat, he must have blacked out. The meat is arranged on his plate like something from a bonafide steak house. And cooked to perfection. He always preferred his steak to be bloody. And she didn't disappoint.

"Honey," she calls from the kitchen. "Would you like seconds?"

With a mouth full of succulent meat, he stands from the dining room table and makes his way into the kitchen, where his wife has her back turned away from him.

"Just a moment," she says, her voice seductive and melodious. "Just have to cut off another piece!"

When she turns to him with the knife in her hand, it is inserted just over her breast muscle. Blood running like wine. Her left breast hanging two inches from her belly button. She cuts back and forth, back and forth, until a tender piece of breast meat comes off, landing in the skillet.

She made sure to give him the leanest piece.

He has to think about his cholesterol, after all.

"Oh," she says, her smile bright and wide. "We can't forget the butter and garlic, now can we?"

John can't help but be mesmerized as she works. Flipping and seasoning the steak. Melted butter glistening and sizzling.

Judith cooks the steak on both sides. A few minutes. Not a second longer. And it's ready.

The plate is in his hands. The aromas of the steak filling his nostrils. Making his mouth water.

He wolfs it down. Like a dog who's been denied meat by an abusive owner. He savors every last bite, licks the plate clean of the decadent juices left in its wake.

Just when he thinks he's satiated, his wife turns her smile on him. "Ohhhh, I think someone's still hungry."

Her hands cup the area where her breast should be, at the bleeding muscle fibers that now call to his primal instincts.

Before he realizes what's happening, he's like a baby suckling at its mother's teat. Gnawing and tearing and chewing as she pets his head. As he has his third meal.

"That's it, baby." The shushing noises she makes are oddly soothing. "Let Mommy fix it."

As John's dream self takes in his new favorite type of steak, he wakes screaming.

John screams himself awake.

It's still dark. The clock reads 4:30am in the morning. His wife is fast asleep next to him.

Carefully, he makes his way out of bed, cursing under his breath, doing his best to keep his groaning to a minimum. When he sees his neighbor's windows are all dark, he shuffles his way over to his writing desk.

Quietly, he turns the desk lamp on.

He writes: "*I had a terrible nightmare. I don't put much stock in the meaning of dreams. But I think maybe God is trying to tell me something with this one. Perhaps that what my neighbor is doing might corrupt us all. Might lead us straight to the fiery pits of Hell.*"

John looks at the bed. The wife is still asleep.

He continues writing: "*My so-called wife didn't even hear me scream! Damn ear plugs she bought after she complained about my snoring! What would she have done if I was dying?*"

It's then he notices light filtering through the window, bouncing off his telescope.

John is delighted to see that his neighbor is home after all! He peers through the telescope's eyepiece, and sees him in his art studio, toiling away once again on his so-called "art."

Layer by layer, John watches him add more and more flesh to the armature. It's starting to look like some kind of zombie out of a Hollywood movie.

It's an hour before Emmanuel covers the abomination with a sheet and moves into the back yard.

John watches him go to the shed and take out a shovel. Though he can't see too well with the fence in the way, John's certain he's digging something up.

Maybe a body?

Maybe he's digging a grave?

What kind of a man digs in the middle of the night? How many don't have something to hide?

This goes on until sunrise.

Emmanuel retreats back into his house.

John's already reaching for his phone, dialing the police.

He's got him now.

John's at the window, writing down every single movement he sees his neighbor making.

He can hear Judith stirring in bed, scoffing and cursing.

He doesn't even bother to hide what he's doing. And he can't stop smiling.

"Jesus H Christ, John," Judith says. "Really?"

"This time I've got 'im!" John shouts, turning to her. "I saw that son of a bitch digging up a body in his back yard last night!"

She sits up, holding her head. "I'm sure he was just doing yard work."

"At four in the morning? I don't think so! There's no other explanation!"

"It's been pretty hot this week, I'm sure he was just trying to avoid—"

"Bull-pucky! Why are you on his side?"

She pulls herself out of bed, hands on her hips like she knows everything. "Because, unlike you, I've had actual conversations with him, and he's just a nice man trying to make a living like everyone else."

"Well, the police will be able to tell for sure."

"What?"

"I called the cops!"

"You didn't!"

"Damn right, and they're gonna get to the bottom of this! What sort of man digs in the middle of the night, anyway? No one I know, that's for sure."

"John, you don't know anyone. All your friends at the legion stopped talking to you."

"Bah!" John jumps at the sight of a Henrico police car pulling into the neighbor's driveway. "They're here!"

John manages to hobble his way out the bedroom and down the stairs. He doesn't even bother to get clothes on, he's so damn happy!

"Goddamn it, John, at least put some damn pants on!"

Too late, he's through the door!

The wife chases after him, limping his way across the front yard in his underwear and wife beater, waving the officers down. No doubt, they're going to want to take his statement, and no amount of stomach pain is going to stop him from enjoying this.

"Officers!" John shouts. "That man is a murderer! He's been making things with human flesh and digging up the bodies in his back yard!"

"John!" Judith shouts. "You're embarrassing me!"

The wife hides her face in shame as John explains to the officers about how the neighbor is a cannibal, a member of a secret group of flesh eaters that meet in secret.

Finally! The moment of truth!

The neighbor comes to the door. He scowls at John, showing his canines.

John can only grin and nod at him.

From the corner of his eye, John catches Judith smiling and waving at the neighbor. "I'm so, sorry, Emmanuel, there was nothing I could do!"

"Don't talk to him!" John shouts.

The officers approach Emmanuel. At first, John expects things to escalate. Expects his neighbor to run for his life.

To John's dismay, he watches the officers calmly explain to his neighbor what the situation is. That they got a call that someone saw him digging a grave in the back yard.

John wonders why they're being so polite to him. Why they're not arresting him right then and there!

Emmanuel invites them inside.

John stands there, waiting with bated breath for them to emerge, Emmanuel in handcuffs.

Much to John's frustration, the cops emerge from Emmanuel's home laughing with him.

He's *not* under arrest.

John approaches the fence. "Hey, officers! What are you doing? Why aren't you arresting him?"

The officers sigh and roll their eyes at him.

One of them approaches his wife. His WIFE.

"Ma'am, can we have a word with you for a moment?" the officer asks.

"Sure," Judith says.

John sits there, watching from a distance, seething as the three of them talk in a hushed whisper on HIS front lawn! On HIS property!

When Judith returns to him, she's got a smug look on her wrinkled, bitch of a face. "Well, I hope you're happy with yourself."

"What were you talking with them about?" John demands.

"They explained to me that Emmanuel keeps late hours, that he can't handle the heat, some kind of medical condition—"

"Bah! Medical condition my foot!"

"All that digging you were complaining about, do you know what he was actually doing?"

"Digging graves!"

"No, John! He was fixing the drainage for his HVAC system!"

"Lies!"

Judith crosses her arms. "You know what else they said?"

John hesitates to ask. She's got that look, like it's gonna be something bad.

"They said this isn't the first time you've done this. I don't know why I'm surprised, really, but they also said that they won't respond to another call, either. And if they do, they're gonna throw your ass in jail for the night for wasting their time!"

As the police drive away, John shakes his fist at the cruiser. "My tax dollars pay your salaries!"

"John!" Judith's practically turning red, pointing at the house. "Get in the house now! The whole gosh-darn neighborhood can see your giblets!"

Emmanuel. He's glaring at John from his doorstep.

"I'm going to catch you!" John shouts. "You hear me?"

His neighbor doesn't say a word. Just sighs, retreats back inside, and calmly closes the front door.

"You know what?" Judith claps her hands and walks away. "Go ahead and stand there half naked for the whole world to see, I'm done."

Why does no one believe him?

Why does everyone side with the ghoul?

Later, John is hunched over his writing desk, praying as he scribbles in his investigation journal that the pain killers he's taken will finally kick in.

He writes: "*He's crafty. I'll give him that much. But there's only so much charm he can display before everyone else will see what I see. But by then, it'll be too late, won't it? And I'll just tell everyone I told them so!*

"*It's what they'll deserve, too! Yes it is!*

"*The woman is giving me the cold shoulder. She doesn't believe me. Of course not. She's fallen for his charms. I'll bet she wants to have relations with him too.*

"*The harlot!*"

When he finishes the entry, he thinks about returning to his investigation. But, instead, his eyes find the tattered book his new friend lent him.

In all the excitement since the library, he hasn't had a chance to read it.

John decides he'd like to take his new friend up on his offer after all.

After all, why should he stomach living under the same roof as a harlot?

He sends the man a message over Reddit. After a short exchange, the man gives him his address.

John is all too eager to leave the house.

John pulls up alongside an older building in Church Hill. The place looks like it's falling apart. The gray-blue paint is peeling off, along with the siding. The fence appears to be rotting in places.

After pulling himself from the vehicle and carefully making his way up the old cobblestone pathway, John reaches for an old door knocker in the shape of a Doberman.

The door opens before John's fist can touch the knocker. Once again, the man's got style. He's wearing an older-style suit again. This one's black with a red tie.

"Why, hello there," the man says. "Come in, come in!"

"How did you know I was coming?" John asks.

The man smiles wide and deep. "Cameras. Can never be too careful."

John nods. "Smart man. Smart man. I hate Richmond. City's full of nothing but a bunch of smug, liberal jerks."

"Indeed, but the food is absolutely to-die-for."

The man leads John into a Colonial-style dining room. The walls and decor are all dark, as if the man doesn't like a lot of light.

"I trust you've enjoyed the book I gave you?" the man asks.

"My bitch of a wife hasn't left me alone long enough to read it!" John shouts.

"Not to worry, my friend." The man chuckles. "This is as good a place to read as any. I trust you brought the book with you?"

John nods.

"Then, please, have a seat, make yourself at home while I cook you a meal. Perhaps later I'll be able to add a few more books to your reading list."

"I can't keep anything down." John holds his gut. "Are you sure this will work?"

"Like I said, my friend, I believe I know what's wrong with you."

"You're not gonna use none of them weird hippie spices or vegan crap, are you?"

"Wouldn't dream of it. No, this is an entirely meat-based remedy."

"Well, well!" John approaches a large, leather recliner and takes a seat. "Now we're talkin'!"

"Relax, my friend, I shall return with a feast." The man bows like some kind of butler before taking his leave.

John takes the tattered book out of his jacket pocket and begins to read.

The first thing that strikes John is that the book is written entirely by hand. Like some kind of journal, maybe. As he reads, some of the words run together in odd ways, and sometimes it's hard to focus on it all.

The book has lots to say about ghouls. Says they were born from the flesh of something called the Black Goat. That she took a piece of herself and gifted it to a chosen few men, the most devout of her worshipers. Those men found themselves transformed by her gifts, and they no longer craved the plants or animal flesh of the Earth, but for the flesh of their former brethren.

But, man did not accept this behavior. This cannibalism. Man drove the ghouls underground, where they made their tunnels, fashioning them out of the bones left in the wake of their meals.

The smell of seared meat, salt, pepper, and garlic fills the air. Tears John's attention away from the book.

To his surprise, his new friend brings him what looks like a steak dinner on a fancy silver platter. The smell. Oh, the smell makes his mouth water something fierce.

He's so hungry.

The pain in his gut. It reaches and reaches. All the way to the back of his throat.

Like a starving dog, he grabs it with his bare hands and sinks his teeth into it. When he rips off a piece of flesh, it's bright red in the center. Medium rare. Just the way he likes it.

Each bite is more succulent, more flavorful than the last. When the meat is gone, he picks up the silver platter and licks the blood and juices till it sparkles like it's been freshly scrubbed.

Then he stares at his hands. The juices and blood coating his fingers. He worries about what the meat might do to his stomach.

John can't help but picture himself hugging the toilet.

But for some reason, his stomach feels fine. Better than it has in a long while. As if the pain was simply…washed away.

"I trust you feel better?" the man asks, smiling bright and wide. Showing his teeth.

John, dumbfounded, nods.

His new friend hands him a handkerchief.

After John cleans himself up, his friend invites him to his personal library, where he gives him two new dusty books.

Each of them just as tattered as the last, with no titles on the covers or spines.

He tells John to read them when he gets home. And to return them at his leisure for another meal.

John thanks him for the meal and the books, and heads home.

When he returns home, he sees the woman left him some vegetable soup. The note on the table says it's got healing properties.

"Bah! Vegan garbage!"

He picks the bowl of soup up, and dumps it in the garbage.

With the wife still at work, John is free to do as he pleases. So he sits in his favorite recliner and opens up one of the books his new friend lent him.

The first book tells him that the ghouls were a blessing by someone named Nyarlathotep. Some Egyptian Pharaoh. The story is that long ago, men from all over the world would come to hear the Pharaoh's wisdom, and if a man proved his greatness, he would bestow upon him gifts from behind the stars.

Ages ago—the book is not specific—one such man came to Nyarlathotep in the hopes that the Pharaoh would cure his leprosy.

Nyarlathotep agreed, so long as the man could complete a trial.

The man would do anything to have his affliction cured so that he would no longer be shunned by society. He was told to go out into the world and bring the Pharaoh his first born child, and to offer him up as tribute.

The man was hesitant at first, but as wicked men will do, the promise of a cure was too much to resist. So the man smuggled his way back into the walls of his home city and stole upon his wife and children, stealing his first born from its mother's breast and riding off into the night.

When the man presented his firstborn child, a girl who still could not speak, the Pharaoh told the man that if he wants to be cured of his leprosy, he will have to eat his child alive.

To take her life essence and add it to his own.

The man did as the Pharaoh commanded, ripping the flesh from the child's bones until they were picked clean.

When it was done, the Pharaoh smiled upon his subject. And told him that his affliction had been cured.

But, Nyarlathotep's gift was anything but. While the man's leprosy was cured, his flesh had changed. He was now a hideous creature, with the head of a jackal and a body made as though interbred between a hairless hyena and a man. He would forever be forced to stalk the land in search of children to feast upon.

Other entries speak of the ghouls as travelers, who are able to cross between the lands of dream and the mortal world.

The second of the two new books has several parts about ghouls. It says they make their nests and tunnels beneath human towns and kingdoms. That they intersect with our sewers to give them easy access to our streets, and our young.

The tunnels are made of materials taken from their victims. Stone, mortar, bones, bricks, you name it.

One passage says the ghouls came from the dreamlands, and are nightmares made real. John doesn't really know what that means.

Another says that they often breed with human beings. That they will often come up to the surface world to steal children, and replace them with babies of their own kind. Half-breeds. Like those tales about elves…the book calls them changelings.

Over time, their features slowly start to change. Sometimes when they reach adulthood, and sometimes when they're much, much older.

Ideally, the changeling matures when they're still living with the foster family. So that they can return their bodies to the netherworld, so that their true family can feast on their flesh and drink of their blood.

John wonders if maybe that's what happened with his neighbor?

He hasn't seen family come visit him. Emmanuel seems to be a loner.

And, now that he thinks about it, his neighbor's features do look strange. Like his jaw is too long, his cheek bones too sharp. That sort of thing.

John eyes the stairs. He'll have to adjust his telescope the next time he's able to observe his neighbor. See if he can tell for sure.

Today, John has pep in his step.

He springs from his bed like a newly-made man. Ready to take on the world…and his neighbor.

When his work in the bathroom is done, coffee is made, and he's got his friend's books in hand, he's ready to get to work. The only work that matters to him.

At first, the woman seems surprised. Her eyes are wide. He can smell her sweat from where he sits reading at his table. For some reason, the smell makes the pang of hunger return to the back of his throat.

He catches a smile forming on her lips.

But, when he moves back to his telescope, and sits on his stool. He sees the smile fade.

The woman doesn't bother to scold him. She sighs, mutters something under her breath, and makes her way downstairs to get ready for her day.

Good. She's learning.

John peers through his eyepiece. He watches the neighbor in his studio, toiling away on his latest creation. Now the bust is nearly complete. It has shoulders, a chest, and a grotesque head. The neighbor's wearing a mask and has what looks like a spray paint can in his hands. Whatever comes out of the can is clear, though, and gives the abomination on the work table a slimy sheen.

Disgusting.

Then, the neighbor's attention is grabbed by something toward the front of the house.

John notices there's a car in the driveway.

The neighbor removes his mask and trots out of the studio.

That's when John sees them. A young woman and a little boy. The boy can't be older than six.

They're both the same color as his neighbor.

But that doesn't mean they're family.

John has a terrible feeling. It grips at his heart, makes his teeth clench tight. Makes his mouth water.

He watches carefully through the telescope as they disappear into the house. Before long he can see their feet in the makeshift art studio. All of them close together.

Doesn't she know what kind of danger her child is in? That this man will take their flesh right off the bone, season it and marinade it, and sear it to an internal temperature of 130 Degrees Fahrenheit?

John can't help but think of yesterday's meal. The thought of getting another medium rare steak makes his mouth water.

No. He's got to stay focused!

Breakfast can wait.

He thinks about the illustrations in the books his new friend lent him; canine-like creatures twice the size of most men snatching up children in their claws and snapping their tiny heads off with their impressive jaws.

Some of them, turning the headless torsos upside down and drinking them like a sweaty jogger might drink from a water bottle.

Soon the feet disappear, moving into what he thinks is the kitchen. All the houses in this suburb are the same. So it *has* to be the kitchen.

He's got to get a better look.

In his mind, he can't help but picture his neighbor boiling the child and mother alive in a cauldron.

His eyes find the binoculars on the shelf not far from where he is. He hops off his stool and grabs them, then runs downstairs and out the door into the yard.

John finds a hole in the fence where he can poke his binoculars through. He's got the perfect view of the living room. And there they are. All three figures. His neighbor, the woman, and the child. The woman and the neighbor look like they're having a grand old time. The child, however, keeps looking into the art studio, at the abomination of flesh and lacquer on the worktable.

His neighbor notices this. Smiles wide. Too wide and too sharp. And guides the little boy into the art studio, where he shows him his work. The mother looks uneasy. Who wouldn't? From here, John can see other works in progress in his neighbor's "studio." Things with too many teeth and pits for eyes. Things with human faces covered in human hair and horns carved from human bone.

The three of them eventually leave the art studio and, consequently, John's line of sight.

He panics.

This is just what his neighbor wants.

He can't help but imagine his neighbor leading them into his basement. A dungeon that goes on and on and on, transforming into a tunnel made from the bones of each of his meals.

As he creeps along the fence, looking for another angle from which he might be able to peer into his neighbor's home, he can't help but imagine the mother and child getting ripped apart. Teeth sinking into their soft, unseasoned flesh. The sounds of chewing and snarling echoing into the depths of that devilish tunnel.

John can't help it.

His body takes on a mind of its own. Climbing and crawling over the fence. Scrambling through the yard in the sweltering Virginia air. Fumbling with the doorknob.

Making his way through the living room, sniffing the fumes coming from his neighbor's "art studio." The horror show there. His eyes can't help but linger on them. So many figures, patchworks of leathery human flesh and hair.

Not the smell he expected.

When he thinks about that. All he can think about is the succulent steaks he was served by his new friend.

When he remembers their juices. The smells of the seasoning, the garlic and the butter and the salt and the pepper…swirling and mixing with the smell of the blood, the look of the meat waiting for his canines to sink right into its—

The pain. In his gut. It returns with a vengeance.

As he hears their laughing, jovial, giggling voices upstairs, all he can think of is the meat. How it tasted.

How it eased the pain in his gut.

The hunger.

When he mounts the staircase, he's crawling on all fours.

His fingers are clawing, digging into the carpet.

The pain is excruciating.

His mouth hangs open, drool pooling and dripping.

John can practically smell them when he reaches the top of the stairs. Their sweat, the oils on their skin. Nature's marinade, he thinks.

When he sees them, sitting on the couch, watching the TV, that's it.

He can't control it.

Doesn't want to.

Like an emaciated animal, he leaps at them. Clawing and biting and tearing.

And then, swallowing.

And slurping.

And biting and chewing and repeating it over and over again.

The woman tries to get away, crawling and weeping like a sheep.

With a swipe of his claw, she slumps to the floor, her blood seeping into the carpet like freshly-spilled wine.

He knows it's over when their screams stop.

He blinks. Glances around at his handiwork.

The ruined faces of his neighbor and his guests.

The neighbor's bleeding, sopping throat and exposed ribcage.

The woman's blank stare, the claw marks all over her legs and back.

The boy's horrified expression and stiff limbs.

He curses Judith.

Her cooking.

Really, this is all her fault.

And he finishes his meal.

Soon, he'll give her a talking to.

One she'll never forget.

Meet the Authors

Matthew Davenport

Matthew Davenport hails from Des Moines, Iowa, where he lives with his wife, Ren, and daughter, Willow. When his scattered author brain isn't earning weird looks from the ladies of his life, he enjoys reading sci-fi and horror, tinkering with electronics, and doing escape rooms. Matt is the author of the *Andrew Doran* series, the *Broken Nights* series (along with his brother, Michael), *The Trials of Obed Marsh*, and *Satan's Salesman*, among other titles. He's also a self-styled student of the Cthulhu Mythos and exercises that influence in his stories and as an editor at the blog Shoggoth.net. You can keep track of Matthew through his X/ Twitter account @spazenport. Matt occasionally updates his blog at davenportwrites.com.

David Hambling

David Hambling is a journalist and author based in Norwood, South London. His fiction, starting with a collection, *The Dulwich Horror & Others*, explores the Cthulhu mythos in his own locale. His novels include the popular Harry Stubbs adventures, also set in the 1920s, and he has previously contributed to ST Joshi's *Black Wings of Cthulhu* collections. He can be found at:
https:// www.facebook.com/ShadowsFromNorwood/

Philip Hemplow

Philip Hemplow is a cosmic horror and science fiction writer from Yorkshire, in the UK. His previous works include the novella collection *Spoiled Children*, the novel *Exoteric*, and assorted short stories and audiobooks. When not writing he can be found watching football, running, working at his day job, and complaining about not having time to write more. His output can be found in the usual places.

Eric Malikyte

Eric Malikyte is a neurodivergent author, illustrator, science communicator, and video editor. He has published works in various genres, including Lovecraftian horror, dark fantasy, and cyberpunk. He has written for YouTube channels such as TopTenz, Geographics, and Biographics. He lives in Richmond, Virginia, with his wife and two cats, where he spends his spare time exploring used bookstores, Irish Pubs, and terrorizing the neighborhood children on Halloween. Get a free copy of Eric's debut novel *Echoes of Olympus Mons* here: https://dl.bookfunnel.com/ 1cw07o2uyb

C. T. Phipps

C. T. Phipps is a lifelong student of horror, science fiction, and fantasy. An avid tabletop gamer, he discovered this passion led him to write and turned him into a lifelong geek. He is a regular blogger on "The United Federation of Charles"

(http://unitedfederationofcharles.blogspot.com/)

He's the author of *Agent G, Cthulhu Armageddon, Lucifer's Star, Straight Outta Fangton, Space Academy Dropouts,* and *The Supervillainy Saga.*

Curious about other Crossroad Press books? Stop by our website:
http://crossroadpress.com
We offer quality writing
in digital, audio, and print formats.

Subscribe to our newsletter on the website homepage and receive a
free eBook.